ACKNOWLEDGEMENTS

I am grateful to those I have met in my journey creating this book. You have inspired me to write these words and give a voice to all who have unjustly suffered incarceration.

My family and friends have been invaluable. Not just offering your constructive criticism, but more importantly for your unconditional love and encouragement. So many family members and friends embraced me when life presented its most challenging obstacles. I thank every one of you. This is why we have family and friends.

My deepest thanks to Arthur Schwartz, my friend for almost half a century. He devoted countless hours to helping me make this book the best it could be. His criticism was painful at times, but always resulted in a better paragraph, chapter, and book. I am truly privileged to be the beneficiary of his creativity, insight, and friendship.

> *"It is said that no one truly knows a nation until one has been inside its jails."*
>
> *Nelson Mandela*

CHAPTER 1
Welcome to Hell

It's a cool spring day as Lily turns off State Highway 22 in our rented SUV and heads up a long, winding road toward Federal Medical Center, Franklin.

I don't have to surrender for another fifty-four minutes.

From a distance, the prison looks rather majestic, but as we get closer, the grandeur of the building is replaced with rows of rusted barbed wire and peeling paint.

Not sure of where to go, Lily sees an employee who is planting some seed on the golden-brown lawn and asks for directions. The disinterested employee points in the distance and tells us we need the "Receiving and Departure" area. It's my first time in West Virginia, and it isn't the warmest of welcomes.

All the anxiety of the previous months is escalating from a simmer, to a boil, to the inevitable. If only time could stand still, but the finality of defeat has engulfed us.

Lily and I kiss, we cry, we embrace, we stare, we touch, we cry some more. It's all we can do. Of course, we exchange words, but I can't recall a single word.

I have gone through fifty-five years without a school detention or a speeding ticket. Two years ago, I couldn't walk when I lost all feeling in my legs from multiple sclerosis (MS). Eighteen months ago, my immune system was destroyed by the MS medication. Now I'm on the grounds of a federal prison, about to self-surrender, and I'm supposed to survive a two-year sentence here? How is any of this possible?

My hand hovers over the door handle for a moment as I try to muster up some courage for what awaits me. *Breathe,* I think, as I exit the car. Lily pulls me into a hug and I don't want to let go, but I have to. We slowly release, a millimeter at a time. Tears roll down our faces that have morphed into blank stares. After two years, it's now time.

I slowly walk the last one hundred yards with a cane in one hand and a bag of medication in the other. Before I reach the gate, I stop and turn to my wife of thirty years. She is standing beside the car, her cheeks wet with tears. We wave. She blows a kiss to me. Never have I felt so helpless.

I approach the layers of fencing, which must be fifty feet tall. Barbed wire curls around the top. The building looms in the background, made of many more bricks than windows. A lookout tower stands to the left where I imagine a guard keeps duty at all hours.

This prison houses 2,000 men, but soon will house one more.

My hands shake as I press the button on a keypad that will let me in. And then I wait.

After a few minutes, an officer approaches the gate. He's wearing a utility belt adorned with a bunch of gadgets.

"I'm Jay Keller, here to self-surrender." My voice is quivering.

"Go to the door up there. Someone'll let you in." The prison guard speaks into the walkie-talkie attached to his shoulder, "I got a self-surrender, Keller." The voice on the other end is muffled.

He reaches for a giant key, unlocks the gate, then he follows me as I head up the pathway to the entrance, a heavy metal door. When I step inside, I'm taken aback by the cold feel of the place. Laminate flooring. Walls in need of paint. Scuff marks on both.

A young correctional officer with jet-black hair and a slow deliberate gait greets me. His left eye is clouded over from a cataract. This is my first test of trying not to stare.

"Follow me," he says in a Southern drawl.

We segue through a few hallways until arriving at the receiving area. An older guard is sitting behind a beat-up desk that serves as his footrest. He lets out a large sigh and removes his feet off the desk, then types something on the computer.

"ID," he says in a bored voice.

After handing over my bag of medication, I reach into my pocket. All that remains of my life as I used to know it is a driver's license, which I hand to the guard. He searches through a large box and pulls out my file. He looks at the license, then looks at me. "Over here for some pictures and fingerprints," he says.

When I stand for the photo, I remember the words of a respected friend who said, "Smile for your ID picture. Don't let those fuckers think they won."

All I want to do was cry, but I smile broadly. I've gone from being on the cover of *MD News* to smiling for my prison ID.

"Keller, have a seat in the room behind you."

I'm quickly escorted to a holding area, where I sit on an L-shaped concrete bench. The frigid room makes me shiver. My mind oscillates between everything that I've left behind—a wife, my two children, my career as a respected physician, my friends and family—and what's awaiting me in prison.

I choose to focus on the building: the walls and floors are thick with layers of paint, the room smells musty and old, the ancient radiator has steam valves and a pan to collect leaking water. A rusted stainless-steel toilet is off in the corner. I try to remain calm. My wife's lips are a distant memory. I listen to the two guards debating whether Bill Cosby could have raped all of those women.

"Come with me, next room over," says the guard, as we now enter a small room with shelves filled with prison attire. The door slams shut behind me. "Take all yo' clothes off, put 'em in the basket."

With no room for negotiation, I do as I'm told, following the guard's commands that are spit out in a rush of an unpunctuated sentence. "Now lift yo' arms, turn around, lift yo' left leg, now right leg, lift your scrotum, bend over, stand up, turn around, arms back up, open yo' mouth, lift yo' tongue— Good. Grab some clothes from tha'na shelves behind you."

"How do I know what size?" I ask naively.

Pointing to the different stacks of clothes, the guard says "Shoes go seven to ten, ten to thirteen, and fourteen-plus. Pants 'n shirts are large, extra-large.

Be quick, ain't no one care how ya' look. Gotta walk ya to yo' room."

This is it. My stomach is knotted. My teeth chatter slightly from being in the cold and damp basement.

We begin the arduous journey, first through the bowels of the basement. It's a long hallway, dimly lit by fluorescent lighting, no windows, and no end in sight. With cane in hand, I explain to the impatient guard that I can't walk any faster. Once up a long ramp, we're finally at street level, and I realize how large the prison is. I'm exhausted already.

Finally, we arrive at the Antioch housing unit, a three-story brick facade with countless tiny windows. A middle-aged man is sitting on the railing just inside the entrance to the housing unit. I walk past him wearing my brown T-shirt, khaki pants with an elastic waist, and blue slip-on sneakers. I try not to stare at his neck tattoos of dragons and flames. As we walk by, the inmate chuckles and says "Welcome to hell."

CHAPTER 2
Dazed and Confused

My new room is full of inmates. Eight bunk beds line each side of the room. I suck in my breath. I can feel their eyes on me. The guard locates the empty lower bunk—232L—in the middle of the row and tosses the rolled-up bundle of sheets and a blanket onto a green two-inch-thick plastic mattress.

"Here's your bed, Keller." He turns and walks away before I have time to gather my thoughts to ask the first of a million questions.

My heart is pounding as I try not to stare at the other inmates, but all I can do is stare as if I have just landed on another planet. A glance out the giant windows unveils verdant rolling hills, but my gander is short- lived as I return my focus back to my new room. On a positive note, amidst my sheer fear, I'm happy there are no bars; No cells. Only a giant fifteen-foot-ceilinged room with four colossal wall-mounted fans blowing and screaming, creating a loud background hum.

There are about twenty men of varying ages and ethnicities scattered about. At one end of the large room, a group of young men are joking and laughing like college dorm buddies. An older man is hunched over his cane and looks to be anywhere between fifty and ninety-nine years old. Usually, I can estimate people's ages well, but today my skills are worthless.

Another inmate has dreadlocks extending well past his knees. In the corner is a middle-aged Black man with a scowl on his face, eyes hidden behind sunglasses, his long beard braided into three, and a large wooden Star of David dangling from a necklace. Directly across from me is a bearded middle-aged man calmly sitting in his wheelchair reading a James Patterson paperback.

In the bunk next to me is an older Black man serenely reading the Koran. He's a stark contrast to my sweating palms. I try to slow my racing heart but can't control my body despite repeating Lily's mantra of "just breathe."

I'm confused. Everyone looks healthy in every sense of the word. This is a federal medical prison facility, which means the Bureau of Prisons (BOP) designated you here specifically because of your medical conditions.

With trembling hands, I unwrap the bundle revealing two flat sheets, a pilled blanket, a small transparent hand towel, and a pillowcase. As I labor my way around the bed, I see two men across the room reveling in my state of newbie confusion.

Focus, Jay, focus. Forget your medical problems. Forget you never should have been sent to prison. Let's make the bed now, I mumble under my breath.

It only takes a few moments to make my bed, though I wish it took longer. At least I would have something to do. I sit down on the paper-thin mattress, trying to get a sense of where I am. It's all so surreal.

The man in a wheelchair makes his way over to my bunk. He has brown hair, blue eyes, and a close-cropped reddish beard. "First day here?"

"It is. My name's Jay. Just got here."

"I'm Ryan, been here about a year. Where'd they have you before here, Oklahoma City?"

Confused, I explain my wife drove me here this morning.

"Oh, lucky—self-surrender, if you want to call that lucky. What other prisons have you been at?"

"None, this is my first day in prison—ever."

Ryan raises his brows. "I barely remember my first day. I was too out of it. Anyway, it's not too bad here—usually. I was locked up in county for thirteen months. What a dump that was. This is much easier time, relatively speaking. You'll get used to it. Where you from?"

"New York," I say affirmatively.

"Thought so, your accent's a little different. How long you got?"

"What do you mean?"

"How long a sentence?"

"Oh, twenty-four months minus fifteen percent good time."

All of a sudden, I remember my lawyers told me not to discuss the details of my case. A flush of anxiety washes through me. This will be a slow learning curve.

Ryan smiles. "Two years—that's a drunk stop. Ya know, by the time you sober up, you're outta here. A two-year sentence is nothing around here."

Nothing? Two years seems like a lifetime. The conversation with my lawyer is echoing in my head, all the things I was told not to do, the first being: *Don't ask what someone is in for.* But I'm grateful that someone is extending a bit of kindness, and I want to continue the conversation. Besides, Ryan seems like a decent guy.

"Ryan, how long you have?" I ask hesitantly.

His smile exposes a few vacancies in his line of dentition. "I got a twenty-year sentence, served about two so far."

I gasp. *Twenty-year sentence.* I can't even wrap my mind around that. I'm dying to know what he did, but I've been warned not to ask. I just stare at him, unable to form words.

"Yeah, lotta time to go," he says with a laugh. "No secrets here, you'll hear anyway. Got caught robbing a bank with a bomb on me. The feds counted the bomb as a weapon of mass destruction."

The least threatening-looking guy in the room spews words that scare the hell out of me.

"Ryan, I have to confess, you're the first bank robber I've ever met."

"Oh yeah? Quite a few in here."

Those words offer no comfort. I look at my wrists and can see my pulse beating. My breathing is rapid and shallow, and my legs are twitching out of control. Very discreetly, I say, "This place has more of a college dorm vibe than a prison. Is it true that you have to be sick to be sent to a federal medical center prison?"

"Who told you that?"

"My lawyers. My wife and I also attended an orientation put on by the BOP. That's what we were led to believe."

A month ago, Lily and I attended the Bureau of Prison orientation. We were sitting in a stuffy room with no air-conditioning as the man from the

BOP told us what to expect. I was to be sent to a Federal Medical Center (FMC) because of my health conditions. I remember worrying about my multiple sclerosis (MS) and how my lack of a working immune system would fare in prison without my personal team of medical experts. For the first time, it dawns on me that if I didn't have medical problems, I would have served my time in a "camp," a low-level prison with no walls or fences. But here I am, sent to a rather hardcore prison for a crime I was totally unaware of.

Ryan shakes his head. "Nah, maybe half are here for medical reasons, the other half is just here. Locals, protective custody, sex offenders—a big melting pot of misfits. Nice that you have a wife. Two years is doable for her. Much longer and the marriage falls apart. Any kids, parents, family?"

"Two kids, grown. Both parents died and my one sister is estranged from the family. Glad my parents aren't alive. My circumstances would have killed them." Suddenly feeling brazen, I ask, "Mind if I ask why you need a wheelchair?"

Casually he responds, "Took fourteen bullets during the robbery."

What the fuck am I doing in this place? The rest of the inmates seem happy and healthy, and the one person I meet is in a wheelchair because he was shot fourteen times during a bank robbery while carrying a bomb. My bounding heart has a mind of its own as I try to digest this latest revelation in a calm manner.

"I'll tell you about it later," Ryan responds. Maybe he can see the shock written all over my face. "I can't ever walk again, if that's what you're wondering. What happened to you? What's with the cane?"

"I have some balance issues from multiple sclerosis."

"Got it. A good friend of my parents died from MS. Anyway, you should get ready for chow."

"For what?"

"Chow, ya know, dinner."

"How should I dress?"

A smile curls at the corner of his mouth. "That's funny. In your best prison garb, which means you'll go as you are. If you push my wheelchair, I'll show you where we eat when it's time."

Ryan pivots his wheelchair and heads back to his bunk, which is across the room and one bunk to the right. I'm alone with my thoughts with not a single possession to my name. I focus on my bed. I was given a pillowcase but no pillow. I sigh, knowing there is no one I can call in this place that's going to bring me a pillow.

Just then, a scent of buttered popcorn replete with the distinctive odor of baked trans-fat wafts through the air. The odor is enough to knock me over, which would not have required very much. I'm more exhausted than I have ever been in my life from the stress of being completely disoriented. It's the first time in my fifty-five years that I've truly feared for my life. I've seen movies and TV shows that take place in prison, and it's never a pleasant depiction. My imagination is running wild with the fear of being beaten to a pulp, raped, tortured, never seeing my loved ones again, permanent disfigurement, getting infections, having more MS attacks.

I can no longer be vertical as I sink into the abyss of a weak mattress and even weaker bed springs. I think back to a wretched hotel room where Lily and I stayed years ago in Newport, Rhode Island. Unbeknownst to us, we arrived in Newport on the eve of the deciding seventh race for America's Cup, the most important yacht race in the country, and couldn't find a decent hotel room. That hotel room has always been the benchmark for horrible accommodations—until now.

Fear is the only thing keeping my eyes from closing. Despite my baseline level of terror, my eyes close for maybe a minute before I appreciate that I had dozed off for a few seconds. I prop myself up but can barely hold my head up. I study the details of where I am.

There are sixteen bunk beds circa 1950, metal frames with collapsing springs. Each one is numbered and labeled *U* for upper and *L* for lower. I have a lower bunk, which I have to believe is more desirable since I don't have to climb up and down. Each side of the room has windows eight-by-five feet divided by numerous panes. A trap section in the center falls away to allow airflow. It's a cavernous room with old plaster walls and a fifteen-foot-high ceiling that's interrupted by two-by-four beams, also of plaster. Everything is painted in the dullest shade of construction gray except for the retrofitted sprinkler system, which has bright red pipes that crawl across the ceiling in two rows. Many inmates hang from the sprinkler pipes in order to do their pullups. Three smoke detectors and four light ballasts also are tucked in-between the beams. The periodic flashing of the smoke detector is directly in my line of vision if I'm supine on my bed. Only the floor has a hint of brown in its linoleum tiles, a slight deviation from the gray tones. Rust rings where bed frames have been moved add another hue of brown. Most areas are covered in paint, but the walls and ceiling have the texture of an adolescent's face with pimples in full bloom. A few areas are peeling, revealing previous shades of red, blue, and green. Alongside each bed is a cheap gray plastic chair purchased from whoever was the cheapest vendor.

Behind the bunks are tandem beige lockers. Each inmate has a locker, which is twenty inches deep, thirty inches wide, and thirty-six inches high. All of my possessions for the foreseeable future must fit in this tiny locker. Fans are mounted high and blow from all four corners, plus there are individual bedside fans scattered throughout the room.

The northern end has a card table where six men are playing dominos. They argue loudly, incessantly, and entirely incomprehensibly except for the obligatory "motherfucker" every six to ten words. The southern end has several men in their twenties in here for who knows what. This is as close as they will get to a college dormitory, so unlike me, they're happy as could be, much to my utter amazement. How could anyone be happy in here? One of the millennial's voice is a perfect double for Edward G. Robinson's. His back has a large tattoo with one word, Peckerwood. At the top of each of the bedposts are short green winter coats, but now just collecting dust. Lastly are the radiators, originals from the 1920s, and covered in layers of dark gray paint. The bottom horizontal bar has eighty years of dust baked onto it. This is my new home.

The man in the next bed is signaling for my slumberous body to stand up. I unintentionally ignore him. Finally, he taps me on the shoulder and firmly tells me to stand up. I listen and realize everyone in the room is standing.

Suddenly, a guard bursts in yelling something unintelligible as he walks down the corridor of the room counting the inmates. Everyone stays standing so I do as well. Then another guard—a female somewhere north of two hundred and fifty pounds—repeats the procedure of the first guard. When I see everyone relax and scatter, I sit down on my bed, thankful my legs didn't give out.

Everyone is either talking or laughing, but no one else appears as disconcerted as I am. Actually, they appear quite content. My preconception was that the federal medical center where I'd serve my sentence would be like a hospital surrounded by a fence. That is how my lawyers and the BOP described it. It's clear this place isn't a medical center at all. Not even close. I'm in prison.

CHAPTER 3
My First Night

I push Ryan into the elevator for our ride from the second floor down to the first. Once the doors close, the elevator begins to shake, making me more nervous. After a painfully slow ride in an antiquated elevator that probably hasn't been inspected for decades, the doors open to the first floor.

"Just lucky the elevator is working. It's broken as often as it works," says Ryan.

"What do you do when it's broken?"

"I manage. I get someone to carry my wheelchair down and I either use crutches and my one good leg. Sometimes I crawl on my butt. Like most things in this dump, you get used to it. Don't think the warden will let me call Amnesty International."

I push Ryan out of the housing unit and back toward the main building. He tells me where to go, but I'm mentally retracing the steps I made with the guard earlier today to get a feel for the layout of the place. It looks so different now—the hallway is dimmer and narrower. It's funny how our perceptions change.

When we enter the main building, Ryan says, "Just go through the metal detectors and you'll be in line for dinner. I'll see you after dinner."

Inmates in wheelchairs have a separate dining room. Now I'm alone standing in line for dinner, not just alone, but completely discombobulated. All psychological cues from my first five decades of life are suddenly invalid, gone. I replay in my mind a scene from *Shawshank Redemption* when Andy DuFresne sits down to eat his first meal in prison alongside seasoned inmates.

"Just breathe," I whisper. Shell-shocked but standing, inertia places me in the cafeteria line. Looking at what the men in front of me are doing, I mimic their actions by grabbing a tray and a spoon and fork rolled up in a napkin. I shuffle in line as the inmate behind the counter shovels food—rubbery green beans, mashed potatoes, and mystery meat—onto my plate. Tray in hand, I make my way into the dining room, where I'm the only Caucasian. It's packed to the rafters as panic sets in. I fill my water glass and walk by a table when a middle-aged dark-skinned man nods at me and slides over.

"This seat open?" I ask.

"It's your seat now, my man."

I quickly sit down next to him and stare at the limp and gray food, not that I have an appetite. I'm probing for words so I can converse with him, but I'm coming up empty. My problem is solved when his baritone voice asks, "Just get in today?"

I look up at him. "Few hours ago."

"Where you comin' from?"

"New York."

"Which prison were you at? Why'd they send you all the way down here?"

"Oh, I live in New York. Self-surrendered today." His eyes grow wide. I suppose I will have to get used to that reaction.

"Where are you from?" I ask.

"Mobile, Alabama. The name's Carl, but everyone calls me Mo."

"Jay. Nice to meet you."

His name and registration number printed on the front of his shirt are illegible, which leads me to assume he's been in prison a long time. Mo has that "prison smarts" look and has probably dined with dozens of newbies over the years. We exchange pleasantries for a few minutes as I pretend to eat, moving food from one side of the tray to the other.

"How long a sentence ya got?" Mo asks.

I remember Ryan confirming that sentence length is a fair-game question, but I don't want to offend this guy. I pause for a few seconds before responding. "Twenty-four months."

"Sheeeeeet, that ain't nothin'. You just a tourist."

GLENN LESLIE

"A tourist?"

"Anyone under three years is a tourist, a short-timer. Come on, you seem like a decent guy, I'll give you a quick tour of the place after chow so you can at least know where the fuck you are."

Mo has a healthy appetite. My only goal is to look as if I'm eating. *Appetite* is nothing but a Scrabble word at this point.

"What you in here for?" he asks with a mouthful of food.

Without hesitating, I calmly reply, "My case is still pending. Lawyers told me not to discuss the case."

"Okay, that's cool."

I'm ambivalent. Am I supposed to trust the second guy I meet in prison? On the other hand, Mo is a charming seasoned veteran who might be able to help me.

We bring our trays to the dishwashing area, leave the cafeteria, and head down the main hallway. I try to appear casual, but I'm scared out of my mind, on high alert. Mo shows me the library and a few other locations adjacent to the cafeteria.

"Come on, I'll show you the indoor rec area in the basement. It's always busy this time of day."

"What do they have in rec?" I ask with the authority of a church mouse.

"Everything—weights, machines, crafts, chapel. Let's go down, it's cool."

I'm fearing the worst. After I'm raped, I'll be cut into little pieces, disposed of, and vanished off the face of the earth. Why didn't I just say I had to get back to my unit? Maybe because I'm not sure of how to get back. Following Mo, we make our way down a congested stairwell that opens to the cavernous basement area. The *only* comfort to me is that it's crowded everywhere we go. Maybe I won't be carved up, or at least not here. Mo is fist-bumping every tenth person, so part of me thinks I've aligned with the right guy.

We enter a room where a few men are working out on bicycles. "Here's the spin room, behind that you got treadmills. Full court hoops over there. Pool tables—always busy at night, and make sure you play by the house rules. Down there's the chapel."

We walk down a long corridor, not quite as crowded but still busy. My eyes are drawn to the aged pipes half covered in what looks like asbestos. A smell of chemicals hits me, the kind of chemicals used in nursing homes to disguise odors. The crowd is now sparser as we turn the corner and approach the chapel.

"Are there any cameras in this prison?" I ask.

Mo chuckles. "Ah, pretty observant. Nah, this place is old-school. Only prison I've been in that doesn't have cameras everywhere. They have cameras in visitation and outdoor rec area. That's it. If a fight breaks out anywhere else, the guards have no way of knowing."

"Got it." My body clenches at the thought that I could be attacked and beaten, and there would be no video evidence.

Mo informs me of what time church services are. *Do I give off the vibe of a church-going guy?* Just then, the chapel door swings open and a man towering at six-five with piercing green eyes exits and warmly greets Mo. "What up, dawg?"

"Chillin', showin' a rookie around. You workin' tomorrow?"

"Bright and early." The large man turns to me. "I'm Lou, when you get in?"

Anxiously but controlled, I respond, "Few hours ago, the name's Jay."

"Hey, Lou, can you make sure my man Jay gets all new clothes tomorrow morning?" Mo asks.

Lou nods. "Be in laundry at eight a.m. and I'll fix you up good. Gotta run."

I'm shown a few other highlights before meandering back to where we started. For a moment I relax, then put my antennas right back up. We come to a crowd of sweating men in desperate need of a shower. The stench of body odor is overpowering.

Mo puts his arm out to stop my momentum. "We gotta wait here till next move, about five minutes. Anyone tell you about *macs* yet?"

"Macs? No, what's that?"

"That's money, bro, gotta learn *macs*."

Mo goes on to explain that there is no real money in prison. Inmates buy "macs"—a bag of vacuum-packed mackerel fish—at commissary and use it as currency. In 2004, federal prisons banned cigarettes, so inmates had to find other means for trade. However, I can't imagine why a bag of mackerel is so coveted.

"One mac costs one dollar. Haircut, two macs. Poker, we play for macs. Football game, we bet macs. Unused stamps is the other currency, but I'll tell you another time. I lay some macs on you tomorrow till you can buy your own," Mo says.

At the top of the stairs, Mo directs me back to my unit, pointing in the opposite direction where he's going. "Don't forget, laundry at eight."

I laboriously find my way back to my bunk and reality hits me. I'm in this place for two years, sleeping on this uncomfortable bed, in a filthy prison surrounded by society's outcasts, dumbfounded as to why everyone appears relaxed. Thoughts race through my head at dizzying speeds. For the first time in my life, I entertain the thought of killing myself if things get really bad. *Deep breath, deep breath,* but it isn't working. The once-quiet domino game in the corner has escalated into an all-out shouting match. What do I do when the fighting starts? I have no books, no watch or clock to tell me what time it is, no pillow, no toiletries, and no identity other than an eight-digit ID number. Exhaustion envelopes me as I struggle to keep my eyes open. Ryan told me that I must stay awake until the nine-p.m. count, so I sit there, struggling to keep my eyes open. Finally, the count comes and goes uneventfully.

Now I can recline in earnest and perhaps get some sleep. Brushing my teeth or washing up before bed is not an option. Fully dressed other than my slip-on sneakers, I scurry under the blanket, resting my head on a rolled-up towel. As fatigued as one could possibly be, it's impossible for me to doze off. Fear keeps me on constant vigil, but I'm not sure for what. No one else's hair is standing on edge. No one else shows the slightest bit of anxiety. A goal-oriented man, I set a lofty goal: be alive come sunrise. That's my goal. Now the mechanism. I'll stay awake all night on full alert. I've never feared for my life as much as I do on this first night in prison. Every person walking by my bed is a potential assassin.

Seconds swell into minutes, which amass into hours. Without a watch, I'm clueless about time. The room is dark and filled with snores and other strange sounds—the heating pipes possibly. At some point, a guard with a flashlight comes into the room and shines his light on every inmate. Thirty seconds later, a second guard does the same. This procedure is repeated three times throughout the endless night. I think I dozed off for a few minutes. The difference between wakefulness and sleep has been obliterated.

The man in the bunk above me tosses, turns, and bounces all night long. Each movement creates loud squeaks from the rusted springs. I feel claustrophobic, as if the world is crushing down on me. How much longer until morning? Outdoor floodlights pour through the windows, but I need to see sunlight.

Delirious, confused and disoriented, I start to notice different sounds and rustlings. No sunlight, but a few people are deliberately stirring around. More people wake up and groan and stretch. It must be morning even though it remains dark outside. And then it's official: I've survived my first night in prison.

CHAPTER 4

The Con Is On

It has only been nineteen hours since I kissed my wife goodbye. It feels much longer than that. My back hurts from a restless night, but I made it. I have no comb, so I simply run my hands through my hair. Good enough for prison. Each pore on my body feels like a mini pothole. I walk to the one bathroom that is used only for urinating and close the door. I'm instantly overwhelmed by the smell of urine. Someone missed the toilet and peed on the floor. A centipede traverses the puddle with ease. Instead of brushing my teeth, I swish water around my mouth before spitting it into the rust-stained sink with the broken faucet levers.

I'm surprised that there's no official business I need to do, like meet with the warden or a case manager, or someone. Instead, I begin my journey to the laundry area in an effort to get my official prison garb. With my head down, I retrace my steps so I don't have to ask anyone. I find the basement and the laundry area. A sense of accomplishment puts a smile on my face.

Lou is standing behind a large workbench. His face brightens when he sees me. "How ya doin', New York? Go right through that door. Give me five minutes and I'll be right with you."

The warehouse-sized laundry room is lined wall to wall with metal shelving. Within half an hour, Lou has me completely outfitted with three khaki slacks, four brown T-shirts, a pair of steel-tipped boots, four khaki shirts, underwear, socks, a belt, a winter coat, and two laundry bags. I thank Lou for his help and leave the laundry area with a cane in one hand and a laundry bag stuffed with my new wardrobe in the other. The walk back to my housing unit is long and arduous, but at least I've accomplished something other than pulling an all-nighter.

Each inmate is given a small locker for storage, which is usually behind the bunkbed. Just after I place all my clothes in my locker, a tattooed inmate approaches me, and a wave of anxiety courses through me. It's the same man who'd said, "Welcome to hell," when I first arrived. I recognized the dragon tattoo on his neck.

"I'm John, a friend of Mo's. He said you were a good guy, so he wanted me to check on you. I see you got your clothes."

I breathe a sigh of relief and try my best to be cool. "Nice to meet you. Jay Keller," I say. "I'm slowly settling in as best I can."

"Mo said he wanted to lend you ten macs until you get on your feet and get to commissary, which isn't for five more days."

"Thanks anyway, but I should be okay until next week. Really."

John shakes his head. "You gonna need macs. Just take them and pay him back when you can. Mo said you're good for them."

"I'll be fine. Thanks anyway."

John doesn't know how to take no for an answer because he doesn't listen to a word I say. While I'm arranging my clothes in my locker, he places ten macs on top of the locker. By the time I turn back to John, he's already left the room. I didn't think this through fast enough, and now I'm involved with Mo and John and whoever else. *Shit. Bad move, Jay.*

I place the macs in my locker while I try to remain calm. I'm distracted by laughter across the room at Ryan's bunk. I head over and he introduces me to another inmate, Diaz.

"Hi, Jay," Ryan says, wiping the tears from his eyes. I wonder what they were laughing at. "Ya gotta laugh when you're around Diaz," he clarifies.

Diaz quickly pipes up in Spanglish. I catch the last thing he says: "I'm Diaz, heard you just got here."

Diaz is a five-foot-two, jovial, fifty-year-old rotund Puerto Rican inmate with deep blue eyes. His resemblance to Humpty Dumpty is striking.

"Where you from?" I ask.

"Florida, but I grew up in the Bronx. Where you from?" His accent is a combination of the Bronx mixed with a southern drawl, the pace blistering.

"New York state. Westchester County."

Diaz immediately launches into a soliloquy about growing up in the Bronx near the famous Arthur Avenue, his Puerto Rican–Spanish heritage, his ten kids, nine grandkids, his wife, and why he's a Puerto Rican with blue eyes. I do my best to absorb it all, content to simply be part of a conversation. Ryan and Diaz know each other well. They try their best to size me up by peppering me with a barrage of questions. I, too, have to laugh at the mania of Diaz, my first chuckle in prison. Then things get serious.

"What was that guy doing by your locker?" Ryan asks.

I'm taken aback by the sudden change in tone. "John?" I ask, my voice cracking. I feel like I'm about to be scolded and I don't know why. "He lent me some macs to hold me until next week."

Ryan and Diaz glance at each other, and Diaz is smiling while shaking his head. There's no need to ask, as their facial expressions tell me I've fucked up.

"Did I do something wrong?" I ask, sporting a defeatist attitude. I've only been here a day, so how would I know any better?

Ryan leans in and lowers his voice. "Listen, I've been here over a year. Never had a problem, but that's because I avoid guys like John. He's trouble, a career criminal. His hustle is selling cigarettes, but who knows what else he's into."

The color drains from my face as I turn to my new best friends, much to the bemusement of Diaz who's doing a poor job of containing his laughter.

"What should I do?" I ask.

Diaz starts in, "First, *never* accept a gift in prison. No one gives you something because you're a nice guy. You're in prison! Second, give 'em back right away. Whaddaya think, Ryan?"

Ryan nods. "Have to agree with Diaz. You fucked up taking the macs. Nothing in here is free."

Frantic, I tell them about my dinner with Mo last night and anything else I can think of. My heart is skipping beats.

Less than one day in prison and I screwed up. I beg for advice. "What do I do?"

Diaz replies, "Tell you what I'd do. Give the macs back. You don't even have a lock on your locker yet. John can come back when you're not around, take his macs, and still say you owe him ten macs."

"Diaz is right," says Ryan. "Find John or Mo, and give the macs back."

Diaz sees the fear on my face and calmly suggests, "Let's go up to my room and ask my cellie. He's been here about four years. Good guy. Might even know Mo if you're lucky."

I'm grateful these two men are watching out for me but fearful they may be conning me.

Diaz and I enter his two-man, eight-by-ten-foot room. His roommate in the upper bunk is named Ken Brady. Ken is handsome, dark-skinned, and six feet tall with a shining shaved head. He's muscular and athletic, his white teeth are perfectly straight.

Diaz says, "Ken, meet Jay, he's new here. Got in yesterday and needs a little advice." He turns to me and I can feel my cheeks burning. "Why don't you tell Ken the whole story."

I rehash the story and wait for a response. My nerves are getting the better of me.

Ken dangles his legs from his perch of the upper bunk. "You ever been to prison before?" he asks calmly.

"No," I say sheepishly.

"*Never* accept gifts from someone you don't know really well. You're kinda asking for trouble. I don't know a Mo, but I do know John. He's a scumbag, so there's a good chance his friend Mo is a scumbag."

Diaz sighs. "Whaddaya think he should do?"

I can't believe I have gotten into this much trouble without doing anything. All I wanted was to stay to myself, stay out of trouble, and do my time. It's clear now that things don't always go as planned, especially in prison.

"Best case scenario, give 'em back. A simple thanks-but-no-thanks," Ken says.

Diaz agrees, and it's decided that I will give the macs back—something I am not looking forward to. Thankfully, we change the subject. Ken takes an interest in me, perhaps because he appreciates that I'm not your garden variety inmate at FMC Franklin.

"How long is your sentence?" Ken asks.

"Two years minus good time, one year of supervised release after that."

"That ain't nothin'. What'd ya do, jaywalk in front of an angry or bored fed?"

My legs are spasming again, so I sit down on the lone plastic chair. "I'm uncomfortable talking about my case."

"Listen," says Ken, "I've been here for four years, and I know a lot of the guards, including the CO on duty tonight. I can walk down there now and have him tell me all about you. Secrets? Not in prison."

I feel another surge of adrenaline. Am I to trust these two men I barely know? I think back to my last phone call to my lawyers before Lily and I left for our drive to West Virginia. Both lawyers were adamant that I shouldn't tell anyone about my case. But I have to say something.

"I owned a small office building and rented space to a commercial laboratory that did some bad stuff. The feds thought I was part of their illegal scam, and in the end, I didn't have the resources to prove the negative. Eventually I took a plea, one count of commercial bribery." I tell them my story with as broad a stroke as possible so as not to divulge I'm a doctor and not violate my lawyer's advice to keep my mouth shut.

"For *that*, they put you in prison?" Diaz's eyes are wide.

"Listen, I don't need to know all the details," Ken injects. "Years ago, I was a gym rat. Now I'm a library rat. It's all about culling the herd to feed the system. The US had thirty federal laws in 1790. Now, we have about 5,000 criminal statutes and 300,000 regulations. The government can make anyone a criminal—if they want."

"Exactly. The U.S. Attorney had a narrative and wasn't going to let facts get in the way," I reply.

"Motherfuckers!" says Diaz.

Ken continues, "I don't know you or what you did to end up in here. What I do know after four years here is how the system works. This place—every prison—is filled with guys whose cases hinge on *nothing* but the feds getting false or exaggerated statements out of co-conspirators. Who wouldn't

macs this evening. When you go to commissary, you can pay me the other ten macs you owe me," Mo says.

"I'm sorry, what other ten macs?" I ask as my voice cracks ever so slightly.

"My fee for getting your new clothes done right away. Nothing in here is free. Musta told you that when we ate together. Gotta go, you'll see John tonight."

Mo moves with the rest of the crowd as soon as the rec yard opens. Swarms of men move past me armed with water bottles, weight-lifting accessories, and sneakers. I'm relieved, but still uncertain and frightened about what it all means. In a best-case scenario, I pay the ten macs and Mo leaves me alone. In a worst-case scenario, Mo demands more and more from me. When will it really end, if ever?

CHAPTER 5

Worried Sick

I've always been a worrier. I drove my mother crazy when I was five years old and about to start kindergarten. She had to talk me off the ledge because I was so worried about starting school without knowing how to tie my shoes or tell time. The concept that school was to teach you how to do things went right over my head. My mother used the month of August to teach me how to tie my shoes and tell time proficiently. Now I was ready and willing to tackle the academic pursuits of half day kindergarten.

I walk into the Antioch Unit worried over my interaction with Mo. I feel duped, stupid, and fearful of inmates perceiving me as naïve or weak. Diaz approaches me as I get to my bunk, talking a mile a minute while I'm rehashing what Mo just said to me. Ryan joins soon after. I'm barely listening to Diaz when I notice the scars on Ryan's arm and his atrophied left leg. How did I not notice that yesterday? In an effort to interrupt Diaz's incessant babbling, I quickly chime in, "Ryan, how long have you been in a wheelchair?"

"Let's see," he casually responds, "about ten months here, fourteen months in county jail, and two months in the hospital. What's that, about two years?"

"You were in the hospital for two months?" I ask inquisitively.

"Nah, more like three to four months."

Diaz claps his hands and shouts, "Come on, man, tell him the whole story. It's a great story."

"I'm not trying to be nosy," I say, and it's the truth.

Diaz blurts out, "It's no secret. Everyone in Broward County, Florida,

26

knows about it. I first met Ryan in county jail. Believe me, there are *no* secrets in prison."

Ryan holds his hand up as if to silence Diaz, and it works. "All these gunshots wounds are from robbing a bank," he says as coolly as if he was giving someone directions to the nearest Starbucks. His arm is littered with circular scars.

"Come on, really? Don't fuck with me," I say stupefied.

An animated Diaz adds, "All true. We have at least five other bank robbers just in this unit. Ryan's story is the best."

Ryan laughs. "For once, Diaz is right. Besides, it's no secret." Ryan launches into a monologue to a mesmerized stranger in a strange land as he tells his story while I sit on the edge of my bed with my jaw open in awe.

Ryan was a single, college-educated, well-traveled guy with health insurance who was well paid to manage a chain of restaurants and bars in Florida. When he was thirty-nine, he became clinically depressed. Shortly thereafter, he began to hear voices, increasing in frequency over time. With no history of mental illness, Ryan ignored the changes and instead started conversing with the voices.

Although financially comfortable, he never saw a doctor, and he and his inner demons decided to extort money from a local supermarket chain. He threatened to taint several high-volume items unless the supermarket gave him $5 million. When the money wasn't paid, he exploded a pipe bomb in the middle of the night in front of its flagship store. Ryan emphasized he never wanted to harm anyone with his bombs.

It's not hard to make a bomb, apparently. The bomb worked so well that the voices told him to take a bomb into a bank and rob it. Ryan entered the bank on December 14, 2013. He unzipped his jacket in front of the bank teller, exposing a bomb that was hanging from around his neck, handed the teller a handwritten note that demanded $40,000. Ironically, it was the same bank branch where he did his personal banking. The teller returned with the money but made sure all the silent alarms were triggered. By the time Ryan opened the door to exit the bank with the $40,000, several policemen were standing on the sidewalk with their guns drawn. They commanded he lie face down on the sidewalk, hands fully visible. Every second that passed, more and more emergency vehicles arrived, including a SWAT team and a helicopter. There were enough vehicles to quell a coup in most third-world countries.

Ryan lowers his voice and says, "I was face down, and I didn't know how many vehicles and personnel descended on the bank. I remembered a police officer telling me not to get up. Not caring if I lived or died, the voices told me it was time to get up. And so I did."

Diaz pretends he is holding a gun and shouts. "*Pop—pop, pop, pop*. Take that, motherfucker. Another inmate downstairs actually saw the whole thing while he sipped his morning espresso across the street from the bank."

"Thanks for the sound effects, Diaz," Ryan says with an eye roll. "As I began to get up, I heard the police yelling at me, 'Stay down.' I didn't. Thirty bullets were fired at close range, fourteen landed in me. The bomb never exploded because it was only a fake. The last thing I remembered was being loaded into the ambulance knowing that somehow, I would survive the shooting. My instinct was correct."

"Fourteen bullets, close range, and you lived? That's amazing," I say.

"I guess so, but it's all old history at this point. Now I have to figure out a way to survive in prison for another seventeen years. That's no easy task either."

I'm mesmerized by Ryan's story. Never in my wildest dreams did I imagine being friends with someone like Ryan, a man who committed a crime that landed him in prison for twenty years. I hung around social elites, fellow physicians, business leaders, and attended highfalutin fundraisers and events. But strangely, Ryan's story was honest and real. It felt like the first true thing I had heard in a long time. At the same time, I was still worried about my debt to Mo. I needed to know what to do, so I changed the subject from the grandeur of bank robbery to banal petty prison extortion. Finally, I decided to defer to Ryan and Diaz's prison instincts.

"By the way, I ran into Mo on my way in here tonight."

A laughing Diaz asks, "Did he ask you for a blowjob yet?"

I pause, not knowing if Diaz is joking or not. "I'm freaked out enough. Is that what he'll want from me?"

"That's only if you're lucky," Diaz snickers.

"I told him I don't need the macs so he can take them back. That's when he told me he'll have John take them back, but I owe him ten more macs as payment for arranging to get my prison clothes right away."

"Nah, he ain't gonna let you off that easy," Diaz says, and Ryan agrees. "By the way, every inmate gets new clothing their first day in prison. With or without Mo, you could have walked down to laundry and they'd give you fresh clothes."

I know they're right, which worries me. "Jay" and "lucky" were two words that haven't been used in the same sentence for a few years now.

The four-p.m. count goes uneventfully. A count, always conducted by two guards, is how the prison knows everyone is accounted for, twice daily on weekdays, three times on weekends. Feeling like a seasoned veteran, I know to stand up for count when everyone else does. After count, I just want to sleep. It's been over thirty hours since my arrival. Exhaustion is getting to me. I check with Ryan to see if there are any other obligations before dinner, and I'm informed it's all leisure time now. In fact, it's the beginning of the weekend. My first weekend in prison, my first weekend away from loved ones. My life as I know it has been hijacked for two years with no way out.

I return to my bed but still too nervous to let my guard down. I lie there, my head swimming. Some time passes before Diaz stops by and tells me that we'll go to dinner together. I've realized something about my new friend: Diaz needs to share his prison smarts with anyone who will listen to him babble. Why not listen? I'm the one who's in desperate need of prison survival skills.

Diaz is in full jabber mode while I tune in and out of his weekend ramble. I oscillate between Diaz's monologue and noticing my environment in exquisite detail. I stare at the bunk bed above me with its rusted springs, torn plastic mattress, and remnants of illegible graffiti. My own bed is no less disgusting. Internally I debate if rusted springs are better than no springs. I'm in disbelief of the entire scenario. I wonder if I could have fallen any farther.

"What you gonna do to get Mo off your back?" Diaz asks.

I turn my full attention to him. "Maybe he'll take pity on me and just call the whole thing off."

"Yeah, about as likely as the Vatican opening a Planned Parenthood office in Rome. Listen, giving the macs back to John tonight is a good first step. Then next week you'll buy ten extra macs to pay for Mo's laundry fee. That's all you can do, dude, other than pray Mo won't try to torture you the entire time you're here."

"You trying to help me or make me feel worse?"

"Rest, wash up, and I'll be down in an hour to go to dinner. Promise I won't charge you anything for showing you around while we walk to dinner. You can't worry about everything in here or I guarantee you'll go crazy. One day at a time, hear me? See ya later."

I'm now all alone in what seems like a Russian Gulag right out of Aleksandr Solzhenitsyn's *The Gulag Archipelago*. He eloquently described the unsanitary conditions, meager food, hard labor, and violence. It was where Stalin placed his political opponents, doctors, writers, artists, scientists, Jews, and hardened criminals.

If I die tonight, would anyone ever know what happened to me? I survey the room, which is nicknamed the "Bus Stop," as this is a dumping ground for new inmates, inmates just back from Solitary, inmates kicked out of their rooms, or inmates who just want to be in a central location in order to keep their finger on the pulse of all that goes on in the unit.

Despite not sleeping for well over thirty hours, I dare not close my eyes. Besides, I know within an hour my new best friend Diaz will be escorting the rookie to dinner. I spend my time gazing, but not staring at each inmate. What did they do to land themselves here? Do they deserve to be in prison? Each man has a story, a sad story. It has to be a sad story, otherwise they wouldn't be in here.

Before I know it, Diaz is standing over me. "Thought for sure you'd be asleep," he says. "You gonna spend your entire sentence here without sleeping?"

I look up and smile. "If I thought I could do it, I would. Just a guess, but at some point, my body will crash. How are you doing?"

"I'm fine. I'm always fine, but I've been doing this longer than you. It's the weekend, so enjoy your first prison weekend."

I sigh. There's a first for everything, but I'm still unsettled to think that I have so many "firsts" in prison. "Diaz, how long have you been in prison?"

Diaz bites his lip. "Well, I've been here for almost a year and before that I was in county jail for almost two years. Three fuckin' wasted years. Six more to go."

I'm so astonished every time I hear how long someone received at sentencing, or how long they have been in prison, or how long they have yet to go. Despite that reality, how I will survive a day, a weekend, a week, or a month all seems insurmountable.

Another young inmate approaches my bunk. He whispers something to Diaz, and before Diaz can introduce him to me, the inmate introduces himself.

"Hi, I'm Shane. You look like you're new to this unit. Where'd you come from?"

I introduce myself and tell him I'm from New York.

"No, I mean which prison did you come from?"

These "standard" prison questions amaze me; everyone I've met has asked what prison I came from. I still have so much to learn. "This is the first," I say. "I self-surrendered yesterday."

Shane looks surprised. "Wow, second day in prison. Very cool, man. And you're already listening to Diaz's bullshit? Nah, just kidding. Diaz is good people, especially for a Puerto Rican. Anyway, you're welcome to come to church tomorrow. I'm an usher and pretty involved with the church. It's a good community that helps a lot of guys in here. You should check it out. Besides, you have nothing else to do."

"Thank you," I say genuinely, "I'm not the churchgoing type—but thanks anyway."

"Cool. If you change your mind, come see me. First room on the left when you go around the corner. Diaz, I'll see you later. Go easy on the new guy."

Shane vanishes. I follow Diaz to the cafeteria, rather entertained by his descriptions of all facets of prison life. Judging just by grammar, Diaz sounds as if he has minimal higher education. Yet through my eyes, Diaz is the smartest person I've ever met. This guy knows everything about prison. He floats from one conversation to another, in English and in Spanish. He appears to know everyone and everything. I feel lucky to have met this guy. Like many things in life, sometimes you just have to have faith in people, and I believe Diaz can help me a lot. He also entertains me simply by his manner of speech, a cross between Joe Pesci and Robin Williams.

The dinner goes uneventfully as I try to absorb all of Diaz's wisdom. Diaz, on the other hand, is just as amazed at my naivety regarding life in prison. I am, in his eyes, the most ignorant man he's met in a long time. Fortunately, he likes me and certainly feels sorry for me. He goes out of his way to help me transition to my new life.

On the way back to the housing unit, we notice that everyone is coming back from the outdoor recreation area, which is supposed to be open for another three hours. Diaz stops one of his many friends, a man with colorful neck and face tattoos. In Spanish, he asks why everyone is leaving the rec area on a nice spring evening.

Diaz explains to me the outdoor rec area is closed because there was a stabbing.

"A stabbing?" I ask. "How common is that?"

"It happens. Listen, this is prison, just another day in paradise. Stabbings are part of prison life. That's how disputes get settled. That's how caged animals settle things. It's not too bad in here compared to other prisons, but it happens. Don't worry. If you don't get into disputes or have gambling debts, you'll be fine."

Those words are of no comfort to me. My mind immediately goes to the worst possible place. The macs I owe to Mo—does it end in a stabbing? I keep thinking about my ties to the outside world: a wife, two children, friends and family, colleagues. I was a well-regarded and well-known physician, a community leader. My goal, once I learned of my twenty-four-month sentence, was to make it out of prison with my health intact. Thirty-six hours in prison and I'm wondering how long it will be before I get stabbed and killed.

Diaz sees the color drain from my face, the fear, the newness. If he's going to help me, he has to give me some hope.

"Stabbings are rare in here."

"Where I come from, stabbings are nonexistent," I say in a shaky voice.

"I hear you, man, but forget where you come from. You're in prison, just like everyone else. No one's gonna stab you unless you do something stupid."

"Like owing macs to a stranger?"

"Come on, let's go back to the unit and I'll show you how the computers work."

He starts to walk away, but I'm frozen in place. He turns around and sighs. "Jay, look at me—no one's gonna stab you. You're gonna live. You just need to learn what it takes to survive on this side of the fence. It's a whole different set of rules you gotta learn." He has comforted me a bit, but I can't get it out of my head that someone was stabbed.

We walk to the unit and enter a small room that has about ten outdated computers. The screens are smudged and the keyboards look beat up, but they're functional.

Diaz gets on a computer and gives me a quick tutorial. Again, I'm mesmerized with Diaz's fluency of prison life. Two seats over, a large muscle-bound inmate stands up from the computer and walks away. He has a large bicep swastika tattoo. The word *fuck* is tattooed on the back of his left calf, and the word *you* on his right calf. *Get me out of here.*

I thank Diaz profusely for his tutorial. Now the fatigue is becoming overwhelming. I can barely rise from the computer chair. We have forty-five minutes until the nine o'clock count. If I go to bed before nine, I will never wake up for count.

"I'm going to head back," I say.

"See you soon, my man," Diaz says, and we part ways.

Instead of going upstairs to my room, I wander into the enclosed courtyard that is just off the computer lounge area. The courtyard has six picnic tables where assorted inmates are engaged in chess, dominos, checkers, and bullshitting. There is an obvious racial divide, as the whites congregate with whites, Blacks with Blacks, Latinos with Latinos. I know no one, so I walk aimlessly around the courtyard, listening to snippets of different conversations.

Suddenly I see a familiar but unfriendly face heading toward me. It's John. An adrenaline surge wakes me right up. To my surprise, John's smiling, almost laughing.

"You lucky son of a bitch! You are one lucky dude," John says in a mocking manner.

I'm confused. I don't know what he's talking about, and I feel anything but lucky.

"Mo's in the SHU. How fuckin' lucky can you get?"

Ice crawls through my veins. The SHU stands for Special Housing Unit. Most people on the outside know it as solitary confinement. I know it's never where you want to be.

"What happened?" I ask, trying to keep my voice steady.

"Mo got into a fight earlier tonight in the rec yard. All I know is one of the guys was stabbed, but they're both in the SHU. Probably both be shipped out to a higher security prison for a stabbing."

My eyes are wide. "Do you know what the fight was about?"

"Nah, probably some kinda debt. Maybe the kind of debt you would have had with Mo. But with Mo gone, you're home free, you lucky motherfucker. Mo isn't a bad guy, but extortion is kinda his thing. Maybe you would have gotten him off your back, maybe not. Either way, you lucked out tonight."

Standing there motionless and exhausted, I breathe a sigh of relief. A twenty-thousand-pound weight was lifted from my shoulders as John walks away whistling.

CHAPTER 6

Precious Sleep

Not having slept in over two days, everything is becoming blurry. Sleep-deprived and delirious with fear, I remain in the courtyard. I know I have to sleep, but I'm still too afraid to close my eyes. I have visions of someone putting their hands over my mouth and suffocating me while I'm sleeping. The interior courtyard is the better choice for staying awake until the nine o'clock count.

It's a beautiful spring evening, and every table in the courtyard is filled with a full complement of inmates. Defaulting to what I know, I inspect the flowers planted around the perimeter. Canna lilies, hostas, Echinacea, anemones, day lilies, yarrow—all familiar to my love of gardening, all familiar to life in Westchester County. Lily and I have spent countless hours toiling in the garden. Now I'm trying to seek pleasure, beauty from a few plants that abut the twenty-foot-high brick walls of the courtyard.

"Nice lilies, right?"

I turn to see a tall man in his late sixties with his arms clasped behind him, also admiring the plants.

"Few more months and I'll be back home in my own garden," he says confidently. "Love to be in my garden with a cigar and a cold beer. Used to pay the gardeners lotta money to make everything look just right. Won't be able to afford that when I get out, but I can still have a cigar and a beer."

"Sounds good to me," I say as I size him up. We have a common interest in gardening, which is a good start.

"You're new here, right? When did you get in?" he asks.

"Two days ago."

"Where were you before that?"

This time I know he isn't asking about my old life and where I lived. He's asking which prison or jail I was transferred from. I now know the difference between jail and prison. Jails are usually for short-term stays, although that can often mean up to a few years. A jail is where you wait to be tried or sentenced or transferred. Once you are found guilty, which they always do either via a plea or a trial, you are then transferred to a prison where you serve the remainder of your sentence. Prisons, on the other hand, are designed to house inmates for long periods of time.

"Self-surrendered," I say confidently.

"You're lucky, at least about that. I was in county jail for two months. You think this place is a shit hole? You should live in a county jail. As bad as the food is here—and it's horrible—try living on bologna sandwiches and grits for two months. Finally put me in shackles, flew me from Pittsburgh to Oklahoma City. Stayed there for a week without any of my meds. Then, back in shackles, I got to fly Con Air to this place. You in the Bus Stop?"

"Yeah. Pretty noisy place," I respond, trying to contain my anger.

"Ah, you'll get used to it. You get used to a lot of things in here you never could have imagined. How long a sentence you got?"

Diaz was right; it's okay to ask someone how long a sentence they have. It's not okay to ask what their crime was. Quite an education I've gotten in just two days.

"Twenty-four months."

"Oh, white-collar bullshit? I got twenty-four months too."

"Yeah, total bullshit, but I'm here," I say assuredly. Sure enough, my new friend looks relieved and far friendlier when he hears I'm in for a white-collar crime. The fact that I have a short sentence and I self-surrendered tells everyone I can't possibly be a cho-mo. We exchange pleasantries. His name is Alan, and I like him already.

"I know it seems like you'll be here forever, but time does go by quickly," Alan says. "Before I know it, I'll be back home. Got less than a hundred days left."

It's time for count, so we part ways. A smile creeps onto my face. I'm amazed. Alan did it. He survived prison. I'm in awe and envious that he's at the tail end of his sentence and I'm just starting mine.

I slowly make my way up to my bunk on the second floor before count starts. Across the room, Ryan is rummaging through his locker with a towel draped over the back of his neck. There are a few minutes before count, so I decide to chat him up.

"Getting ready for count?" I ask as I approach.

"Nope, getting ready for bed. I like to read a chapter or two before I crash. They have me on these meds that can put a herd of elephants to sleep. I'm amazed I wake up at all. Haven't you noticed I sleep all day?"

Now that he mentioned it, I did see him sleep like a hibernating bear this afternoon, but then again, a lot of guys spend their time sleeping.

"If I were you, I would try to get some sleep tonight," he says. "You got bags under your eyes. You can't *not* sleep. Besides, with a little luck, no one should bother you at night. I mean that. Odds are you'll be fine. This place may look weird and scary—and it is—but it's not as bad as you think. Really, man, you'll be fine."

Not as bad as you think are the words he uses to comfort me? I receive no comfort from those words, but I know he's right. I have to sleep. I'm just hoping I won't suffer too much before someone decides to kill me. I'm rooting for someone to kill me quickly, if that's my fate. Only two days in here and I don't care if I live or die, resigned to the reality that I won't be able to survive my sentence. My life has already been pointlessly taken from me by an overzealous Department of Justice who then handed me over to their enforcer, the BOP. Please make the execution quick.

I decide that once count is over, it will be time to close my eyes. I always believe that no matter how bad a day is, the morning always comes. Hell, the sun came up the day after the Boston Red Sox finally won the World Series after an eighty-six-year drought.

Someone at the end of the room shouts, "Walking," and everyone stands up for count. Two guards, one fatter than the other, walk through the Bus Stop mumbling numbers as they count each inmate. Their cheeks bulge with chewing tobacco, each holding a cup where they periodically spit into. Fat and Fatter exit the room as unceremoniously as they entered. A minute later, one of the guards shouts, "clear," at which time everyone goes about their own activities.

I tell Ryan that I'm going to sleep and he assures me once again that I'll be fine. He'll see me in the morning.

I already know Mo is in the SHU. Ryan tells me it's safe to sleep, so what do I have to lose other than my life? Fully dressed, teeth not brushed, and a hand towel rolled up to serve as a pillow, I lay supine on my bed, staring up at the rusted springs above me. Fatigue has won out over fear.

CHAPTER 7

Train Wreck

I stretch my legs and arms; grateful I survived the night. I see daylight. I see people scurrying about although most roommates remain asleep on Saturday morning. Ryan is already dressed and ready to go to breakfast, but first he comes over to congratulate me. So as not to disturb the sleeping inmates, Ryan whispers, "I told you nothing would happen if you went to sleep." What I'm learning to appreciate is that that there's safety in numbers. There are potentially thirty-one eyewitnesses to my execution. Perhaps that is what keeps some of the peace in here.

Grabbing my hand towel and a tiny bar of soap, I head to the bathroom. Perhaps *bathroom* is too generous a word. There are two bathrooms near the Bus Stop, each to be used by one person at a time. Since doors and locks are prohibited, a shower curtain serves as a door. When someone occupies the bathroom, the shower curtain is closed and a mop stick angled diagonally across the opening letting people on the outside know the bathroom is occupied.

There is a shower, a toilet, a urinal six inches from the sink, and a sink with a mirror above it. The mirror, circa 1940, is clouded over and thus useless. Mold covers the tiles and other surfaces. A few areas are devoid of tiles and plaster, exposing old pipes and asbestos linings. All the fixtures and faucets are in varying states of disrepair. A large fan is on the outer wall overlooking the courtyard. The dust on the fan blades has to be an inch thick. The wires are fully exposed. Having been forewarned, I'm wearing a pair of worn-out flip-flops Diaz gave to me so my feet will never have to be in direct contact with the floor. The smell of the bathroom can choke a donkey and all its offspring. One more thing to get used to.

I turn both handles of the faucet. Much to my surprise, scalding hot water comes out. I adjust the broken handles to finally arrive at a usable temperature. The water feels delightful on my face, so I wash my face before running my wet hands through my hair. I gaze in the mirror but realize the futility of using a mirror that doesn't reflect an image. I quickly pee, brush my teeth, and get the hell out of that toxic petri dish. I remove the broomstick, open the shower-curtain door, and see three or four inmates waiting in line for the bathroom. Ryan is one of them. He gives me a fist bump as I silently walk past him making my way back to my bunk. I'm fifty-five years old sharing a room with thirty-one strange men, locked behind rows of barbed-wire fencing, stripped of my identity, dignity, and basic human rights. The guards, hired to ensure I don't escape, are mostly inbred tobacco-chewing angry hillbillies. If things could get any worse, I'm at a loss to describe how. I've fallen as far as one could fall. A fall from the top rung of society seems to be a longer and more painful descent than for most of the people who are in here, many of whom have lived on the fringes of society. My crash is painful.

I relax on my bunk, needing a few moments to gather myself before I face the day. Ryan is reading a book, but I need to interrupt him with more questions. Oddly, a man who was shot fourteen times while robbing a bank with a weapon of mass destruction has a rather calming effect.

"I have a quick question for you," I say as I sit in the nearby chair. "Because it's the weekend, I hear there's an extra count at ten."

"Yeah, weekends and holidays always have an additional ten a.m. count. Don't ask me why, but that's what they do here."

"Anything else different on weekends I need to know about?"

"Not really. Did anyone explain 'move' times to you?"

I shake my head. There is still so much to learn.

Ryan explains that "move" times are nothing but suggested move times by the management. Moves allow inmates to move from one location to another every hour on the half-hour—for instance, 8:30, 9:30, 10:30, etc. The guards give you ten minutes to go from one location to another before locking the doors, so wherever you are, you have to stay there until the next move.

I feel frustrated. Since I've arrived, neither an administrator nor a correctional officer has pulled me aside and explained all the rules and regulations. I was just thrown into the deep end without a life raft.

"Why isn't any of this basic information explained to me by the staff?"

"The staff at this prison doesn't give a shit about you," Ryan says. "They're as lazy as the sentences are long and they lie like a rug. Safe to say after living here a year that I've never seen a group of people so incompetent, lazy, and disrespectful as the people who work at FMC Franklin."

"So we don't talk to the guards at all?" One of the first things I noticed was the lack of guards. Other than for count, there's never more than one guard in Antioch to watch three hundred men.

"You can talk to them, but remember they're never your friend. Wait until you meet your case manager, counselor, and unit manager. They make the Three Stooges seem like Florence Nightingale. These are just bad, angry-at-the-world people, and they want to make your useless life a little more miserable."

My breathing quickens and I feel overwhelmed. I've been too preoccupied to process everything going on around me, much less meeting with my case manager. "I heard there's an orientation for inmates," I say.

Ryan bursts into laughter. "It would be very easy to sit you down, explain the rules, and make the transition smoother. But that's not what happens here. Don't *ever* expect *anything* from this worthless staff. They suck and that's just how it is. They hate us, we hate them. Get used to it." Quickly changing the subject, he says, "Have you met the German yet?"

Ryan points to an older inmate, about sixty-five, who is trim, has a white beard, and a stern look on his face.

"No. I've seen him around. He's only two bunks away from me but seems to be in his own world. Does he speak English?"

"Oh yeah, his English is good, just with a thick Nazi accent. He's only been here a few months and keeps to himself. He's been down for a pretty long time. Think he was transferred from another FMC, but who knows. Seems pretty healthy to me. It's interesting, but you'll meet a lot of guys who really don't talk to anyone. Everybody does their time differently."

Ryan says the German has "been down," which means how long he's been in prison. If someone asks how much "paper" you have," it refers to how much probation you got once you're released. Nothing here seems to make sense.

"By the way Jay, you got a GED? They'll bust your balls if you don't. Make you go to all these stupid classes until you pass. I think the prison gets money for pretending that they teach you enough to pass the GED test. You got one or not?"

"I'm good," I say slowly. "I graduated high school." For some reason, I don't want to tell him I went to college, let alone medical school. Maybe I don't want to share my past with anyone. Maybe it's too depressing to talk about everything I have lost.

"Cool. One less form of torture. Before you know it, you'll be getting out of this place unless they kill you while you're in here." Ryan grows serious. "No shit, a lot of guys die in here. Really sad. You'll see when you go up to medical for your arrival physical. It's a shit show. They sent you here because of your multiple sclerosis?"

I nod affirmatively but choose not go into the details of my broken-down body. Seven years ago, I was diagnosed with multiple sclerosis, a progressive disease that attacks the central nervous system. Each attack affects a different part of the brain or spinal cord, meaning you lose a piece of your nervous system. My first attack left my feet numb, my speech slurred, and my hands uncoordinated. Another attack weakened my legs, offset my sense of balance, and left me profoundly fatigued.

I remember when the neurologist first told me of my diagnosis, only a few hours before thirty people were coming to my house for a Passover dinner. My immediate reaction was one of devastation. I wasn't thinking about several of my patients who had MS but lived relatively normal lives. My focus was on my father's best friend who was wheelchair-bound, blind, and died by his mid-forties from MS. My focus was on how many things I loved were going to be altered for the worse. In this prison, I will be going to the medical clinic three times a week for an injection in an effort to prevent future attacks, if they give me the medication.

In an effort to change the subject, I ask, "Is getting a pen and paper difficult around here?"

My father grew up a few blocks from Yankee Stadium. He attended Lou Gehrig Day, July 4, 1939 when Gehrig gave his epic farewell address. Forty years later, we went to the second tribute to Gehrig, a brainchild of Yankee owner George Steinbrenner. It was a poorly executed, worthless tribute. When the event was covered in the NY Times, I wrote a letter to the editor expressing how disappointed we were. The letter got published and that was the beginning of my passion for writing. Lily too loved to write. Since both her mother and father's families settled in Palestine in the 1850's, she grew up communicating with her many Israeli relatives via hand written letters.

Ryan reaches into the bowels of his locker and pulls out a writing pad. "Here, you can have this. I got plenty of pens too."

Wow, a pen and paper. This is my mental escape from the horror of a third-world prison. It's as if Ryan has just handed me the Holy Grail. I rush back to my bunk, unsure of how closely they review outgoing mail. I know all outgoing letters can't be sealed. Is that to check for contraband, or do they read every letter? Who cares? "Go to it, Jay. Tell the world what it's like," I say with an angry passion.

Dearest Lil,

It doesn't quite seem as I imagined. I've entered a new world since I last saw you. Okay, I don't even know where to begin. My only goal at this point is to stay alive another day. Tomorrow I'll worry about tomorrow.

I hope you and the kids are all well. I miss saying, "I love you." I miss sharing a bed with my wife of thirty years. I miss hearing what Sara and Richard are doing as they launch their careers. One day, when this nightmare ends, I will tell you I love you face to face.

The building looks like the movie set from the film *Shawshank Redemption*, built in 1925 and without a renovation since. It's strange, but it's a real prison, not at all like we were told. The food is inedible, especially for me. Imagine, I haven't had a salad or piece of fruit since I arrived. I'm in a large dorm room with about thirty other men along with a few rats, mice, and cockroaches. There's no air-conditioning. I still haven't received orientation yet, so it's trial by fire and word of mouth. They have yet to give me Copaxone, diazepam, Lovaza, Crestor, or Bactrim. No one seems to care that I'm not getting my meds except me.

Much to my surprise, there is actually a room full of guitars including three classical for use by the inmates. I'll need you to mail copies of my sheet music.

As if I don't have enough stress, I have to live with a big lie. I haven't told anyone I'm a doctor. There are too many stories of inmates being extorted, and I don't want to put a bull's-eye on my back. I've learned to just say it was a "white-collar" crime. Maybe someday I'll come out of the closet and be able to be honest about my past.

I'm really wrestling with the heavy Southern accents and constantly have to ask people to repeat things. People think I'm pretty stupid.

It's an interesting mix of inmates with about forty percent incarcerated for drugs, fifty percent sex offenders, and ten percent all other. Regardless of the offense, psychiatric disease is rampant. When all the psych hospitals were closed in the eighties, it didn't mean mental illness disappeared. It just moved from the psych hospitals to the prisons. What a train wreck.

I miss you more than you know, and cannot wait until I'm free.

Your loving husband,
Jay

CHAPTER 8

A Caged Asylum

Diaz is eager for me to go to breakfast with him. I have nothing else to do but go with the flow of the day. No plans. No projects to work on. No phone calls to make or return. No one to text or email. No one to meet with. Just survive this asylum. At least I had a fair night's sleep. I don't recall waking up with leg cramps, the guard's flashlights, or anything.

Diaz leads the way with his characteristic right-tilted gait, looking like Humpty Dumpty about to roll over to his right. I love the guy, but I already know I can only take him in small doses.

When we get to the bottom of the stairs, we see the correctional officer exit his office looking as if he has a massive hangover. I look for a chair to sit and rest my painful legs when suddenly the CO shouts, "Chow!" That's the signal he will open the door of my housing unit and release us for breakfast.

I hate the word "chow." It sounds as if we're farm animals. A crowd heads to the exit much like a herd of cows marching to their execution. For Diaz, this is just another breakfast. For me it's my first. At home I rarely have much more than my morning cappuccino for breakfast. Am I really that naïve or just hoping that it would be like a New York diner? Once again, I'm wrong.

We wait in the long cafeteria line of almost a hundred prisoners. My mind focuses on inmate after inmate as they leave the cafeteria and have to pass those of us waiting. Limbless, bandaged, wheelchairs, odd-looking, scary looking—they all walk by me. Diaz starts to laugh.

"What's so funny?" I ask.

"I'll tell you when we sit down. It's a great story," he whispers.

45

Just then, two longhaired inmates with a distinctive female wiggle saunter by. I have a revelation and poke Diaz in the side. "Holy shit! I thought this was a men's prison. I just saw two ladies go by."

"Oh yeah, forgot to tell you there are a bunch of trannies in here."

"Trannies?"

"Ya know, transgender dudes. Think that's Emerald and Samantha who walked by. Their real names are Emmet and Samuel. They're changing from dudes to ladies. BOP says if you got a penis, you go to a men's prison."

I watch Emerald and Samantha walk away from my line of vision. I can't fathom the daily perils they face with transitioning from one gender to another, while incarcerated.

The breakfast consists of generic cereal flakes, a large piece of chocolate cake, a biscuit, and a half pint of skim milk. Cake for breakfast? Diaz confirms this is normal in here and then crumples up the cake, pours it on the cereal, and pours milk on top of both. As I look around, most of the inmates mix their cake, cereal, and milk to form a breakfast treat. My breakfast is really just playing with the food with my plastic fork and spoon. For obvious reasons, there are no knives in this place.

In my mind, Diaz is a prison savant. While he simultaneously carries on conversations with people at the surrounding tables in English and in Spanish, my mind wanders to when I was a little boy in my parents' house. With each season, my mother would bring home the most delicious foods, long before the term "seasonal cuisine" was used—persimmons in the late fall, Comice pears and ruby red grapefruits in the winter, artichokes in the spring, cherries in June, melons, peaches, and plums in the summer. My daydream is short lived.

"Jay, Jay, have you heard of hooch?" Diaz asks with a mouthful of cereal. I tell him I only know it from movies, and he laughs. He enjoys laughing at me.

Hooch is the inmate word for homemade alcohol. Inmates take fermentable sugars, i.e. an apple mixed with water and yeast. They store it in a place where the guards won't find it while it ferments into a consumable adult beverage. Sometimes it will be in the HVAC ducts, a garbage dumpster, or a toilet tank.

Inmates used to be able to steal yeast from the kitchen, but the prison stopped supplying yeast for this reason. Now, the yeast comes from the fat folds of the overweight inmates. They scrape the yeast from their richest fat fold and sell it on the black market. Apparently, there is one man in Antioch whom they call "fatman," the major supplier of grade-A hooch yeast. If it's who I think it is, the man must wear a size seventy-two sport coat. He's enormous.

"Remember when I was laughing in line? Almost forgot to tell you about Frankie One Stamp," Diaz says in a low voice. "He was standing about three or four people in front of us. Anyways, Frankie is kind of an underground celebrity in some circles. Let me make it clear: I know who he is, but I don't really *know* Frankie One Stamp. Catch my drift?"

"Just spit it out," I say in a sharp tone. I'm glad I have met Diaz, but the man doesn't know the meaning of the word silence.

"There are two currencies in this prison. You learned about macs the hard way. The other currency is stamps. Each stamp is worth forty-nine cents, or two stamps equals one mac. Macs are more common, but some people trade in stamps. Remember I told you how everyone has their own hustle, doing whatever they have to in order to survive in this dump?"

"Yeah."

Diaz leans in even closer. I can see the pores on his nose. "Well," he says, "for one stamp, for forty-nine cents, Frankie One Stamp will give *anyone* a blowjob. That's how he got his name. Want me to introduce you to him?" He bursts into laughter.

"Come on, you're shittin' me. Is that really true?"

"Swear to God, Jay, this place is filled with crazies. And just when you think you've met them all, someone crazier comes along. This place is fucked up."

Diaz is almost done with breakfast. In the corner of my eye, I spot something lying on the floor about ten feet away. "What's that?" I ask.

Diaz chuckles. "What do ya think it is? It's a dead rat. They gotta eat too, right? You'll get used to it. Lot of rats, lot of mice around here. Guys who work in the kitchen and warehouse say it's filled with rats. Trust me, they're the least of your problems. They're harmless."

Now I've really lost my appetite.

After breakfast, I lie on my bunk, wallowing in my mass of self-despair, feeling all alone, feeling sorry for myself, confused, angry. Pick a negative adverb or adjective, they all apply. Yet, this place is too dangerous to let my guard down. I must remain focused and vigilant.

The Bus Stop offers an interesting perspective of the housing unit. It isn't really a room but rather a wide hallway with bunk beds lining each side. People pass through from one part of the unit to another. There is no regard for the fact that this is where people like myself actually live. As people pass through, they maintain conversations, arguments, yell from one end to the other, carry their trans-fat-laden food, or engage in an occasional pushing–shoving incident. This is where I live. Five other strange men live within three feet of my living space.

I miss my king-sized bed I shared with my beautiful wife. Our bedroom had six tall windows overlooking the backyard. The peaceful sound of our small pond and waterfall was just below the bedroom windows with frogs croaking throughout the night. That was then, this is now.

There is a beacon of light in all of this darkness. Throughout breakfast, while I was trying to ignore Diaz's disgusting stories, I couldn't stop thinking about what I would write to Lily. I can't scare her by telling her everything but I'll write down my thoughts. My letters can be a sort of therapy session on paper, to help me sort out what I'm thinking and feeling, to document what goes on in this unspeakable place.

Dear Lil,

It's only my fourth day here, and I'm not yet capable of describing what has been taken from me, but hopefully someday I will. I'll try my hardest to stay healthy, and that will be the challenge. It makes every other life challenge a mere walk in the park. I've never read the *Divine Comedy*, but I think I now understand the meaning of *Dante's Inferno*.

I thought I was going to a federal medical center and it would be like a hospital with a fence around it. Everyone would be here because of a medical malady. Not even close. Some guys look like they're in rough shape. I've seen blind guys, limbless guys, demented, stroked out, you name it. Psychiatric disease is rampant in here. However, many are normal, at least physically speaking. So far, I haven't seen anything that would make me call this a medical center and everything that would make me call it what it really is: a fucking prison. Plain and simple.

If that isn't enough, I'm now being told the medical care here sucks. Guys die left and right. My head was spinning when I first arrived. Now it's ready to explode. I hear the medical care at the university, about fifteen minutes from here, is better. This place is nothing but a large triage center and any real care is done at University Hospital. I hope I'm seen by the neurologist and immunologist at the university within the month.

I have a bottom bunk since a top bunk would be a guaranteed disaster for an MS patient. The tiny plastic mattress is limp, and everything squeaks when the guy on top moves. Sleeping is not easy, especially since I can't have any diazepam for my leg cramps. You can imagine how few hours I sleep between high ambient noise, voices galore, leg cramps, fear, and guards checking all the beds three times a night. Commissary is only open to me on Wednesdays, so I won't have a watch until then. All the calls, letters, and emails are monitored both ways, so be nice. I don't want to stay here any longer than I signed up for. It's been cool so far, so no air conditioning hasn't been a problem, but that will change soon, and for me that will be an upcoming battle. I'm waiting for commissary day and will eat nuts and prunes rather than sloppy cafeteria starch. Don't share the details with the kids quite yet. All hands-on deck!

I miss you something awful. Don't ever forget about me.

All my love,
Jay

I spend the afternoon in the four-acre outdoor rec area trying to look at ease despite being wound as tight as a top. At the northern end of the yard is a large baseball field with a dirt infield. The center of the rec area is filled with several handball and volleyball courts. The southern end has side-by-side basketball courts, a bocce-ball area, and horseshoe pits. The basketball courts have rims and nets, but the pavement is filled with divots and barely visible court markings. There are scattered cement picnic tables throughout the yard. Unlike the rest of the prison compound, the rec yard is spacious and that's what I yearn for. I can easily wander from location to location, sun to shade, noisy to quiet. Beyond the barbed-wire fences are beautiful green hills, sparsely populated by humans but confirming there is a world on the other side of the fence. This brings me comfort.

Suddenly, I start to panic because I realize that no matter what, I have to stay within the confines of these fences. Perhaps there are about ten acres comprising the entire prison. My world for the foreseeable future is limited to ten acres. I feel like a zoo animal confined to a cage. Regardless of the size or living conditions, I'm a caged animal. I think about all the turtles, fish, reptiles, and amphibians that I housed as a child. Now I see the cruelty of my childhood hobby through completely different eyes. I seek to justify my actions by immediately claiming how different humans are from dumb animals. Maybe that's true, maybe not. That only raises a much broader issue, which is why I'm here. I understand many people in here have done horrific things to other humans and need to be separated from society. But what about me and all the other non-violent first-time offenders?

Every judge and prosecutor should spend a short period of time as a prisoner so they know what they are sentencing people to. Why am I separated from society? I pose *no* threat to society, and yet I'm treated exactly the same as the man three bunks down who killed two people in a drug deal gone bad. In my effort to make sense of all of this and observe my new environs, I've done nothing but intensify my level of anger at the system that placed me here. How could I possibly survive and endure a two-year sentence while living in this caged asylum? God, I hate this place.

CHAPTER 9

Meet Dr. Mengele

A beautiful Sunday evening has a different feel when you're in prison. I haven't been able to communicate with my wife by phone or computer. Only my counselor, Ms. Newham, can give me a password, which I will use to log on to the computer or make phone calls. She also gives out pillows, approves visitors, and who knows what else. Despite her "being at work" on Thursday and Friday, no one has seen her in almost a week. I'm told it's very typical in that she prefers hiding rather than being in her office in the housing unit, helping the inmates whom she is supposed to "counsel." Other staff members say she's "around," so be patient. Patient? No pillow, no phone, no computer, and I'm supposed to be patient?

Before I came in here, Lily and I researched the prison. The BOP website said I would have a case manager, a counselor, a unit manager, and even a staff psychologist. On the surface, and having lived in the real world, that all sounds rather positive. Lily has no way of knowing it's all a façade for public consumption. She has to have wondered why I haven't called or if everything is okay. In addition to my angst, I'm also feeling hers.

I try to remember the last time I was out of communication with my wife for these many days. It's a first. We have both gone on separate vacations. I often would attend medical conferences, but we were always in touch. This is new territory.

The last night at home before I turned myself in, we were cuddling up on the sofa in the living room. She couldn't stop crying. I never saw her break down like that. Lily, a woman always in control of every situation, had lost it and I had to do everything possible not to follow her.

"It's going to be okay," I said as I ran my fingers through her curly hair.

"I'm just so scared." She looked up at me, and her green eyes were sparkling. I memorized her face, those few freckles on her cheek and her pouty lips. I didn't want to forget what she *really* looked like.

"I'm going to be fine, I can handle it," I reassured her, but I was freaking out. I had never been so scared.

I took off my gold wedding band and placed it on her left middle finger. "I'll be back for this," I said.

Although a wedding band is permissible in here, I didn't want to risk losing it or someone stealing it. From my reconnaissance, having a wife immediately puts me in the minority. I've met several men who are thankful to be away from their wives. I'm not one of them. My marriage to date has been joyous and gratifying. Our core values are in unison. We've always been on the same page with childrearing. Lily is a fabulous cook, an empathetic woman, an accomplished professional, which makes this experience even more painful. How and why has this happened? I try to put myself in her shoes, but inevitably I obsess over my own predicament. *Focus, Jay. Be alert. Be strong. It won't last as long as your sentence says.* But nothing eases the pain, the omnipresent fear, the anxiety.

While in the courtyard, I strike up a conversation with Jeremy, a kind man from just outside London. His British accent is a welcome anomaly to the painful brand of English that surrounds me.

"I once lived in London," I tell him, but quickly realize I can't tell him the real reason I lived in London. During my last year of medical school, I spent four months completing all my electives at the Royal Free Hospital on Pond Street, the summer when Prince Charles started dating a young woman by the name of Lady Diana Spencer. I pivot quickly. "So, West Virginia must be quite a change for you?"

"Certainly the accents," he responds.

"What kind of business were you in?" I wonder if the question is out-of-bounds, but he seems undisturbed.

"I owned an electrical engineering company based in Maryland and

London before the wheels fell off the bus. It started out as a tax case between two business partners. Once the feds took the case over—well, I learned the meaning of the American idiom, 'Making a federal case out of nothing.'"

What a welcome relief Jeremy appears to be. He's about my age, has been married for a long time, and he also believes that he doesn't deserve to be in prison, especially this horror show. The first conversation you have with any inmate is always rather guarded, each one checking out the other: *Will this person bring harm to me? Can this person be of help to me? What does he really want from me?* I like to think I'm a good judge of character, and I get good vibes from Jeremy.

"Looks like the *call-out* list is out. Want to check it out?" he asks politely as only a British gentleman can.

The *call-out* list comes out every evening. The list provides the names of inmates and whatever appointment they have for the next day, such as a medical or dental visit, or a visit with the unit staff. When someone first arrives here, he will have many more call-outs than someone who has been here for years. Basically, I need to pay attention to this list every day.

I also discover that everyone in prison must hold a job within the prison for which you will be compensated *twelve cents an hour*. No, that is not a misprint. It just adds to the list of things people should have told me before I entered my new world.

I follow Jeremy to check the call-out list, which is located on a table just outside the CO's office. It's organized in alphabetical order by last name. Sure enough, I have one call-out. I have to be in the medical clinic at ten a.m. on Monday. Jeremy speculates it's probably for my entrance physical, which includes blood tests and whatever else the doctor deems appropriate. Everyone has a physical when they arrive.

"I must warn you that the medical staff is a far cry from what you're used to, so don't mistake this visit for a visit with a *real* doctor."

Once again, my nerves are on edge knowing I'm in need of competent health care because my life depends on it. I thank Jeremy for his help and go upstairs to crash on my bunk.

Having an agenda for tomorrow is a welcome change. Wandering aimlessly day after day wears me down even further. Despite what everyone has told me about the poor medical care, I somehow want to believe it's an exaggeration. Plus, I know my way around healthcare.

An inmate a few beds over is being discharged tomorrow. As is common when someone's discharged, they give away or sell whatever they can. This man gives me half a writing pad. He's hosting a stream of visitors who all want to say good-bye and wish him well. I'm envious of this man. Will I ever be in his shoes? If nothing else, it's nice to fantasize about my departure date.

The next morning, Ryan tells me where the medical clinic is located, and much to my surprise, I find it without incident. Rather than using the elevator, I choose to use the stairwell. My dislike of elevators dates back to when I was a medical resident at an enormous 1,300-bed VA Medical Center. We had to share the elevators with patients who were leaking from every possible orifice and/or medical device attached to them. This place is very similar, so although stairs are difficult for me, it beats the alternative of sharing the elevators packed with broken-down inmates.

The clinic feels all too familiar. It has all the sights and smells of a VA hospital, any of the 152 VA hospitals throughout the country. They're all the same, and this place is no different. I sign in and take a seat in a packed waiting room.

This is most unpleasant since there's nothing but inmates in varying degrees of disrepair. A few men have open wounds, some are coughing, others are yelling at the staff who are sitting behind a wall of thick glass. No one's happy, everyone's miserable, patients and staff. It dawns on me that I should always carry a pen and paper as there's so much to write about. Now I know for next time. No magazines, no TV, no cell phones, no smiles. The man sitting next to me is easily four hundred pounds. He, like many of the inmates, uses an extra-wide wheelchair to get around the sprawling prison. On the other side of me are two Spanish-speaking young men who are on the brink of a fistfight. Another man sits in a motorized wheelchair baring a below-the-knee amputation of his left leg. There are bandages on his lower right leg but his infected ulcers peek through.

An hour and ten minutes later, a nurse calls out my name. I make my way to the triage area. She takes my vital signs before dismissing me back to the waiting room where I wait another hour and a half. Finally, I am called to see the doctor. The nurse tersely says, "Keller, second door on your right."

I walk into the exam room where the doctor has his back to me while he types away at his computer. A few minutes pass before he turns around to look at me. He's in his mid-forties, grossly obese, bald, rather unattractive, with visible beads of sweat on his forehead despite being in an air-conditioned office. He sizes me up for a few seconds before going back to typing for another minute or two. *What odd behavior for a physician.* But, I'm willing to give him the benefit of the doubt. After all, I'm in this medical center for medical care, not to become best friends with the doctor. Finally, he turns to me and begins his medical history taking.

"Your name is Keller, 45632-067, brand new here?" he asks with a thick Southern drawl. He's as disinterested as a police officer directing traffic at a football game, waving his arms with authority but with no real care.

"Yes. Just got here a few days ago."

"Okay, let's go through your medication list. Don't want to get it wrong and have to do this whole thing all over again. Crestor, five milligrams a day for your cholesterol; diazepam as needed for leg spasms; baby aspirin daily; Lovaza, two grams twice a day; vitamin D, 5,000 units a day; Copaxone, forty milligrams sub-Q three times a week; and Bactrim DS, three times a week. What the hell are the Copaxone and Bactrim for?"

I already have a bad feeling about this guy.

"Did you read my medical records?" I ask in a non-confrontational tone but don't get a response. "I'm sorry, doctor, but what is your name?"

"Hey, I ask the questions around here, not inmates. What's the Bactrim for? And the name's Dr. Huff."

Recognizing this is quickly deteriorating and taken aback by his hostility, I try to regroup while answering his question.

"I take the Bactrim for my immune deficiency, I've—"

"You got AIDS? Wow, that really sucks."

This is not going well. "It's a little more complicated than that," I say. "What happened was—"

"Yeah, yeah, we'll get to it. Let's try to get through your med list. You take the Lovaza for high cholesterol? That's a non-formulary drug, so you can forget about getting that. Same with Crestor and diazepam. You ain't getting none of that."

"The Lovaza is for familial hypertriglyceridemia," I state matter-of-fact.

"That's a mouthful. What's the Copaxone for? Ain't familiar with that drug."

I clench my fists. All the inmates were right. This is a frightening medical clinic.

"It's for multiple sclerosis."

"Is that one of those million-dollar specialty drugs?"

"It's a lot. About $500 an injection," I reply calmly.

"This country has gone to hell in a hand basket. My mama can't afford her medications after working her whole life for the school system and our government spends $1,500 a week on medication for scumbags like you. What the fuck!"

"I'm not a scumbag, if that makes it easier to understand."

Huff contorts his face even more. "Wrong, mister. Believe me, you're a scumbag otherwise you wouldn't be in this hellhole. Anyway, how long you got MS?"

"About seven years. It's all in the records that were forwarded to the BOP. I even brought an extra copy, which I handed to the intake nurse." I try to remain calm, hoping that he will come around and exhibit a sliver of humanity.

"You got MS and AIDS, and you're just starting your sentence? Man, wouldn't want to be in your shoes. How'd you get both?"

"As I started to say, when I was first diagnosed with MS, they placed me on a newly approved drug called Tecfidera, dimethyl fumarate. The FDA approved it a month before I started it. After about eight to nine months, my neurologist noticed that my lymphocyte count was down to almost zero. This was a known side effect of the drug, and sure enough the FDA had announced two deaths resulting from lymphopenia the same day my doctor saw the low lymph count. He ordered a CD4/CD8 count, and my CD4 count was thirty-seven, just as low as most AIDS patients, but I don't have AIDS, just an old-fashioned immune deficiency. A normal CD4 value is over five hundred. I stopped the Tecfidera immediately and an immunologist started me on Bactrim to prevent Pneumocystis pneumonia. About a month or two later, I was started on Copaxone. Unfortunately, the CD4 count never returned to normal and now I'm in prison."

"You know a lot about this," he says casually.

"That's because I was a doctor before I came in here."

He freezes, then stares over at me, glaring with his beady eyes, his eyebrows arched. He adjusts his large frame on the stool and inches toward me.

"Let's get one thing straight. In here, you're not a doctor. *We* are not colleagues. In here, you're *nothing*. You're just another fucking low-life inmate sent to this shithole because you fucked up in the real world, so get used to it. I repeat: You ain't no doctor in here and hopefully never will be again. The sooner you realize this, the easier it will be for you. If you want to pretend to be a doctor in here, I will personally make you pay, so don't even try. Ever! Believe me, I can make your pathetic life even worse than it already is, and you've fallen pretty far, my man. Did I make myself clear?"

My cheeks burn as anger courses through my veins. "Crystal clear," I say sheepishly. I'm stunned a physician can be this cruel, this uncaring, this mean-spirited. I understand this is a prison, but why work here if you despise everyone you have to treat? Or is he simply sadistic? Perhaps he's a distant relative of the infamous Dr. Mengele, the Angel of Death from the Auschwitz concentration camp.

I was so hoping to have a medical ally while I served my sentence. I wasn't expecting or in need of special treatment. I just need an advocate who would help my medical conditions while incarcerated, someone I could count on to help me if my medical status worsens. Instead, within a few minutes of the first meeting with my doctor, I realize he despises me. I want to scream and cry at the same time. I'm back to square one where the only person who is going to come to my rescue is myself.

He turns his back to me and types away on his computer while not saying a word. Beads of sweat continue to pour down the side of his face, his breathing is labored, and his scrub suit is two sizes too small. Not a pretty sight, but my thoughts are racing about how I'm going to get my non-formulary drugs. I learned from the BOP orientation that there is an appeal process so inmates can receive non-formulary medication. However, the appeal process for medications would have to be initiated by Dr. Huff. I don't see him looking to help Team Keller.

I suddenly become aware of the big picture. I pleaded guilty to a crime I was unaware of nor had any intention of committing. The plea deal was my best–worst option. I have complicated and serious medical conditions my doctor could care less about, and I'm in a disgusting, filthy prison that's disguised as a federal medical center. The medical clinic for this enormous prison complex isn't half the size of my old office. It's all a façade that inmates are going to receive the care that they need. The reality is just the opposite. My goal all along remains exiting from this prison in relatively the same physical condition as I entered. Now I'm consumed with doubt that I will ever get out of this place alive. What if I get sick? Am I dependent on Dr. Huff's clinical acumen to save me? If that's the case, kill me now.

"Can we discuss the non-formulary meds? I was told by the BOP that there's an appeal process," I say in a steady voice.

"You're right, Keller. There is an appeal process and it starts with me. So far, I have no reason to go through that process. We'll get some blood tests. Based on that, *I* make the decision as to whether to appeal for a particular medication. If I were you, don't get your hopes up. They rarely give approval," he says with a sadistic smile.

"What about diazepam? That costs nothing."

"No way! Too much abuse potential in here. If we gave it out for anxiety, the whole fuckin' prison would be on it."

"But I need it for leg spasms from the MS, not anxiety."

He shrugs. "No one dies from leg spasms. You're not getting it."

"That's the only criteria you use around here? Whether someone needs a medication to stay alive? I can't accept that as an answer," I say defiantly.

He cocks his head to the side and huffs and puffs. "You are either really stupid or you just don't get it. You have to accept it because this isn't the real world where you may have been a big-shot doctor. This is a prison! You better learn to accept a lot of things or you won't survive in here very long. I'm supposed to be impressed that you know which meds you should be on? You're in prison, dude. Discussion over."

"What about my Copaxone?"

"For some reason, that expensive shit is on formulary so you'll get it every Monday, Wednesday, and Friday. Hop up onto the exam table. I have to examine you."

Slowly I get up out of my chair and onto the exam table. His sweaty body moves closer so I can truly appreciate the body odor emanating from this grotesque man.

As he holds his thumb forcefully under my eyebrow, his entire exam consists of listening to my heart for ten seconds with his stethoscope placed over my breastbone. He then asks me to take a deep breath. After two breaths, he says, "You can step down now." He completes the physical exam in less than twenty seconds. And I'm the one who's a criminal?

I sit back on the chair while he returns to another five minutes of computer work before he turns his attention back to me. "We're done now. I ordered an EKG, an echocardiogram, chest X-ray, and blood tests. You'll be on callouts for those. Don't miss any of the appointments or I'll make sure there's disciplinary action. By the way, I know what you're thinking. Don't think you can complain to your unit manager that you don't like me and want another doctor. You don't got no choice of a doctor in here. It's prison, and you're stuck with me. If inmates had a choice, I wouldn't have any patients, but that's the nice thing about being a prison doc, I don't have to pretend to be nice to dirt bags like you. Five more years and I'll leave here with a nice, fat pension. What are you going to have in five years, more prison time? And that's only if you're lucky enough to survive this place. Lotta guys don't."

He's dead wrong about that. I will survive this place.

CHAPTER 10
Licking My Wounds

I follow the signs back to Antioch Unit in a daze. Although it's a beautiful day to spend in the courtyard, I need my bed so I can lick the wounds given to me by Dr. Huff. I can't stop thinking about what a mean-spirited, depraved man I have as my doctor. Being a physician worked against me, but he's the first person in here I told what I did on the outside. I remain fearful of telling others I'm a doctor, thus labeling me as a "rich guy," an extortion target. The one nice thing about prison is that everyone dresses the same and no one has any possessions that really are worth a damn. In that regard, everyone is pretty much on even footing. Call me a skeptic, but this place is just a little too scary to tell everyone my life story.

Tattooed John passes through the Bus Stop and comes over. "What's doing, Jay, getting adjusted?"

"Still trying, John," I say.

"Nice, you remembered my name. Anyway, are you good on macs or do you need some until you go to commissary?"

"I'm good for now, but thank you," I say a tad sarcastically.

Does he really think I'm going to go down that path again? He has to have known the angst I went through after Mo lent me the macs. I'm too new at this to try to predict what someone else is thinking.

"I'll see you around, Jay."

No sooner does he walk away in search of his next target when Diaz appears, a comforting sight after being verbally abused by Dr. Huff. "I met the infamous Dr. Harley Huff today," I say.

"What did that fat fuck have to say for himself?" Diaz says with a laugh. "Did I ever tell you the first time I met him? This is a great story." He pulls up a plastic chair before I have a chance to answer his questions.

When Diaz first got here, he was assigned to the Q4 unit, which is the one hospital-like area in the prison. It has about thirty beds for the really sick inmates.

"My defibrillator was all fucked up and I was in big-time heart failure. It was firing when it shouldn't have and some other shit, so they stuck me on the Q4 unit with all the other pathetic sick fucks. Most were there dying of cancer, AIDS, hepatitis, or some other shit. Anyway, there's a doctor in charge of the Q4 unit, but he was on vacation, so who comes around dressed in filthy scrubs? Dr. Huff. He stood over my bed looking at my chart but didn't say anything, so I said to him, 'Who the fuck are you?'"

"He looked at me and said, 'Who the fuck am I? I'm Dr. Huff. Stuck filling in for Dr. Miller, so you better hope you don't get too sick. You Diaz?'"

"'Yeah. Hey, what's with the attitude? I'm a sick guy.' That asshole glared at me and said, "You should have thought of that before you committed a crime. Then you wouldn't have to worry about being here. But too late for all that. I'm just gonna renew your meds. By the way, I see you've been here a few months already, so you probably heard a bunch of shit about me. Well, guess what? It's all true. I am a motherfucker, so don't try any shit with me. I'm hired to babysit you scumbags, and you ain't getting no favors out of me. Don't even think about pain meds."

I reach into my locker for my pen and paper.

"I was shocked the doc would talk to me like that, you know? So I said, I'm not asking for any favors. I'm cool. I thought they was just exaggerating about you being an asshole."

"It's all true. Don't fuck with me and we'll get along fine," he boasted.

"That was the one and only time I had seen Huff as a doctor. I saw him in the hallway every day that week, but he never came back into my room. Wonder what medical school Porky Pig graduated from—probably Dumbfuck University, and I bet he was last in his class. There's no way that guy could ever make it on the outside as a doctor. This is the *only* place that will tolerate his shit."

I'm in shock. The more I hear about Huff, the angrier I get. "This is a pretty disgusting place to be a doctor," I say. "Bet there's a whole backstory about how he ended up working here. How much longer you got in here again?"

"Shit, about seven years."

"Seven years," I repeat incredulously. "I'm really sorry to hear that."

"You're sorry? There's no way my heart is gonna last seven years in here. I got a condition called cardiomyopathy, which they think was caused by a virus, but no one is really sure. I had good docs in Florida, but that doesn't help me now."

"Not with guys like Huff running the clinic."

Diaz explains that he has an ejection fracture of eighteen percent. That's the amount of blood the heart can pump out each time it beats. It should be over fifty percent, so his heart is on its last leg. His doctors talked about doing a heart transplant on the outside, since that's really the only cure for his condition. But the BOP would rather have him die than pay for a heart transplant.

"There are some bad motherfuckers that make the decisions around here," Diaz says, and there's sadness in his tone. I'm beyond angry. The system is broken.

"The title of *doctor* is a term of veneration, and Huff doesn't deserve an ounce of respect," I say.

I proceed to regurgitate the details of my office visit with Huff. Diaz laughs continually, albeit an angry laugh. For a while, we go back and forth comparing notes. Diaz tells me about the other five doctors who work here. Basically, all are misfits, but Huff has the worst reputation. He knows the system and knows what he can get away with.

After Diaz floats away, I immediately crash on my bunk, my heavy prison-issued boots placed under the bed. I'm exhausted. Ali, a skinny middle-aged Black man, engages me in conversation for the first time since I've been here. He is a practicing Muslim and an active member of a large Muslim community within the prison. He rarely talks to anyone, spending most of his time reading the Koran or other religious commentary.

"Couldn't help overhear your conversation with Diaz," Ali says. "I'm stuck with Huff too, and let me tell you, that is one mean motherfucker. He's sort of a cross between a spitting king cobra and a hippopotamus. Be careful with him."

"Thanks for the heads-up," I say. I'm not a betting man, but I would bet that everyone has a story about Huff.

"Let me tell you what he did to me," Ali continues. "I was transferred from Terre Haute, Indiana, to get a hip replacement. Spent a few days at University Hospital, came back here with a prescription for ten more days of Percocet written by the surgeon. Well, that wasn't good enough for Huff. He thinks we're all just looking for drugs to help us pass the time. Son of a bitch refused to write for Percocet and told me I'll be fine using Tylenol or Advil from the commissary. You're new here, but hopefully you've seen enough to know that no amount of arguing or logic will ever change these motherfuckers."

We talk for a good half hour. Turns out Ali has one more month to go on a fifteen-year drug sentence. He describes himself as a low-level drug dealer from D.C., rarely used drugs, but it was a way to make decent money. He then gives me a rather coherent and articulate overview of how the prison system in America works or doesn't work, depending on which side of the fence you're on. Unlike the emotional diatribes of Diaz I've been listening to for a few days, Ali is very matter of fact in his descriptions. Being in prison for fifteen years, he tells me he trusts no one and I should do the same. He's even more critical of the staff saying how they treat us like shit and are proud of it.

"Always be on your toes, stay out of trouble, and you'll be fine," he says.

A central theme early on is there are three ways you're guaranteed to end up in a fight: gambling debts, TV channels, and telephone calls. I was never a gambler, and TV could easily be avoided. Telephone calls are a curious reason to fight, but as the days go on, I realize people don't like waiting in turn for the phones and that's when the fights break out. A less obvious source of trouble is the interaction with the guards and staff. If you piss them off, for any reason, they will make up some excuse and have you thrown in the SHU. Dr. Huff, in retrospect, was telling me if I cross him in *any* way, he will have me thrown in the SHU. I never thought for a moment that he was bluffing.

Dear Lil,

Today I experienced the worst doctor visit of my life. I hoped being a physician would have helped me but instead he chose to hold it against me. He never examined me. He never did a neurologic exam, never asked me about my immune status, didn't care about my medical history, and hadn't read a single letter from any of my New York doctors. He said he wasn't interested in what they had to say because it wouldn't change anything he did in here. He didn't do anything other than make me angry at the world. He's a horrible, evil man, and this is who I'm stuck with. He is the most unprofessional physician I have ever met, but more importantly, there was an element of sadism in his mannerisms and speech. I was scared shitless in his office because he made it clear that he didn't care if I lived or died. This is my world.

On a lighter note, I often wake up disoriented thinking I'm home and you're lying next to me in bed. Then I realize where I am and I'm filled with melancholy. Can't wait to be back home.

I love you madly, love to Richard and Sara. I wrote to them separately.

Jay

CHAPTER 11

Contact

Eight days after my arrival, I finally get to meet my counselor who holds the passwords for me to use the phones and computers. Ms. Newham is a middle-aged Black woman with absolutely no interest in her job or even faking that she cares.

I'm sitting in her cramped office that's overflowing with paperwork. She's sitting behind a cluttered desk, and there's a bookshelf behind her with pictures of cats and her family. The walls are packed with an odd collection of Native American photos.

"I got here last week and was told that you can give me a password so I can use the phone and computers. It's really tough not being able to speak to—"

"You're in prison, Mr. Keller," she snaps. "Put on your big-boy pants and get used to it."

That's it? Get used to it? I know I'm in prison. I don't need Ms. Newham to tell me that.

"Ms. Newham," I say as relaxed as I can given my state of anger, "I just need a password and then I'll be out of your hair."

She sighs. "What's your Registration number?"

"Keller, K-E-L-L-E-R, 45632-067."

She quickly scrawls a few numbers on a piece of scrap paper and hands it to me, then points to the door where I'm to exit her office. I feel as if she just handed me a pound of truffles.

"Thank you, Ms. Newham," I say with a smile even though I'm burning up inside that this woman made me wait eight days for a task that took her less than thirty seconds.

I have to find Diaz so he can show me how the passwords work since there are three separate passwords written on the paper. Shit, he's not in his room. His roommate Ken is there, working on his appeal but offers to help.

We walk downstairs to the main room with the phones and computers. Within a few minutes, Ken connects me to the outside world. We confirm the $195 I handed to the intake officer is in my account. After thanking him profusely, I head straight to the phones. It's the middle of the day with most inmates at work, so the phone room is empty.

I dial Lily's cell number only to hear it go to voicemail. But oh, the sound of her voice! I want to burst into tears. Then my heart drops. How could she not answer? How could she not have her phone dangling from a necklace? How could she not do everything possible to make sure she's available for my call? My boosted spirits are instantly deflated. Diaz told me I have to wait a half hour before I can make another call. In reality, if the call didn't go through, I could have kept trying. Leaving a voicemail is not possible, so I walk upstairs. I return to the phone room thirty-five minutes later only to be thwarted a second time, still no answer.

It dawns on me that I should write down what I want to say knowing I will only have fifteen minutes to tell her everything. All calls are automatically terminated at the end of fifteen minutes. I could speak for hours, but I have to be selective. I use the downtime jotting down notes, revising it, writing more notes, and finally consolidate it to five "must discuss" topics.

I waited eight days only to hear her voicemail message? What I don't appreciate is how closely monitored the calls are. All calls are recorded, and at a later time, the guards have to listen to all the calls as part of their job description. This makes me fearful that if I said anything negative about the prison, the guards will retaliate against me at a later time. I will have to be somewhat cryptic in letting her know I'm living in a third-world dungeon. Should I insert grammatical errors she knows I would never use? Oh my god, I'm beginning to think like a criminal only eight days into my sentence. On the other hand, I'm afraid to tell her how horrible it is because some asinine guard will beat the shit out of me when he gets the chance.

Once more I make my way down to the phone room. As I enter the dirt-encrusted stairwell, I see a thirty-year-old wheelchair-bound man resultant from spina bifida on his hands and butt making his way up the staircase. I offer assistance, which he declines because he's one step away from making it to the second floor. "Damn elevators are broken more than they work," he mumbles. What a tragic sight, a gross indifference to human rights.

The phone room is still empty. I dial a third time, this time I hear her voice.

"Jay?"

"Lily, where've you been?" I'm shaking.

"Oh, Jay, I'm *so* sorry I missed your calls! I was in a meeting without my phone. I'm never without my phone, even when I'm in the bathroom. It's so good to hear—"

"Lily, listen we don't have much time and I want to tell you everything, but won't be able to, so listen closely and let's try to make the most out of each call. We have about fourteen minutes left. I don't know how, but *somehow* you have to get me out of here. Call whomever you think can possibly help, but you must know that this isn't a medical center—it's nothing but a real prison. There is *no way* I'm going to last in here for eighteen months."

"Jay, are you okay in there? I was so worried when I didn't hear from you."

"Today I'm okay, but it's rough in here." I look at my notes and fly through my list. "How are the kids doing?"

"They're good, Jay, a big help to me. Sara's lab is up and running. Wish I was more conversant in stem cell research. She's good. Been dating a new guy, but I haven't met him yet."

"And Richard?"

"Hard to believe he's a working lawyer. His swearing in to the Bar is next week. Short ceremony, so I'll try to sneak away from work. They both call me every evening to make sure I'm okay but can't wait to hear I've finally been in contact with you."

And just like that, the one-minute warning buzzes in my ears. "I love you,

Lily. I miss my beautiful wife and can't wait to hold you. Look at me, my life reduced to having a fifteen-minute phone call with my wife. We still have each other. They can't take *that* from us. This is really painful for me, Lily." As the tears begin to flow, I end by telling her, "When the rest of my life is through, the finest thing I've done is simply loving you."

"And I love you too, Jay. I'll do everything I possibly can to get you out of there. I'm here for you." I end the call by telling her to read all my letters closely and read them more than once.

We say our tearful goodbyes before being rudely cut off by a system that allows for fifteen minutes and not a second more. But at least I heard her voice and was able to alert her to some of my obstacles while minimizing my disdain and disgust of our judicial system. Hopefully Lily will have caught on, but I can't imagine I was able to hide my emotional state very well.

I want to smile and cry at the same time. Yes, we heard each other's voices. But she's in New York and I'm in Bumfuck, West Virginia. I didn't get to share a fraction of what I wanted to say, plus I was prudent about speaking freely on a monitored telephone call. While thoughts are fresh in my mind, I immediately compose a letter to Lily, telling her the details I didn't have time to verbalize.

> Dear Lil,
>
> What a treat to speak to you!
>
> Another day in paradise, rainy and cold. Here's what I didn't have time to say. I'll begin by describing the characters I live with. There are many factions so I'll use generalizations. Since drugs dealers and "cho-mos" (child molesters) make up the majority of the population, they deserve the most words.
>
> The cho-mos are rather easy to spot in that many just look like they are of that ilk. Most are white but of all ages and simply odd or creepy in appearance. However, they are usually quiet and respectful. The drug contingency is either Black, Hispanic, or hillbilly.
>
> The Black group is incredibly boisterous, watch a boatload of

TV, or play board games. Their heads are either shaved or in dreadlocks. They use the word "motherfucker" as Valley girls use the word "like." It's their filler word.

Of the white inmates, either a shaved head, a ponytail, or a braided beard pass for fashion. There's no shortage of Nazi tattoos. There are only a few white-collar guys here who spend much of their time reading.

The Hispanics might be the wildest of the inmates in terms of loudness and unruliness. Many have minimal command of English, so I suspect my interaction with them will be limited. They're really scary, but it's harder for me to accurately describe why they evoke the most fear. Perhaps it's the eyeballs tattooed on the back of a shaved head or a striking king cobra tat rising up the neck. But my best friend, Diaz, is Hispanic, and he's great!

Speaking of tattoos, regardless of one's ethnicity, tattoos are ubiquitous. People are covered in them with facial tats almost being mainstream. I assume they aren't concerned about their appearance at a job interview. Some of the inmates are limbless, many in wheelchairs, all with really sad stories amplified by our judicial system as you and I know all too well. By the way, P.O.W. in here doesn't mean prisoner of war. It stands for Pedophile on Wheels, which is a euphemism for a cho-mo who requires a wheelchair. Lil, only now do I realize our lawyers were clueless in regard for keeping me out of prison on medical grounds. No matter what the ailment, you're going to deal with that ailment while in prison. No one gets a pass for medical reasons. They didn't even get that right.

The other omnipresent danger is the staff. I've never seen so many malcontents in one location. Everyone seems to hate their job and take it out on those who are helpless to do anything. It would be very easy to predict their behavior if they worked in Dachau circa 1943. If they could get away with taking us out back and shooting us, they would perhaps be more content and have more job satisfaction.

So that's the playing field, complete with land mines and time bombs. My job is to avoid the sundry traps at all cost and walk out of here alive. Your job is to use every imaginable resource to get me out of here. If I could spend just one day less in here, it would be worth the effort. Maybe someday we will figure out how I ended up here and why. As much as I'd love an answer to that question today, my focus is on survival for now. Make sure you save my letters in case I ever want to write about this nightmare. Send my love to Sara and Richard.

Your loving husband,
Jay

CHAPTER 12

Splashed

In a relative sense, the room is quiet in the middle of the night but sleeping remains nearly impossible. Nighttime leg cramps from MS, stress, fear, guards with flashlights, and who knows what else keeps me awake. Massage the legs, stretch the legs, calm the mind, try to go back to sleep. That's my routine. While partially sitting up to soothe my legs, I see two men walking down the center aisle of the room. They are wearing wool hats with eye cutouts pulled over their heads and faces. The smaller man is carrying something. The men move slowly and stealth-like. When they get to the bunk before mine, one throws the contents of the plastic basin onto the man next to me.

I sit up fully, which comes as a surprise to the hooded men. They throw the remaining contents of the basin onto my bed and race back down the corridor and out of the room.

I gag. A horrific smell permeates the space, a smell you would expect to find if you were to open a septic tank. One by one the inmates wake up, curse the smell, and curse the interruption to their sleep.

"What the fuck?" someone shouts.

I feel some sort of liquid, and my stomach turns. I get up, afraid to touch anything.

The man in the next bed who bore the brunt of the basin contents doesn't talk to anyone. That's his thing, so I've had no interaction with him up to this point. Everything in prison changes in a split second.

"You okay, man?" I ask incredulously to the stranger who lives three feet from my bed. "What the hell just happened? What did they throw on us?"

Ali, who's on the other side of me, answers for him. "You just got splashed! Man, this is a bad one! Splashing is when someone takes their shit, piss, and fish juice and throws it on another inmate. Usually the cho-mos are the ones who get splashed the most. But it's also a good way of retaliation if someone fucks with you."

"Splashed?" I ask in my naïve innocence. "This stuff is horrible!"

"Ahh, man!" Ali quickly grabs a towel to cover his face in order to shield himself from the penetrating stench. "Looks like you just got a little, not as bad as the guy next to you. Motherfucker, no one's gonna be able to sleep in this room tonight. Better get rid of your bedding."

The room erupts into groans and curses. I can hear someone retching and my stomach turns again.

Ryan wheels over with a towel wrapped around his head as he surveys the damage. "Sorry this happened to you but, this *is* prison. It's usually the cho-mos that get splashed."

"But I'm not a cho-mo," I say in earnest protest.

"Yeah, but whoever did this probably doesn't know and just profiled you as a cho-mo. You're white and not a drug dealer, so until proven otherwise, you're a cho-mo. Just how it is. And tonight, they were doing two-for-one and you got caught in the crossfire. Pretty sure the guy next to you, Steve, is a cho-mo. Lucky you didn't have much land on your bed."

"I saw them walking toward me but didn't think anything of it."

"Did you see who it was?" Ryan asks.

"No, I only know a few guys in here, and they were wearing ski masks. Just saw two non-descript figures."

"They probably saw you sit up and ran before they got a full splash on you. Who knows?"

Steve, who absorbed a full splash, is busy stripping his bed calmly and deliberately. He still doesn't engage anyone in conversation or ask anyone for help. How can he stay so calm? His bed just got covered with the most foul-smelling stuff imaginable and he's acting like his four-year-old just wet the bed. On the other hand, I have smoke coming out of my eyes and ears but don't know what to do next.

"Should I go down to the CO and tell him what happened?" I ask in my bewilderment.

"Of course, you *can*, but I wouldn't do it," Ryan says forcefully.

"Why the hell not?"

"First rule of prison: anticipate all the consequences of anything you do or say. Put your ego away and roll up all your bedding. I'll show you where to throw it out and where they keep the cleaning stuff. Gotta get rid of this smell so everyone in this room can get back to sleep."

As I slowly and carefully roll up my bedding, I can see my mattress is unharmed. Steve didn't fare as well. Ryan and I go down another hallway and arrive at a large utility room filled with cleaning chemicals, brooms, mops, and buckets. I throw the bedding onto another dirty pile of bedding before heading back to my bed.

"Tell me why I shouldn't go to the CO. I just got splashed, goddamn it!"

"First of all, the night guard doesn't give a shit you got splashed. If you do go to him, he'll have to write up an incident report and put you in the SHU."

Prison rules are so infuriating. "Why would *I* have to go to the SHU?"

"Jay, it doesn't matter," Ryan says in an annoyed tone. "They'll put you in the SHU for *your* protection. Could be a month or two before they do an investigation. They won't find anything because no one will snitch them out. Then they'll finally release you. Meantime, you'll be rotting away in the SHU. Ain't pretty, Jay."

"Fuck," I say helplessly. "I can't believe this place."

"There's another reason you don't go to the CO. It labels you as a snitch, which is the lowest form of an inmate. It's not a label you want any part of, which is why no one in their right mind would do it."

"How can I be called a snitch? I don't even know who did it. I just want another bed to sleep in tonight with new sheets."

Ryan runs his hands through his hair in a frustrated matter. "Doesn't matter, Jay. You go to the guard, you're a snitch. No good will come of it, and the guard probably won't give you fresh sheets because he's pissed you made him work. He'll have to write up an incident report which fucks up his whole night. The only thing keeping inmates out of the SHU is the guards are too lazy to write someone up for every little incident. In the scheme of things around here, this is a little incident. Things like this just have to be settled among inmates. It's just how it is."

I'm tired and frustrated. "Where the hell do I sleep tonight? Is that too much to ask?"

"There's an empty top bunk mattress in the Bus Stop next door. Let's do that right now before Steve grabs it. If your mattress doesn't smell, take your old mattress and we'll switch them out right now."

"What about bedding?"

"Not tonight, Jay. Be thankful we can get a new mattress for you. In the morning you can go down to laundry and tell them what happened. They'll give you fresh sheets and you won't have to spend time in the SHU."

Sure enough, Ryan is right, and there is a fresh unused mattress next door. I get back to my bed just in time for the five-a.m. count. Ryan, being zonked out on psych meds, falls right back to sleep as if nothing ever happened. I'm too wound up for sleep. I sit on the side of the bed as Fat and Fatter walk through to do their count, oblivious to what happened tonight. "Jesus," one of them says, "it fucking stinks," but that's about it. No one was hurt, no one dead, no reports to write.

Little by little, I see signs of morning light. My heart may have slowed a tad, but my worry gene is in high gear. Were they targeting me, or was I splashed because I woke up and saw them? Are they going to come back to fully splash me? Do they think I'm a cho-mo? What do I have to do to convince them that I'm not a cho-mo, wear a sign? Will the day-guards find out what happened and put me in the SHU anyway? Who did the splashing? The unit is locked, so it had to be someone in the unit.

More light, and a few people begin to stir. Will I be a target for as long as I'm here? Is it a stigma with other inmates that I was splashed? What if Steve decides to go to the guard? Will I still end up in the SHU?

My mind is whizzing along, and no matter how I try to control things, I can't. My pulse is bounding. *"Please don't have a breakdown. You have every right to have one, but don't. Be strong, Jay. Find the strength somewhere, Jay,"* I whisper to myself. But nothing works to calm me down. I can't help but wonder if they will try to extort me. Is this the beginning of my torture?

CHAPTER 13
Searching for Normalcy

There's no shortage of advice when you are in prison. Deciphering useful from non-useful is the difficult part. I'm in a situation where I need all the explanations, all the insight, all the wisdom other people have because they have lived in prison for an unconscionably longer period of time. All the norms, social and psychological cues, of my past life are now invalid. All that gave me comfort is gone. All the daily freedoms I had are gone. I'm now told when to sleep, when to eat, where I must be, where I can't be, and if and when I can communicate with the outside world.

Everyone talks about finding a routine, which helps to pass the time and even normalize time. I know it's too early to be in any routine, as I still have a ton of medical tests to go through, meet with the psychologist, the dental clinic for a baseline evaluation, and who knows what else. I can't be assigned a job yet until I'm cleared medically, and that I'm told will be done by the neurologist rather than Huff.

I'm never one to have difficulty staying busy or finding things to do. I had work, hobbies, friends, family, kids. I was always busy. That was then, this is now. My entire past has been vacated, gone the instant I walked through the initial prison gate. All the people I knew who were part of my old routines, who helped me thrive for so many years, vanished. Who doesn't want to thrive? I have to leave all the old people behind and find new people and new routines to help me survive this nonsensical hell.

The prison has almost two thousand inmates but is broken up into eight different housing units. For the most part, you socialize with the people in your unit. That leaves about three hundred inmates in my unit. From that reduced number, there are only a few white-collar inmates, meaning, I have to expand my comfort zone by finding things in common with people from all walks of life. Diversity is no longer a catch phrase; it's my new home. Diaz is hardly white collar, but he has offered more information and help than anyone else. Ryan is helpful but sleeps most of the day because of his psych meds. The others are all a work in progress. No one embraces you because you have a sad story. Other inmates embrace you only if you have something to offer to *their* stay in prison. Diaz's roommate Ken has been pretty helpful and will often sit by me when I'm alone in the courtyard writing in my notepad.

I'm fascinated by Ken's backstory. He grew up in the seventies in Grand Rapids, Michigan, and his fourth-grade class was part of a forced busing project. From fourth grade through high school graduation, he was bused to a white school district. He vividly recalls the bottles and rocks being thrown at his bus as he drove through white neighborhoods. As a result of busing, he told me he's entirely comfortable around white people. Many of his friends growing up were white. He played sports on teams that were mostly white. Sleepovers were at white homes in the wealthy suburbs, and he hosted sleepovers at his house. According to Ken, no matter how tough some of the Black guys may want to appear in front of me, they are actually extremely uncomfortable around white people. They have spent their entire lives either in the "hood" or in prison. Through no fault of their own, all they know is the Black culture, which includes its language, dress, mannerisms, and norms. He's the first person to tell me how intimidated they are of people with an education. It scares the hell out of them.

Ken is forthright about why he's in prison. He committed mortgage fraud (according to the U.S. Attorneys) and was given a fourteen-year sentence, four down, ten to go. This is a man who went from lower-middle class to a millionaire in a twenty-year period. His children went to the University of Michigan on athletic scholarships. He personally financed a basketball academy for underprivileged kids complete with a travel schedule, fancy uniforms, and coaching. He spends day and night working on his *pro se* (for himself) appeal on the basis of previous inadequate counsel. He shares his case and appeals with me. I'm blown away by the professionalism of his appeal, all from information he's learned while serving his sentence. Whether or not it will help him in the long run remains to be determined.

Diaz and Ken share a room in A/C Alley, the eight rooms in the entire unit that have air-conditioning. I can't believe I'm in an FMC that houses federal inmates with serious medical conditions, but ninety-five percent of us live without air-conditioning. They always invite me to hang in their room so I can get away from the oppressive West Virginia summer heat. Despite both being my new friends, I share very little of how I ended up in an FMC with them. I just keep it simple and say I'm a businessman from Westchester County who got busted by the feds on a little-known charge along with many other local businesses. Although I'm still fearful of divulging too much, in reality, no one is interested in other people's cases other than to know the broad strokes. Details of most cases are a yawn because everyone in here is a victim of the system in some way, shape, or form. But to feel as if you have friends is huge. They translate so much of the craziness for me. As much as is possible within the confines of prison, I trust them. I realize I have to trust people—to a point.

I have been here for almost four weeks. I'm beginning to accept this as my new home for the foreseeable future. It's quite a contrast from my previous home, which was beautiful, filled with colors, art, plants, with life. Every day is a struggle. From a medical point of view, the fatigue from MS is killing me. It's not the usual "I'm tired today" fatigue. It's down-to-the-bone incapacitating fatigue. Every night I struggle to stay awake for the nine o'clock count. My goal for each day is making it to the night count signifying I've passed another day.

As usual, someone in the Bus Stop announces the guards are coming for count and everyone in the room must stand up at the side of their bed. The guards walk past me and are about to leave the room when one of them suddenly turns around and walks back. It's Officer Beecham. He's particularly malignant.

He stops at my bed. "What's your last name?" he barks.

"Keller," I choke out, not having a clue what's going on.

"Open your locker."

I don't know what's happening. I'm frightened, but not panicked. I open the locker filled with all my possessions and step back. I'm thinking he has me mixed up with someone else and is looking for some form of contraband. What a naïve idiot I am. He's not mixed up at all. He knows exactly what he's doing: inflicting terror on a new inmate.

Without pause, he proceeds to empty my entire locker. Every item gets tossed to a different location of the room, each landing on the grimy floor or someone else's bed. I don't know what's going on, but the rest of the room is rather amused. They've seen this before, especially from Beecham.

"Keller, turn around, face the window, lift your arms up."

In no position to argue, I turn around as he proceeds to pat me down.

"Empty your pockets now. Ain't got all night."

With my pockets inside out and empty, his mission still isn't completed.

"You forgot to turn your pass in before the four o'clock count. Don't ever forget and fuck up my night. So, where the hell is the pass, you dumb fuck?"

"I'm sorry, but I thought it was in my pocket. I'll have to look for it," I stammer.

"Damn right you will, and you better find it. If I don't have that pass back by midnight, you're gettin' writt'up. Bring it to my office if you find it."

With that, he turns around, proud as a peacock, and continues to the next area of his count.

I'm shaking as I collect all my belongings and reassemble the order I had in my locker. Because the lockers are tiny, one has to be extremely creative and organized in storing personal belongings. As soon as the guard storms out of the room, everyone goes about their business as if nothing has happened. No one other than my wheelchair-bound friend Ryan offers to help. My fatigue is suddenly replaced with anxiety, sadness, anger, and hatred, thoughts that are hardly conducive to getting a good night's sleep. He couldn't have just asked me for the pass? He knows I'm new. Rookies make mistakes. But this is a different species who works here. These are people who get pleasure from seeing someone squirm from inflicting pain on others. They define sadism. The worst part is that they are employed by a bureaucracy that condones and champions their sadistic behavior. It's all normal on my side of the fence.

Once I finally have time to go through my clothes in a methodical manner, I find the missing pass in the crevice of a pocket of my khaki slacks. I make my way down to the CO office where Beecham has a stupid smile on his face, his feet up on his desk.

"Had you goin' there, Keller, didn't I? Just kiddin' with ya."

This guard isn't an anomaly, a rare bad apple. This is the norm and thus my new norm. Trying to deal with these halfwits in any peaceful manner is nearly impossible. No matter what my answer is to a question, it's wrong. I can do no right in their eyes. I think it's quite enough punishment to be separated from society and leave your life behind. In a civilized society, separation should be adequate punishment.

Yet, I'm quickly learning in America, separation is not sufficient punishment. Rather, it comes daily in dimwitted incidents like the locker raid, solitary confinement, or a million other ways they inflict just a little more punishment. I used to think I was a strong person with endless energy to endure whatever it took to complete a task. I now doubt my capacity to endure this sentence.

CHAPTER 14

Lieutenant Shatner

It's a Sunday with a bluebird summer sky. The outdoor rec yard is the only place other than the indoor rec area where you are permitted to play a guitar as long as you can get the instrument and make it to the outdoor rec yard within a single ten-minute move. Despite my slowed gait from MS, I get a guitar, play outside for two hours, and now have to return it to the music room at the next ten-minute move. I make it quickly, return the guitar to the stoic inmate who's in charge of the instruments, and head back to my housing unit.

I pass through the main building and I'm now outside. The inmates walking in the opposite direction all seem to be looking at me, but I don't think anything of it. I'm more concerned with making it back to the housing unit in time. Finally, one of the inmates gets my attention and tells me I need to turn around. Behind me is Lieutenant Shatner, foaming at the mouth.

"Why didn't you stop when you heard me yelling at you, boy?" screams Shatner.

"I'm sorry, but I didn't hear anyone yelling at me or I would have stopped," I say very calmly and innocently.

I have never been a military-type guy, and a few of the prison veterans here can't help but compare similarities of prison and military. The regular guards, who are mostly ex-military, are analogous to privates. Up the chain of prison personnel come the sergeants followed by the lieutenants. Lieutenants have power in the prison and you do not want to cross them. Throwing you in the SHU is an Olympic sport for them. The lieutenants are seen and make their presence known. Just below the warden (general) come the captains. They're far less visible, but they have the final say on how the prison is run at any point in time.

"I've been yelling at you the whole time. You think you can just ignore Lt. Shatner? Give me your ID and follow me to my office!"

"Lieutenant, can you at least tell me what I did?" I say as my calmness is slowly being replaced by anxiety.

"Don't you worry, inmate. I'll tell you what you did when I'm good and ready. You can either follow me to my office or I can walk you to the SHU right now."

Opting for the former, I enter his office and he slams the door behind me. He demands I follow closely, which I do, eventually reaching his private interior office. He looks at my ID, then looks at me before tossing my ID onto his desk.

He has a thick Southern accent, a well-earned beer belly, a flattop crewcut, a booming voice, and sunglasses that he wears backwards on the top of his head even though he works inside. He reminds me of a quintessential marine drill sergeant, and he probably was one at some time. Federico Fellini would have recruited this guy in a heartbeat to star in one of his films.

"Listen here, Keller. You disobeyed a direct order from a lieutenant. Not just any old lieutenant, but Lt. Shatner. Now that don't sit well with Lt. Shatner. That's why you're in my office until we sort all this out. You follow me, boy?"

How bizarre that this man is calling another man easily ten years his senior "boy," but in this setting, anything passes for normal. I've been called much worse since I've been in prison. I have bigger problems than semantics, and I still have no clue why I'm being held hostage by this guard who refers to himself in the third person.

I gather all the false pleasantries I can and ask, "Lt. Shatner, did I do something wrong that has offended you?"

"There you go, boy, that's a good place to start. You sure as hell offended me. You not only offended me, but you broke a prison rule. Lt. Shatner don't like it when some stupid inmate breaks a prison law. That's why they got me in the Mainline hallway to make sure no rules ain't be broken. Now I can tell from your accent that you ain't from around these parts, you a Yankee. That could be a problem, but that's up to you."

"It won't be a problem, sir, I can assure you. Just maybe we can resolve this problem if I know what I've done to offend you." I'm scared shitless he's going to put me in the SHU, but I have to contain from laughing at this over-the-top character. *Speak slowly and thoughtfully, Jay.*

"What did you do for work when you were on the street?"

"It's all in my record. You can read all about me." I try to remain calm and cooperative.

"I could do that. In two minutes, I could know all about you—every last detail. However, I'm asking *you* what you did on the outside, and last time I checked, you ignored what Lt. Shatner asked you. So, what's it going to be? You gonna tell me, or make me work to get the same information? If Lt. Shatner has to work extra hard to git the same information, that's not gonna make him very happy. See what I'm sayin', boy?"

"I hear you loud and clear, sir. I was a well-respected physician for thirty-two years before I came here." It feels strange to say that out loud.

"Let me guess, you were just a little too free on writing those narcotic prescriptions? That's what all the doctors are in here for these days. Although, I remember one doc a few years back who was finishing a twenty-year sentence. Son of a bitch hired someone to kill his wife. Too bad he hired an FBI agent. He was pretty beat up by the end of his sentence. I'm telling you."

"No, sir, no drugs were involved. In fact, I was entirely unaware a crime was being committed. I'm a 'generated defendant' for a purpose that isn't quite clear to me yet. Maybe I'll figure it out someday. For right now, sir, I'm an inmate at FMC Franklin, no more, no less. Just another inmate doing my best to survive prison. It's not an easy task, sir."

"Well, that might be the first sensible thing you said today. You're right, you ain't no overpaid doctor. Not in here. You just another inmate. With a little luck—and it does take luck—maybe you walk outta here someday." Lt. Shatner's attitude has shifted ever so slightly in my favor.

"Sir, can we discuss why I am here?" I say in as non-threatening voice as possible.

"We sure can, boy. You were walking in the hallways with a hat on. No inmate is allowed to wear a hat inside. No inmate can have their hands in their pockets. No sunglasses allowed indoors. We got rules in this prison, and it's your job to obey every fuckin' rule. I'm *sure* someone told you about wearing hats inside when you went to your orientation class."

Fashion in prison is very limited and for the most part is dictated by what the commissary sells. I bought a baseball hat and sunglasses for when I'm outside in the rec yard. Diaz warned me that the commissary sells out of items frequently so buy them if they're in stock. His exact words were, "Hats sell faster than hot pussy on Mother's Day." Sure enough, I had to wait several weeks, but I was finally able to purchase my very own baseball hat yesterday. Not only will the hat shield me from the intense southern sun, but combined with sunglasses, it shields me from my surroundings by making me more anonymous.

And now I'm getting in trouble for it.

"With all due respect, sir, I have yet to attend my orientation class. I've been here well over a month but still haven't had a call-out for orientation. Of course, if I knew that wearing a hat inside was against prison rules, I certainly wouldn't have done it. I want my time in here to be as uneventful as possible."

"You speak well, boy. Respectfully. I like that. The problem is I have a reputation to maintain, and everyone saw Lt. Shatner pull you out and bring you into my office. Everyone has to know that you don't fuck around when Lt. Shatner is on duty. And everyone knows you can't wear a hat inside the main prison. Guess you gonna have to spend a little time in the SHU."

"What?" I swallow the lump in my throat. "We both know it was an accident. I'm new. I was never given orientation. You know I didn't disobey a law intentionally. Lt. Shatner, I meant no disrespect to you or any other prison official. I simply didn't know of a rule that prohibited wearing a hat inside this building. Now I do, and it won't happen again. I can't go to the SHU over this. Let's be reasonable. For very legitimate medical reasons, I can't go to the SHU. Please, think about this."

Lt. Shatner pauses for a few seconds before leaving the office altogether. I remain alone in his office for what must have been a half hour before he finally returns with a smile and a hint of whiskey on his breath.

"Well, boy, this is your lucky day. I'm going to offer you an alternative to the SHU. If you leave here on the next move and head back to your unit, you don't have to go the SHU." The scent of alcohol is now a certainty. "If anyone asks why you ain't in the SHU, what are you gonna tell 'em?"

"Well, sir—" I pause, searching for the right words. "I was given a second chance by Lt. Shatner *only* because I hadn't been to orientation class, which was an administrative oversight. It should have been done within the first two weeks of my arrival at the latest. Being the fair and reasonable man that he is, he let me off with a stern warning. How does that sound, sir?"

"Not the best answer, but not bad. I think we settled this issue, so as soon as the next move starts, get the fuck out of my office."

"I can do that, sir."

With that, I wait a few more minutes in the outer area of the office until the move starts. It always feels good to leave the presence of a full-blown psychopath. Today is no exception. This is one man, among many, I know I must stay clear of.

CHAPTER 15

No One Really Cares

Sweat drips down my back and I groan from discomfort. It's 110 degrees in the Bus Stop, and the heat is beginning to take its toll on me and my MS. I can feel the strength draining from my body just as Superman feels when standing near kryptonite. That's when I decide to take Diaz and Ken up on their offer of visiting their room to escape the oppressive heat. I also have to get their take on the latest rumor of another stabbing in the rec yard.

"Diaz, man, I thought you said this place was safe. This is the second stabbing since I've been here!" I say more in anger than in disbelief. I collapse onto the plastic chair, relishing in the coolness of the air-conditioning.

"Hey, the first one was Mo, and he was a known full-time hustler scumbag who pissed off a lot of peeps. This one started as an argument on the handball court, ended in a stabbing. It happens. I've been here over a year, and believe me this place is relatively safe compared to other prisons. But let's be honest, man, this isn't a Chamber of Commerce meeting hall, it's fuckin' prison, dude."

Diaz never ceases to amaze me. He only has a ninth-grade education, but he always seems to be able to read people and read situations.

"How'd you know I was in the Chamber of Commerce?"

"I didn't, Jay, I was just talking out of my ass like I always do, but I can see you in a nice suit, hanging out with other business dudes. So, you were one of those guys?"

"Yeah, did it for years. Was even president of a regional Chamber for four years. Seems like a lifetime ago. I used to be somebody," I say as a rush of sadness fills my already depressed body. I've fallen as far as one could fall.

Ken chimes in, "I too did the Chamber thing for about a year. It was too much of a white club for me. Got tired of all those extra looks. Ya know, a little 'Who the fuck invited the Black guy'? I was cool with it. Got bored after a while so I quit goin'."

"Ken, you've been here for almost four years. How many stabbings have you seen?" I ask, hoping he will add a broader perspective.

"These are the first in probably about three months. I remember more when I first got here, but it's been pretty quiet lately."

"If you say so. Still seems like a dangerous place to me."

"You gotta remember that stabbings in prison are really commonplace."

"How common?" I ask with utmost naivety.

Ken loves to pontificate, so this is right up his alley. "Let me tell you, in penitentiaries, or even mediums, you got guys who know they're never getting out of the criminal justice system. They have *nothing* to lose. Ya hear me? *Nothing*. Their release date says *deceased*. No one on the outside gives a shit if they ever come home. They've been down for so long, they don't even know anyone on the outside. Don't know the stats, but there are prison murders every single day in America. I had a life before here, a good life. You, too, had a real life. It means nothing in here. You get stabbed, the BOP fills your bed with another unfortunate soul by tomorrow."

Ken continues educating me about the morbid subject of prison violence, including rape and assaults. His soliloquy provides an extra layer of fear. He speaks eloquently and honestly about the risks of being incarcerated in America. Bedtime banter like this I don't need, but I have to be polite to my hosts. Only as it approaches count time do I put an end to Ken's oratory skills.

"You guys have been a bundle of joy tonight, but I'll digest your words back in the heat of the Bus Stop. It's almost time for the night count." I get up slowly, say my goodbyes, thank them for the air-conditioning. The moment I step outside their room, I'm blasted by the heat.

It hasn't taken me too long to realize that count time is more a "suggested count time." It's whenever the guards decide to get off their asses, load up with a wad of fresh chew, and do count.

I sit on my bed, sweating through my shirt, and write Lily a letter. It's my favorite pastime.

Dear Lil,

I've crossed the five-week mark and I'm still vertical. It's almost time for the nine o'clock count and the room is well over a one hundred degrees. You can imagine how my MS-riddled brain is reacting to the oppressive summer heat. Nonetheless, writing to you always gives me pleasure. Thinking about us gives me contentment. Seeing and holding you would be joyous. Sharing a bed with you, divine.

I just had a conversation with a couple of veteran inmates. I thought about telling them how I went from being on the cover of *MD News* to being photographed for my prison ID. Aside from the esteemed Dr. Mengele and a crazy lieutenant, no one knows I'm a doctor. I've really had to restrain myself, even bite my tongue when inmates start throwing around medical issues and have no clue what they're talking about. So far, I've been able to get by just by saying I was a businessman and that's fine. No one really cares.

I'm the only one who cares because I hate living a lie. I have to assume many others lie about their past. In here, with so little contact to the outside world and no internet access, you can be anyone you want. Chances are no one is going to call you out or know who you really were when you were "on the street." This is a world unto itself, with its own set of norms, rules, and fears. I am fearful of many things in here: the guards, the inmates, the lack of medical care. Even in relatively quiet times, you never are truly at ease. It's simply too insane a place to ever be at peace. It's peace that I seek, more than anything else.

I love your letters as they remind me that there is life beyond this living hell. With a little luck, we will resume the splendor we had for so many years together. Be sure to give Sara and Richard a big hug. I'm enjoying all the mail I receive from friends, family, and patients. Yesterday I received fifteen letters, and according to the guard, fifteen letters in one day is an FMC Franklin record. More to follow.

All my love,
Jay

CHAPTER 16

The Feel of Terror

I didn't appreciate it at the time, but my attorneys were proactive enough to have me approach the feds instead of the feds approaching me. By doing so, I was never arrested, which may not seem like a great consolation prize, but it was significant. The more people I speak with in here, the more I realize I never had to face the "shock and awe" of being arrested in a raid by federal agents. So many inmates describe in detail the day they were arrested. Guns drawn and aimed, scores of agents, doors knocked down, blinding lights, search warrants flashed, handcuffs, threats, and hyper-testosteroned SWAT teams. If that isn't enough trauma, you are most likely placed in a disgusting county jail by the end of the day where you remain for months on end.

Rick lives a few bunks down from me. He's a thirty-year-old weed dealer whose upper-class Maryland neighborhood was awakened one morning by the wrath of the SWAT team on full display. That meant assault vehicles, battering rams, enough ammunition to execute a military coup of many nations, and most importantly, the arrest of a harmless stoner.

Years later, inmates can laugh about the absurdity of their fateful day, but I always wonder about the motivation behind such displays of power. Monica Lewinsky was extracted from a Washington, D.C., restaurant by twelve armed FBI agents. The more stories I hear, the more thankful I am that I never had to experience such indignation. I've had my share of indignations throughout my contact with the criminal justice system, but never the full shock-and-awe treatment. In the end, the motivation has a common thread. If you give boys toys to play with, especially new shiny toys, they will play with their toys, and they will terrorize.

Today, I terrorized myself.

To everyone in here, I'm a greenhorn barely getting my feet wet in my first prison, yet I feel as if I've been in prison forever. I was so excited when Ryan gave me the paper and pen, and I started to carry it with me everywhere. Why? Because everywhere I go, everything I do, everyone I meet, is a story. I quickly earned the reputation, justified or not, of being a writer. I want to describe everything I possibly can. These stories have to be told. Most of America has no idea what goes on behind the walled fences and barbed wire. Now I have the opportunity to tell these stories. It also helps me pass the time as I have few friends and even less energy to do things.

Sometimes complete strangers approach me to ask me if I want to write their story. I usually oblige unless they are overtly psychotic. An inmate introduced himself to me when I first arrived but hadn't yet had a pen and pad. Within a minute, he was able to tell he was a member of the Knights Templar, knew the location of the Holy Grail and the Arc of the Covenant, and has seen the Shroud of Turin. That would have been a good story to write about, but he was transferred or discharged before I could tap his brain.

When I first arrived, it was all about the arrival. Now I realize that people come, and people go. Ali is getting released in two days and will return to Washington, D.C. In his late-forties, he has spent the last fifteen years behind bars for petty drug trafficking. His Muslim faith supposedly transformed him, so hopefully he will carve out a life on the outside. I heard that someone I saw yesterday in the cafeteria is also being released today. At first, I was only aware of people coming in. Now I appreciate that people do leave prison.

I spend Saturday morning in the outdoor rec yard with my notepad and pen. After I write some return letters, I indulge in simply journaling, describing all that I see in the yard. For me, everything is new and fresh, and of course bizarre. One odd-looking person after another walks by my table, which is situated just beside the walking track. Despite the cloudless sky and comfortable temperature, the yard is rather empty. That's okay by me. There's still plenty to describe. Then comes *recall*. That's when everyone must empty the yard and return to their housing unit for the ten-a.m. weekend count. I never understand why recall is a full forty-five minutes before ten o'clock count, but no one consults me.

Back in Antioch Unit, I find an empty computer terminal and check my emails. Lily described her Friday night, which was far more interesting than mine. A few other people had emailed me, so before I know it, I'm absorbed in responding to all the emails. I'm smiling and laughing at some of the emails, feeling good.

And this is where I messed up.

"Yo! What floor you live on?" asks an inmate whom I've never seen before.

"Second floor," I say rather confused as to why he's even asking me such a mundane question.

"Look around you, you see anyone?"

I look around and realize I'm the only one left in the computer room. I still don't fully appreciate the gravity of my predicament.

"It's count time. You gotta get upstairs for count or you're fucked, man," he says with a chuckle.

Boom. A rush of adrenaline hits my body. I can feel the surge of all my fight-and-flight hormones that have been part of humanity for hundreds of thousands of years suddenly rushing to every cell in my body. If I were a cartoon character, my hair would have stood straight up. Sheer terror. I remember Diaz and Ryan telling me, "Whatever you do, don't fuck up the COs' count. That's automatic time in the SHU."

I can't believe I could be this stupid, this casual, that I forget all about the count. I race to the door leading to the second floor. It's locked. Shit! I go to the second exit door. Also locked. How could I have done this? The inmate who alerted me sees my state of terror and says, "Try the elevator, man." I run to the elevator, which is usually broken, but it's working today. The doors slowly open to the antiquated elevator and close even more slowly. The ride from the first to the second floor is painfully slow and wobbly, easily the longest elevator ride of my life. All I can think about is being in the SHU with no medication and even more squalid living conditions. It feels as if decades are passing with each second. Finally, the elevator doors open and I rush to my bunk. Everyone is already standing for count.

"Ryan, did they count yet?" I ask, panting.

"Where the fuck have you been? No, you're lucky, they haven't counted yet."

No sooner did he get the words out when the door flies open as the guards begin their count. My heart is still racing. Sweat from my armpits oozes down. I can't turn the surge of hormones off, but I do breathe a big sigh of relief knowing how close I came to missing count.

Ryan wheels himself over to my bed. "What happened to you?"

"Oh my god, I can't believe how stupid I am. I was on the computer and totally spaced out about count. I got involved with emails and never noticed the room had completely emptied. If some guy on the first floor didn't say something, I would have missed count. I can't believe how close I came to landing in the SHU. How could I be that careless? Definitely my most terrifying moment since I've been here."

"Scarier than when you thought Mo was gonna extort you till you had nothing left, and then kill you?" Ryan says with a compassionate smile.

"I think so. I think so."

CHAPTER 17

Out of the Closet

It's a random weekday evening in the courtyard, and I'm enjoying a few moments of relative quiet when Ken sits next to me.

"I got it, man. I got it," he says, smiling from ear to ear.

"Got what?" I wonder what constitutes good news in a prison.

"They designated me to a camp. I'll be transferred in a few weeks to a federal camp about two hours from my home in Michigan."

"That's great news. I'm happy for you. I'll miss you, but I'm happy for you."

Ken goes on to explain the details of his transfer. He has a fourteen-year sentence. You can't go to a camp unless you are under the ten-year mark. He asked for the transfer as soon as he crossed that threshold, and, amazingly enough, they granted the transfer.

A Federal Prison Camp (FPC) is more laid back, with many white-collar criminals, no specific "move" times, and overall, much more freedom and relaxed atmosphere without walls or barbed-wire fences. His family will only be a two-hour drive away from him. At FMC Franklin, they are about ten hours away. Years ago, camps had the reputation that they were country club prisons with golf courses and tennis courts. That era has long vanished, and although it's better than FMC Franklin, make no mistake about who runs the camps: The Federal Bureau of Prisons. Ken of course, is hoping, like so many people in here, he will be released once he wins his appeal, but the odds of that happening are the same as winning a Powerball lottery. Nonetheless, he focuses on all the positives of his transfer.

From that moment on, Ken tries to spend every free minute talking to me. There are times I believe it makes Diaz uncomfortable when he sees Ken and me together. Yes, even in prison you still have to massage egos. I never truly understand Ken's intentions. Perhaps it's nothing more than being able to converse with a non-psychiatric person, such as those he associated with in the real world. Who knows? With unlimited time, I always proofread his *pro se* appeal paperwork. I never mind because it actually feels good to be useful. For my adult life, I always felt useful. Being in prison makes me feel useless and irrelevant, a mere trivia question for those who knew me in the past.

Often Ken will come down to the Bus Stop, which is really slumming it compared to his air-conditioned wing. He stops by my bed, pulls up a plastic chair, and chats. I admire his ability to remain so even keeled amidst the squalor of a prison. We talk politics, family, sports, criminal justice, society, race, you name it. Like so many people in here, I am astounded by Ken's optimism while facing so many years of incarceration in front of him.

Having a Black friend also helps to buffer the invisible walls that exist between whites and Blacks and Hispanics. He always goes out of his way to introduce me to his group of friends and thus I'm more accepted by some whom I would otherwise never have gotten to know.

After a long dissertation about his family, Ken says to me, "So that's my family. Don't know what else to tell you about them. Tell me about your wife. I'm sure you can remember. It's only been a few weeks."

"Don't overestimate. It seems like years ago when I last saw her."

As I rummage through my scrambled brain to find the right words, I don't appreciate how long I'm taking to respond to what Ken views as a lay-up question.

"Come on, man, I'm being transferred in another week. I asked you about your wife, not your kindergarten teacher."

"Right, my wife. How to describe my wife? Ever hear the question, 'If you're stuck in a foxhole in battle, who's the one person you'd want to be stuck with'? That would be Lily. She's a beautiful woman in every sense of the word, inside and out, graceful, elegant. More a classic beauty than a bombshell beauty. Warm, smart, great mom, can recall statistics like no one else, sensual, makes me laugh. Talented sculptor. Runs a Human Resource department for a large accounting firm in New York. No, here's how I'd summarize her, true story. My office had about twenty-five employees, mostly all women. They did a survey: 'If you were getting married again, who would you want to marry?' A few George Clooneys, Brad Pitt, and names like that were talked about. But the winner was, by a large majority, Lily. That's who they all wanted to be married to, which is pretty extraordinary for a boss's wife. That's Lily."

"She sounds special," replies Ken.

"She is, but there's another side to her. A few weeks before self-surrendering, we went to the movies. An older woman behind us never turned off her phone so it would ring and ring. Finally, on the third or fourth call, sweet Lily turned around and said, 'Can you please turn off your fucking phone?' Don't cross Lily."

I briefly wonder if I am saying too much about Lily and my worry gene gets triggered. What if someone on the outside learns about her or my kids and wants to extort me?

The days move along at a snail's pace. Ken's transfer is postponed by a few weeks; the BOP never has to give an explanation. I'm spending time with Ken but also more time with the handful of white-collar inmates who live in Antioch. Spontaneously we arrive in the courtyard for our evening "vent" sessions. There is a fine line between venting and simply complaining about everything. I'm depressed enough, and I certainly don't need to listen to everyone else's whining. We all know it sucks to be in prison, especially this cluster-fuck of an institution. One local inmate describes the management of FMC Franklin in his best West Virginian vernacular. "This place couldn't manage two pigs fucking in a burlap sack." If the whining is part of a funny story, then we all laugh. When it is rambling vitriol, it's exhausting. Overall, it's a fun pastime that gets me out of the sultry Bus Stop.

"Hi, Jay, what ya doin' tonight?" Ken asks as he sits down next to me in the courtyard one evening. After a string of hot, humid days, today's a welcome cloudy day. Before I have a chance to answer, he lays out some paperwork he wants me to critique.

"You gotta read this. I was in the law library all morning and found case precedent that will really help my appeal. Check it out."

I start to tackle the six or so pages of legalese. Just then, an inmate I haven't seen before joins us at the table. He's Caucasian, small, around five-five, one hundred and thirty pounds. He's missing several front teeth and *odd* looking, for lack of a more precise adjective.

"Just get here today?" Ken asks the inmate.

"Yeah, flew in on Con Air with about thirty other guys. Been in county for a year and a half."

"Hey man, the name's Ken, and the bookworm over there is Jay. Welcome and good luck here."

"I'm Jarred. How long you've been in here?" he asks Ken. I can tell he's nervous.

"I've been here over three years. Jay, how long you been here?"

"Too long, maybe a little under two months. Still trying to figure things out. It takes time. This is my very first prison."

The answer surprises Jarred as it does so many. For most inmates, at minimum, they do a chunk of time in a county jail either after their arrest, awaiting bail money, waiting for their trial, or waiting to be designated by the BOP to a long-term prison.

"How do you like this place?" Jarred asks me.

"If I can editorialize for a minute, I think it's a squalid third-world prison run by a morally bankrupt government agency in the business of unnecessarily ruining the lives of tens of thousands of citizens. If you ask me the same question when I'm in a bad mood, I'd probably have worse things to say. But it's where we are, so let's make the best of it."

Jarred seems to be in shock.

Ken chimes in, "I've been in worse places, but this place is pretty run down and doesn't run with the efficiency of some other prisons. You'll be okay in here."

I want to finish reading Ken's legal papers, so I let Ken explain to Jarred the ins and outs of FMC Franklin while I wade through Ken's latest legal treatise. Half listening to the conversation and half reading the papers, Ken's commentary makes me smile every so often.

"Yeah, here for medical, got Hepatitis C and a bunch of other stuff," Jarred mumbles sheepishly.

"Well, good luck. One thing this place is not known for is its medical care. Everyone thinks they give real medical care because this is an FMC. They don't. Right, Jay?"

"He's right about that. They put out a nice façade but don't really do what they should. I'm up in medical a lot for my injections, so I see what goes on, or more accurately, what doesn't go on. Somehow, they get away with it. I think that 'dot-gov' label helps."

Being a direct and to-the-point kind of guy, Ken is not going to let Jarred off that easy. Especially since Jarred already has opened up about his Hepatitis C.

"What other medical problems you got? Am I going to get Hep C from you by living in the same housing unit? You're making me nervous here, Jarred," Ken says with a smile.

"I don't think so. They're also treating me for HIV."

"What the fuck! You got HIV and Hep C? Anything else I need to know," Ken exclaims, now a little less jovial. "Listen, you have your problems, I have mine, Jay has his. We all got problems. Jay, me, we're both cool. But if I was you, I would keep the medical things to yourself. Just say you're here for *medical,* and no one needs to know more, especially the animals in here. By the way, you gay?"

"Well—yeah, that's how I got HIV and hepatitis," Jarred replies hesitantly. He seems annoyed at himself for being so open once Ken explained that he needed to be more discreet. Now the horse is out of the barn, down the street, and into the next county. He gets up, asks us not to say anything, and slowly walks away.

Once he's out of range, Ken turns to me with his eyes bulging. "Holy shit, that guy is fucked if he thinks they're going to fix his problems here. Wouldn't want to be him. Glad I'm being transferred so at least I don't have to worry about catching anything from him."

Then it happens. It isn't premeditated. It isn't rehearsed. It just happens.

"You won't catch anything from him," I say authoritatively.

"How the fuck do you know?"

"Because Hep C is transmitted through blood contact, usually sexually or from sharing needles. I trust you won't do either with Jarred in the few weeks you have left here."

"Got that right. Even if I was gay, I wouldn't put my dick anywhere near his rotting teeth. Not my type. But I do kinda feel bad for the guy. Being in prison with HIV, with Hep C—he's a walking bull's-eye. Wonder if you die from Hep C?"

"Usually you don't. If you're treated properly, there's a ninety-five percent cure rate."

"Who are you, the Surgeon General?" Ken asks in a more confrontational tone.

"Fifty to eighty percent of people who contract Hep C go on to develop chronic hepatitis. Of those people, fifteen to thirty percent will go on to develop cirrhosis within twenty years. That's usually what kills them. The good news is that if you do receive proper treatment, which takes anywhere between twelve to twenty-four weeks, there's a ninety-five percent chance that six months post-treatment the virus can't even be detected. It's called a 'sustained virologic response.' Without treatment, not so good." It's cathartic to hurl all those statistics.

"You just happen to know those stats like that, or are you pulling them out of your ass? How'd you know all that?"

"That's what I did before I landed here. Was a doctor for thirty-two years, internal medicine."

"Damn," Ken says with a broad smile. I can tell he's blown away by my secret. "Now that I think of it, you've said a few things I wondered how the hell you know all that. Guess I figured you were some smart, well-educated Wall Street guy or something like that."

"Have nothing to do with Wall Street, just a physician—or at least I used to be."

I'm relieved I no longer have to hide who I am. I have enough problems just surviving the chaos of this place.

"So, tell me, Jay, what are you really in here for? Too many narcotic prescriptions like most of the docs in here?"

"No. It's a long story that *I* barely understand, but I have no problem telling you the details if you're interested. Let's just say I'm a run-of-the-mill generated defendant used to advance the career of some prosecutor. Simply collateral damage. I was naïve, I was stupid, but my intent was never criminal. I can bitch and moan forever, but it won't change a thing. We've all been lassoed by the feds."

"Come on, man, let's hear it," says Ken. "We've got time before we have to go in for count."

"Remember when I first got here and I told you that I rented space to a lab that did some illegal stuff?"

Ken nods. "I do, although I remember being more interested in whether or not you were a cho-mo."

"Well, in my office building, I rented space to this lab, which I believed was a legal arrangement. I found out later that over one hundred other doctors also rented space to the same lab. Maybe it was legal, but the government said it wasn't. That's all the matters. The lab, which received about a quarter of my lab specimens, overbilled the insurance companies. If I ordered tests A, B, and C, they would bill for A, B, C, D, E, and F. They made millions. I should have paid closer attention, but I didn't. Was too busy taking care of patients."

"Okay, but why are you in here? Why not lock up the lab owners and call it a day?"

"The simple answer is 'overzealous prosecutor.' This is where prosecutors really have power. They can pick and choose which cases and people are prosecuted and which cases and people aren't. Listen, I get the purpose of the law because money does influence thinking. Conventional wisdom is a financial arrangement with a lab or radiology facility could influence how a doctor orders tests."

"Did you know what the lab was doing?"

"Not at all. The feds knew I *never* ordered a single unnecessary test. Didn't matter. I received money from the lab. The government was convinced I knew what the lab was doing, they claimed the contract to rent space wasn't legit, and the whole arrangement was nothing but a kick-back. And, whoever wrote the statute added that even if the doctor had no 'intent to defraud' or had 'no knowledge that someone else was defrauding the government, they're still guilty if their actions led to fraud."

"If the feds are so worried about money influencing thinking, how come they don't lock up every single congressman? Fuckin' lobbyists own Washington. That bribery they condone?"

"Exactly. Legislators pick and choose what constitutes a bribe and what's a political donation."

Ken clicks his tongue. "I've been around this shit much longer than you. I'm guessing you had money for real lawyers. They couldn't get you out of this?"

"No. In the end, I didn't have the resources to prove the negative and the lawyers we did choose were not versed in healthcare law. I would have needed about $1.5 million to defend myself. I had two choices. The first choice: fight the government, and if I lost, I would face ten-plus years in prison and my wife would face jail time too. If I won, I got to clear my name, but I would be flat broke from legal fees and all my assets, including my home, gone."

"Whoa, what did your wife have to do with the case?" he asks.

"Nothing. She deposited the rent checks so they claimed that constituted the Holy Trinity: wire fraud, mail fraud, and of course conspiracy. Bet I'm the only one in here whose "bribes" were part of my financial statements."

Ken whispers a soft "fuck."

I continue, "My second choice: accept a plea, my wife goes free, and I preserve my assets, which would have been eaten up in a legal battle. That's it. The ironic part was that I had already sold my practice and was really enjoying the freedom of not running a business. I was also dealing with more frequent MS attacks, so who knows what would have happened to my ability to treat patients. In the end, I went with the second choice, my best–worst option."

"Okay, man. You're even cooler now than my first impression of you." Ken extends his fist toward me. I reciprocate the fist-bump as we get up from the table and head inside for count.

I collapse on my mattress with a sense of relief and feeling better that I finally told my real story. I have enough prison savvy, relatively speaking, to think the truth about my profession won't come back to haunt me. It's all part of my steep learning curve. Whatever the consequences of inmates knowing my true background, I'm ready to deal with it. Lying, in and of itself, is exhausting, and that's the last thing I need.

CHAPTER 18

Open for Business

It doesn't take long. The next morning, I run into Diaz who's conveniently in the Bus Stop jabbering to Ryan. "*Que pasa*, Jay?" he says with his usual over exuberance. "You and me gotta talk." He puts his arm around me. "I got some doctor questions for you and hope you're open for business."

My heart races a little. "Oh, Ken told you?"

"Dude, I think it's great. I knew you were smarter than those stupid fucks up in medical. Huff might be the worst, but they all suck."

"Tell you what, Diaz. I gotta shower now and then go to medical for my injection. How 'bout we meet in the courtyard after lunch, 12:30? I know you're on a bunch of meds so bring them all."

"Thanks Jay. See you later."

Getting an injection at the medical clinic is always an adventure. All it involves is a nurse handing me a pre-packaged needle and syringe, me walking to the treatment area, injecting myself, and finally showing the nurse I am placing the used needle in the large secured red Sharp box. Yet, often I can sit for hours until the nurse decides to give me my medication. On holidays, the clinic is closed so I have to hunt all through the prison to locate the nurse on call who can open the clinic. Nothing is prison is simple.

Diaz is thrilled. He's going to have an appointment with a real doctor. However, I think I'm more excited than he is. I'm going to be a doctor again, this time in the truest sense of the word—*to teach*. I'm going to be useful to someone, something I think every physician takes for granted while in the midst of their frenetic daily tasks.

I think about two patients I treated for years, Belle Mayer Zeck and William Zeck. Both were prosecutors at the Nuremberg Trials after World War II. Both went on to have long, productive legal careers. Two weeks before Judge Zeck died, I made a house call for him. By that time, he was living in a hospital bed on the first floor of his home. He looked up at me and said, "For the first time in my life, I feel useless." Two weeks later, I attended his funeral.

I arrive in the empty courtyard several minutes before Diaz and seat myself at a table the furthest away from the entrance that will give us the most privacy. I'm not thinking of patient privacy in the conventional HIPPA sense. My baseline paranoia is more concern about the medical staff finding out I'm "practicing" medicine even though it's nothing more than simple advice. Yes, much needed advice that isn't going to be given out by the staff at FMC Franklin.

"Dude, brought my meds, I'm ready," says a jubilant Diaz as he rushes over. "Got a million questions for ya. Hope ya got time for all this shit."

"Time? I've got time. Nothing but time." I place my pen and pad to the side.

"Shit, with all the writing you do about this place, you're gonna have one helluva book someday."

"Let's hope. Anyway, show me your meds. We'll go one by one. I'll ask you what it's for, and you'll tell me what you think it's for and how long you've been on it."

The medication bag has about thirty bottles in it. We labor through each one. His medications reveal a fifty-year-old man with a lifelong history of epilepsy, severe congestive heart failure due to a virus or medication-induced cardiomyopathy, hypertension, a psychiatric history, and few other conditions that are resultant from his heart failure or epilepsy. It turns out Diaz has a defibrillator implanted in his chest and has life-threatening medical conditions. Fortunately for him, he doesn't appreciate the severity of what is going on, which I believe accounts for his happy-go-lucky attitude.

"This is great. They don't tell me shit up in clinic. They always say they too busy. Busy? Doing what? Seeing three patients a day? Eating lunch? I hate those fuckers."

I explain what each medication is for. There are several redundant medications, so I mark those bottles with a large *X*, and next time he goes to medical clinic, he should have his doctor adjust his medication list. We spend two uninterrupted hours going over his medical conditions and his medications. Diaz is a happy camper by the time we're done.

"I almost forgot. Tell me again why you were sent to an FMC," asks Diaz.

"Long story. You know about the MS and you know I have a weakened immune system. I also have the JC Virus. If it ever reactivates, it could kill me."

I do my best to explain the JC or John Cunningham Virus which is a virus that over half Americans have had. No one knows where it comes from but once in the body, it can lay dormant for decades. It has no significance for healthy people, but for those with weakened immune systems, it can kill you. It causes a disease called progressive multifocal leukoencephalopathy, PML for short. Think mad-cow disease for humans.

"Sounds complicated. Anyway, what do I owe you for the consult?" Diaz asks as we stand up to leave the courtyard.

"What are you talking about? You don't owe me anything," I say, bewildered that he would even ask such a question.

"Come on, man, nothing in prison is free, and I ain't gonna be your sex slave for a week."

I chuckle. "That's a good thing, but my father taught me you don't make money on friends or family. You don't owe me *anything*. I mean it. Now get out of here."

"Okay, if you say so. All kidding aside, I appreciate you making sense of all this. Too bad they don't give *you* a job in the clinic instead of hiring all those misfits."

"Remember my first visit with Dr. Huff? That's when he told me I'm not a doctor. I'm nothing but a worthless lowlife inmate who fucked up in life."

"Not to me, Jay. Not to me."

CHAPTER 19

Running a Practice

Prisons are fueled by rumor and hearsay every day. I knew it wouldn't be long before Diaz made sure everyone in the prison—or at least the Antioch Unit—knew I was open for business. I'm okay with that but must do my best not to bring any untoward attention to myself when rendering my medical advice, always cognizant of Dr. Huff's threats.

A few days later, Ken approaches me as I'm writing at a courtyard table. With him is a young, handsome, Black man whom I've seen before but don't know him by name. Ken introduces him as E.

"I told E you might be able to help him with a few things," Ken says.

E eagerly sits down next to me holding a file full of papers.

"Nice to meet you, E. What can I do for you?"

Before E can answer, but Ken interjects enthusiastically. "He needs you to review an autopsy report."

"Who died?"

"Long story," says E. "You got time now to hear it?"

"Nothing but time."

E articulates his story, which is guilelessly tragic, and nobody came out victorious except perhaps the prosecutors. As a student at Michigan State, he was a low-level drug dealer and occasional user. Home for Christmas break, he scored a little heroin. Late one night, he was in a bar when he met two girls who had been partying all night. He knew the girls peripherally so they easily engaged in bar talk. When the bar closed at two, he suggested they continue the party at his house since his parents were out of town. E, the two girls, and two other guys went to his house. He told them he had a little heroin left if anyone wanted to snort some. All five indulged in snorting a line or two. All fun and games.

Shortly after snorting the heroin, one of the girls passed out instantly, fell to the floor, and stopped breathing. Everyone panicked, but E had enough clarity and sobriety to drive her to the hospital just a few minutes away. She was rushed into the emergency room while the four of them sat in the waiting room. Half an hour later, a policeman approached them and informed them the woman had died. Before they even had time to digest the tragic news, they were told they would need to come down to the police station for statements. That was over twelve years ago. E had no idea that sitting in the hospital waiting room was to be his last taste of freedom.

The feds picked up the case. A twenty-year-old young white woman was dead. E was a twenty-year-old Black college student now facing a lifetime prison sentence for first-degree murder. He came from an upper-middle-class family, so he was able to hire a defense attorney, not having to rely on the overworked, underpaid public defenders. In the end, however, he entered a plea. Twenty-five years in a federal prison. That was his best–worst option.

I listened to the details of his entire plight and wanted to scream. Life as a college student, his goal of being a journalist, his time in a federal penitentiary, a dead woman he barely knew. I was dumbfounded and at a loss for words.

After composing myself, I get around to asking him what he needs from me. He wants me to review the autopsy results. To a layperson as himself, he believes a number of items on the toxicology report could have led to her death. The prosecutors claimed "but for" the heroin, she would be alive today. E believes "but for" the other items, she would be alive today. He had given her two small lines to snort, but that's all it took.

I peruse the autopsy report and the toxicology report. The autopsy is unremarkable, but the toxicology showed heroin metabolites, cocaine, ecstasy, alcohol, nicotine, amphetamine, and marijuana. Despite what I may have thought—or anyone may have thought—the prosecutors contended it was the heroin that killed her. In the end, that's all that mattered because E didn't want to face the next sixty-plus years in prison and opted for the twenty-five-year plea. We talk about his case for the next hour, mostly going around in circles.

I can't say definitively it was something else that killed her. It was a classic polysubstance overdose. The combination, rather than one individual drug, killed her. It didn't matter that he didn't know what she consumed earlier that night before he met her. She didn't want to die that night, but she did. He didn't want to kill anyone that night, but he provided the straw that broke the camel's back. Her parents lost their daughter forever.

Within a few days, all three hundred men in the Antioch Unit know I had been a doctor "on the street." My initial fear of being extorted turns out to have no merit. In fact, the opposite is true. I now have something other inmates need: medical knowledge. Diaz isn't the only one who had no clue about his medical condition, medications, or medical needs. I am still new to FMC Franklin, but I realize very quickly that calling this place a medical center is like calling McDonald's fine dining. Everyone has complaints about the medical care. Now word is out in the Antioch Unit that there is someone here who can actually explain things, and he's doing it *gratis*. I now have respect.

Nothing in prison is more important than respect. I can't tell in my short time here how many fights or near fights started with the words, "You disrespected me." When everything in your life has been stripped from you, one of the last vestiges of humanity you have is your respect. Unintentionally, I gained respect. One by one, people seek me out for various medical questions. I have something other inmates need. Sometimes I could give an answer on the spot. Most times they would make an appointment so we would have the needed time.

Some people have their medical records from their last twenty years in prison. They are now handing them to a man who, after only eight weeks, barely understands prison life, can barely remember to go to count, and often cries spontaneously.

Jeremy is the British man who arrived six weeks before me, although he was in a maximum-security prison for four months prior to being transferred here. He has cardiac problems including a pacemaker that was placed in him long before his legal problems. Jeremy has a very calm demeanor despite all the trauma he and his family have been through. I learned from others his situation was a very high-profile case in Great Britain complete with paparazzi following him and his wife everywhere. For the British, his case was about a challenge to the extradition treaty that exists between the US and the UK. The US feds wanted him for a crime that wasn't a crime in the UK so most people couldn't understand why the British government would so easily acquiesce and hand him over to the US.

Jeremy brought me his entire medical record since incarceration in the US. He also brought me something else, Celestial Seasoning teas. I had no idea they had such teas for sale in the commissary until Jeremy offered to share his tea with me until I could purchase my own. The smallest of luxuries means so much when all else has been taken from you. After a few sips of Wild Berry Zinger, we dive into Jeremy's case. Fortunately for him, his entire cardiac workup was performed in the UK so he at least had an accurate diagnosis and treatment plan. As best as I can ascertain, he has a "sick sinus syndrome," which is causing a slowing of the heart or even a stopping of the heart. He hasn't had an attack since the pacemaker was put in, but he is months overdue for a check to ensure his pacemaker is functioning properly. My advice is for Jeremy to go to medical clinic so they can arrange to have the pacemaker checked.

Jeremy is concerned about a recent spate of palpitations, so after my conversation, he makes his way to the medical clinic the next day. He is under the "care" of Dr. Alaijawan, a Nigerian-born woman with a warm smile, which is at least a buffer to her uncaring attitude toward inmates. She is on vacation this week, so he is seen by Dr. Huff.

Jeremy tells me how his appointment went, and it's not surprising.

"We'll schedule you to see a cardiologist," said the disinterested Dr. Huff.

"But you can see from my medical records that I'm more than a year overdue for a pacemaker check. How long will it take to be seen by a cardiologist?" asked Jeremy very politely.

"Whenever the BOP arranges for it. We'll tell you when, so don't make any more visits up here asking 'when.' In my experience, all that does is delay the process. Besides, do you have the expertise to interpret your medical records? Goodbye, Mr. Gordon," Dr. Huff shouted as he started to storm out of the room.

"But you didn't answer my question. I should have had this checked at least six months ago," Jeremey said.

"*Dr. Gordon*, you're beginning to annoy me," Dr. Huff said sarcastically. "Maybe you had one of the jailhouse docs look at your records and they told you you're gonna die unless you get it checked yesterday. Well, their opinion ain't worth a pig's testicle in here. Now get the fuck out of my clinic."

Jeremy was dumbfounded by Dr. Huff's attitude but had witnessed the American justice system long enough to know when something was hopeless. Reason and logic have no impact on Dr. Huff.

Over a meeting of the minds—a.k.a. meeting for tea in the courtyard— Jeremy and I discuss what he should do next. I suggest he wait until his own doctor is back from vacation and hope she is more sympathetic to his case. I also give him specific talking points to tell her that perhaps would be more likely to light a fire under her. We then enjoy our Celestial Seasoning tea and laugh about the absurd façade of medical care that exists at FMC Franklin. We laugh our fears away, at least for a few minutes.

Later that day, shortly after the four-p.m. count, Ken comes by my bunk and hands me his revised appeal motion that he wants me to review. "Can you bring it up to my room later tonight?"

"Not a problem," I say. "Any excuse to get out of the heat of this Bus Stop." The monster fans just move the hot air around and make noise. My requests for an air-conditioned room have been ignored.

Five minutes after Ken leaves, another inmate introduces himself as Travis, and within three minutes I learn he's serving a twenty-year-sentence for child pornography, divorced from his wife, estranged from his kids, has a bad case of Crohn's disease, and always goes to church. Travis is a talker, no doubt, and a rather normal-looking guy if you were to run into him in a shopping center. But the longer he talks, the more I want to place him in the "creepy" category. Ten minutes into his monologue, I question whether he is here to ask a medical question or to tell me his life story.

"The other problem I got is a really bad anal fistula. That's what they called it at the last prison I was at. Can I show it to you, see what you think I should do?"

Thinking quickly for once, I respond, "That's not really my area of expertise. I was an internist, you know, internal organs like the heart, lungs, liver, kidney. Fistulas are treated by surgeons."

"Can't you just take a quick look at it anyway? You gotta know more than those quacks up in medical."

I take a step back. "Sorry, man, I just don't know much about fistulas. You're welcome to ask me any other medical question, and if I know the answer, I'll tell you. If not, I'll tell you I don't know."

Travis's face contorts in anger and disappointment. "Ah, thanks for nothing." He walks away, clearly dissatisfied that I'm not able to help with his anal fistula. Go figure.

Later that evening, after reading Ken's motion and making the necessary corrections, I walk up to Ken's air-conditioned room. We discuss his motion *ad nauseam*. Actually, Ken discusses it and I contribute grammar and common-sense issues. It's getting late, and I need to get back for the nine o'clock count. As I get up to leave, Ken asks one last question.

"Isn't it hard to stay sane when you think about how the fuck you ended up in here?"

"In some ways it's easier on this side of the fence. Before I got here, I thought it was just me who got screwed by the judicial system. At least now I see it's not personal. It's culling the herd to feed the system. The hotel stays full and the prison-industrial complex runs like a well-oiled machine."

This is what I think about every night, but why I'm in here remains a mystery. This place will break a man down and spit him out until there's nothing left. I carry so much anger, disappointment and rage, but damn, am I trying my hardest to get through it all.

CHAPTER 20

Orientation

A lot can happen over the course of two months. It surprises me that I have been here for over sixty days, but who's counting? Orientation is supposed to occur within the first days of my arrival. It consists of a physical exam, psychological exam, dental exam, and a whole day of orientation from each of the prison department representatives. Unlike most other inmates who have been in numerous prisons before here, I actually need orientation but somehow have been lost amidst the bureaucracy.

The psychological exam isn't an exam at all. It's initially performed by a PsyD intern, and a few weeks later by a PsyD psychologist. The intern exam is more involved—as a budding psychologist, she doesn't take any shortcuts and bombards me with a bunch of non-applicable questions. She's well-meaning and nonjudgmental, but in the end, she's powerless and nothing but a hired data intake clerk. The exam by an actual psychologist is four or five minutes long.

The psychologist beats around the bush until he asks the only questions that have any relevance to him or the prison: "Are you suicidal," and, "Are you homicidal?" Once I answer "no" to those questions, his job is done. The prison now has a record that they have inquired about my mental state and I told them that I wasn't suicidal or homicidal. End of psychological intervention, for the remainder of one's time in prison, whether it's for two months or twenty years.

My dental exam is performed by a staff dentist, the notorious Shaky Jake. It doesn't take me long to figure out the origin of Dr. Jacobs' nickname. His hands have the steadiness of a college freshman after drinking twenty cans of Red Bull. He does comment on the fact I've had regular dental care in the past, a rarity in the prison population. I ask him if I get a reward for having good dental hygiene, but he doesn't even answer me. He just packs up his neuroses, shaky hands, obvious disdain of inmates, and leaves the room.

Lastly, I have a call-out to the Arrival and Orientation (A&O) area. This is where each department representative is supposed to orient the inmates as to how things are done in *this* prison. Most inmates have been through a multitude of prisons and know things are done differently in each one. Even among the federal prisons, there is a lack of uniformity. The warden and other administrators really do make a difference in how the facility is run. For that reason, a representative from each department is supposed to give a five-minute talk about their respective department and respond to questions. Keep in mind most of the staff *hates* speaking to inmates or having anything to do with inmates.

We're all crammed in a room that has a distinct odor of lemon cleaner. There's a long table set up for us to sign-in and then find an uncomfortable metal folding chair for the day. It begins benignly enough with the head of food service speaking about the rules and regulations of being fed. The chaplain tells of all the wonderful services that exist for prisoners of all faiths, plus the rules and regulations of the chapel area. The psychology department puts in their two cents. The recreation staff talks about the most important of all rules in the prison: the dos and don'ts of the weight-lifting area, the written and unwritten rules. For example, you will get kicked out of the weight area if you are not wearing your steel-toed boots. Who knew?

The next to last speaker is from education. Mr. Ford is in his late thirties, muscular with that ex-military look. I recognize him because during move times, he always stands in front of the library other staff members, talking sports, yucking it up, while ignoring the inmates as we walk by. His comments are sad, but his honesty is something I haven't heard since my arrival.

"My name is Mr. Ford from the Education Department. Welcome to FMC Franklin. It's not a bad place, as far as prison goes. Listen, I know you probably heard some bad things about my department. You guys don't really like us, I get it. Truth is, we don't really like you guys much either, but just try to make the best of it. I hope all of you have your GED degree. If not, come see me. I'm usually in front of the library." He walks away, ignoring the five or six hands that are raised to ask him questions.

Last but not least is someone from security who's supposed to tell us the rules and regulations of the prison so we don't end up in the SHU for bad behavior. Sneezing too loudly in front of a guard could land you in the SHU. I hear from other inmates that security usually talks about how to report a prison rape because the prison must maintain the illusion that they are concerned about our safety. They know rape is part of the prison landscape, but they want us to know that there are mechanisms for reporting rapes or sexual assaults of any type. There is no shortage of policies on paper for everything.

Now comes the *Lieutenant Shatner Show*. What transpires confirms my suspicion that working in prisons attracts some of the most malignant personalities society has to offer, of those that are not already in prison. I previously had the misfortune of meeting Lt. Shatner the day I was wearing my baseball cap indoors and he almost put me in SHU. He's someone who clearly enjoys his power way too much, and he loves to scare the bejesus out of people.

I move my seat a foot to the right, placing me partially obscured by a pillar and virtually out of the sight of this full-blown psychopath.

He stands up at the front of the room, his thick neck bulging out of his shirt. "My name is Lieutenant Shatner in case anyone in this room doesn't know me. Remember that name—Lieutenant Shatner—if you remember nothing else about your stay with us here at FMC Franklin." All the other inmates are bored to death. I feel like I'm watching a Fellini movie.

His hands are clasped behind his back, his sunglasses are on the back of his head while he struts his stuff, silently and slowly pacing in front of his new inmates, relishing the moment. As for the inmates, no one wants to hear him because he's the last of twelve speakers.

"Okay, everyone stand up or you get a shot."

A shot is a disciplinary mark. If you get too many shots, you can be placed in the SHU or transferred to a higher security prison.

He waits a few seconds for everyone to follow his command as he swaggers back and forth. "I want y'all to carry yourselves like *men* in here. See, this man here? He's properly dressed. If you dress like this, you won't have any problems with Lt. Shatner. But if you choose to dress like this piece of excrement"—he points to an inmate who is standing in front of him with his pants down past his ass and a misbuttoned shirt—"then Lt. Shatner will be all over you like a fly to shit."

I roll my eyes.

"Let's talk about visitation. Behave yourself in visitation! Do y'all hear what I say? See, this one inmate in visitation used his two little kids as a picket fence while his old-lady friend slobbed his knob right there in visitation."

The crowd bursts into laughter and cheering.

Shatner is pissed. "Quiet down, you fuckers! As I was saying, the inmate thought he could pull that over on Lt. Shatner, but Lt. Shatner happened to be watching all this on camera. We watch everything, especially ol' Lt. Shatner. I ran down to visitation, pulled him out, and laughed all the way as I walked him right to the SHU. And he now spent a good few months there in the SHU, lost all visitation rights for the rest of his stay here, no commissary for six months, all because he thought it was okay to get his knob slobbed in visitation. Ain't gonna happen here, we clear on that? No knob slobbing in visitation!"

He turns his back to us before turning back around. "We got more rules. Mr. Keller, stand up."

Busted. I stand up in disbelief that Lt. Shatner knows I'm in his orientation class. Son of a bitch.

"Mr. Keller, would you like to share with your esteemed colleagues another rule you learned since you been here?"

"Yes sir," I say as I stand at attention. "Wearing a hat or sunglasses is forbidden inside any building. I can assure everyone that Lt. Shatner has no tolerance for rule violations."

"And what's the penalty for wearing a hat indoors?"

"Time in the SHU."

"Thank you, Mr. Keller. There's a man who knows what happens if you break a rule in front of Lt. Shatner. You can be seated now."

I was never a fan of people who refer to themselves in the third person but this guy, in a perverse way, amuses me. Clearly, no one admires Lt. Shatner as much as Lt. Shatner does.

"Now, I know there are drugs in here. Lots of drugs. I get it. Y'all like to get high and that's what gave many of you an admission ticket to stay here. I was born on a Monday, but it wasn't last Monday. I know everyone who deals drugs in here. No drugs! Ya hear me? Or I'll walk y'all to the SHU and I'll be laughin' the whole damn way."

I don't doubt this man. He lives to escort inmates to the SHU. He paces in the front of the room for over a minute not speaking, just wearing a huge smile. "Who's in here from a Pen?" he asks, referring to a penitentiary. "I worked a Pen for six years. Most men here couldn't make it in a Pen. See this pocket?" He holds out the left shirt pocket of his uniform. "That was for my pack of Newport Menthols."

He pauses for a moment and glares at the crowd. "Lt. Shatner don't smoke, never did, but I always carried my Newports. I used to pay the inmates with cigarettes who helped me take care of problem inmates. I can tell you about this now because it was years ago and the statute of limitations damn run out. That was the old Lt. Shatner. I'd walk by the cell of one of *my men*, put a few cigarettes under their cell door, and tell them which inmate needed a whooping. Sat in my office listening to the radio until sure enough, I'd hear 'medical emergency in cell 223,' then I knew it was taken care of. Hell, one time, the poor sonna' bitch got shanked and died a few days later. Nothin' easy about bein' in prison, so behave yourselves in here. Don't do anything stupid!"

Everyone in the room except me has tuned this guy out long ago. They probably have met many depraved guards like Lt. Shatner. I admit, I'm enjoying the *Lieutenant Shatner Show* on one hand, but I realize he isn't fabricating stories to impress people; he's simply boasting of his career highlights. He goes back to his strut, pausing only to adjust his superfluous sunglasses.

"Hey, if Lt. Shatner offended you, too bad. I know you're all tough dudes in here. Hell, sometimes you may even want to get even with me. When you finally get out of here, go look me up. That Google thing's a son of a bitch. Y'all can find out anything on Google. Y'all can find my address and come on over to my house. Just remember though, when you show up, I'll be waiting for you on my porch with a .357 Magnum in one hand and a cold Bud in the other. I'll pull that trigger and shoot you right there. Yeah, I'd love that. Might even shoot you a second time. Once you down on the ground, I'll piss in the hole I just made in your head. Lt. Shatner ain't afraid of you punks. Whew, not really sure where I was going with that, but Lt. Shatner don't lie to you. I'm a straight shooter. Act like men, carry yourself like men. But really, I'm a nice guy. I'm approachable. Ya'll got a problem, come see Lt. Shatner. Talk to me before you do anything stupid. I'd rather see you in the hallway than in my office. Well, y'all have a good day now."

Lt. Shatner leaves the room with a spring in his step. My prison orientation is completed.

CHAPTER 21

New Room

"Keller, come with me," a pudgy CO tells me one afternoon.

Oh, man, this can't be good. A hot flash rushes up and down my body. Have they found out I'm giving inmates medical advice? Have I messed up in some other way?

I follow him down the hallway toward my counselor's office and another hot flash washes over me. I enter and see Ms. Newham hunched over her desk. When she looks up and sees me, she grunts and tells me to take a seat.

"Mr. Keller, how are you today?" she asks as she rifles through some papers.

Shocked that she's even trying to have a conversation with me, I stumble over my words. "F-fine?"

She raises a brow, unamused. "You're going to be moving from the Bus Stop to the room you requested. You can transfer after four p.m. count."

An inmate named Bruce Hellman, who runs the yoga class, lives in an eight-man room and has a roommate who was being discharged. Bruce lobbied the other men in his room that he had a suitable replacement. He approached me with a sales pitch that being in his room should help me sleep because the room is quiet, no arguments over a game of dominos or cooking food throughout the night. There's a general level of respect for each other in a smaller room. And unlike the bus stop, there's just less traffic in this part of the unit.

I didn't understand at the time, but if someone is leaving a room because they are being discharged, the other people in the room want to choose who should replace that person, otherwise, a random person can be placed in the

117

empty bed. There's an incentive to being proactive in replacing the departing roommate. When Bruce first met me in yoga class, he pegged me immediately as a potential replacement. Over the next few weeks, he was active in forging a genuine friendship with me, which is how I ended up in his room.

Aside from leaving the chaotic Bus Stop, the best part of the move is my new roommate, Bruce. He's in his mid-sixties, fit and athletic, with a warm smile. I liked him immediately. After the first yoga class, he came up to me and introduced himself.

"You look like you know a lot of important things," he said to me, smiling.

I laughed; it was the most interesting greeting I'd received so far. Putting humility aside for a moment, I replied, "I do know a lot."

At his peak, Bruce was a wealthy guy who lived large. He had money, a McMansion in Bucks County, Pennsylvania, a love of sports, a wife and two kids, and well-traveled. As unjust as my sentence is, Bruce has an eighty-four-month sentence for some form of insurance fraud. He tried explaining it to me, but I never really grasped what he had done when he owned an insurance agency. Bruce thought about going to trial but ran out of assets. Unless you have been through it, you cannot imagine how the wrath of the federal government can drain you in every sense of the word.

He moved his family from a McMansion to an apartment and eventually chose to enter a plea. According to him—and I have no reason to doubt him—the prosecutors changed the plea deal at the last minute and his wife, Iris, got a two-and-a-half-year sentence as well, which she only recently finished. His two children, in their late-twenties, had both parents in federal prisons. This is what I mean when I frequently recite an old Blues song that *someone is always worse off than you.* Nonetheless, Bruce always smiles, cracks jokes, and goes to his job every evening in indoor recreation. I still remain ineligible to work until I'm assessed by a neurologist.

As it turns out, Bruce and I have a fair amount in common, especially by prison standards, so forming a friendship was easy and genuine. Bruce was an outstanding football player throughout high school and apparently good enough to get recruited by Penn State as a linebacker.

"You played football at Penn State? Must have been exciting?"

"It was, but I wasn't big enough as a linebacker so I was a backup for a year and then quit. Didn't take me long to appreciate that despite being six-one, two hundred and twenty pounds of solid muscle, I was too small. Guess you heard by now who recruited me?"

"Come on, Bruce, I lead a sheltered life in here. Who recruited you?"

"I thought everyone knew. Jerry Sandusky, Penn State's most famous pedophile who's now serving a life sentence. As if doing prison time isn't hard enough, I'm now labeled as being one of 'Jerry's Boys.' Anyway, instead of football, I learned the insurance business on an academic level. Hey, did you hear the one about the one-eyed pirate?"

Bruce helps me load up my belongings onto a small dolly before making our way up to the third floor. "Guys, this is Jay Keller," he says to the roommates who are in the room at the time. It's a small room for eight men, but he insists on giving me a detailed tour. Bruce is clearly the de facto mayor of the room.

My new eight-man room—thirty-by-eight feet—is a penthouse compared to the Bus Stop. An improvement, but a long way from the Ritz Carlton or even a Comfort Inn. First of all, it's on the top floor of the prison, so it's really hot. It's a long, thin room with two big fans positioned at each end of the room. I'll suspend my personal fan from the bunk above me so it will sit about two inches above my body. No matter what, it's hot as hell, which affects my MS. That's a big negative. The other negative is sharing a tiny room with seven other men. I'm way too old and yet, I'm only the third oldest.

As for the positives, it's a very quiet part of the housing unit and we have a bathroom just for the eight of us. Sharing a bathroom with eight men instead of forty or fifty is a step up. We also have a cleaning service, which means having the room cleaned twice a week. A little stereotypical, but we pay the Mexican inmates sixteen macs a month to do the cleaning. That's their hustle.

When I lie in my bunk and look up, I see food and bugs splattered on the ceiling but have no clue how either became adhered to the twelve-foot-high ceiling. There is a non-functioning radiator right next to my bed, which Bruce encourages me to use.

"You can use it as a nightstand, but listen to this. Prison rules state only the Holy Bible can be left out during the day. Put your books away until after the four-p.m. count and make sure you put them away before 7:45 in the morning."

"Thanks. Would not have thought of that on my own."

Four bunks, eight men. One bathroom with a door (no locks of course), a sink, a separate toilet, and a shower, all built in 1925. The toilet, from that era, is about fifteen gallons per flush. They tell me the best feature of the whole room is the radiator in the bathroom, which serves as a great towel warmer during the cold weather.

Bruce was sent to an FMC because he has Crohn's disease, which keeps him in the bathroom for large swaths of time. His bunkie also has Crohn's, so they call each other "cronies." Nonetheless, Bruce, with his big heart, makes everyone smile and laugh despite the fact that all of us are in prison.

The other six men in the room are a cast of characters.

"Gerald is a meth-head whose brain and body are both fried, and I mean fried," Bruce explains. "He's on a twelve-year sentence. His vocabulary is reduced to being able to say 'fuckin' aye.' Above him is AJ, who is leaving in a few weeks after finishing an eight-year sentence. I assumed he was gay, as I always saw him with his gay lover. Turns out, he's going home to a wife and son. They call it "gay for the stay.""

"Gay for the stay. Got it."

"Above you is twenty-seven-year-old Jimmy serving five years on child pornography charges. He's smart, tech savvy, and handsome but will forever be labeled a CP sex offender. Was in the Navy when he got caught with it on his computer. Navy dropped the charges, but two years later the FBI knocked on his door and arrested him. Great guy."

Now I understand why everyone calls me a tourist. Twenty-four months is nothing in comparison.

Bruce continues, "My bunkie Shane has a ten-year sentence. Joe Mack, in the next bunk, has thirteen years. Above him is Derek, fourteen years. All three are here on various charges of CP. I think Derek's case was true child molestation because he never talks about it and reeks of creepiness."

"Should I be worried about him?"

"Nah, you're about fifty years too old for him. Last, but not least is our 'room polyp.' He's about my age and batshit crazy. A few times he's come after me with his padlock in a sock. The other guys stopped him otherwise I would have had to beat the shit out of him."

"What's his deal?"

"Really angry man who introduced himself as Dr. John Clarkson, a PhD from Princeton in organic chemistry plus a master's degree from Duke in biochemistry. I was suspicious of him immediately since he couldn't even conjugate the verb *to be*. Found out he's a preacher from Lubbock, Texas, who went to Africa to recruit a sex slave for himself and friends. He's about halfway through a twenty-year sentence. Eight guys all living in a tiny polluted fishbowl."

***

The weeks move along. On most days, surviving in prison is the most difficult feat imaginable. You must control your mind in order to control your time. If you don't master your circumstances, you're bound to be mastered by them. With the luxury of a new room, settling into a routine becomes more easily defined. Make no mistake, having a routine is critical for surviving a prison sentence.

Every morning, I awake at five, listen to NPR radio broadcast by the UWV while drinking my instant black coffee and preparing my hips for yoga later in the morning. If all goes well, the guards open Antioch's doors at six. My first stop is the music room to get my guitar.

Brett Randall's prison job is running the music room, a large closet lined with forty-five guitars (three classical), a few bass guitars, drumsticks, a fiddle, and a large standup bass. You can't get an instrument without an ID and Brett's approval. He was a professional guitarist before prison yet has a total disdain of inmates who aren't as proficient a musician as he. Brett barely talked to me my first few months. He barely talks to anyone. Everyone is greeted with his scowl. He stays in that closet writing and playing music from six in the morning until eight at night, returning to his room only for mandatory counts.

Every morning I have to hand Brett my ID in exchange for a guitar. I practice for the next two and a half hours straight. No breaks. No interruptions. I start each session with practicing scales, a great way to regain coordination of my hands which have been affected by the multiple sclerosis. Major, minor, chromatic, pentatonic, and Segovia scales. Hours and hours of mind-numbing scales, all while sitting in a filthy stairwell of the indoor rec area.

There is no such thing as a bad practice session because aside from the musical component, I need to regain dexterity of my right hand. I was unable to play the guitar for over three years after the first MS attack. My right hand lacked the fine motor skills needed to play the instrument. On the recommendation of my guitar mentor, I returned to playing the simplest of pieces in my repertoire. Months went by but I was seeing improvement in my ability to play more difficult pieces. Now that I have a lot of time, I play every day, regaining as much coordination as possible. Even if I'm not playing the musical pieces well that day, my hand is slowly showing more and more coordination. For me, every practice session is a minor victory.

My usual practice spot in the indoor rec area is a litter-strewn, graffiti-covered stairwell, which is part of the defunct prison morgue. There are two plastic chairs, one for me and one for my music book. I tape sheet music to the railing using address labels for tape. The bottom of the railing serves as my footstool. Electrical wires protrude from the plaster walls. Some lead to lighting fixtures or outlets, others lead nowhere. The acoustics, however, are outstanding.

Less often, I go to the indoor rec area in the evenings to practice. The mornings are quiet, but the evenings are noisy, crowded, and chaotic. Close to my stairwell is a hallway we call the Nerdery where all the cho-mos congregate every evening to play Dungeons and Dragons and who knows what else. Frankie One Stamp is a regular at the Nerdery.

After music comes yoga class, which lasts from 8:30 to 10:00. I return back to my room at the ten o'clock move for a shower before heading up to the medical clinic for my injection. That carries me to lunch.

Afternoons are spent either in the education area or Dr. Gerard Jobin's meditation class. There's a designated area for education, but unless I bring my own reading and writing materials, there is no education. Dr. Jobin is a staff psychologist who holds a meditation class for inmates three days a week. The session is for an hour with usually eight to ten inmates in attendance. The first half of the class is talking about whatever the inmates or Dr. Jobin would like to discuss. The second half is for meditation.

Dr. Jobin is a middle-aged man who holds a PsyD degree and has been with the BOP for several years. He is the only staff member I've encountered who has empathy for inmates, is non-judgmental, and speaks openly about how poorly the BOP functions as well as the entire US criminal justice system. He's a breath of fresh air. Recognizing most inmates have never meditated, he teaches all of the basics and hands us the tools to meditate and be mindful. Most importantly, he often reminds us about the futility of ruminating on a past that can never be changed.

After four p.m. count, I either do more reading, writing, or play the guitar. I'm asleep as soon as the guards conduct their nine o'clock count. There's plenty of time for all my activities, socializing, and self-reflection. Prison is the perfect place for self-reflection.

Unlike many men in here who have serious regrets about their heinous actions, I don't. I made a stupid mistake by having a financial arrangement with a laboratory but never was there criminal intent. The feds should have viewed this as a civil matter, not criminal. Although the financial arrangement did not change the actions of my medical practice one iota, the feds still wanted their conviction. However, I know I never conspired to commit a crime. My actions, through the myopic eyes of the U.S. Attorneys, constituted a crime that had to be punished to the fullest extent of the law. That's all that matters. That's why I'm in prison. I was collateral damage. My self-reflection leads elsewhere. Survival.

There are always a handful of teachers, at every level of education, you remember because they were exceptional. I reflect on the words of Joseph Brezina, my high school Latin teacher. He would often tell me, "Jay, you must exercise the muscles in the gymnasium of your mind." Funny how years later I recall his exact words and -isms. He could not have known I would need to exercise my mind while in prison, but he was absolutely right. The advice of forty years ago is more relevant than ever. If I can stay busy, focused, productive, and healthy, I'll survive this hell.

Weeks earlier, one afternoon in the outdoor rec area, an inmate named Manny stopped to listen to me while I was practicing my classical repertoire. He was taken by Bach's "Gavotte en Rondeau" and asked if I wanted to sit in with The Convictions for a song or two. The Convictions are a musical group of five or six inmates led by an extremely talented troubadour by the name of Manny Richards, a paunchy middle-aged man who was a professional musician on the outside. He's friendly, socially engaging, and loves to perform. The Convictions perform every Sunday night in a hallway set up with chairs from the nearby chapel. I started to watch them most Sunday nights. For two hours they played rock songs of the fifties, sixties, and seventies, all with intricate vocal harmonies. They weren't just good; they were sublime, all under the musical stewardship of Manny Richards.

Manny and I agree that I'll perform one solo classical piece and one Beatles' song with the band. On Thursday evening, I go down to the indoor rec area to practice. I want to get some extra practice time in preparation for my performance with The Convictions a few days later.

There I sit in the noisy indoor rec area, amidst the cockroaches on a filthy floor, trying to get my right hand up to speed for a performance later that week. What I have learned was that the more I practice, the better the coordination and speed of my right hand.

I play a lot of music over the next few days. The Saturday before I am going to perform, I ask Brett, the music room guru, if he'll listen to me practice. Only after hearing me play Bach's "Bourrée in E minor" by memory does he recognize me as serious musician. From that moment on, our relationship changed.

The next night, I play with the Convictions, Bach's "Bourrée in E minor" followed by a classical rendition of the Beatles' "Norwegian Wood." My right hand cooperates, and I perform well, hiding most of my mistakes. The other guest performer that night is a big, burly three-hundred-and-fifty-pound man named Michael Pudretski who sang three songs. He has a voice from heaven, absolutely mesmerizing. I end up accompanying his vocals for several other performances.

I'm quite sure I'm Brett's only friend in the entire prison. He's finishing up a ten-year drug sentence. Brett's survival routine is practicing music, ten hours a day, every single day. He has written 2,755 songs while in prison. He rarely engages in conversation with anyone, as that would cut into his practice time. Not only does he speak to me on most days, he makes sure I have fresh strings for my guitar, which he doesn't let anyone else use. For ten years, in his own way, serving his own needs, Brett controlled his mind and thus his time.

One day while starting my morning musical routine, Brett shares with me that it's his last month. I'm genuinely happy for him. I pick up my guitar and start to play *Pachelbel's Canon.* He spontaneously reaches for his guitar and joins in with fabulous melodic solos. For the next ten minutes, we make beautiful music, increasing the tempo and slowing it down. A few inmates who are waiting to get an instrument listen, polite enough not to interrupt. I wish I had a recording of that duet.

One of the men waiting for a guitar that day was Luis Gomez, a middle-aged finance guy serving twenty-five years for creating a Ponzi scheme. After hearing me play with Brett, he approached me and asked if I could perform at the Spanish Heritage Month ceremony, as he was the organizer of the event. "Can you play a few songs while people are getting their seats and a song between each of the speakers?"

I had over two weeks to prepare a repertoire, which was just enough time. There's a big difference between playing a piece in the stairwell and performing it for others. A performance forces you to bring the piece to another level. The performance in and of itself was fine. Most people listen to a few measures and move on. What I didn't appreciate was the respect I gained from the Hispanic community, a group of people with a different language who had little use for someone from the white community. Between the opening and closing ceremonies, I performed four times. Never once was I harassed by anyone from that community.

CHAPTER 22

Death Threat

Yoga was another major passion of mine while in prison. Not only is it where I befriended Bruce, which led to me transferring out of the Bus Stop, but it also helped my body combat the effects of MS. Bruce and I were reminiscing one evening about the first time I attended prison yoga.

I remember Bruce giving the backstory of those who regularly attended yoga. Billy Jo was the inmate who persuaded the recreation department to sanction the class, meaning we had yoga mats and a designated area for us to practice, indoors during the winter and better space outdoors in the spring and summer. Billy Jo spent years in a US Penitentiary in Beaumont, Texas, which is where he developed a legit yoga practice.

"Don't be fooled by Billy Jo. He's been down for twenty years, ten more to go," says Bruce.

"A thirty-year sentence? What the hell did he do?"

"Big time weed smuggler. He lived on a farm he owned in Guadalajara, Mexico. Once processed, he had a fleet of six airplanes that flew the weed into the US for distribution. He was netting well over a million dollars a month. When I met Billy Jo, he looked every bit the age of a man who was pushing seventy, but extremely flexible and a very capable yogi."

"What about the other regulars?"

"All good guys: Harry was a smuggler from Florida, Jose a gang banger from Chicago. I'm in charge of entertaining the class. You've been here long enough to know everyone has a story."

I started to practice yoga about a year before prison. For all of my life, I always did some athletic endeavor. I was a runner, a skier, basketball player, baseball player, black belt in karate, you name it, except golf. Two weeks before my first MS attack, I was playing in my Tuesday night men's league basketball game. I played for years so most people there knew my game. That night I was worse than terrible, dribbling the ball off my foot, couldn't make a layup or jump shot, and couldn't explain it. The following week, my game was just as bad, maybe worse. A week later, I was in the midst of a full-blown MS attack, which at the time, the doctors thought was a stroke of unknown etiology. After playing basketball for about forty-five years, I never walked onto a court again. Eventually I was diagnosed with MS and had to make many adjustments in my workouts. That's when Lily suggested yoga.

Lily had been practicing yoga for about fifteen years and loved it. She hired one of the instructors she knew from her yoga studio to give me a few private lessons before I started classes at the studio. There was a lot of vocabulary to learn, and it was different from all the competitive sports I had done. Nonetheless, I took to it immediately in that it was something physical I *could* do in spite of my new physical limitations. I wasn't particularly flexible, it didn't come naturally, but I worked at it. I started going to the studio regularly, plus I practiced at home. As an MS patient, balance and core strength were the two things I had to improve on. My leg strength was diminished and my right-hand lacked strength and coordination, but yoga gave me something to focus on toward restoring what I had lost, and hopefully preventing further deterioration. Having stopped working because of my physical deficits, yoga was soon part of my daily routine.

Now I'm in prison doing yoga with Bruce, Billy Jo, and a cast of other characters. In a million years, I never could have predicted this. There is great comraderie among us. We all have obstacles, we all have demons, and we are all are angry at the system that placed us here. But for an hour and half each day, we escape our hell.

Billy Jo was beginning to develop serious knee issues and was told by the University Hospital that he was heading toward a total knee replacement, sooner rather than later. This meant Bruce was running the class most days, but he, too, needed occasional relief. A few weeks ago, Lily sent me some yoga material, so I began to make up my own yoga routines. When Bruce asked if I could lead the class once in a while, I said, "Sure, no problem."

I'm challenged the very first day I lead the class indoors, not by my fellow yogis, but by one of the basketball players. We have half the basketball court designated for yoga during the cold weather. A few minutes before the 8:30 indoor class, I retrieve all the yoga mats from the cage where they're stored and start to lay them out when I'm approached by an irate inmate.

"What the fuck do you think you're doing with those mats?"

"I'm laying them out for our eight-thirty yoga class. We have half the court from eight-thirty to ten."

"Really? No you ain't! We running full court. Get those fuckin' gay boy mats off the court, asshole."

"No way," I say defiantly, "we have this court reserved all winter for indoor yoga. I'm not going to debate you. You can play half-court like they do every other morning."

"You deaf or you stupid? I said we playin' full court this morning. What you gonna do about it?"

"The way I see it, I only have two choices. First, we fight it out. You'll probably kill me and spend the rest of your life in a Pen, twenty-four hours a day locked in a cage, and you'll never play basketball again. Or I go to the CO and explain my predicament. You see, I don't give a shit if you think I'm a snitch or a rat. For the next hour and a half, I'm a yoga instructor, which is what the Director of Recreation wants me to do. So, get the fuck out of my face. We're doing yoga with or without your blessing, asshole."

I start to walk away, heading in the direction of the CO office, when the inmate yells, "Fine, use the court for your faggot cho-mo yoga class with all your cho-mo friends, motherfuckin' snitch."

Bruce caught the end of my death threat. "Ah, don't worry about him. I know him. He's being discharged tomorrow."

Everything in prison is a struggle, even a yoga class.

It's not long before I'm leading the class about four times a week. Unlike Billy Jo and Bruce, who do the same routine every day, I change things up, which is greatly appreciated by the other inmates. More importantly for me,

I run the class based on what I want or need to do on a given day or am capable of doing since weakness and fatigue are part and parcel of MS. The class has grown to seven or eight inmates a day, and on a good day, sometimes ten. One guy even showed up on the recommendation of his prison doctor who told him she had heard there was a good yoga class at FMC Franklin he would benefit from. Bruce and I have a nice collection of yoga journals in our room. We share interesting articles or poses with the other inmates. Like most insurance salesmen, Bruce knows how to sell, so he did all the recruiting for the yoga class. He could sell snow to an Eskimo and convince anyone how they would benefit from yoga.

Like everything in prison, and in life, nothing stays the same. Bruce's physical appearance begins to change although he denies it. Mentally, Bruce is as enthusiastic as ever about yoga, but physically he appears weaker and frailer. He's lost weight and now has more of a pallor to him. When I first met Bruce, he was muscular and robust. He still does yoga on most days and still makes us listen to all his bad jokes.

"A fish walked into a bar. The bartender asked him what he'll have. The fish responded W-A-T-E-R." Bruce cracks himself up every time he tells that joke. I laugh, seeing how much Bruce enjoys the joke despite everyone else not even understanding the joke.

If on some days he skips yoga, it's because he wants to get some extra sleep. The more I do yoga, the more I enjoy it, and the more I appreciate my physical limitations.

When the cold weather comes, we have to move the classes indoors. While outside, we get to see the sky, breathe fresh air, and feel some warmth on our bodies. One downside is the BOP gun range off in the distance. It's very common to hear barrages of gunfire as the guards practiced their mandatory one-week per year of target practice. We all know if the guards could get away with shooting us, they would have gladly done it. We also see planes fly overhead, which leads to endless fantasies.

Indoor yoga is more challenging. Not only is it incredibly noisy, it's filthy beyond belief. You do your best to stay exactly on your mat. I can't wait for the warm weather and the move back to outdoor yoga. As bad as it is being indoors, I still appreciate doing yoga every morning despite living in a dungeon.

Dear Lil,

Today was a first. I touched my fingers not just to my toes but all the way to the floor. I don't think I could even do that in high school. Maybe the tight hamstrings from thirty-plus years of running and basketball are finally loosening up. Anyway, it felt good to see a change for the better. I haven't had too many of those moments in these last few years. I did the balancing flow routine you sent, which was a big hit with the class.

This morning I asked the female guard at indoor rec, as she made her way to do her morning inspections, if she wanted to join us for yoga. She replied, and quite accurately I might add, "Hell, I wouldn't get on those yoga mats in a Hazmat suit!" But somehow we all make it work. We all benefit from our practice, we all escape the hell we live in for an hour and a half a day, and we all are witness to the benefits.

I will write more soon, but give my love to Sara and Richard. I miss you all and can't wait to walk out of this "medical center." So far, no major infections so I remain in one piece.

As usual, all of my love from your loving husband,

Jay

CHAPTER 23

First Visit

Only a couple of months have passed since I entered prison. By my account, I've been here my entire life, barely able to remember what it's like not being in prison. After finally getting BOP approval, Lily has made plans for a weekend visit with my beautiful daughter Sara. Despite the BOP pontificating on paper how much they encourage inmates to have visits in order to maintain family ties, they do everything possible to impede visits. They devised a point system to limit the number of visits, and the visitation area is only open at certain hours on specific days. Having said that, I'm counting the days until I see Lily and Sara.

A few days before the expected visit, Lily emails me that very dear friends of ours are on a long drive from New York to Florida and they will make a detour to West Virginia. They want to see me, but also take advantage of the unique opportunity to actually visit someone in prison. I'm bursting at the seams. Evelyn and Frank Daniels are dear friends, so there's no doubt this will be a splendid weekend. The timing is perfect such that they will all have dinner together Friday night, visit me Saturday morning, and the Daniels will hit the road after their visit. Lily and Sara will then visit with me all day on Sunday as well. Sometimes things just work out like this.

Saturday morning comes and I can barely contain myself. I wait in front of the COs' office to be called to the visitation area. When I met Lily, she was living in a studio apartment on Bleecker Street in Greenwich Village, working in finance at Merrill Lynch. Her facility with numbers steered her to finance but her passion was with the arts. I smile as I recall a weekend when I stayed at her apartment on a Friday night. We awoke Saturday to a city blanketed in snow. We walked from Bleecker Street up to Madison Square Garden in almost two feet of snow. This woman, I was gradually getting to know, loved the cold weather as much as I did, knew how to dress for it, and appreciated the beauty of a fresh snowfall.

On our walk she talked about living through the rough winters when she was an undergrad at the University of Vermont. Lily honed her skiing skills on the frigid Green Mountains. She took pride in knowing how to stay warm. A walk to midtown in the snow—piece of cake. Lily and I discovered we both had simple tastes. We didn't aspire to belong to country clubs, wear designer clothes, or drive fancy cars. We both enjoyed movies, live music, and traveling. She too was a skier so winters were about going to the mountains rather than the warmth of the Caribbean like most of our friends, either Vermont or the Rockies.

Lily and I played in the snow as there were very few vehicles in the streets, made snow angels, and walked for blocks with snow up to our waists at times. She looked so beautiful in her big boots, long coat, flowing scarf, and a big furry hat.

When we finally got back to her apartment, she removed her mittens, hat, down coat, and ran her fingers through her hair. Despite the wind, snow, and wearing a hat, I looked at her as her thick curly hair perfectly framed her beautiful smiling face.

My roommates warn me that the visitation area, like the rest of the prison, is old, filthy, noisy, and the vending machines are filled with food from the early seventies. I don't care. After the guard calls me, I show my ID, and sure enough I'm allowed to enter the visitation area after a very brief pat-down. As soon as I walk in, I immediately spot the two most beautiful women I have ever laid eyes on. I can't contain the tears, and neither can they. It's a glorious reunion. We all sit down at a table, but the guard immediately comes over and lets us know that the inmates have to face the front of the room at all times where they are in full view of the guards who are seated high up in their barricade.

The room is a non-descript square filled with about eighty or so plastic seats, small laminate tables, weight-bearing pillars, and an alcove for the vending machines. The guards are in the front of the room perched in their bunker that resembles a judge's bench. There's a male and female guest bathroom, plus a smaller third bathroom for inmates to use. Security cameras hang from multiple sites.

Lily is wearing a white top and has her curly hair pulled back at the nape of her neck. Her green eyes are sparkling with tears of sadness and joy. Every night before I go to sleep, I imagine my wife's face, and she's always smiling at me, and now she's sitting across from me and it's more than I can ask for.

At twenty-six, Sara's looks are strikingly beautiful, with her thick wavy black hair and dark eyes both contrasting her light skin, a honey-sweet voice, and most importantly, her warm heart.

After I compose myself and wipe the tears from my eyes, I realize the Daniels aren't here. "What happened to the Daniels?" I ask somewhat disappointed.

Lily is staring at a nearby inmate who has a large eyeball tattooed in the middle of his forehead.

"Lily, don't stare," I whisper. "You've never seen an eyeball tattooed on someone's forehead?"

Lily flashes a nervous smile. "Didn't mean to stare, but how can you not? Do you know that guy?"

"No. Think I'll keep my distance. What about the Daniels?"

"Frank went to the emergency room with kidney stones early this morning and hopes to be here later," she says with a smile. "We told the guards we may be joined by two others that are part of our group, which is why they sat us at this larger seating area."

I'm a little sad about not seeing the Daniels, but I'm with my wife and daughter. I feel great, almost human! I'm invigorated in a way I haven't felt in the longest time.

"I'm going to see if the vending machines are really as bad as I've been told. I'll bring back what's edible," Lily says.

Sara puts her arm around me. "I like the beard, Dad. You going to keep it?"

"Probably not now that I have a mirror in my new room. When I didn't have a mirror, shaving was too hard."

"You look better than I was expecting, but you've lost weight. What's it like in here, Dad?"

"Good question," I say as I gather my thoughts. "Remember when Dorothy and her friends finally make it to Oz? The great and powerful Wizard was trying to intimidate them with smoke and fire and scary sounds. Then Toto pulled back the curtain that was shielding the Wizard, exposing him as a feeble, ordinary old man frantically pulling levers, switches, and dials."

"I loved the movie, but what does that have to do with what it's like in here?"

"Everything. I now see the Justice Department for what it is, and it isn't about justice as I used to believe. It's an antiquated bureaucracy hell bent on ensuring every bed is filled, prosecutors focused on advancing their careers, staff looking for the easiest way through their days, profits being more important than human rights, and sentences not based in reality. No matter what the conviction, it follows you the rest of your life and prevents you from truly rejoining society. I could go on for hours. Look around, Sara. Most people need mental healthcare, education, job training, and alternative punishments. Placing humans in cages only ensures more criminal activity because damaged people damage others."

"I'll take your word for it." Sara surveys the room more closely.

"Tell me how you're doing. Mom says your lab is in high gear."

Sara's one smart cookie. She studied evolutionary biology as an undergrad and went on to get a PhD in molecular biology, with her interest being in hematopoietic stem cells. "Yeah, it's really taken shape. We have a few hundred of our thrombopoietin-knockout mice, and I've finally gotten the hang of using the flow cytometer so I can analyze the frequency of hematopoietic stem cells. I like most of the people I work with—there are a couple of weird PhD candidates, but that comes with the territory."

"Not many people you can talk to about your work," I chuckle.

"No. I keep things very vague on first dates."

"How's Mom doing?"

Sara looks around for a quick moment, and I notice she's nervous to make eye contact with anyone. "She's doing the best she can. At first, she cocooned in her bedroom, but now she's accepting more dinner invitations and things like that. She said she feels like a widow going out to dinner with married couples."

This breaks my heart. "And you, sweetie?" I ask, keeping my voice steady.

"I miss you—but I'm fine. Compared to you, I have it easy. Seeing what a rundown place this is and how scary some of the people are in here will give me a few more things to worry about."

"I'm learning to survive, but there are just so many variables I have no control over. My life has certainly changed. It's never the changes we want that changes everything. Anyway, Mom says you and Richard have been great to her."

Richard is my son. He's a good son, smart, and now in his first job out of law school, working his ass off for a large New York firm.

"We try to come out most weekends. We don't count days—we count weekends until you're home. We're biding time, you're doing time. Mom said they put ten more doctors associated with the lab in prison since you've been in here."

"What a misuse of power, unnecessarily destroying lives. Anyway, Mom appreciates your help. You're a terrific daughter."

Just then, Lily returns, and I'm in awe of her beauty. She's just so effortless. I'll love her forever.

"Find anything in the vending machines?" Sara asks.

Lily rolls her eyes as she places a few drinks and edible items on the table before sitting down next to me. "These nuts are rancid!" exclaims Lily after consuming just a few bites.

The time flies, interrupted twice by the guards. The first time is about two hours into the visit when I hear my name called over the loudspeaker asking me to come up to their desk. Not thinking there's a problem, I go up and am verbally assaulted by the guard known as Tight Shirt. He got this nickname because he always wears extremely tight shirts in order to flaunt his muscles. I was warned about this psychopath, but like most things in prison, you can't believe it until you witness it. He tells me that my wife and I can't drink out of the same water bottle.

"Okay, sir, it won't happen again." I have no idea why until I explain this to my posse. They conclude it must be a mechanism in which contraband is exchanged. Not being a criminal, I never think like a criminal. An hour later, I get called up to the desk again. This time, Tight Shirt is fuming mad as if I had just stolen his supply of anabolic steroids.

"You and your wife cannot eat the peanuts out of the same bag. You have to put them in separate bowls. You screw up once more, Keller, and I'm gonna throw you and your friends out of visitation. You'll lose visitation rights for a year. Got it?"

I clench my fists. "I'm sorry. This is my first time to visitation, and no one told me about these rules. I'm not trying to disobey orders. Anything else I should know about?"

"Yeah, read the fuckin' rules, moron. Now get the fuck out of here, Keller."

I walk back to Lily and Sara like a scolded puppy. Puppies don't know what they did wrong, only that they did something wrong. When I spread the word, Lily and Sara look up at the guards with scorn, which probably doesn't help matters. Nonetheless, we resolve not to let a pair of lowlife guards ruin our visit, and it doesn't. We have a great time, true joy. We laugh endlessly, cry on occasion, and exhibit veritable love. I hold hands with Sara and Lily. We are even able to put our arms over each other's shoulders, as long as I'm facing the guards. It's emotional for all, but especially Sara. I try to imagine what it would be like if I was visiting my father in prison. That probably explains her spontaneous tears. I love when Lily or Sara would rest their heads on my shoulder. Simply blissful.

I so want to slow time down, but the clock above the guard's desk ticks on. When I look into my wife and daughter's eyes, I realize more than anything that it is relationships that give meaning to my life, to all of our lives. Here I am, an inmate in a federal prison sitting in a dingy visitation area of a prison, thinking how fortunate I am to have so many significant and relevant relationships.

"Do they have educational programs for the inmates here?" Lily asks.

"The educational programs exist on paper only, all a façade for public consumption. Here you have a collection of people who need education more than anything else. They have the time to devote, they want to learn, but the system fails them. I was just reading an article that compared prisons with and without educational programs. Those with education programs are safer, have lower recidivism, and have increased chances of job acquisition after discharge. But the administration here doesn't care."

"That's terrible!" Sara says. She pauses for a moment, looking over my shoulder. "Do you know the inmate who takes the photos in here?"

Any inmate who wants a photo with a friend or family can ask this inmate to take their picture in front of a seasonal backdrop, as long as you can pay for the photo with a coupon purchased in advance at the commissary.

"I don't know him but see him playing basketball a lot. My roommate Bruce told me his backstory last night. Would you like to hear it?"

They perk up because so far, every tale I tell them is more jaw-dropping than the next.

"He used to be a police officer in Memphis. After investigating several bank robberies over the years, he decided to become a bank robber in retirement. He successfully robbed thirty-eight banks. Got caught on the thirty-ninth. He's now serving a twenty-five-year sentence. Can't make this shit up!"

Minutes turn into hours and inevitably visitation is ending. Now it's time to say our goodbyes. I will see my wife and daughter tomorrow, which makes me want to cry again. It was a successful visit.

No one told me in advance that all inmates are strip searched on the way out of visitation. Just in case I had the time of my life with my guests, the visit has to end with a strip search. The prison is concerned that guests will supply inmates with contraband. The most common items of contraband in the prison are cigarettes, real alcohol, drugs, and the most dangerous of all, cell phones. Do they really think an inmate can put a cell phone and a carton of cigarettes up their asses? All the contraband in the prison comes through the front door when the guards show up for work every day. They're searching the wrong people if they truly want to stop the flow of contraband.

It's the best night's sleep I've had in long time. Having such love and support is so nourishing to the soul, and seeing my wife and daughter just brings to light how much it's missed. Yes, they support me from afar, but there's nothing like seeing them in the flesh, holding them, kissing them, knowing our hearts are connected.

***

I wake up the next morning with a skip to my step, eager to see Lily and Sara again.

"Still flying high?" Bruce asks. He just got out of the shower and his hair is slicked back.

"I don't think I've felt this elated in such a long time. I even slept well."

Bruce smiles. "There's nothing like seeing family. And pretty ones at that. We're stuck looking at all these ugly mugs 24/7."

I laugh. Bruce has the ability to make me laugh harder than anyone else.

I place myself by the COs' office for another visit with Lily and Sara. Some time passes and I never get called. *Maybe they're running late.* I start to get anxious. I know they're in town. I saw them yesterday. There's no one I can ask—the room is sealed off, I can't get in or call anyone. So I sit there and wait—and wait—and wait.

It isn't until several hours later when I realize our visitation isn't happening. Frustrated and worried, I finally reach Lily on her phone. She's crying and rightfully so. When she and Sara showed up early in the morning for visitation, the same guards who were there yesterday, Tight Shirt and his sidekick Dopey, refused to let them in. They knew all too well that they had flown down here from New York. So why didn't they let them in? Because they had the power to deny them. They cited that the Daniels represented a different visit from Lily and Sara. Of course, Lily explained the Daniels never showed up, but they still counted two separate visits in their warped, malicious minds because we never informed them the Daniels weren't coming. Those BOP sycophants can see in the visitors' log that the Daniels never signed in, but it doesn't matter. The guards claimed I had two additional visits Saturday, so all my visitation points were used up.

This isn't an isolated event. This is prison. Inmates are powerless, and the guards and staff have absolute power over everything. Every inmate knows that with absolute power comes absolute abuse, and this is no exception. The guards saw how we enjoyed seeing each other as they conspired how to deny our visit the next day. They did just that and there is *nothing* I could do. I'm furious without any way to vent my rage. I head back to my room where I spend the rest of the day in a fetal position listening to my radio. I can't wait for the day to be over.

"Back already?" Bruce asks as he enters the room.

I explain what happened and feel my blood pressure rising. Yesterday I was on cloud nine and today I feel like burning the place down.

Bruce is angry on my behalf. "Tight Shirt is like an angry viper. He's a poorly educated redneck whose former wife is none other than the unit secretary for Antioch. She divorced him to marry another guard at this prison, a handsome, happy-go-lucky Black man. Guess it was too much for Tight Shirt to handle, so he unleashes his anger on the downtrodden of the earth—us inmates. I'm sorry that happened."

It takes days for my anger to calm down to a point where I can have a decent conversation with anyone. You want to believe that people are inherently good, but prison is the perfect breeding ground for the bad eggs—those lost souls who get off on seeing others suffer. I don't believe there is any hope for them, and I start to lose faith that all will be right in the world.

CHAPTER 24

Where's the Compassion

In addition to yoga and playing guitar, there's plenty of time to read in prison. Friends and family send me all sorts of books. When else have I had the luxury of reading three books a week? In my readings, I stumble upon a program in the federal prisons called Compassionate Release. It sounds great on paper. The BOP can release an inmate if there is a legitimate reason why an inmate should be released from prison. I believe I can follow the protocols and convince the BOP why I shouldn't be in prison, all in the name of *compassion: a feeling of deep sympathy and sorrow for another who is stricken by misfortune, accompanied by a strong desire to alleviate the suffering.*

From 2007 through 2012, 39,000 federal inmates filed for Compassionate Release. Twenty-eight got approved. Six died before they could be released. That means of the 39,000 who sought compassionate release, only 0.0005 percent were released. It begs the question, is there just no legitimacy to their claims, or is there no compassion on the part of the BOP? My months in prison have provided the answer.

Once a week, we're served eggs. The other six days we are fed a combination of cheap starch or starch-plus-fatty protein. I love eggs, but more importantly, because seventy-five percent of the brain and nervous system is made up of fat, I need to consume healthy fats in my diet. What better way than via eggs. Sunday lunch—and only Sunday lunch—is when they serve eggs. If you look at the official BOP menu, you will see cheese omelets once a week, scrambled eggs another week, and perhaps a spinach omelet the following week. Like most of what the BOP publishes, it's all for show.

Usually we are given two hardboiled eggs a week. I don't really care how they are made; I'm just happy to have eggs.

I'm standing in line one Sunday morning with a few friends. As we approach the food line, Paul, who is standing in front of me, turns to me and says, "I can't believe they're giving us only one egg today." He's upset and getting angrier with each inmate who leaves the food line with only one egg. When it's his turn to be served, he asks the guard who is standing behind the inmate servers, "How come we're only getting one egg today?"

The guard, six-two and three hundred and fifty pounds, says, "You're lucky we feed you at all!"

Enraged by the answer, he flips his tray over right in the food line, storms out of the cafeteria, and heads back to Antioch. In retrospect, Paul behaved admirably. His anger was taken out on the tray, not on the guard. I don't think the guard said anything that he and most of the guards don't believe. We *are* lucky that they feed us at all. They have no compassion for what it's like to be an inmate.

One man I know applied for Compassionate Release, and, amazingly enough, the warden approved it. His name was Harvey Ross, an eighty-five-year-old gentleman, and I use that word in the truest sense of the word. Harvey was serving a three- or four-year sentence for a problem arising from his construction of a federal housing facility. Initially he was sent to a camp in Arkansas closer to his home in St. Louis, but as his health deteriorated, he was transferred to FMC Franklin. He walked with a cane, had a full head of white hair, and most of all, he was dignified. Before I ever met him, he had applied for Compassionate Release.

His appeal stemmed from his wife of sixty-one years who needed a lung transplant due to progressive pulmonary fibrosis. A lung transplant is an arduous undertaking at any age, but she needed her husband to help her after she was released from the hospital. The warden approved it and sent the paperwork to Washington, D.C., for final approval. As the weeks advanced and Harvey remained in prison, his daughter made calls to D.C. to find out why it was delayed. She employed her local congressman to aid the family. Week after week, she was unable to get an answer from anyone in D.C. as to why Harvey wasn't being released.

Harvey's health began to deteriorate, and he was shuffled back and forth between the prison and University Hospital. That was how I really got to know Harvey. I served as interpreter between him and what the medical staff was telling him. He had two cardiac stents in addition to a multitude of other procedures. We talked a good deal about his medical issues, but what really bonded us was baseball. Despite my being a generation his junior, we talked about our love of baseball, before money hijacked the sport. He loved Stan Musial and the St. Louis Cardinals. The Cardinals had a rich baseball history, which we discussed ad absurdum. He was amazed I could name the starting lineup of the 1968 Cardinals who went to the World Series. Those dialogues made both of us feel free. They stabilized his medical problems, but his daughter was unable to make any progress in Washington. Harvey was discharged from prison on the day of his original release date, not one day sooner.

No one knew who obstructed the process, but it wasn't a computer glitch. It was done by a human who offered no compassion to a man who served his country well. His wife wrote me three months after his discharge telling me Harvey had died. I often think of him.

I take my tray with one egg and find a spot at a fairly empty table. I have no doubt that Paul is grumbling in his bunk. He's a man who is always grumpy and yearns for two eggs a week. Then again, I understand some of his anger, as he still has a few years to go on a ten-year sentence for a bank crime. Paul owned a bank and made the fateful mistake of temporarily using client funds to finance bank activity. I understand why such laws exist, but a ten-year prison sentence seems excessive. What makes it more painful is the case of Governor and Senator Dan Corbath of Connecticut who committed the same crime as Paul only on a much grander scale. Corbath took $1.6 billion of client money to cover a bad bet his hedge fund made on Portuguese bonds. He served no jail time and only paid a fine.

Paul is from South Bend, Indiana, about a six-hour drive to FMC Franklin. He's a veteran of our prison and knows how to survive. He's expecting a visit from his son and daughter-in-law in a few weeks. Paul hunted down the laziest of the lazy, Charlie Willis, a unit counselor. It's amazing how a fulltime employee is never in his office. Mr. Willis will show up a few hours a month, do what he needs to do, and then disappear. When Paul happened to see him at his desk, he pounced.

Paul explained that his son and new bride were already approved for visitation, and he needed Mr. Willis to correct his daughter-in-law's change of name, as she already had a new driver's license with her new name. Mr. Willis listened, and without saying a word, opened his computer. Paul had already written the name change on a piece of paper and handed it to Mr. Willis. After a minute or two, Mr. Willis announced, "All done," and handed Paul the newly printed visitation list. Being the proverbial cynic, Paul looked closely at the visitation list and saw the gross malfeasance inflicted on inmates.

The name was corrected. That should have been the only computer field that was ever opened. But it wasn't. Mr. Willis opened a second field—the address field—and changed the home address from 91 Elbert Street to 6 Earhart Street. Why would he do this? He knew that after a six-hour drive, his daughter-in-law would not have been allowed in visitation because the address on her driver's license and the address on the visitation list were different. Only a depraved person would have thought of doing such a thing, yet these are the people paid by Paul's tax dollars. Fortunately, Paul spotted the error and Mr. Willis, kind of caught with his pants down, made the appropriate corrections. I heard later the visitation was uneventful.

My case manager, and one of two case managers for the Antioch Unit, is Nikki Williams, who brings out the worst in everyone. Compassion is not her forte.

Nikki Williams has an important job as a case manager. As the name implies, her job is to manage the case of each inmate. Every visit, release date, restitution payment, education, job, obtaining a social security card, room assignment, transfer, etc. is controlled by the case manager. They wield enormous power over your stay in prison, so it's very common to ask a fellow inmate in the Antioch Unit, "Who's your case manager?" If the answer is Nikki Williams, her name *always* has a story attached to it.

My favorite was when the Deputy Attorney General of the United States asked her to scan four pages of notes an inmate (my British friend Jeremy) possessed and forward it to him. Her response was, "Do you know how busy I am. This is my first day back from vacation. I don't understand why the inmate can't go to the library and make copies." There is universal disdain for this woman.

Ms. Williams is in her mid-forties and somewhat attractive, until you interact with her. The hairdo is circa 1985, and who knows where she buys her cosmetics. The makeup is put on with a trowel, the hairdo has enough hairspray to stay in place through a tornado, and her clothes never fit properly or the alterations have come undone unbeknownst to her. There are a million Nikki Williams stories, all of which could fuel an entire book, but T-Bone's story captures the essence of Ms. Williams as well as any. Suffice it to say that Nikki Williams's lack of compassion forced this forty-year-old man, who had been incarcerated forever, to lose it with her.

"You fucking bitch!" he screamed at her when she refused, for the fourth time, to sit with him for ten minutes, after he spent months preparing a *roadmap for success* upon his release. She pressed the alarm on her belt that all staff members carry. That was only the beginning and the mildest of his tirade. The guards arrived within a thirty seconds and escorted T-Bone to the SHU where he remained for his final eight months in prison. It's amazing an inmate has never killed her.

CHAPTER 25

How Low Can I Go?

An hour before the nine-p.m. count on a Sunday, the CO places Monday's call-out list outside his office for all to peruse. Mondays are the busiest day for call-outs. Diaz and I, already waist deep in discussing the facial tattoos of tonight's guard, walk over to the call-out sheet. I hate having any call-outs. If it was up to me, other than my standard Monday–Wednesday–Friday call-outs for MS injections, I'd be happy never to have another call-out. My desire to fly under the radar takes all priority. No such luck tonight. In addition to my medical clinic call-out, which I have every Monday, I have a call-out to Medical Records at 7:30 a.m. I'm confused by this.

"What does it mean to have a call-out to Medical Records?" I ask Diaz.

"Not sure, did you request medical records?"

"I did two days ago. I got a response they received my request and I'll be contacted in about three weeks when they are ready for pick up." I periodically request my medical records, which the BOP is obligated to produce. I like to read what is in the records before mailing them back to Lily for safekeeping.

"That's strange, 'cause we know those lazy fuckers don't work overtime in order to get Jay Keller's medical records prepared in record time," says a smug Diaz. "I bet they need you to sign a form or something like that."

I believe Diaz. What he says does make sense, so I don't give it further thought. After checking for any newly arrived e-mails, always a source of pleasure, I say good night to Diaz, make my way up the forty-six steps to my room, and begin to organize myself for tomorrow. I place all my pills—six of them that I will take at lunch—into toilet paper, which I then place in my

145

uniform front pocket. This way, I won't forget to have my pills, which are best taken with meals. I write the 7:30 a.m. call-out on my homemade calendar in case I wake up tomorrow and forget I have a call-out. I do everything I possibly can in order to be in the right place at the right time, do the right thing, and make my stay here as uneventful as humanly possible.

At 7:30, I show up at Medical Records, show my ID, and take a seat in the little waiting area outside the office. A few other inmates are there, and they have no idea why they have a call-out to Medical Records. That should have been a clue that something isn't right, but I still have no reason for alarm. As we all sit around, I pull out a paperback I placed under my shirt and begin reading.

After half an hour, a woman comes up to us, confirms our names, and simply says, "Come with me." We do just that, although I'm getting a bad feeling in the pit of my stomach. We journey through the prison basement until we arrive at the Receiving and Departure area. I finally recognize where I am, the same area I spent my first few hours in prison. In fact, the same guards are here.

"Can you tell me why we're down here?" I ask of the woman who escorted us and is hastily about to leave the area.

"Med trip," she answers curtly before disappearing.

"What's *med trip*?" I ask the guy sitting next to me on the bench.

"You new here?" he responds, rather incredulous that I don't know what a med trip is.

"Four months."

"Med trip means you're going to the University Hospital to be checked by one of their doctors. They're better than the docs here, but they still ain't winning no prizes if ya know what I mean."

Now I understand why I have a call-out to Medical Records. It's the prison's obsession with security. No med trips are announced in advance. After all, if I have advance warning, I could arrange for my escape with the use of a helicopter, an armored car, or perhaps a Harrier jet.

Finally, after almost five months, I'll actually see a real doctor. Convinced it's going to be a neurologist, I begin to make a mental list of all the things I want to tell the doctor, all the lack of care I've endured. I hope not being part of the BOP, he or she will be someone I can tell what really goes on behind the barbed-wire fences. This could be a good day.

Two hours later, I hear a guard yell, "Keller, get your ass over here."

Slipping my book back under my shirt, I walk through another locked door where I'm confronted by a guard who looks like the twin brother of the Grim Reaper. He has a huge wad of tobacco in his mouth while he proudly carries a bottle of Mountain Dew to collect his spit. His physique personifies the meaning of BOP, or more accurately, Belly Over Pants. His arms and neck are covered with hideous tattoos of gruesome images, and he's wearing mirrored sunglasses to work in a windowless room in the basement of a prison. *Just breathe, Jay, just breathe.*

"Lemme see ya ID."

I hand him my ID, which he never looks at before handing it back to me. With his mirrored sunglasses, he can't see anyway.

"See that last room down there?" He points. "Well, that's where ya gotta change. Move it."

"What am I changing into?" I ask innocently, but that seems to irritate him more. He's confused as to whether I'm just another stupid inmate or if I'm challenging his authority. Either way, I'm not looking good.

"Don't matter, just change in a top, bottom, and slip-on shoes, then come out so I can search ya. Wait, let me search ya first."

He makes me turn around, put my arms up in the air, and pats me down before releasing me to change my clothes. He tosses my book from under my shirt into a large garbage can. It wasn't a great book.

The room is the same dressing room when I first arrived and had to wear a uniform that defined me as a new arrival. I guess they use the same uniforms for med trips, but I'm becoming more fearful of further angering this guard. The sizes are XL, XXL, and XXXL. I reach for the XL.

"Turn around, arms up, spread your legs," he says.

"But you just searched me," I spit out before I have a chance to censor myself. I know I've screwed up, but his reaction is calmer than expected.

"I did. But there a'lotta bad dudes in this place, so when I ask to search you, you supposed to say, 'Yes sir.' Got it?" He makes another deposit of tobacco juice into the can of Mountain Dew.

"Yes sir." I'm boiling up inside, but there's nothing I can do. Nothing. You have *no* rights in prison, and you are always in the wrong. Why can't I remember that?

He walks me to another door, unlocks it, and leads me outside although still in a caged area. I'm standing outside, not far from the spot where the gates opened so I could enter the prison on that fateful day. I turn to look at the spot where Lily was parked as she waved goodbye to me. Man, I want so badly for her to be there to take me home.

The guard opens a zippered bag and pulls out long metal chains, lots of clanging, lots of unraveling. Before I know it, he's putting cuffs around my ankles. He proceeds to attach the metal shackles around my waist a few times before saying, "Put ya hands out in front."

"What are you doing? I have the lowest level custody in this prison. This shackle stuff isn't for someone like me. Look at my paperwork, I'll show you where it says 'Custody Level 1.' I'm telling you the truth."

"The only truth around here is what I say is the truth. Ya got that, boy? If I say you a Level 4 Custody, then you a Level 4. Don't you go thinkin' ya know better than me. We ain't discussing this any further, otherwise you gonna do explaining when you in the SHU. Besides, I don't much like Yankees, always thinkin' they know best. Hate Yankees—always have, always will." He spits into his Mountain Dew collection container and my stomach turns.

Following his commentary, he puts me in full shackles so I'm in chains from my ankles all the way up to my shoulders. Once it settles in as to what has just transpired, I now feel the tightness around my wrists and ankles from the squeezing cuffs. Asking him to loosen everything is an option, but not a good one. He could make them even tighter I suppose. This is a losing battle. I just stand there, saddened and helpless.

"Ankles and wrists okay?" he asks.

"Wouldn't mind if they were a little looser."

"Put your hands out front."

After fumbling for his keys, he undoes one cuff. "Thanks, that feels better." No sooner did I get the words out, he tightens the handcuff even more than it was before, the metal compressing my forearm bones as tight as he can adjust them. He does the same to my other wrist and each ankle. Each limb is screaming out in pain as I do my best to not show my discomfort. I gaze at trees, passing cars, and a few stray cats, anywhere but at my captor.

In a few minutes, a van arrives with two other BOP goons who are to escort me to University Hospital for my visit. They order me into the van, which is almost an impossibility being shackled as tightly as I am. I inch my way into the back of the van. When the guards get bored of watching me struggle, they lift me by my elbows and throw me onto the bench seat. My head hits hard into the opposite door, but no one is the least bit concerned with my *what-the-fuck* comment. They slam the doors shut and head out of the prison compound. No seatbelt. No conversing with me.

I look out the windows, which are covered with metal wiring, but at least I can see where I am. It's the first time I've left the prison since I arrived about five months ago. We're driving on the same road Lily and I drove on when she brought me to this hellhole. Here I am, months later, and things are only getting worse. I'm in full shackles in the back of an old van along with two oversized musclebound guards who would just as soon throw me out on the side of the road and let the turkey vultures have a feast. I hate this place, and I hate these fucking guards.

The van stops just short of the medical center. The driver exits the van while the other guard plays a game on his cell phone. Ten minutes later, the driver returns with two big cups of coffee.

"Who'd you bet on?" the guard says.

"West Virginia by seven and a half points. It's a safe bet," the driver says smugly.

Upon arriving in front of a large office building, which is part of the hospital complex, I remain in the van while the two BOP guards converse with two other guards who work for a private service responsible for our custody while we're out of the prison. Eventually they pull me out of the van, and we make our way into the building. Here I am, in full prison garb and shackles, being led through the corridors and elevators of a respectable medical center. The guards have guns visible for all to see. I'm a sideshow for all the other patients as they wonder what kind of man I am to be in such a predicament.

We make it to the doctor's suite, but much to my surprise, I'm not seeing a neurologist. My appointment is with Dr. Beth Jones, a clinical immunologist. *Okay, think up a whole new set of questions for the immunologist.*

In the hour or so I'm sitting in the waiting room, the guards initiate conversation with me. They are both former guards at FMC Franklin but now work for a private agency to earn extra in their retirement, and very easy money they tell me. Being retired, they're a little looser in their references to the atrocities that occur in FMC Franklin, a little more honest, a little more sympathetic.

A mother enters the waiting room with her son whom I guess is around eight years old. He's a bit hyperactive but within reason, clearly fascinated with my shackles and armed-guard escort. I can tell he wants to see the shackles up close, so he feigns looking for a magazine. As he inches his way closer to me, his mother yells, "Get back here, Steven. That's a *bad man* over there. Come here right now!"

I sink into my chair. This might be the lowest moment of my life. Those words hurt more than any physical pain I've experienced. I want to curl up in a fetal position, close my eyes, and exit my earthly existence.

"Mr. Keller, Dr. Jones will see you now," says the perky twenty-something medical assistant, and I'm relieved to get out of the waiting room. The two guards help me up, because the shackles make it difficult to go from sitting to standing.

I'm escorted down a hallway and into a small room where I sit in the chair next to the desk. It's a comfortable consultation room adorned with the obligatory diplomas on the wall behind the doctor. Dr. Jones graduated from the University of Kentucky School of Medicine and did her Allergy and Immunology training at Northwestern. Okay, well trained.

A few moments later, Dr. Jones enters the room with a warm smile. She extends her hand to shake the hand of a new patient, but that's not going to happen with the iron jewelry I'm wearing. She smiles when she realizes the folly of the situation and just says, "We can forego the handshake." She takes a seat opposite me.

"Nice to meet you, Dr. Jones, I'm Jay Keller," I say confidently as if I'm introducing myself to a colleague. Unlike Dr. Huff, she's respectful and non-judgmental, as I had hoped would be the case.

The visit progresses nicely. There really is no physical exam to do for an immunologist. She's intrigued with the combination of medical problems and even admits she doesn't know much about the effects of Tecfidera on the immune system. Giving a prognosis is thus impossible, just as my immunologist from New York had said. As we get into the specifics, she pauses before asking me what I did for a living before I was incarcerated. I'm forthright and tell her what I did and briefly described how I ended up in prison.

"They put you in prison for that?" she asks. "I have to tell you, I never paid much attention to anything to do with criminal justice. I doubt you did either. Anyway, a friend, colleague, and doctor of mine—an orthopedist—got into a bunch of trouble from the feds."

"What egregious act did he commit?"

"His wife accepted gifts from an aggressive MRI facility. It might have been a few thousand dollars in gifts over a year or so. They threatened to put him in prison, but in the end, they suspended his license for a few months and he had to pay an obscene fine, something like half a million dollars. He was devastated by the whole process, was ready to quit medicine. You must have had a rough time too."

"Had a rough time? Yes. I *have* a rough time every single day. Any idea what a dump that place is? Any idea about the doctors they have working there?"

She smiles and simply says, "I've heard stories. Sorry you're going through this."

With that we progress through my medical history and what to do going forward. Because the guards are with us and hearing every word, I chose my words carefully before proceeding. "I'm sure you will have to issue a report of your findings to the prison staff. Make sure you are very detailed about the dangers of a CD4 count in the thirties combined with all the other factors. Please be concrete in your recommendations."

What I try to convey is for her to write a report stating that I shouldn't be in prison at all given my medical conditions. I believe her to be sympathetic, but how much she can push them is an unknown.

"Oh, I do have one other question. You know, we do see inmates from time to time. I personally don't see many, but they're usually not in shackles. How come they put you in full shackles?"

"No logical reason other than the guard in the departure area wanted me to have an extra special day. I'm supposed to have the lowest level of security. If I didn't have medical issues, they would have just sent me to a federal camp."

I glance over at the guards; they remain silent, but look stiff in their posture.

"So, you got extra punishment for being sick?"

"Yes, I did. Very nice meeting you. I hope your consult will have some influence on the powers-that-be at Franklin."

She smiles and wishes me good luck. "We'll skip the handshake."

With that, the guards escort me past the curious eyes of the waiting room patients, the corridors, and elevators until we reach the original BOP guards waiting for me in their steel-caged van. All four guards exchange pleasantries and paperwork before I'm stuffed back into the van. Heavy metal music is blasting from the radio.

As we pull away to make the fifteen-minute drive, with a nothing-to-lose attitude, I ask the guards, "No seat belt?"

The guard in the passenger seat slowly turns to look at me. "Only time you get a seat belt is when I put it around your neck."

No other words are exchanged.

Back at the prison, the two guards hand me to my friend in R&D who still has his trademark Mountain Dew bottle filled with tobacco juice. "You were right there, Yankee. You were supposed to be low custody. Guess I didn't see that this morning. Hope you had a good med trip."

He unshackles me and releases me to go back to the Antioch Unit. Even by prison standards, today was a rough day.

CHAPTER 26

Lockdown

Dear Lil,

This will be a week of writing letters if the rumors are true. They say we may be on lockdown all week because of some security infrastructure work. I can read. I can write. That's it. Time is moving at a snail's pace.

Everyone has a story, one sadder than the next. The first time I witnessed someone leaving prison, it was an anomaly to me. Now it's the norm. Most of the time you are so sick of seeing the same people and their idiosyncrasies around you every single day that you're happy when they leave. Unfortunately, they're replaced with someone else you will grow weary of in a short period of time. That's just how it is here. What's harder to understand is the prison-industrial complex that remains such a stain on our culture and society. Aside from my own plight, every day I witness gross injustices. Other times, it's atrocities that fall under the heading of "business as usual."

Yesterday was another sad day at FMC Franklin. Duke was a large man, six-two and six hundred pounds. Duke loved to eat. He would go to commissary with two empty laundry bags (everyone else used one) and filled both of them with carbohydrates of the unhealthiest variety. I got to know him through my friend Ken. Duke was one of many low-level drug dealers from the West Virginia area. He had over ten years to go when I first met him. Duke was a happy-go-lucky man, but I never saw Duke happier than the one time I saw him in the visitation area with his wife and kids. He was at the medical center for his profound sleep apnea, morbid obesity, lymphedema (chronic swelling of the legs), hypertension, and a heart that had trouble supplying his heavy weight. He was a "patient" of mine in that he would often ask my opinion on a multitude of medical issues. Despite his serious medical problems, I always enjoyed his optimism and hearty laugh.

I didn't know him as a smoker, but sure enough the guards found cigarettes in his locker on a routine shake-down. He might have just been selling cigarettes for some extra commissary money. Who knows? Lily, there are only two ways to obtain cigarettes. You can buy real cigarettes for the equivalent of $10 a cigarette. Those cigarettes are brought in by the guards and sold at a handsome profit. The other method is more creative.

Most of the guards walk around with a wad of chewing tobacco in their mouths and a container to collect the spit. Eventually their containers fill up and they toss them into the garbage. Inmates comb through the garbage, collect the tobacco juice in the container, and bring it back to their housing unit. They put the juice in the microwave oven until it's reduced to a tarry, sticky substance. Next, they take this residual tobacco product and roll it in rolling paper. In prison, that means pages of the Bible. These previously chewed tobacco products are now made into cigarettes and sell for $3 each.

The guards know who smokes, where they smoke, when they smoke, and when they need a new supply. I suspect the bootleg cigarettes compete with the cigarettes supplied by the guards, so the guards crack down on the bootleggers by periodically sending some poor soul to the SHU for dealing cigarettes. Duke was this week's sacrificial lamb. Duke's roommate, Maris, went down to the COs' office to notify the staff that Duke's nighttime breathing apparatus didn't go down to the SHU with him. The CO just scoffed at Maris when told about the oversight and the need for Duke to use the machine at night.

Early next morning, I'm up in medical clinic getting my injection when a nurse comes out and tells us we all have to immediately evacuate the medical clinic. No explanation is given, but when you're a prisoner, no explanation is expected. After waiting in an adjacent area for over an hour, we're finally allowed back into the clinic area. I receive my injection and resume my day just a little later than usual. It wasn't until lunchtime when I learned why we were evacuated.

During medical rounds that morning in the SHU, the doctor didn't like the way Duke looked. He decided to have Duke checked in the medical clinic. Whenever anyone from the SHU has to go up to the medical clinic, the entire clinic has to be empty of inmates. The SHU is in the basement of the prison, which means the guards had to use an elevator to move Duke from the basement, up two stories, to the medical clinic. Except the elevator was broken, which is often the case in this facility. Plan B was to wheel Duke up the ramp that led from the basement to ground level and from there they could take another elevator up to the clinic.

They started to wheel Duke up the long ramp when the nurse noticed he was no longer breathing. CPR was immediately started, but in the chaos, Duke rolled off the stretcher and onto the floor. This enormous six-hundred-pound man was now lying face down on the ramp as they tried to turn him over to give him CPR. Duke died on the ramp. I'm sure the BOP sugarcoated the sequence of events that led to his wife being a widow and his children losing their father. Duke came, now he is gone.

Somehow, I remain safe.

All my love,
Jay

Dearest Lil,

Today is day two of the lockdown, although I was allowed to go to the medical clinic for my injection.

Seated in the waiting room, I watched the line of diabetics receive their injections, the nurse never once cleaning the skin with alcohol. As soon as the nurse called me in and waved my injection container to get my attention, I walked back in the treatment area to find an empty stretcher. On the first stretcher was a man I recognized. His name was Donald Hemmer, a seventy-year-old man serving his second prison stint. After escaping from a prison camp that had no fences, he was a free man for fifteen years living incognito in Florida. His wife died of natural causes and soon his business failed. He was now homeless and without medical care. What does one do? He went to the nearest US Marshal office and turned himself in. He was glad to be in FMC Franklin, complete with lodging, food, and "medical care."

As I walked past his stretcher, I noticed he was very still with his eyes closed. He was hooked up to an EKG machine. My eyes went to the EKG graph like a hankering alcoholic would turn to a full bottle of whiskey. The EKG was bold and clear. He had ST segment elevation in leads II, III, and aVF. He was having an acute inferior-wall heart attack.

The nurse in charge saw me gawking at the EKG. She didn't reprimand me as expected. Instead, she put her index fingers in both ears and said to me, "Don't tell me what it shows. Just get your injection and leave!" She shook her head knowing what the EKG revealed. I walked to the last stretcher, gave myself the injection, and walked back to the nursing station to show them the used syringe. As I placed the needle and syringe in the Sharp box, I asked the other nurse who was not privy to the EKG incident, very innocently "Are any of the doctors in the clinic this morning?" She replied, "No, I think Dr. Alijawana will be here in the afternoon." I thought about going back to say something to Mr. Hemmer's nurse, but I didn't. My inaction has haunted me since.

I never saw Donald Hemmer again. Some come, some go.

I love you forever,
Jay

Dear Lil,

Day three of lockdown. Last night I received a letter from Steven Bariletti, an ex-inmate I was friendly with when I first arrived. I remember him well because he made me laugh, no easy task around here. I remember the evening before his discharge, hanging with Steve in the Antioch courtyard. He was imitating all the prison hoarders by saying, "Are you gonna finish that meatloaf? Mind if I take it? Can I have that banana? Mind if I take that egg? You gonna eat that hot dog?" I recall that evening because it was the first time since I entered the prison that I had a big belly laugh, laughing uncontrollably at nothing but his silly scenarios. For a period of five minutes, we laughed our hearts out. Even while living in a third-world prison, we managed to laugh. I was saddened when Steve left but I was very happy that he was able to leave this hellhole. Everyone is sincerely happy whenever it's someone's time to leave. How could you not be?

Steve is a fifty-year-old Floridian who worked for years as a manager in the defense contracting business. He is smart and witty. His Crohn's disease is rather severe, which is why he was sent to a Federal Medical Center. He has a wife from Slovenia and two very young children. Like many in here, he went from being financially stable and successful to having nothing. Once the feds get hold of you, most likely, you lose everything you've ever worked for, defined only by your worst deed.

Steve's bitterness stemmed from the fact that he never cheated the government but was the scapegoat for a prosecutor who knew a crime had been committed but needed a donkey to pin the tail on. Steve was the donkey. The reason he wrote to me was to say that he had been exonerated. It turned out he was able to finally prove, after serving eighteen months in prison, that the prosecutor had lied. He was able to get a circuit judge to compel the DOJ to hand over five thousand pages of documents. In those documents was the evidence to exonerate him. Had he not been smart and tenacious, he would not have been exonerated. You develop a pretty good sense of who deserves to be in prison and who doesn't. Steve, like me, should never have been incarcerated. That is one reason for our friendship. Nonetheless, his career has been ruined, his bank account emptied, and his wife moved back to Slovenia with their children. He never found out if the prosecutor was disbarred for making an innocent man into a criminal.

It goes on and on, Lil, just like my love for you.

Jay

CHAPTER 27
My Cousin Vinny

After five months, I have a great flow of communication with the outside world. I receive mail virtually every day, as well as books and magazines. I also have a group of people who are on my email list. Whether I want to or not, I know what's going on in the outside world. One of my most stalwart writers is my cousin Donnie. Although he lives in California and I live in NY, he is my closest living relative. Both my parents are deceased and my one sister hasn't been seen by a family member in years.

Donnie and I always enjoy our time together. His dad, Harry, my father's older brother, was one of those guys who could take over a room when he entered. He was handsome, quick, and funny. For many years, especially when Harry lived in Las Vegas, his closest friend was Vincent Gallardo, whom I heard about for years. Vinnie, according to Harry, is as smart as any Harvard graduate but spends his career in the casinos of Las Vegas in every capacity, including being a casino owner. He *is* Las Vegas.

Harry died at the age of sixty-seven from colon cancer. His funeral was in New York, quite close to where Lily and I lived. After the funeral, we invited all the out-of-towners—and there were many—back to our house. It was a beautiful July afternoon. That was when I met Vincent Gallardo. Vinnie and his friends had the appearance of mobsters of the first degree. Our home suddenly looked like a casting call for *The Sopranos*. We talked about Harry, and I could feel Vinnie's loss; his sadness was palpable. Lily turned the house into a catering facility as only she could. My daughter and Donnie's daughter, close in age, performed a dance routine for everyone's viewing pleasure including all the mobsters. Harry was right: Vinnie was smart and like Harry, funny as hell.

One day, I check my email before going to bed and read an email from Donnie. He tells me Vinnie got busted in Baton Rouge for possession of an unregistered silencer and was being transferred from a penitentiary in Louisiana to FMC Franklin to finish his six-month sentence. Unregistered silencer? Who even uses a silencer? Do hunters need one so they don't disturb the other deer? Donnie didn't know the exact date of Vinnie's arrival, but he would let me know. He said he would also forward a recent picture of Vinnie so I could recognize him. I was excited but I also knew there were eight housing units at this prison. Unless he was in the Antioch Unit, the only place I would see him would be in the rec yard or the cafeteria. I would have to be on full alert.

About three weeks later, I'm down in the Bus Stop, my original room, visiting Ryan. We often swap books and catch up on life. I look up and see a guard escorting Vinnie to his new bed, right next to Ryan's. The guard throws his roll-up onto the bed before quickly disappearing.

I rush over to him. "Vinnie! I heard you were coming but didn't know when. I'm Jay Keller. Remember me? I can't believe you're here!"

Vinnie smirks. "I'm here all right. How old is this place? Looks like a relic from the Civil War."

"I thought I'd have to search you out and here you are, right next to my friend Ryan!"

We share a great big hug. We aren't relatives but it's the next best thing. It's the first time in eighteen years we've seen each other. My spirits are immediately lifted. This is a surprise visit that will last forty-five days.

Vinnie is in his early seventies, on the short side, a bit plumper than I remembered, a full head of gray hair neatly combed back, and very distinguished looking. We happen to be in prison, but I can just as easily envision this man walking into a boardroom in a suit and tie and sitting at the head of the table to initiate a corporate board meeting. I introduce him to Ryan and immediately take the roll-up from his arms.

"Let me help you with that. You don't need to wrestle with everything the way I had to." I flash back to my first day in prison, the fear, the confusion. I won't let Vinnie suffer any more than he has to.

"Thanks, pal. How's Lily and the kids? I remember going back to Vegas after the funeral telling everyone about your daughter's dance routine."

"Everyone's good, thanks."

He looks well, but older. Who doesn't age? I can tell that Vinnie is going to be fine. He never spent time in prison until a few months ago, but he already has a swagger about him that just says, "Don't fuck with me."

"Hey, Keller, ain't ya gonna introduce me?" says Diaz as he strolls through the Bus Stop for his afternoon social rounds.

"Of course, man. This is my cousin Vinnie, Vincent Gallardo. Vinnie, this is the one and only Orlando Diaz."

They shake hands, eying each other. "You guys cousins?" asks a perplexed Diaz.

"Not really, just friends. Haven't seen each other in eighteen years. Vinnie was best friends with my uncle. Now he's in this dump. Be extra nice to him, Diaz."

"Sorry you gotta be here, Vinnie," says Diaz. "It ain't too bad here, I've been in worse, but it's pretty bad. Anyway, nice meeting you. A friend of Jay is a friend of mine. Anyone ever tell you ya look like Joe Pesci, only better looking?"

Vinnie laughs at Diaz's unfiltered words. "Actually, you're the first. But I've met Joe Pesci, had dinner with him. I'll tell you about him some time."

For once in his life, Diaz is speechless. He walks away mumbling something in Spanish, sporting his characteristic right-sided tilt.

"You've just been introduced to the Director of Misinformation," I say as we start to put sheets on the bed. "I love Diaz, and he helped keep me afloat when I first got here, but that boy doesn't always get his facts straight. Take everything he says with a grain of salt."

I get Vinnie oriented as best I can, sharing every bit of knowledge I have about how this place operates. Helping Vinnie is helping me as much as it's helping him. I'm useful. Over the next few weeks, we eat together whenever possible. I feel like I'm dining with the Don.

Vinnie adjusts quickly. He's surprised by three things here. The first is the wanton filth of FMC Franklin. Secondly, the quality of inmates. When he was in the penitentiary, he expected to be surrounded by crazy, badass, angry men. He thought a lower security prison would be different. What surprises him is the high percentage of crazy people here. We discuss how prisons have become the de facto "mental institutions" since most were closed down in the eighties. FMC Franklin wreaked of mental illness. Lastly, it's a poorly run prison. Quoting one local West Virginian when speaking about the "management" of FMC Franklin, "They can't find a mouse running around in a bass fiddle."

My favorite time with Vinnie is hanging out in the courtyard of Antioch. Vinnie would hold court, telling one hilarious story after another. One evening, Andy Alteri, a Canadian held hostage by our Justice Department, made a reference to the movie *Casino,* which is all about Las Vegas. Vinnie then spends the next hour describing the real characters the film was based on. He told us how the real-life Ginger, Sharon Stone's character, was more beautiful and savvier than Sharon Stone was portrayed in the film. The real Sam Rothstein, played by Robert DeNiro, was a savant when it came to the point spreads of sporting events. The sociopathic Nicky, played by Joe Pesci, was even crazier and more depraved in real life. He knows the backstory of every character. He gives all of us an education about the glory days of Las Vegas before it was taken over by corporations.

Vinnie gets along with everyone, probably because he fears no one. The guards tell the inmates what other inmates are in for, which is one reason no one can hide anything, especially the cho-mos. Everyone knows Vinnie came in under the O/C umbrella, Organized Crime. No one is going to test Vinnie, plus he carries himself well. However, you also don't want to cross him. Even Officer Beecham, our daytime CO, never hassles him. Beecham is a dumb, drunken hillbilly who couldn't make it in the military so he became a correctional officer as a place to park his troubled past. Beecham does have his fan club of inmates who buy his cigarettes, cell phones, and who knows what else. If you're a customer of his, he's your best friend. To the rest of us, he's a nightmare. He's the guard who threw my locker contents all over the Bus Stop simply to amuse himself.

Vinnie spends a lot of time in the library, which has a decent variety of books and old newspapers and magazines. During the week, you need a pass to go to the library. It should be a simple process, but nothing is simple in prison. In theory, you give the CO your ID in exchange for a pass. When you return the pass, you get your ID back. Simple.

I'm just happy to have Vinnie around—there's a familiarity with him that I don't get with the other inmates, and it's because he knows members of my family. Every day I'm in prison is a reminder of the separation from my family. Hanging with Vinnie lessens the pain.

One day, I'm sitting in my room writing in my diary when Diaz walks in with a concerned look on his face.

"Beecham gave your cousin Vinnie a rough time getting a pass today. Don't worry, Vinnie stayed cool."

"What happened?"

"I was behind Vinnie waiting to get passes from Beecham. The door to his office was open, but Beecham had his head on the desk like he was sleeping.

"Vinnie said, 'I need a library pass, Mr. Beecham,' very calmly and politely. Beecham raised his head, looked at Vinnie, and put his head right back down. Vinnie turned to me and whispered, 'What the fuck?'

"Then Vinnie took a step closer and said to Beecham, 'Just need a library pass, sir, then I'll be out of your hair.'"

"Beecham didn't even raise his head. A minute went by before Vinnie knocked on Beecham's desk and repeated his request.

"Beecham raised his head and glared at Vinnie with bloodshot eyes before shouting, 'You stupid or what, Gallardo? I ain't givin' out passes this afternoon. Passes are a privilege that don't extend to inmates today.'"

"Vinnie just stood there. 'What fuckin' part of what I just said don't you understand?' Beecham slurred. 'Get the fuck out of my office and close the door on your way out! Fucking inmates!'"

Once again, I'm irritated, which is par for the course. Nothing in prison is easy, and you're made to feel like an ingrate when you request simply the basics.

Vinnie told me what happened later that afternoon. Beecham, despite his delinquent behavior as a correctional officer, is the head of the local union of correctional officers. He's pretty much untouchable. He's just one of many who make each day in prison a little more painful. I calmed Vinnie down and told him to go to the library in the evening when you don't need a pass. He took my advice.

I met Vinnie later that night in the courtyard of Antioch. I was back from indoor rec while Vinnie spent the evening in the library.

"That library's fucked up," Vinnie says as if he's telling me something I don't know.

"Let me guess, it was noisy and filled with crazy people," I say with the wisdom of a seasoned prison vet.

Vinnie nods. "That's not a library. Guys were playing cards, another group looked like the executive committee of a *Star Trek* convention, and a fight broke out over a pencil sharpener. It's fucked up. This one guy sat down next to me excited as hell because he just crossed the threshold. Only fifty-seven hundred more days left on his sentence. That's over fifteen years! I congratulated him and went back to my book. What a fucking train wreck."

"I told you, Vinnie. I go there only if I need a specific book or I need air-conditioning. That's it. The cast of characters is right out of *Cuckoo's Nest.*"

Vinnie has a couple of medical problems that landed him in FMC Franklin, the most serious of which is his trigeminal neuralgia and the facial pain associated with it. However, for a man of seventy-three, he looks good. Last night he came up to my room, the "Penthouse," as Bruce calls it, to ask me my medical opinion. He noticed some blood in his urine the last two days that made urination painful at times.

"I would have it checked tomorrow at sick-call," I say without room for wiggle. Sick-call is where any inmate can be seen by "someone." It's really nothing more than a glorified triage center where the nurses either tell the inmate to get an OTC product at commissary or arrange a call-out with their doctor. On occasion, they will treat the problem right then and there.

I explain to him the process of sick-call, all the logistics, so he can have a less horrible experience. I have to be there for my injection, so I would probably be able to see him in the clinic at that time. By the time I arrive Wednesday morning, Vinnie is being triaged by the nurse. There's no privacy or HIPPA laws in prison, so the whole waiting room hears everything. Vinnie doesn't see me sitting in the waiting room, but I certainly hear him when he encounters a dismissive nurse.

"I've had the blood in my urine for about three days," states Vinnie.

"Does it hurt when you urinate?"

"Yeah, enough to bring me up here."

The bored nurse responds with a perfunctory, "Well, blood in the urine is common every once in a while. I don't think we need to take up the doctor's time with that. Go to Commissary and get some Tylenol or Advil, and drink a lot of water."

That isn't the answer Vinnie wants to hear. Standing over the diminutive nurse on the other side of the glass, he says, "Ma'am, I've been on this earth for seventy-three years! I've never had a menstrual period in my life, and I sure as hell don't think I'm having one now. Are you trying to tell me the blood in my urine is just part of my menstrual cycle? It isn't! What do you take me for? And Commissary is closed all this week in case you didn't read that memo! I need to see the doctor right now."

Vinnie storms out of the clinic never realizing I'm sitting in the waiting room. Sure enough, the nurse made an appointment for Vinnie to see the doctor later that afternoon where he was diagnosed with a small kidney stone.

I love being around Vinnie. He makes the unbearable just a little more bearable. Everyone loves the guy. He's even able to win over some of the sourest of guards. Overall, Vinnie passes his time by keeping a low profile, reading a lot, and walking the track in outdoor recreation. And before you know it, it's his last week of prison.

In the home stretch of prison life, Vinnie runs into trouble. He tells me the story but he can't stop laughing at himself.

It was nine o'clock count and Vinnie was engrossed in a TV show. By 9:20, the guards were getting ready to start their count on the third floor when they saw him sitting in front of the TV.

"What do you think you're doing here?" the guard asked incredulously.

"Oh, just watching a show on banana farming," he replied in a nonchalant tone.

"Did you happen to notice that you're the only inmate in this room?"

Vinnie paused and looked around. "You know, now that you mention, it is pretty empty."

"So that means you're not gonna go to count tonight? You'd rather go to the SHU?"

That was when he realized he totally forgot about count. With three days to go, he spaced out count. "Could I be any stupider?" he says to me as he imitates the look on the guard's faces.

"Holy shit, Officer, I forgot all about it. I'm really sorry. Did you guys count already?"

"Not yet. Do you know how lucky you are that we're starting on the third floor tonight?" the guard snapped.

"I'm *really* sorry, officers. Hey, listen, pal, I'm going home next week. Didn't mean any disrespect, sirs. But tell you what, next time you come to Vegas, you look me up, Vinnie Gallardo. I'll make sure you're treated like an A-list celebrity. You'll have the best time."

This story proves just how hard it is to be mad at Vinnie. Even the ill-tempered guards ultimately laughed it off so there never was any punishment.

On Vinnie's last morning, I walk him down to the exit door of Antioch. He's all set to head to the Receiving and Departure area. Who's the last person he sees in Antioch Unit? None other than Officer Beecham.

"Heard you're leaving us, Mr. Gallardo," says Beecham. "Hope you behave yourself this time. Have a good trip home."

Vinnie gets right in his grill and says, "Damn right I'm leaving. You'll still be in this shithole for years." Vinnie takes a step closer to him. "Listen, Beecham, you better hope we never meet on the outside, you fuckin' drunk! One day, when you wake up in a hospital with two broken knees and a rearranged face, but have no idea how it happened or who did it, think back to how you treated me and all the other helpless inmates at FMC Franklin you wouldn't even give a fuckin' pass to. So fuck you, Beecham, I'm out of here."

Vinnie flashes a big smile at the stunned correctional officer before he makes his way to the Departure area where his ride was waiting for him. He called Lily to let her know I was safe and doing okay. You have to love Vinnie. My forty-five-day reprieve is over.

CHAPTER 28

What's a Stem Cell?

With Vinnie gone, I have more time to write. Sitting alone in the courtyard well before the night count with my pen and pad, my thoughts and my writing are beginning to morph into some sort of organized book, or at least it is in my head. I try to write down every story I hear and will put it all together when I leave here. How did people write books for centuries without word-processing tools? I've gained a fresh respect for writers of all eras. Vinnie has only been gone a week but it feels much longer. Diaz strolls by and sits.

Diaz and I watch as Joe Hatch makes his departure rounds. Joe is the poster boy of untreated mental illness. He is finishing a six-year sentence for bank robbery. He went into a bank, passed a note to the teller, and left the bank with a few thousand dollars. He got into his white Cadillac, which was parked right in front of the bank, and drove a few blocks to Whole Foods. Despite being at least a hundred pounds overweight, Joe loved everything about Whole Foods. With a wad of cash, he began his shopping spree, which ended when the local police arrested him the second he exited the store. Joe drove me crazy because he was an incessant talker who had nothing of interest to say. However, I feel sorry for him because his mental state is so bruised and fragile, the product of a drug-addicted mother and unscrupulous foster homes.

"Leaving tomorrow, fellas. Back to a halfway house in Florida. You boys stay safe in here," says Joe as he extends his hand to me and Diaz.

"Nice sharing time with you, Joe. Good luck and stay in touch. You'll be missed around here," I say as I give a wink to Diaz.

A smirking Diaz adds, "Maybe I'll see you in Florida if I ever get out of this shithole. Take care of yourself." He gives Joe a hug.

Once Joe leaves, Diaz places his hands behind his head and stretches out his arms. "One less psycho around here. Too bad he'll be replaced by five others. What are you writing about tonight, Jay?"

"I was writing about Frankie One Stamp, not that I've had any interaction with him. I was also going to write about our burgeoning cockroach population. But after saying goodbye to Joe, I would be delinquent if I didn't write about Joe Hatch. He doesn't need prison time; he needs a psychiatrist. Vegas has Joe a 7:1 favorite for being back in prison within the year."

"I hope I get to read your book someday. If you want a bestseller, make sure I'm in it," says Diaz with a big smile.

"You'll be tall, dark, handsome, smart, funny, and rich in the book. Does that work for you?"

"Hey, did you hear about the guy in Henworth Unit, the motherfucker who hung himself?" Diaz changes the subject.

"I heard something but didn't know who they were talking about. Did you know the guy?"

"Heard the guy kept saying he was going to kill himself, but no one gives a shit in this place. They'll have his bed filled by tomorrow afternoon."

Just then, Officer Beecham comes storming into the courtyard and starts yelling at all of us to clear the courtyard immediately. Sure enough, the guards are beginning a shakedown of Antioch Unit, which means we all have to move to the outdoor rec area after a quick pat-down. I'm exhausted so I immediately seek out an empty bench until we're allowed back into Antioch. Diaz takes a seat next to me.

"Heard they found Soldier with a cell phone. He's fucked if that's true," chirps Diaz. "This is the third shakedown this month." He shakes his head. "Hey, Jay, ya know how I'm always talking about my kids and my old lady? How come you never talk about your kids?"

"Who wants to hear about people they don't know? Besides, they're good kids but not all that interesting to a stranger. Just starting their careers."

"Bet your daughter's really hot. Is she?"

I smack Diaz on the side of his head. "Come on, man, she's my daughter. Have a little respect."

"Where does she work?"

"Okay, I can tell you're not going to let this go until I tell you about her. Sara's my youngest. She's going for her PhD at Columbia University in molecular biology."

"What the fuck is 'stem cell'?"

"You know, the cells that grow the stems of flowers," I say, hoping his confusion would end the conversation.

"Must be smart. Does she look like you or your ol' lady?"

"I'd say a mixture, best of both. Don't get your hopes up. She has a boyfriend. She's an independent soul, loves to travel, and wise beyond her years. Good kid, talented artist, but never has enough time to paint or sculpt. I miss her a lot."

"Shit, look up at the windows of the Bus Stop," says Diaz. "You can see the fuckin' goon squad doing their thing. Hate those motherfuckers, especially Hatter. He lives to find contraband. saving America, one stolen apple, one cigarette, one gambling slip at a time. Heard he was a sniper in Iraq. Wonder how many women and kids' heads he blew off?"

It's now approaching midnight with no end in sight to the shakedown. Diaz wanders off for more stimulating conversation than I'm offering, but inevitably he makes his way back to my bench where I've just finished a letter to Lily. My energy level is at zero.

"Heard we'll be able to go back in soon," says Diaz.

"I'll believe it when I'm lying in my bed. Until then, it's you and me."

"Listen to this. I'm working in the library today and this dude is looking for a book to read. He pulls out this book called *Pearl Harbor*. It has planes, flames, and sinking ships on the cover. He says, 'Do you know what this book is about?' I say, 'Dude, you know, it's about Pearl Harbor.' I get a blank stare from the guy. Son of a bitch never heard of Pearl Harbor."

"Nothing surprises me around here."

"Hey, you never told me about little Jay? We got time. What's he into?"

"You mean my son Richard? Started learning jazz and riding the unicycle by sixth grade. He gave us a run for our money in high school when he used to brag how none of his friends were in the top eighty percent of his class. Richard was always a great athlete, but by high school he would rather get stoned with his posse than do anything else. Only sport he continued was skiing."

"Sounds like my type of guy, same crowd and all," replies Diaz, "except for the skiing. Never met a Puerto Rican that skied."

"When he was nine years old, he spent one winter in a ski racing program in New York State. The coaches said he needed to move to Colorado to train with the best. They all referred to him as a 'skiing savant.' But as much as he loved to ski, he hated the competition part. Guess he made the right choice since most top ski racers end up with horrible injuries."

"He as smart as you?"

"Smarter. He won't have to go through life wearing the scarlet letter of being a felon. Went to college in Michigan where he majored in philosophy and jazz, law school in New York, has a job, and is off our payroll. He taught me, and says to this day, 'There are only two types of days: good days and great days.' My time in here has challenged that saying."

"Two kids. Has to be easier than raising ten like I did."

"Diaz, who told you to have ten kids? To quote W.C. Fields, 'I love my cigars but I take them out of my mouth once in a while.'"

Our laughter floats in the air.

CHAPTER 29

Mengelized

It's an exquisite autumn morning as I sit outside in the courtyard with a few friends, sipping coffee, admiring the sky. Today I left the indoor rec area early in order to get dressed in time for my call-out at 8:30 a.m. with none other than Dr. Huff. I assume the visit is to go over the blood tests, EKG, and echocardiogram results, all of which were ordered over five months ago.

At the next move, I make my way up to the medical clinic. The waiting room is packed. I assume it's an overflow of patients from the morning sick-call, which runs from seven to eight in theory only. I sign in and take a seat far away from everyone. The clinic is no place for an inmate who doesn't have a functioning immune system. I learned early on that the wait can be painfully long, so I always bring reading or writing material.

I'm finally called into the treatment area at 11:30, three hours after my appointment time. Another hour passes before the infamous Dr. Huff graces me with his presence. He walks right past me, flaunting his girth and body odor, before sitting down at the computer. His back is to me just as in my first encounter. A good ten minutes pass while he's doing whatever on his computer.

"Okay, let's go over your test results," he finally says. "Hmm, echo good, EKG good—"

"Did they see the atrial aneurysm on echo?" I ask in a non-threatening way.

Without even rechecking the echocardiogram report, he tersely replies, "Echo is normal. Your labs are all good, you had your PPD test, chest X-ray is normal, flu shots are starting in two weeks. You're all set. See you in three months." Only then does he turn to face me, probably to watch me squirm.

"That's it?" I ask incredulously. "I have a few questions for you if that's okay."

"Make them quick." He gestures with his hand for me to move things along.

I start with the easy questions like what exactly were my lab results. As it turns out, they aren't normal, as my cholesterol and triglycerides have risen toward dangerous levels since I haven't been getting any meds for these conditions.

"I understand Lovaza and Crestor are off-formulary, but can't you make an appeal to the BOP?"

"I could. Next question."

I'm driving one hundred miles an hour down a dead-end street, but I can't help myself and proceed to ask more questions. No one else is going to be my advocate.

"What about a cholesterol-lowering med? I was on Crestor, five milligrams a day."

In a moment of sanity, he replies, "Yeah, I can put you on Lipitor. Not a problem."

"Actually, it *is* a problem. If you read my record you would have seen that I've had an adverse reaction to Lipitor. That's why I'm on Crestor."

He grits his teeth. "Where the fuck do you think you are? This is prison, dude, and you're getting Lipitor. Reading your medical records from your private docs ain't gonna change nothing I do in here. What's your last question?"

The anger is coursing through me. "I have a few more questions. They won't take too long. Can I have an air-conditioned room? The heat is killing me. Come on, you know heat is like kryptonite to MS patients."

Dr. Huff scoffs. "Get the fuck out of here, dude. Did you think they were sending you to a five-star hotel with room service? You get what everyone else gets. You should have thought of all of this *before* you went on your crime spree. If you didn't break the law, you wouldn't have all these problems."

I want to say, *thank you, Dr. Obvious*, but I realize the conversation is deteriorating and I have to change tactics. "Dr. Huff, can we review the actual lab numbers?"

"No."

"Okay then, last thing. Can we review what the immunologist at University Hospital said? I read her note when I got a copy of my medical records. According to her, I should be in a 'clean and germ-free environment.' This place is hardly clean or germ-free, and if you read what my immunologist in New York said, you would know that putting me in prison is a time bomb."

As much as I try remaining calm, I'm speaking faster and louder than I want to. Huff turns his back to me and types away on the computer.

"Listen, Dr. Huff. I don't have an immune system to fight things off. My biggest fear is getting PML, and you don't seem to give a shit about it. There are twelve letters in my file about PML, including the latest from your own consultant."

"Hold on there, Speed Racer, what the hell does PML stand for?"

"Oh, okay. First of all, it's an obscure disease. I never heard of it before I came down with MS," as I try to reassure his insecure fat ass that he isn't stupid and that we're talking about a rare disease. "It stands for progressive multifocal leukoencelalopathy, PML for short. It's caused by the John Cunningham virus, JC virus. The best analogy I can give you would be mad cow disease. I tested positive for the virus. There's a really high mortality if the virus reactivates."

"Fuck. You got some bad shit going on!"

"Thank you for reminding me."

I have to stop talking and start doing more slow breathing before I say something I know I'll regret. Here I am, filled with nothing but hatred for this man sitting a few feet away from me. I'm repulsed by his attitude, his looks, his contempt of me. I want to kill him, slowly and painfully.

"Listen, Dr. Huff, I need your help. I just don't get why you're not giving attention to my problem. Read the letters, it's all there. I don't get a second chance with PML. Who do you think is going to take the blame if something goes wrong with me?"

That gets his attention. He glares at me with arched eyebrows, then he reaches for the telephone while still forcefully gazing at me. In all my naivety, I actually think he's having a moment of clarity and recognizes I might have been right. I think he's going to call to have someone bring in the medical records for him to read.

"Hi, this is Dr. Huff up in medical. I need security up here right away. I've just been threatened by an angry inmate. Okay, thanks. Yeah, STAT."

I'm stunned and can't move.

"Get out of my office right now, sit in the waiting room, and wait for them to bring you to the SHU, asshole. Goddamn loser, no inmate threatens me. Out of here, now!"

I jolt back, unaware my body is getting up when my mind is still trying to process what just happened.

"What threat? What are you talking about, Dr. Huff? I just need some help. Is that asking too much?"

Dr. Huff gets up and takes a step toward me as I leave his office. He slams the door behind me. I can't believe how quickly things escalated. My lips are closed, but daggers are coming out of my eyes as I head into the waiting room. Before reaching the waiting room, I stop to ask the nurse for my Copaxone injection. She has no idea what had just transpired, so she reaches into the medication cart and hands me the injection plus an alcohol swab. I take the needle, lift my shirt, locate the correct injection site, and plunge the needle into my abdomen. I need about two minutes to correctly inject all the medicine. Dr. Huff's voice is booming as he comes barreling down the hall.

"What the hell is he doing? I told him to sit in the waiting room. Who the fuck does he think he is disobeying an order from an officer? Into the waiting room, Keller, now!"

With the needle still at a forty-five-degree angle into my stomach, I walk to the waiting room and find a seat. I still need another minute to finish the injection when two guards walk into the clinic. They go to the front desk and ask who they have to transport to the SHU. The nurses don't say anything because Dr. Huff immediately makes his presence known. Pointing to me, he says, "He's the one who threatened me. Get him the fuck out of here. I'll bring the paperwork down to your office in a few minutes." He then pokes his head into the waiting room and growls, "Have a good time in the SHU, *Mister* Keller."

"Come on, Keller, let's go," says one of the tattoo-covered officers.

I can't believe this sequence of events as I'm being escorted by two guards, each one holding an arm. We take the elevator to the first floor and into the lieutenant's office. The guards escort me into the lieutenant's inner office and place me in a chair. I sit where I'm told, left by myself for easily half an hour.

Finally, Lt. Tomlin enters the room and sits at his desk. "You know, I can bring you right down to the SHU," he says very matter of fact.

"But I didn't do anything! I was just telling Dr. Huff that—"

The lieutenant cuts me off. "Tell me your side of the story, calmly."

I take a deep breath. "We were sitting in his office reviewing my recent blood tests and some other tests," I say slowly, but I can't remain calm.

"I will say this for last time, Mr. Keller, stay calm and just tell me what happened."

I delve into details of my case. I tell him *exactly* what I said to Dr. Huff, trying to repeat things word for word.

"Lieutenant, there were no threats, physically or verbally, and that's the truth. When Dr. Huff wouldn't answer my questions, I finally had asked him, 'Who do you think is going to take the blame if something goes wrong with me?' Somehow, he considered that a threat of legal action against him. I just wanted him to address my medical issues. This is a medical center. That's why they sent me here. For that I have to go to the SHU? That's crazy."

Lt. Tomlin turns his attention from me to his computer. My guess is that he's looking into my profile. For the next few minutes, my mind wanders into what living in the SHU will be like. Will I get my meds? What's the food like? I heard it's always freezing. What are the guards like? My mind goes to the worst possible scenarios. Meanwhile he continues scrolling through the computer. Finally, he looks at me and says, "You used to be a doctor?"

"Yeah, used to be," I say humbly. "I used to be a lot of things. Now I'm just an ordinary inmate serving my time, trying to avoid trouble."

"Doctor inmates always seem to have problems with the BOP doctors. We see that a lot. Reality is, you can sue anyone. Me, a guard, a doctor, anyone you want. I could bring you to the SHU right now, but the final decision to put you in the SHU will be up to Lieutenant Ferrant. He'll be back in around an hour. Go back to your unit for now. We also need to read Dr. Huff's account of what happened. We'll call for you in a few hours."

I leave the office knowing I'll be heading to the SHU. When I get back to the courtyard of Antioch, I tell my friends what happened. Naturally the other inmates take your side, but my situation really resonates with them. Why? Because most of them have had a negative experience with Huff well beyond the normal level of harassment we receive daily. Even in prison, I think the expectation is that doctors care about the welfare of their patients. Not Huff.

Shortly after the four-p.m. count, the CO comes to my room telling me I have to report to the lieutenant's office right now. "Get your ID and meet me in my office."

Fearing the worst, I speak with my roommate Bruce. We arranged a system so our wives would call the other if Bruce or I went to the hospital or the SHU. It's worked in the past when Lily called Bruce's wife, Iris, when Bruce was in the hospital. Now Iris will contact Lily. Sometimes the stay in the SHU takes on a life of its own, so I make sure Bruce has my locker combination and access to all my possessions.

Bruce is visibly upset. "That fat fuck Huff, he's the one who should be in jail. You can do this, Jay, you're a strong guy." He places his hands on my shoulders and wipes away a tear that is slowly rolling down my cheek. "Want to hear a few of my new jokes before you leave?"

I smile. "Save the jokes so I have something to look forward to when I get out of the SHU." We both smile.

I make the slow trek down to the lieutenant's office. There's no such thing as a good day in prison. At best, the day is uneventful. However, there are bad days, and then there are really bad days.

I knock on the door, and an officer tells me to have a seat in the waiting area. A half hour later, Lt. Ferrant, a six-four rotund Black man with a voice like James Earl Jones, signals for me to come into his office. He takes one look at me and says, "Rough day today?"

175

I can't hide what I'm feeling or thinking. There's a slight tremor to my hands, so I clasp them behind my back.

"Do you want to hear my side of the story?" I ask innocently.

"No. Got all the details from my CO. I'm good."

I take a deep breath. *This is it;* I think.

"Okay, Keller, I read your statement. I read Dr. Huff's. I read your file. You know what this is all about, Keller?"

"No, sir, I don't." I barely have the strength to get the words out.

"You see, this all comes down to five letters. D-R-E-G-O. Just five letters."

"I'm sorry, sir, but I don't follow what you are saying."

"Dr. Ego. D-R-E-G-O. It's a classic case of doctors having their egos clash. You think you know best. Dr. Huff thinks he knows best. Doctors tend to have big egos and usually they clash. That's what this is all about. I read through your statements and what Dr. Huff wrote up. Hard to believe you both were part of the same conversation because the accounts are so different. But I've worked here for twenty-eight years, seen it all, heard it all. I think I have a solution for you if you're willing to work with me."

"I'm with you so far."

"Don't do anything. Go back to your unit, relax, call it a day. Today is Tuesday. Next Monday, you'll send an electronic cop-out to Dr. Huff. In that cop-out you'll apologize for the misunderstanding and assure him it won't happen again. If you can do that, this whole incident ends right here. No time in the SHU, no reports to fill out—get what I'm saying?"

"Yes, sir, I can do that." I bite my tongue. It's another example of pleading guilty and apologizing for something in exchange for a lesser sentence. In this case, it means I won't spend time in the SHU. I can live with that. "No problem, I'll wait until next week and contact him electronically. Can I go back to my unit now?"

"Good decision. Keller, forget about ego in here. It will only get you into trouble. If it was any other doctor, I would have been tougher on you. Like I said, I've worked here forever and know all the players. Have a good day and stay out of trouble," he says while escorting me to the door.

As I make the long, slow walk back to the unit, I feel nothing but relief.

Today, I escaped trouble. In prison, anything and everything can go so wrong, so quickly, so *never* let your guard down for a second. Always think two–three–four moves ahead as to what the consequences of your actions or words could bring. Forget about right or wrong. Just focus on consequences. Living in prison is like living in Tornado Alley where one minute all is calm and the sky is beautiful. A few minutes later, a tornado rips through your life leaving a wake of destruction. In prison, tornadoes aren't a seasonal threat; they're a daily threat.

CHAPTER 30
Three-Tiered Bunks

How do you recover from endless harrowing experiences? Routine. I'm in the stairwell of indoor rec, playing guitar when Brett, the inmate who runs the music room with an iron fist, tells me I have to return the guitar because there is a total prison recall and lockdown, meaning all inmates have to go back to their rooms. Another day, another recall.

I thank Brett profusely. There are no loudspeakers for announcements, so it's possible that I could have been playing music in a dead-end stairwell and have had no clue that the rest of the prison was on lockdown. That scenario would not have ended well.

I make my way back to Antioch walking with my head down. I always have to walk like this so I don't step in someone's spit. Everyone spits. It's just how it is. I once asked the warden why ubiquitous spitting is permitted in a federal medical center. He replied, "I've never seen anyone spitting in all my years here."

As I make my way back to Antioch, I try to get an explanation as to why we were having a recall. No one ever really knows, but most fabricate something. The guards, even if they know, will never tell us. The CO in Antioch did say there was going to be a count so we should stay in our rooms. So much for my morning. The other bad thing about lockdowns is getting my injection. The COs will typically say, "Well, that's your problem."

Diaz informs me what he thinks is going on. "Heard there was a power failure so they have to fix it before someone tries to escape. Ain't like they have electric fences anyway. Hell, we're lucky we have toilets that flush. Ya doin' okay, Doc?"

"Yeah, I'm fine," I say as I make my way up the stairs. "Stop by after count so I can give you a new book. I've had some good ones mailed in last week."

Back in my room, I sit on my bed listening to the radio when a guy from next door comes in to ask me a question. His name is Ed Rondell, a new arrival, a young man maybe thirty years old. I've spoken to him briefly a couple of weeks ago, but today he comes by with a specific medical question. He's at FMC Franklin because he has Factor V deficiency. This leaves him prone to forming blood clots in his legs, lungs, or anywhere else. To treat this, he's on a common blood thinner, warfarin. He asks me how often he should have a blood test in order to assess the efficacy of the medication. As always, I'm happy to be useful, so I tell him what I think and he appears pleased with my response. Before he's about to walk away, I ask him what he thinks of the medical clinic here.

"This place is worse than the prison I was in before, and that wasn't a federal medical center."

Everyone knows there is no real medical care that goes on here, but everyone is helpless to do anything about it. On paper, it's one of six federal medical centers in the US. In reality, they lost their accreditation as a medical center because of lack of air-conditioning, non-functioning elevators, staff-to-inmate ratio, too many bunk beds, among a bunch of other reasons.

"How long a sentence do you have, Ed?"

"Did one year, have about eight to go or so," he says very casually.

I don't know why, but no matter how long I'm in prison, I'm always amazed at the length of the sentences. Here's a young kid who will spend his thirties in prison.

"I know, it really sucks," he says as his demeanor changes. "They love nailing white-collar people to show the country that they aren't just putting people of color in prison. Tried fighting it, but in the end, ran out of money."

I know there's more to the story, but I figure he will tell me if wants to, or he'll abruptly end the conversation, which happens frequently.

"I just finished my second year of med school when I got busted," he offers up. He now has my attention.

I'm surprised by his answer, but since he's put that on the table, I can ask more questions. "What did they bust you for?"

"Came down to misuse of federal grant money. I was an MD–PhD candidate at Indiana University, did a lot of lab work, and next thing I knew I was in handcuffs. You can imagine how tough it was on my parents."

"Yeah, I have kids your age. Really sorry to hear it."

"Gotta make the best of it, what else can I do? Been working out a lot. Bruce invited me to your yoga class. I'll make it one of these days."

"Sure, whatever works. What prison were you in before here?"

With that comes an answer that tragically defines the whole system. "Meehan, up in Michigan. Was okay there but thought I would die in the transfer to here."

"Michigan to West Virginia? Long trip?"

"Yeah, Michigan to here via every possible torture chamber."

"Here I am, a twenty-eight-year-old lab geek living in Meehan Federal Correctional Institute for almost a year. You know, you learn how to get by. I thought when I first got to prison, I'd tutor some guys, so I went down to the education area, told him my educational background, did my undergrad work at Northwestern, blah, blah, blah. Meant nothing to him. Head of Education looks straight at me and says, 'Listen, the quicker you learn that prison is nothing but a place to warehouse people, the easier your time will be. Have a good day.'"

I offer Ed a plastic chair to sit in.

"Ten months into my sentence, I learned I was being transferred here because of my Factor V deficiency. I wasn't happy, but we have no say in anything. Parents were even more bummed because I'd be further away."

"How was the ride down here?"

"Listen to what they made me do. Don't forget, I'm a non-violent lab geek with no criminal record. Nothing. Anyway, US Marshals came for me, gave me a T-shirt and paper pants to change in to. Remember, this is February in Michigan. They loaded me onto a bus with guys who scared the hell out of me for an hour ride to the airport. They took us out of the bus to stand on the tarmac surrounded by four marshals pointing rifles at us. I stood on that tarmac, fully shackled in thirty-degree weather, for over two hours until I was put on Con-Air. There was barely any heat on the plane, everyone was yelling, I was freezing. It sucked. We flew to the Oklahoma City Transfer Center."

"Heard a lot of guys spent time there," I add uselessly.

"Well, I never spent time there because the prison was completely full. They took me and seven other guys in shackles and stuffed us back into a van—four on one side, four on the other. Felt like Kareem Abdul-Jabbar sitting in the middle seat of a fully packed economy-class airline seat. We drove another hour to get to some shitty county jail where I stayed for a full week, no meds I might add."

"What was that place like?" I'm mesmerized with each tidbit of information.

"It was like a concentration camp for the misfits of society. There were thirty beds total, ten three-tiered bunks."

He explains there were thirty-six inmates in one room. Six of them had to sleep on the linoleum floor that hadn't been cleaned since the Carter administration. Only a thin blanket served as a mattress, blanket, and pillow. If someone transferred out, then you moved to a bed. No one was given a pillow. If an older or disabled inmate couldn't make it up to the third tier, they slept on the floor.

"I had a third-tier bed, which is difficult when you're on blood thinners," Ed says. "The lights were on 24/7, the TV blasting 24/7, and we were in this room 24/7."

"Bathrooms, showers, mess hall, anything?" I ask.

"Nothing. There was one toilet in the middle of the room that we all had to use. They fed us through the food slots, and all we had the entire week were bologna sandwiches on white bread. Breakfast, lunch, and dinner."

My stomach turns at the thought. "Did they give you any meds?"

"No, that's the other thing. After five days I noticed my left calf was swelling and getting warm. It was a blood clot."

I'm appalled at the lack of care in the prison system, an absolute disgrace.

"I was scared shitless, but what could I do?" Ed continues. "The guards didn't give a shit. Thought I was gonna die right there in that run-down county jail. Leg improved on its own, but it scared the hell out of me. If that clot broke off, I was done. On the eighth day, they put me back on Con-Air and flew me to here, of course with three stops before they called my name to get off. Think it was my worst week of prison by far."

"Well, I'm glad you survived," I say, and I truly mean it. I hear these stories and it seems like a miracle anyone survives.

"And you? Hear you have a short sentence."

"Yeah, two-year sentence, but I'll spend only eighteen months here, two months home detention, I think. Rented space to a lab that did some bad things so the feds threw a net around everyone. The punishment of me and the other doctors was way too severe but you know our justice system. Hard not to be bitter."

"I'm exhausted from being bitter. Trying really hard to let go," says Ed.

I nod my head, but I'd be lying if I didn't admit the bitterness I still harbor. I tell Ed how I met a guy last week who's from Oklahoma and had friends who knew Timothy McVeigh, or so the story goes. According to this guy, McVeigh knew there were going to be kids in the building the morning he set off the bomb. That was one reason he picked that building. McVeigh knew the statistic that fifty percent of children of federal employees will become federal employees themselves. He wanted to kill the present *and* future generation of federal workers. While I don't agree with that sentiment, or terrorism of any kind, it just goes to show how much hatred people have for our government.

We bonded over the insanity of the criminal justice system in America. I, of course, have to editorialize on the prison-industrial complex, but despite the statistics I can now quote, it's all preaching to the choir. With Bruce's salesmanship, Ed soon became a yoga regular.

CHAPTER 31
Witness to Murder

It's a brutally hot day that would make anyone irritated. I feel increasingly hostile with every bead of sweat that slips down my back. Bruce and I are sitting in the stifling hot room with ten other inmates while we wait for Officer Michael Stallard to teach us about horticulture. Naively, I thought I would learn about horticulture.

The course is three hours a day, Monday through Friday, for ten weeks. One hundred and fifty hours of learning. I haven't learned a damn thing. Even though the class technically started two weeks ago, I invite Bruce to join the class with me to get hours of programming (education, in prison lingo) since the teacher has yet to show up and wouldn't know Bruce missed the first two weeks. The day Bruce joins, the tenor of the class changes from a boring classroom to a comedy club. Bruce and the inmate "instructor" swap endless jokes while everyone else either sleeps, reads, or wanders around the greenhouse area. Now about two months into the course, Officer Stallard has so far only appeared for a total of two hours, and there's only three weeks left. He's well paid to do nothing. Many inmates are in prison for fraud in some way, shape, or form, yet Officer Stallard is fraudulent in his teaching duties and stealing taxpayers' money year after year.

One day, to everyone's surprise, Officer Stallard moseys in with an iced coffee and a yellow notepad. It's so hot I just want to sleep. Dark circles are prominent on Bruce's tried-looking face.

"Let's just write in your notebooks today," Officer Stallard says, and the room erupts into groans. "Unless you want to be in the hot sun for three hours?" Another officer pops his head in the classroom so Officer Stallard excuses himself to join the other guard.

We shuffle in our seats, pages flipping, pens writing. I scribble and doodle, not planning to write anything for the allotted time while Bruce continues to flaunt his endless list of bad jokes.

After an hour, Officer Stallard returns and announces he will end class early because something urgent has come up. He says we'll have to make up the time next week, though we all know that's a lie. At the end of each class, we usually stop at the greenhouse, talk to some inmates, and wait to be released for the 3:30 recall prior to the 4:00 count. Bruce and I are hanging out by the greenhouse when we notice a stocky and very animated inmate swinging a broom at a row of beautiful potted canna lilies.

"What the hell are you doing?" I ask him. I've never seen him before.

"What am I doing? Look at the size of that motherfuckin' bee. Biggest motherfucker I ever seen. That damn bee has the largest motherfuckin' stinger coming out its motherfuckin' face. I gotta kill that motherfucker!"

He swings his broom, trying to kill the bee before it attacks him. He's relentless! There is a problem, however. It isn't a bee at all. It's a beautiful hummingbird trying to do what it is genetically engineered to do: pollinate canna lilies. Bruce and I burst into laughter.

After recall, we're back in the room. Bruce tells the story about the giant bee and everyone laughs. I'm lying on my bunk while he imitates the inmate swinging the broom. Maybe it's the lighting, but Bruce's temples appear to be indented. In medical vernacular, it's known as "temporal wasting," very common in cancer, AIDS, and anorexic patients. But Bruce doesn't have cancer or AIDS, and has the appetite of a horse.

That night, I'm having trouble sleeping. I can't shake the image of Bruce's worn-out face. Things suddenly start making a whole lot of sense, though I don't want it to be true. I think about the last few weeks. Bruce has lost weight. He isn't balding, but his hair has become noticeably thinner. *How am I just realizing this now?* Last week, it was difficult for Bruce to stand on one leg without falling over in yoga class. His stamina is non-existent and he no longer challenges himself in class. There are other signs such as the extended naps. Waking up, going to breakfast, and coming back for a two-hour nap is excessive by anyone's standards. Lately, he chooses to nap rather than go to yoga class. That's not Bruce. He loves the yoga class, or as some inmates refer to it, the *Bruce Hellman Show*.

The next morning, I decide to confront Bruce. After breakfast, we're milling about in the yard and I pull him aside. I place a hand on his shoulder and look him in the eye.

"We're good friends, right?" I say, and he nods. I want to approach this in a way that won't offend him, but I'm genuinely concerned about him. "I've noticed a change in you over the last few weeks. Are you feeling okay?"

Bruce sighs heavily. "I haven't been feeling well."

"Listen, and you don't have to agree, but every inmate has the right to request their medical records. Would you be willing to request your records so I can go over them with you?"

Bruce agrees, and I feel somewhat relieved. At least now I feel like I can help him in some way.

A few weeks later, Bruce hands me a manila folder with his medical records, and I pore over them with a fine-tooth comb. His weight loss of over thirty pounds is documented, which explains the temporal wasting, but what really stands out is his level of anemia. A healthy man normally has a hemoglobin of around fourteen. Bruce is at eight and had been for almost two years.

"What did medical say about your anemia?" I ask him bluntly. We've stayed behind in the room while everyone is out in the courtyard.

"Not much. I remember the doctor mentioning it once, but he said it was probably from my Crohn's disease."

I furrow my brow in confusion. "Your Crohn's hasn't been active since I've known you. When was the last time you had rectal bleeding?"

"Don't know, few years ago."

"You're in medical every three months. Did anyone say anything about your weight loss? You've lost thirty pounds in eighteen months, and I know you eat. You haven't missed a meal since I've met you."

Bruce shakes his head. "You know the doctors don't talk very much to us. No one seemed concerned."

"Well, I'm concerned, Bruce. We have to figure out why you're so anemic and why you're losing weight." What I don't tell him is that anemia and weight loss, combined with hair thinning and temporal wasting, is cancer until proven otherwise.

"I'm due for my three-month check any week now," Bruce adds.

"Good, write down what I'm going to tell you so you'll remember what needs to be asked when you go there."

I make Bruce write down five questions in order of importance and in his own handwriting. I have more questions, but I know there's no way the doctor is going to leisurely let an inmate get his money's worth out of an office visit.

Over the next few months, all the signs that I've noticed are even more exacerbated. He doesn't get any answers out of medical. His doctor is Dr. Huff, which makes things even harder.

One night, Bruce gets up to use the bathroom as he is inclined to do five times a night. Suddenly, we all wake up from a crashing sound in the bathroom. There's Bruce, lying in the shower, completely disoriented. It appears that he grabbed the shower curtain and pulled it down on top of him. The other roommates and I get him back to bed minutes before the five-a.m. count. Moments later, the lights go on and the guards start their count, but the confusion in the room makes their count more difficult. Once their count is correct, the guards leave, never once asking if the inmate we are hovering over is all right.

At 6:30, I take Bruce to sick call. His mental status is better—not perfect, but better. Jennifer, a friendly nurse, is on duty, and I breathe a sigh of relief. I know her fairly well from my visits. Her eyes widen at the sight of Bruce slumped over.

"What happened?" she asks.

"He hasn't been feeling well for months. He collapsed last night in the shower," I say. Then I explain his medical history and hope for the best. It's against prison rules to stay with another inmate once he's in medical, so I head back to do my morning routine.

Bruce spends the day in clinic. I don't see him until just before the four-p.m. count. I was hoping they would have transported him to University Hospital, but that was asking too much. They did bloodwork, an EKG, and a chest X-ray before sending him back to Antioch Unit.

The next night Bruce has a similar incident, and again a few days later. Bruce had a follow-up visit scheduled three days after I brought him to clinic that first morning. He went for his appointment only to find out Dr. Huff is on vacation and the covering doctor, Dr. Angela Morano, is fully booked. He's rescheduled in ten days. That visit never happens because I bring him back to sick call after his fourth fall at night. This time, not the doctor, but the nurse practitioner looks at his labs from last week, sees a hemoglobin of 7.1 and a precipitous decline in kidney function. He arranges for Bruce to be brought to University Hospital after the four-p.m. count. I promise Bruce I will have Lily contact his wife, Iris, and let her know what's going on. He's shipped to the hospital for a lengthy one-week stay.

I'm a bundle of nerves, feeling completely helpless. Bruce is my friend, my confidante, and to see him so sick and weak is distressing. What is happening to Bruce is my worst nightmare—being in this godforsaken place and no medical "professional" caring whether you live or die. I just hope for the best for Bruce, and I'm eager to see him.

A week later, everyone is thrilled to see Bruce back, except the poisonous German in the room. Bruce is a fervent Zionist Jew and Gunter is a Nazi sympathizer. Eight grown men in a small room is never easy.

He looks weaker, thinner, and the skin of his jowls is sagging. His arm is bruised from an IV. But at least he's smiling. I want to hear all the medical details, but Bruce only wants to tell everyone how well he ate at the hospital: filet mignon, lobster bisque, ice cream floats, prime ribs, and on and on. Everyone who's stops by to welcome him back gets the same earful about the culinary delights of the hospital.

Finally, we address his medical issues. "I had nine kidney stones in my left kidney," he says in a raspy voice. Bruce was being treated by the head of urology, Dr. Rudin, a man Bruce liked and trusted very much. "Dr. Rudin told me he removed six stones but was unable to remove three other larger stones. The doctor needed to order different equipment to extract the remaining stones."

I'm a bit more skeptical. I know that every surgeon orders a CT scan prior to surgery so they know exactly which instruments will be employed. My guess is that the doctor tried to get by with the parts he had, it didn't work, and so he sent Bruce back to FMC with stents (plastic tubing) leading from his kidney to the outside, covered with bandages, which must be changed twice daily in the medical clinic.

Bruce tells me that during the one-week hospitalization, he never got an answer about the anemia and weight loss. But they certainly fed him well. It was also discovered that Bruce had a fracture of L3, a lumbar vertebra that must have been broken on the first night he fell in the shower. The medical clinic at FMC Franklin never ordered an X-ray on the area where he had the biggest bruise. Then again, it's only a big bruise to someone who looks at that area, and no one had looked. Also, the urology department sent Bruce back with a prescription for three weeks of Percocet. Huff decided Bruce didn't need it when he could just as easily be treated with Advil from the commissary.

As Bruce waits for the return trip to the hospital, his clinical status quickly deteriorates. He develops fevers, most likely from the stents getting infected. He's supposed to have had them removed within two weeks, and it's almost eight weeks before Bruce returns to the hospital. All of the stones are finally removed, as well as the pus that had accumulated in the kidney area. In fact, Bruce had to have the entire kidney removed. Once again, Bruce ate well, told his bad jokes to new people who cared for him, but never got an explanation about his anemia and weight loss. Upon discharge, the urology resident told Bruce that when they examined the kidney under the microscope, there were some cancerous cells that would need to be followed up on with the oncology team.

I would lie awake at night, knowing that Bruce was sleeping just three feet away in his current state. It haunts me, this feeling that I should be helping, but I can't. Bruce continues to make light of a bad situation. He sleeps all the time, loses even more weight, has aged dramatically, and has shown nothing but a downward spiral. I've seen enough to know this won't end well, and it breaks my heart.

"How ya feeling today, buddy?" I ask him one morning. My new morning routine is getting him tea and sitting with him. I enjoy this time with him.

"You know, I don't feel too bad," he said, though I know he's lying. Pain is written all over his face. "Did I ever tell you about my father?" he asks.

I shake my head. Bruce and I talk about a lot of things, but his father isn't one of them. I noticed in conversation that he refers to him as "him," but I never wanted to push.

"Well, he was a bastard to my mother, a serial philanderer," Bruce says. His eyes get sad. "My mother kicked him out several times but he was always able to sweet-talk his way back. Guess that's where I got my salesmanship skills from. But I loved him. I mean, how could I not? He's my father, after all."

"Was your father as funny as you?"

"Much funnier. Did stand-up comedy in some of the Catskill hotels and local Philly clubs. Laughed my ass off when I was around him. He always practiced his new routines on me."

Lily has developed a relationship with Bruce's wife. Iris, who did thirty months herself in federal prison, knows all too well about the medical neglect of inmates. On my urging, Lily convinces Iris to visit Bruce, which of course has to be approved by the BOP. No inmate is supposed to have contact with anyone who has a criminal record. That's getting harder and harder to do these days in America. Luckily, they get approval, so Iris and Bruce share a two-day visit. Lily tells me later that Iris couldn't stop crying when she hugged Bruce, feeling nothing but the bones of a once strapping athletic man.

Bruce is so weak he can barely stand up without help. I'm scared for him. Everyone in the room can feel the tension and sadness in the air. Bruce keeps making statements about "having had a good life," or, "I had a great family." He falls two or three more times. Bruce can't walk more than twenty feet without being in pain or totally exhausted. Finally, an inmate in Antioch who knew Bruce peripherally stole a wheelchair from the prison wheelchair repair shop. Normally, the medical clinic must authorize an inmate to have a wheelchair, but since Bruce has had no follow-up visits with medical, Plan B was to steal a wheelchair for him. Within a few days, it's clear that Bruce isn't able to keep up with his activities of daily living. I do what I can—I gather people who know Bruce well and put together a schedule of inmates who can push him in his wheelchair to meals, pill line, or wherever he needs to go. Sadly, there's no intervention from the medical department.

About a week later, Bruce starts having hallucinations. At first, we all think Bruce is trying out some of his poorer jokes. Then he's having longer periods of stupor where he is no longer alert or oriented. He will lie or sit in his bed, and his body just twitches or he mumbles for long periods of the day. I'm not sure if he knows my name anymore.

"Bruce," I say as I hold up a glass of water to his mouth. "You need to drink."

There's a cloudiness in his eyes as he stares at me, but I'm convinced there's some recognition, because he listens and drinks the water. "Thanks, Jay," he says.

It's not long before he's not eating and he can't clean or take care of himself. However, there are other times when he puts together periods of lucidity. I'm conflicted about approaching a staff member. There is also the fact that Bruce, when lucid, always says he is fine and capable of caring for himself. Reality is that he has withered away to nothing but skin and bones. It's amazing to think back and imagine his days as a Penn State linebacker or even just a year earlier when he was doing headstands and handstands in yoga.

Finally, Bruce has progressed to a point where I can't stand by and watch anymore. I wake up one morning to Bruce moaning and thrashing in his bed, having hallucinations. I ask Ron, another yoga practitioner in Antioch, to take a look at Bruce. After confirming my observations, the two of us go to the Case Manager Nikki Williams. She feigns interest and even says she wants to talk with him but won't make the effort to go up to see him. Gritting my teeth, we race up to the room, place Bruce in a wheelchair, and wheel him to Ms. William's office. She takes one look at him and gasps. Horrified by Bruce's appearance, she calls up to the medical clinic.

Unfortunately, but predictably, medical doesn't do anything on an immediate basis. Then the unthinkable happens. It's the four-p.m. count, and Bruce has to stand up. Ms. Williams is one of two officers conducting the count when she witnesses Bruce collapsing to the floor. Nonchalantly, she calls medical on the radio, and finally, for the first time in over a month, the medical service comes to see Bruce. Once count clears, he is wheeled to the medical clinic.

I never saw Bruce again.

CHAPTER 32

Judged by Your Worst Deed

The days pass in a haze. I'm utterly destroyed by the loss of my friend. We were told four days later that Bruce had died on the Q4 unit. We only knew he had died when the guards came to his room—our room—to collect *all* of his personal belongings.

I'm grieving. Bruce comes to me in dreams. Or I hear his laugh and I'll turn around and he's not there. Even yoga has lost its magic without Bruce.

Dear Lil,

It's really been sad around here. Everyone saw Bruce deteriorate and die. It moved a lot of people because Bruce knew a lot of people, crossed social/racial lines, made everyone smile, and now he's dead. My friend was murdered, I know who did it, yet there is nothing I can do. It has happened so many times since I've been here, and I fear it will continue to happen. I've never felt so helpless.

Watching Bruce deteriorate as he did without the medical service knowing or caring was hard for us to digest. His last weeks would have been much worse if it wasn't for Bruce's friends in Antioch Unit. We tried to do what we thought was right: we wrote letters to the Joint Commission, tried contacting an attorney at the Aleph Group, which helped incarcerated Jewish inmates, but it was very limited what we were able to do from prison. Lack of information and the culture of prison retribution by the staff put an end to our efforts.

I am sad, angry, and yet I'm relieved. He suffered greatly toward the end. In that respect, his death is a relief. It just felt so wrong, all those months, even years, when they should have known there was a serious medical problem and everyone in medical turned a blind eye to him. No one saw him as a man, a father, a husband, a friend. Bruce was marked by a scarlet letter, *F* for felon, as a criminal, judged not by his life accomplishments, but only by his worst deed, a deed defined by the Department of Justice. It's taking me, and everyone, a long time to get over Bruce's decline.

I know you have spoken to Iris many times. Please reach out and let her know that Bruce was crazy about her. From the first day I met him, he spoke so fondly of her. It hurt him so much how she suffered and probably will for the rest of her life.

He had a son and a daughter. He coached Carol's softball teams for years. She got her nursing degree and has launched her career. It would be great if you could get the phone number of his son, Don, and call him. Bruce was so proud of the gym he opened. Bruce said the gym was running successfully, making money, and Don was doing charity work. I got the feeling that his success was not as predictable as Carol's. Let them know how proud Bruce was of all they have done. He loved his family deeply and they must all know that.

It makes me contemplate my life. Prior to this fiasco, I had done some great things in my life, none better than having you for my spouse. If this could happen to Bruce, it could happen to anyone.

All my love, forever . . .

Jay

CHAPTER 33
Another Attack

The first of every month is always a mini-celebration. It means another month has been completed. All sentences are expressed in months—twenty-four months, one hundred months, three hundred and sixty months—so everyone now has one month less to go, myself included. Since I started off as a "short timer" by federal prison standards, I'm in the home stretch. I have just over a hundred days to go.

I awake at 4:50 a.m., which means I hear the last ten minutes of the BBC *Newshour*. Listening to the BBC is enjoyable and gives a different, less American–centric viewpoint to world events. I make my coffee and I'm back in bed by five when NPR starts their broadcast. Something doesn't feel right with my left arm, but I can't quite define it. I'm more concerned with my cup of black coffee, the morning news, and sitting in a half-lotus position as part of opening up my hips prior to the 8:30 yoga class which I'll be leading. As the NPR show progresses, so does my awareness of the numbness in my left arm. Many times, I wake up with numbness in an arm due to positional compression, but it always resolves within a matter of seconds. My bed can never be confused with a real mattress.

This morning the numbness persists after I am up for over an hour, even after I rotate and shake the arm and stretch the fingers. I justify it by thinking I must have slept on the arm in an odd way. By the time I go downstairs to wait for the guard to release us out for the six-a.m. move, nothing has changed. The arm and fingers are still numb. The computers are down for maintenance, so I never get to check my emails. If I did any typing, I would have known something was amiss. The guard releases us and I head to the music room, knowing Brett is being released in two days.

"Good morning, Jay, what are you working on this morning?" Brett asks as he organizes the music closet.

"Still trying to memorize Bach's "Jesu, Joy of Man's Desiring," but my brain is for shit these days. What are you gonna write about this morning?"

"I spoke to my girls last night. One of them is having boyfriend issues, which gave me a few ideas. Wanna work more on that Joe Pass number this afternoon before I go to the half-way house."

"I'm happy for you. See you later." I take my guitar and head up to the filthy but acoustically balanced stairwell.

I usually start every morning doing scale exercises, but this morning it's obvious I have *no* coordination, no control over the fingers of my left hand, and very little sensation. No matter how I try to move them, it's as if they have an independent brain controlling them. Only five minutes pass before I put up the white flag. My left arm is numb from the elbow down and my hand is completely uncoordinated. That's when it dawns on me something is seriously askew. Everything sort of hits me all at once. I realize the extreme fatigue of the last few days is related to this morning's events. I'm having another MS attack. *Shit!*

With my music book in one hand and the guitar in the other, I race to the music room to return the guitar. A surprised Brett asks, "No practicing this morning?"

"Brett, I think I'm having an MS attack. My hand is completely numb and I can't control my fingers."

He turns a bit pale. "So what do you do now?"

"To start, I'm not going to waste my time practicing this morning. I'll set up for the yoga class, but someone else will have to lead it. Guess I'll go up to medical clinic, which I have to do anyway to get my shot and see if they'll give me steroids. This really sucks. I actually thought I was going to make it through my sentence without an attack." I show Brett how difficult it is for me to touch my thumb to each of my other fingertips.

"Wow, that's pretty fucked up. Good luck up in medical. Let me know what happens," he says with sincerity and concern.

It's early enough in the morning that I still have time to make it to sick call, which runs on a normal day from 6:30 to 7:30. Sick call is always a shit-show where the wretched of the earth show up with their acute medical problems and the staff does their best to deflect, rather than fix, their problems. On a typical sick call, they see about thirty-five inmates in a seventy-five-minute period. That's about two minutes per inmate, two minutes of nurse time to be specific. Although there is a doctor in the clinic for sick call, the reality is no one ever sees the doctor. The nurse decides who gets treated and who gets "referred elsewhere." If the nurse can treat it, she does. If she can set them up for a future appointment, she does that. And if by chance it requires a doctor, maybe she lets the inmate see a doctor. I'm around the medical clinic enough to know the doctor is rarely there for sick call. If Dr. Huff is the doctor that day, you can be sure he's downstairs stuffing his face in the officers' mess hall.

When I get to the clinic, I'm feeling a bit weak and trying to remain calm. I sign in and wait. Finally, the nurse calls me. I go up to the triage area where she takes my vital signs, blood pressure, temperature, pulse, and oxygen saturation.

"What's your problem, Mr. Keller?" she asks with as much interest as a TSA officer.

"I lost feeling and coordination of my left hand."

"That's it? Doesn't look like you're having a stroke. You look fine to me. I can make an appointment for you with your regular doctor if you like."

I have never seen this nurse before. Some of the other nurses know me and know I have MS. No such luck this morning.

"I have MS and think this could be the beginning of a new attack. I really need to see a doctor and get some steroids in me as quickly as possible."

"I'll tell you what, I'll send an email to the nurse practitioner on-call telling them your situation."

"That's it? You'll send an email to a random nurse practitioner who doesn't know me and maybe I'll get a response next month? I need to treat this ASAP. I don't think you appreciate what's going on here."

She scrunches her face up. "Listen, the NP usually gets back to us the same day so just sit tight and I'm sure you'll be fine."

"That's not good enough—Ms. Brandon," reading her nametag. "I need treatment now."

"Listen, you're in prison and I have about ten more patients to go. Either you take a seat back in the waiting area or I call security. Your choice."

I'm fuming and can't hold my tongue. "This is bullshit! You get paid to take care of our medical problems. It's wrong!"

I storm out of the triage area and wait to leave medical clinic at the next move. All I can do is scheme how I can get the needed medical attention. I know I'll be coming back to the medical clinic at 10:30 for my injection.

Back at the room, I shower before searching through my locker, which contains eleven letters from my doctors in New York. A few of them state exactly what is needed in case of an MS attack. I find those specific letters from my two neurologists and will take them to medical clinic. It all depends on who is going to be working later.

Clean and fresh from my shower, letters in hand, I go back to medical clinic at the 10:30 move, my normal time slot for showing up at the clinic. I sign in as usual and take a seat where I can see into the treatment area to view who's working this morning. I cringe when I see Huff, pacing back and forth, tossing a rubber ball against the wall as he saunters about. I also see Mr. Morton, a sympathetic NP, and Ms. Hurst, an RN who at least knows me. Okay, things are looking a little better.

When my name is called, I go up to Ms. Hurst who hands me my Copaxone injection and asks me if I need help giving it. We move to the treatment area and I inject myself in my arm with her assistance retracting the skin for me.

"Ms. Hurst, I was up here earlier during sick call. I think I'm having an MS attack. Ms. Brandon said she was going to send an email to the NP, but I can't wait. I need to start steroids right away. I have letters in my pocket from my doctors stating what needs to be done."

"I'd like to help you, Mr. Keller, but what can I do? You just have to be patient."

"Can I at least show you the letters?"

She looks around nervously. "Listen, Mr. Keller, I can't break protocol. Protocol is sick call, which you did. Now you're waiting for a response. I have to get back to my desk. I'm sorry, but good luck."

Just then, Mr. Charles Morton walks into the treatment area searching for supplies. Mr. Morton is a tall, slim Black man, an NP who's finishing up his PhD at West Virginia University. We know each other because a few months back, I helped him on his research project about prostate cancer. I also know he's going to leave the BOP as soon as he has his nursing doctorate. He already has a job lined up.

"Mr. Morton, can I have a minute of your time?" I ask, trying not to sound too frantic.

"Good morning, Mr. Keller, what's up?" He has his back to me as he searches the drawers while I explain my predicament to him.

He quickly turns to me with sympathetic eyes. Unlike most who work the medical clinic, he appreciates my dilemma. "Who's your doctor?" he says seriously.

"Huff," I reply.

"Shit, too bad. I don't have to tell you that's a problem." He ponders for a few seconds while I pull out my letters. He takes the time to read where it states the need for IV steroids. He looks me in the eye; I see compassion there. "Tell you what, Dr. Huff is here—somewhere. Let *me* talk to him. I have a better chance of getting something out of him than any inmate does. Meet me back here at the 12:30 move. I'll see what I can do."

It's a ray of hope. Mr. Morton, who has one foot out the door of the BOP, knows what a horror show Huff is. Everyone knows, but no one does anything about his juvenile behavior and disdain for inmates. I leave the clinic to go to lunch feeling a bit more optimistic, but I've been in this place long enough to know no one gives a damn about the health of inmates. I keep trying to get my fingers to touch my thumb. Thumb to pointer finger. Thumb to middle finger. Thumb to ring finger. Thumb to pinky—that's the worst.

With my food tray in hand, I walk to the dining room as I scope out the staff who are working the Mainline. At lunchtime, administrators rotate standing in the main hallway to handle any problems inmates may have. That's only in theory. In practice, the administrators—and there's no shortage of administrators on payroll—stand around talking to each other and do everything possible to avoid interacting with inmates, let alone address or fix their concerns. I spot Mr. McVeigh, an RN who is an assistant warden in charge of the medical service. I put my tray down at a table and approach him. I know who he is but never have had any interaction with him.

"Good morning, my name is Jay Keller. I'm in Franklin because I have multiple sclerosis. This morning I realized I'm in the midst of a new MS attack and I can't get anyone up in medical to treat it. I've been up there twice already this morning."

McVeigh takes a step back. "Whoa, whoa, whoa—back up. You're standing too close to me, and get your hand out of your pocket when you speak to me."

I back up two feet. "I'm just reaching for some letters from my doctors stating what to do in case of an MS attack while I'm in here."

"We don't go by outside letters. We have a good medical staff here, very capable of treating your needs."

My heart is racing, my cheeks are warm. *Remain calm,* I think, but it's becoming difficult.

"With all due respect, sir, I was a doctor on the outside. I know what needs to be done. I'm just trying to get some steroids in me as soon as possible, just like it says in these letters, so I can minimize the damage to my nervous system. I'm hoping you might be able to help."

"You just told me you've been to medical twice today. What did they say?"

"An email would be sent to an NP stating my problem and the NP *usually* gets back to them the same day. *Usually* won't help me. I need to get steroids into me as soon as possible."

It's obvious by the partial sneer on his face that he wants no part of this conversation. "You're still too close. Back up. That's better. You've been to medical, and it sounds as if they are working on it, and I'm sure they will come up with a solution. There's nothing else I can do for you. Mr. Keller, don't forget, you're in prison."

With those words, he walks away, leaving the cafeteria area entirely just in case I might have pursued him further. I love being reminded that I'm in prison, as if it's the kind of thing one forgets about.

After the 12:30 move I'm back at the medical clinic for the third time. I take a seat in the waiting area after telling the nurse I'm here to meet Mr. Morton at his request. Within a minute, Mr. Morton appears and ushers me away from the other inmates.

"Listen, I spoke to Dr. Huff. Here's what he said. Number one, he told me you're a piece of shit. Secondly, he's not comfortable giving IV steroids. I told him I read the letters outlining the dosing directions, but he didn't care. I did get him to prescribe oral prednisone for you, which should be at the medicine window before dinner. That's the best I could do. I don't know if the med window will give you the whole bottle or not. It's not a controlled substance, but who knows what they do. It's better than nothing."

Only a slight wave of relief washes over me, but I'm grateful to Mr. Morton. I thank him for his help, knowing that to a starving man, half a loaf of bread is better than no bread. Oral steroids are better than nothing, so now I wait until dinner when the med window opens to get my steroids.

Mr. Morton is a man who chose to help me rather than be an obsequious henchman. He listened and went to battle for me against Huff. He is experienced enough to know if I was the one interacting with Huff, I never would have gotten anything other than an appointment with a neurologist in a few months. My problem is not unique. There are many men with very serious medical problems who get ignored when they need help. I needn't look any further than Bruce. I can curse and fault the BOP all I want, but in the end, it isn't the BOP. It's human cruelty, fellow humans unwilling to help fellow humans.

At five o'clock, after a ten-minute wait at the med window or "pill line" as it's called, I'm handed sixty milligrams of prednisone. The pharmacist isn't willing to give me the entire bottle. Again, I have to be content with what I have, and sixty milligrams is better than nothing if I hope to minimize the damage of a new attack. After dinner, I go down to the music room to talk to Brett and update him on my daylong battle. Inmates are never surprised by the gratuitous cruelty of the BOP. Just business as usual.

"When do think you can play again?" Brett asks very innocently.

"Good question. I'll have to get back to you on that." Brett actually put his guitar down so we could talk. Yes, Brett paused during practice time, to be human. That is when I discover his girlfriend on the outside has MS. That's why he was always curious about the disease.

That night I take an allergy pill I have in my locker. I keep it in reserve because it helps me sleep. Every once in a while, usually after a very upsetting day—and there are many—I will take an allergy pill and sleep through the night. Tonight, with sixty milligrams of prednisone (cortisone) newly arrived in my bloodstream, a little sleep aid is in order. It works.

The next morning, I go to the pill line, stand there with all the psychotics who need their psych meds, and approach the window when it's my turn. I show the pharmacy tech my ID and she returns, only this time she hands me the whole bottle of prednisone. I'm now free to titrate the dosing to my needs, and I don't have to stand in pill the line every day.

As I sit in the cafeteria, I look at the instructions on the bottle. "Sixty milligrams a day for one week, fifty milligrams a day the second week, forty milligrams a day the third week, and thirty milligrams a day the fourth week." What a bizarre way to prescribe prednisone. What a fucking idiot Huff is, but for once, his ignorance and incompetence work in my favor. I have plenty of prednisone to take over a seven- to ten-day period, as I choose to dose it.

Thankfully, the attack never progresses beyond the symptoms of my left hand. Within twenty-four hours of noticing my symptoms, I have one hundred and twenty milligrams of prednisone in me. I conscientiously wean myself off the prednisone over a week's time, and then start my own physical therapy for the attack—playing the guitar. The coordination and numbness of my left hand persists, but I know from previous attacks that aggressive physical therapy does lead to recovery. To me, that means scales, lots of them, every scale I ever learned, two to four hours a day. I play endless monotonous scales, all in an effort to get my left-hand working. I have a fantasy that the BOP will arrange for me to see a neurologist, but like most fantasies, it never materializes.

Every Monday, Wednesday, and Friday I still go to the medical clinic for my injection and see Dr. Huff in the clinic. We exchange glances, but nothing more. Not once does he ever ask how I'm doing. No surprise there; he doesn't care and certainly isn't going to feign caring. His disdain of me is evident in every glance.

With numbness and discoordination, I continue to play the guitar for hours a day. Within a month, I'm back to playing actual songs, albeit with a change in fingering on some songs. My left pinky seems to have a mind of its own and has to be compensated for. I learn to adapt just as I learn to adapt to being in prison. As my playing progresses—because that's what four hours of practice a day will do—I'm aware of a new norm. Since my first MS attack, my right hand was always a tad slower than my left. After this most recent attack, the speed and dexterity seem to have equalized, a balance I begin to enjoy.

CHAPTER 34

In the Flow

Dear Lil,

I'm in the home stretch—only three months of this hell and I'll be leaving FMC Franklin once and for all. The symptoms of my most recent MS attack are waning as I fervently and obsessively practice the guitar, not just in the mornings but later in the day as well, four or five hours a day. Perhaps I am finally in the flow, but it's almost over. I hate being here, but the closer I get to the finish line, it gets a little easier to put up with the daily lunacy of the staff, inmates glued to the TV watching *Jerry Springer*, and fat, shirtless hillbillies playing horseshoes. With a small but good circle of friends, I have found a rhythm, a flow that will take me all the way home until I'm lying in bed with you.

I have to admit, I enjoy what I do on a daily basis. I play music, practice yoga, go to meditation classes, read, write, study. It isn't what I do; it's where I am doing it. As time goes on, however, I begin to understand why things are the way they are. I don't agree or believe things have to be like this, I simply understand the "why." For example, what did I ever know about "mandatory minimums?"

Two days ago, while standing in the lunch line, I was listening to soon-to-be-released inmates. Next week they will be returning to society. Later that afternoon, I wrote seven paragraphs in an op-ed format about mandatory minimums, because for the first time since I've been here, it all makes sense to me. Promise me you will do all you can to publish it, because America needs to know how much injustice there is under the criminal justice umbrella.

I never knew what a mandatory minimum was until I entered this strange, new world. On my side of the fence, everyone knows about mandatory minimums because that's what placed us here. But to someone on the other side of the fence, the term is nothing but a funny combination of an adjective and a noun.

Having built all those prisons (a new prison opened every ten days for fifteen straight years), legislators had to ensure the success of the prison-industrial complex. Every federal crime carries with it a mandatory minimum sentence—the minimum sentence a judge *must* prescribe. Who decides what is the mandatory minimum for a crime? Does anyone vote on it? The same legislators who appropriate money to build the prisons decide on the sentences with input from prosecutors as to what they need the mandatory minimums to be. The problem is the sentences are Draconian. On average, sentences in the US are four times longer than those in the rest of the developed world for similar crimes. Because we are a provincial country, no one knows what goes on in other countries.

Before Ronald Reagan's administration, inmates only had to serve fifty-five percent of their sentences. Reagan upped it to eighty-five percent. Thirty years later, no one has stepped forward to fix it, or admit to its unnecessary, so inmates spend longer times incarcerated than needed.

After over a year here, I understand the purpose of mandatory minimums. They yield power over to federal prosecutors who become the de facto judge, jury, and executioner. US Attorneys make every defendant face unthinkable, unimaginable jail time. Or, you accept a plea deal and receive much less jail time, but you're going to jail. Most indictments—most cases to the tune of over ninety-seven percent—end with a plea deal. Why? Because eventually defendants realize it is their best–worst choice and they take the plea, especially if you lack the resources to mount a legitimate fight. US Attorneys would argue that if they didn't have plea deals, the courts would be backed up. They need the Draconian sentences to force people into plea deals. That may be true. It forces people into plea deals, but has justice been served? I would argue our laws over-criminalize American citizens, and that's what backs up the courts.

More importantly, what has this over-criminalization of America accomplished? We need a criminal justice system because many people do horrible things to other people. I get that, I live with them. I meet people every day who have no business being part of a free society. But the purpose of punishment should always be guided by what is in the best interest of society, not what's in the best interest of the prosecutor or prison-industrial complex.

I come from a scientific background, medicine to be specific. We are always guided by outcomes. What does the data prove? Does Drug A yield a better outcome than Drug B in the treatment of type II diabetes? We do scientific experiments, and if B is a better drug than A, we use Drug B to treat the problem. It yields better outcomes. If Drugs A, B, C, and D yield better outcomes against non-Hodgkin's lymphoma than Drugs E, F, G, and H, we use A, B, C, or D. It's not complicated.

Here's where I get confused. Where is the data when it comes to criminal justice? We've been fighting a war on drugs for over fifty years and what to we have to show for it? Data. Outcomes. Where's the data that shows locking up a twenty-year-old for twenty-five years for dealing crack yields a better outcome to society than locking him up for two years and giving mandatory job training over the next three years? Invest in setting people up for success, not guaranteeing failure! So many people I meet in prison have no chance of success when they get out. They have no marketable skills, no education, barely basic math and English proficiency, no one to help them upon their exit, and unfathomable obstacles because they have a conviction that will follow them forever. That twenty-year-old crack dealer has been locked up for his twenties, thirties, and forties. Prime years. You might as well have sentenced that twenty-year-old to life in prison, because that's where he will be spending his life other than a few brief stints of freedom.

Where's the data to show that putting a first-time non-violent offender in prison for three years gives society a better outcome than one year of home confinement, especially in this era of electronic surveillance? Only with data outcomes will we ever be able to know what's the best punishment of a particular defendant who committed a particular crime. The status quo, based on what "seems right" for a particular crime, isn't working. Further, it seems as if the rest of the developed world has found different criminal justice solutions, often with wonderful success. Our present system works for the prosecutors who can boast of their conviction rate, the number of people they put behind bars, and for how long. It works for the legislators of both political parties who want to appear tough on crime. But it doesn't work for society. It's hurting society far more than it's helping. Most people in prison don't need more time in prison. They need mental healthcare, job skills, education, life-skill training, and preparation for their return to society. Ninety-eight percent of people who enter prison will return to society at some time. America has been tough on crime, but to date I would argue we've been dumb on crime. We can do better.

Lily, it really is the home stretch with only sixty-three days to go. Soon it will be Spanish Heritage month again, which for me, marked a turning point. It was the Hispanic inmate who heard me playing classical Spanish pieces in the hallway and asked if I could perform at both their opening and closing ceremonies. Why was it a turning point? Because many of the Hispanic men whom I truly feared suddenly respected me, would say hello in the hallway, and never bothered me after that first performance. I have a few new pieces for this year.

Diaz, the man who threw me a life preserver when I was drowning, finally came clean with me. I have known him for over a year, but he never spoke about his crime and I never gave it any thought. If someone doesn't want to talk, so be it. One day, Diaz did want to talk. I think it's because he knows I'm leaving soon, so he unloaded on me while we were in the courtyard one evening.

He's serving an eight-year sentence for possession of child pornography. It was his honesty that blew me away. When his mother could no longer care for him, he was placed in an orphanage, Mount St. Mathews in Staten Island, New York. From the ages of four to fourteen, he was mentally, physically, and sexually abused by the staff on a regular basis. Finally, he was transferred to the Jewish Home for the Homeless where he lived in peace other than the scars and trauma that he has carried for a lifetime. He told me, with tears in his eyes, he was fascinated with CP despite all he had been through, analogous to the Vietnam veteran who has to go back to the jungles of Vietnam where all of their trauma occurred. Diaz's story was similar to every other man in FMC Franklin who told me about their CP charges. They *all* were abused as children. It's all making sense. It's all flowing.

When I first arrived in prison, people warned me to behave or I would end up in the SHU. I did behave because that's my nature my entire life. But twice I almost went to the SHU. This is a tough one to comprehend. America is part of an international treaty conceding that solitary confinement is inhumane torture and should only be used for violent criminals, not for random matters of various natures. FMC Franklin uses the SHU for everything. Fever, go to the SHU. Colonoscopy prep, go to the SHU. Cataract surgery the next day, go to the SHU. Arguing with a staff member, go to the SHU. You reported a sexual assault, go to the SHU. The list is endless. I get it. It's wrong, but it's easy. Separate any problem and deal with it at your leisure. Keep peace in prison above all else. Here's the thing: inmates are raped, stabbed, starved, or thrown in the SHU, all within the confines of a prison-industrial complex that's broken, a stain on the American consciousness not seen since slavery. It's wrong, it's illegal, it's unfair. But for the people running the place, it's easy. I vehemently disagree with the overuse of the SHU, but I finally understand why it's so popular with the powers that be.

Reputation and respect are a big deal in prison. I earned the reputation of being a doctor, a musician, a yoga practitioner, and a writer. I always have a pen, and people always want to share their story. I was introduced to Chris Walton, a young man in his twenties. His uncle lives in the Antioch Unit who told me to bring my pen and paper to hear his nephew's plight.

On a beautiful summer afternoon, we all met at a picnic table in the shade where we stayed for three hours, a long time to hear an inmate's story. Then again, I never met anyone serving two life sentences, all because he refused the prosecutor's plea deal of a fourteen-year sentence. A few hours ago, he was a total stranger. Now, because I was perceived by many as an educated writer who might spread the word about criminal injustice, he spilled his guts to me in an unfettered, sincere, and joyful manner. I felt horribly for him but was grateful he shared his story with me.

I never deserved to be in prison, but here I am. Yes, I'm living in a crowded and contaminated fishbowl. It's a horrific experience, the worst of my life, bar none. Yet somehow, today, it dawned on me that I have made sense of it, that I have figured things out, that I'm okay. As I learned from one of the first books I had read while in prison, "Enjoy what is, not what should have been." I'm in the flow, and more importantly, I'm in the homestretch.

With all my love, with a big thanks for all you do, I love you forever.

Jay

CHAPTER 35

Roadkill

They say physicians make for terrible patients. I agree. I've had a low-grade fever for over a week and have been hoping it will go away. I lack the strength to do my daily yoga, and barely have the strength and concentration to play the guitar. My dilemma is this: If I go to the medical clinic with a fever, they will assume I have the flu and put me in the SHU so as not to spread influenza. That would be the worst place for me. Aside from the stress that goes with being in solitary, I hear horror stories from other inmates who have experienced the cruelty and inhumanity of solitary.

When you go to the SHU, you are fully stripped and searched before being given a bright red jumpsuit to replace your regular clothes. You are then placed in a six-by-ten concrete cell, which has a steel toilet attached to a steel sink as well as a tiny shower off in one corner. The bed, attached to the cinderblock wall, is also made of steel with a slightly raised bulge at one end that serves as a pillow. Usually, but not always, they provide you with a sheet, sometimes even two sheets. Considering the average temperature is kept at fifty-five degrees throughout the year, the sheets are entirely inadequate to provide much-needed warmth. The fluorescent lights are left on twenty-four hours a day. Meals are brought to you by the guards who slide the tray through a tiny opening in the door. You are all alone.

Going to the SHU is not an option. I was designated to FMC Franklin to be housed in a medical center, yet they have no facility for isolating potentially infectious inmates other than placing them in solitary. My roommates and other friends have been asking me the last few days why I look so poorly: "Are you sick?"; "Do I want to be checked at medical?"; "Is there anything we can do?"; "Will you be all right?" It's interesting how in the end, you fear being in prison because of your interaction with other inmates, yet they are the only ones who care about your wellbeing.

Nonetheless, I continue to refuse all forms of help because I am, by nature, an optimist. Somehow, I just know the fever will break and I'll be okay. But my roommates, the ones who see me every day, tell me sometimes I talk about things that just don't make any sense. Naturally I shrug it off. My bunkie Jamie, who is now the closest with me since Bruce died, has said I've scared him the last few nights because of what he describes as hallucinations. I'm not stupid. I know something isn't right, but admitting it to myself is entirely different. Am I more fearful of having something really wrong with me or going to the SHU? All the ghastly SHU stories are winning out. I might have something serious, but I'm not going to the SHU, voluntarily.

It's Friday afternoon and time for the four-p.m. count. Normally I would have spent the afternoon in the education area, but instead I just slept. John Tackone, one of the few guards who could be described as fair and well intentioned, is the first guard to count our room.

"Whoa, you all right, Keller?" he asks. "You look like shit. You should get yourself to sick call in the morning."

"I'll be right up. Just gotta finish this equation. Almost done," I say with an inappropriate response that is aimed into space, not back at Tackone.

"What the fuck is he talking about?" asks Tackone as he looks to the other roommates for an explanation.

Jamie can't hold back his concern and says, "Been worried about him for a few days now. He's really been out of it. And you know Jay, Mr. Tackone, no drugs or alcohol are involved. Wish that's what it was. We asked him about going to medical clinic, but he keeps saying he'll be all right."

"He's not all right," says a concerned Tackone. "Look how he's sweating. Does he even know where he is? I'm coming back after count clears and getting him to medical. Keep an eye on him, goddamn it."

I'm lying in bed, drenched in sweat, and hear their conversation but I can't formulate words. All the roommates just look at each other until the second guard finishes his count. All concerned, they proceed to ask me the simplest of questions until they're convinced I don't know where I am or even who I am. Sweat is pouring down my forehead and neck. The more profusely I sweat, the more worried everyone becomes. They all circle around my bed until Tackone comes back to the room with a nurse from medical clinic.

"Oh, now I know who this is," says Ms. Hurst. "I see Keller in medical clinic all the time. Wow, he doesn't look good at all. He's normally a pretty healthy-looking guy, especially for someone with MS. Something's going on, and it's not good. I'll call Dr. Huff once we get him to the clinic."

At the mention of Huff's name, I want to jump up and scream, but I can't.

The nurse keeps staring at me in bewilderment as she and Tackone place me in a wheelchair for the short trip over to the medical clinic. I don't entirely know what is happening, just that I feel so out of control.

"Carry on, guys," says Tackone as he pushes me past them in haste. Once in the clinic, Tackone turns to me. "Hang in there, Keller, gotta leave you to medical now." With that, he walks to the clinic entrance, turns to me for a few seconds before finally exiting the clinic. His concern is genuine, knowing how much medical care gets neglected here every day.

From far away, I hear voices speaking on the telephone.

"Hi, Dr. Huff, it's Beth Hurst from clinic. Listen, I have one of your patients here, a Jay Keller. Do you know who he is?"

"Unfortunately."

"Anyway, John Tackone called me to Keller's unit because Keller was out of it when he went to do count. Also sweating up a storm like a pig in heat. I mean he's hallucinating and just looks like shit. I know him too because I see him up here in clinic all the time for his injections. Solid citizen, respectful, never causes trouble. Anyway, what do you want me to do for him?"

"Call me back after you take his vitals."

"Got it."

Beth hangs up the phone and begins to check my vitals. I've become rather quiet, which makes taking my vitals easy. After a few minutes of entering everything into the computer, she picks up the phone.

"Dr. Huff , Beth Hurst again. BP 100/60, pulse regular at 130, respirations at 20, and his temp is 104.5. Can you come in and see him? This guy is sick." Beth is using the speakerphone so she can enter everything into the computer at the same time. I'm hearing her entire conversation and want to call out.

"You really have to ask me? *No*. I'm in the middle of shopping for a new truck. I'm not coming in for that piece of shit. I'm supposed to drop everything for a fuckin' felon? Come on, Beth. You know better. Tell you what: give him three Tylenols and call down to the lieutenant's office. They can move him to the SHU. I'll make sure someone sees him tomorrow. Are we clear on this, Nurse?"

"Wait, wait—Dr. Huff, I have to tell you—" Then there's a dial tone.

Following the loud click, Beth holds the receiver for a few seconds before mumbling to herself, "Just throw him in the SHU?" Her face is pale and stoic as if she just witnessed a mugging she's helpless to do anything about.

She looks over at me, but I'm hunched over in a chair, staring to the left, laboring for each breath. She places an ice pack on the back of my neck. I respond by looking up at her with a painful smile. I mumble a few unintelligible words followed by a moment of lucidity.

"You've got to get me to a real hospital," I utter as I look directly into her eyes.

I can tell by her ambivalence that Beth's moral compass is being challenged. She's not sure if she takes the easy way and follows the doctor's orders verbatim, or if she challenges his authority by calling a supervisor. She's an experienced nurse who knows when a patient is sick.

She quickly grabs the phone. "Hi, Lieutenant Fuller, Beth Hurst up in Medical. I need a few of you to escort an inmate down to the SHU. He probably has the flu. He's okay for transport in a wheelchair. How long will it be? Thanks. Ten minutes is good."

Damn it. She took the easy way out. Why did I think she would challenge the doctor and entire bureaucracy? I never seem to learn. I have at least ten minutes where it will be just Beth and me.

She spends the next ten minutes assuaging her guilt by talking to me and comforting me. She holds an ice pack on the back of my neck with one hand

and blots my brow with the other hand. She asks me one question after another. "How did you end up in this place? Are you married? Do you have kids? What's your medical specialty?"

I want to give her answers, but most of my answers are unintelligible. Every once in a while, I spew forth a coherent answer much to her surprise. Sometimes I feel as if she's not listening to my answers because she's wrestling with her own code of ethics. Nothing will ever happen to her for following the doctor's orders, but her eyes tell me that she knows this entire situation is morally wrong.

"It's just the flu, you'll be okay," she says, and refocuses on listening to my answers. To break up the monotony she retakes my temperature, hoping that the Tylenol and ice packs have helped. 104.5. No change.

"Hi, Trevor, I thought you were on vacation this week," Beth says to one of the arriving guards.

"Wish I was on vacation but gotta wait till next week. Going hunting with my buddies in Catamount National. What's the deal on this scumbag?"

"Needs to be in the SHU. Probably a bad flu."

"Man, he looks like shit. You know this guy at all?" he says with total contempt.

"Yeah, he has multiple sclerosis, so he's up here regularly for his shots. Was a doctor on the outside. Usually looks a lot better than this. Huff is his doctor, so you know he's in the Lord's hands now."

The two guards, after confirming her sentiments about Huff, radio down to the SHU that they are transporting me. I'm oblivious to my new escorts and continue to babble answers to Beth's questions she asked minutes earlier. Beth and the lieutenants continue their small talk while I'm slumped further forward. The sweat from my forehead dots the sweatpants covering my thighs. A few moments later, I straighten up and start yelling at the lieutenants.

"I need an IV, damn it."

"What the fuck is this dude talking about?" says the guard as he turns to Beth. The lieutenant is now blaming Beth for the inmate barking an order at him.

Turning his attention back to me, he yells, "You ain't gettin' nottin' from me. Ask me one more time and I'll make sure you never leave the SHU. Just shut the fuck up."

With that bit of diplomacy, the guards head for the elevator. As we wait, I can see Beth who clasps her hands in prayer, takes few deep breaths, and sits at the computer to make some entries. Knowing this could blow up in her face, I'm sure she's extra cautious about her computer entry. Anyone who looks at her entry retrospectively will know Beth Hurst did everything by the book, she followed the doctor's orders explicitly, and all the policies of the BOP. What normally would be a few lines of entry is suddenly a short story. Beth knows the system well and knows exactly what's needed to document and protect herself, just in case. As I'm wheeled into the elevator, I see Beth alone in the clinic with her furrowed brow, her head resting in her palms.

Seated in a wheelchair surrounded by two of West Virginia's finest correctional officers, my chair is pushed to the in-take area of the SHU. My two guards are greeted by two more guards who work in-take. With me sitting slumped over, the four guards begin a fifteen-minute discussion about the University of West Virginia basketball program, completely ignoring the reason why they are all in the SHU. Finally, the guards redirect their attention back to me.

"What's the story on this guy?"

"Just here for medical eval. Nurse didn't tell me much more. Probably cause she knew I don't give a shit. Said he had the flu or something like that."

"Is he gonna give us trouble tonight?"

"Who knows. He's a little out of it. Just isolate him and let the docs figure it out in the morning. Only thing I know about him from the nurse is he used to be a doc and has multiple sclerosis. Other than that, nothing remarkable in his file. This is his first time in the SHU."

The guards put on fresh latex gloves before stripping my clothes off and putting me in a bright red jumpsuit. They bring me to my solitary cell, transfer me from the wheelchair to the steel bed, and toss my rollup of two sheets and a few toiletry items onto the bed. I feel relieved to be supine, and the cold temperature of the steel bed feels comforting to my perspiring body. The room is bare, with only two surfaces—concrete or steel—a stark contrast to my former life. Fluorescent lights accentuate my skin pallor.

With a weakened voice, I yell as loud as I can to anyone listening. "You gotta get me to University Hospital. I don't wanna stay here. Call the police to get me out of here. I can't stay here. Anyone even listening to me? You have to get me out of here. Please—"

A guard walks over with a tray of food, which he places in the food slot.

"Shut the fuck up, Keller. I ain't takin' shit from you or anyone else down here. Stop your yellin'. You pissin' me off, boy, do ya hear me, motherfucker?"

I never touch the food tray the guard collects an hour later. I remain shivering, which is of no concern to the guards.

"Tylenol," I say as loud as I could speak, which at this point is barely above a whisper. The guard takes the unused tray but never glances to look at me. And he certainly isn't about to fulfill my Tylenol request.

I survive the night. I was in an out of sleep, in a fever dream. I saw Lily's smiling face, and then darkness creeping up the corners, suffocating me. I hold onto that vision of Lily. I'm not improved when morning arrives. In the SHU, there is no concept of day and night, as all the subterranean rooms are lit 24/7 with bright fluorescent lights. There are no windows in these basement cells, so one cannot detect daylight patterns. Saturday afternoon is when the unit manager and case managers do their rounds on SHU inmates from their unit. The unit manager doesn't know who I am, but my case manager, the despised Nikki Williams, knows my usual appearance rather well. I hear her talking—her voice grates on every nerve. Apparently, she peers into the cell, but she can't see me because my back is to her, and I have no energy to roll over and face her. She can't possibly appreciate my worsening status.

"He's just here for medical, doesn't owe any restitution, no prior disciplinary actions. Let's let medical handle it," says Nikki.

"Okay by me." I recognize the voice of Ms. Brown, the Unit Manager. She's always chewing on a wad of gum, which she regularly uses to mask the scent of alcohol. "I like easy." With that, they disappear.

I remain in a fetal position for the entire weekend. I don't eat, barely drink any water, and exhibit a classic deteriorating clinical picture. My ability to sit up is now an impossibility. You could say the guards check on me because they stand in front of my cell on a periodic basis. What they really check on isn't me, but rather the tray of food they have to be collect. That is the extent of their "checking." The fact that nothing was eaten or drank didn't register with the guards.

On Sunday, a prison staff nurse does her rounds on all the inmates who are in the SHU for medical reasons. Of the medical inmates, most are here because they are to have routine medical procedures such as a colonoscopy, cataract surgery, med trips, or maybe a knee arthroscopy. I'm here because I'm "infectious." When the nurse checks my temperature, I'm still at 103.1. The nurse has never met me before but is experienced enough to know the most important clinical differentiation any clinician must make: *is the patient sick or not*, and if they are sick, *what intervention is needed.*

I'm in pain, and my vision is blurring. I don't know what's happening to me. I continue to doze off—freezing and burning up. I roll over and forget where I am. What happened to that stray dog I saw when I was traveling in Spain near the side of the road where those pretty flowers bloomed? I see red sand falling through my fingers . . .

"Keller, wake up."

I'm floating on the water, my body light. I see Lily, her beautiful face and soft cheeks. Then I see a face, with beady eyes and a greasy mouth . . .

"Keller!"

I uncoil from my fetal position, turn to Dr. Ruiz, and stare at him for a few seconds. I'm snapped back to the moment.

"How ya doin' today, Keller? Battling the flu?" Dr. Ruiz asks.

I'm having some type of out-of-body experience, as I see Dr. Ruiz hover over me in a small room. I see my legs and arms as Dr. Ruiz watches over me.

As Dr. Ruiz examines my face, he says my eyes look like they have some blood in the normally clear white sclera. There are also a few black-and-blue marks on my neck and the right cheek. The puzzled Dr. Ruiz turns to his nurse, "Thought he's here for flu. He looks worse than that."

My vision zooms in and out and before they exit the room, I muster all my energy and shout, "Gotta get me to University— I can't die here. Please help me. Do something. Tylenol, IV, lactated Ringer's, normal saline, let it run wide open, do bloods on me. Coag profile, CBC, metabolic panel, anything, do it all. I can't die like this. What's wrong with everyone?"

Sweat covers my face and neck, the only part of my body not covered by the bright red jumpsuit. Dr. Ruiz turns to the nurse and tells her to give me some more Tylenol when rounds are finished. The two of them sheepishly exit the room, which the guard is waiting to lock. I'm mumbling to myself as tears and sweat roll down my cheeks.

I see Lily again, and I hear her voice. She's calling to me, begging me to come back to her. "I'm almost there. One more step," I say.

Someone is in the room; I can feel it. Someone is hovering over me.

"Mr. Keller, I have your Tylenol. Mr. Keller—Mr. Keller can you hear me?"

Her voice is moving further away, but all I care about is Lily's voice, which is getting stronger. I hear my daughter laughing. I reach out my hand and I suddenly feel nothing.

"Keller's dead! Call a Code Blue. Get a crash cart down here!"

Dr. Ruiz grabs me, starts chest compressions. "Where's the fuckin' crash cart?"

"Medical is on their way. I hear them now," says the uninterested guard.

A newly arrived nurse replaces Ruiz at the chest compressions. Another worker has an AMBU bag over my mouth in an effort to get some oxygen in my lungs. Dr. Ruiz shuffles through the crash cart with Nurse Byrd, the contents of which are falling to the floor in an endless stream of expired vials. They finally secure the needed supplies to start an intravenous line. The only missing supply is expertise. Neither Dr. Ruiz nor Ms. Byrd are able to start an IV line. After multiple tries, Dr. Ruiz turns to everyone and declares the Code to be over. I think my forearms are covered in blood from their botched attempts at starting an intravenous line but I can't be sure. Gravity is no longer holding me. I float a little higher. Blood is slowly oozing out of my ears and mouth, the exposed skin spotted with large areas of black and blue. My lifeless body isn't covered, so my face is exposed, staring at all the onlookers. To the staff who had worked on me, I'm now no different than a dead woodchuck lying on the side of a rural West Virginia road.

The more laws, the less justice.

Marcus Tullius Cicero

CHAPTER 36
Your Worst Nightmare

After organizing myself for the beginning of another work-week, I walk down the hallway and into the kitchen. The ceilings are high, the windows are big and open, but everything feels so empty. Ever since Jay left, the house has felt lonely. Even though it's only been fifteen months, it feels like forever. Sometimes, it feels like he's still here, as if he's just around the corner in the library or seated in front of his music stand playing music. I walk down the stairs leading to the basement. As I sort through some winter clothing I want to bring up, I think back to how much fun I had in my parent's home.

In the basement of my parent's house was a makeshift art studio. It consisted simply of a work table, a potter's wheel and shelving. I sculpted in plaster or clay, and threw my vessels. I called them vessels, which sounded more sophisticated than cups, bowls and vases. It was there I went taking refuge from the turbulence of both teenage life and the late 1960s.

After school and on weekends late into the night, with WNEW on the radio playing nonstop, I would work on my own, indulge in my own mind alternately sorting through social traumas and dilemmas of the day and being in complete blissful distraction. I remember sculpting and throwing clay, pound after pound.

It is to that environment I have continually turned throughout the years, and it is where I find myself now. In my own basement, in my own studio. Looking to make sense out of the mess and the pain. I will do anything to pass the time as I wait for Jay to come home. While covering my new creations in plastic, I smile, flashing back to my earliest memories of sculpting.

How many times did I hear my mother calling down to the basement, "Lily, come up for dinner, sweetie."

I remember one Saturday morning when I was with my father, an accomplished fine art painter, who took me to his favorite art supply store to buy me a new box of clay and all the necessary sculpting tools. The aisles were overflowing with supplies and they had the friendliest staff that seemed to know everything about every item. It was better than the best ice cream parlor.

Just back from the store, I dashed down to the basement and dove into my project. I didn't care that my studio was poorly lit or visited by more than a few spiders, I only remember feeling energized. Despite it being my first month of middle school, I was undeterred by a new school, new teachers, older students and lots of anxiety. I entered an art contest for the entire middle school. I was intimidated by the talents of other students, but I knew I had talent too.

I only had until next Friday to submit my sculpture. It was the first time I remember being obsessed with something. All I wanted to do was shape the clay while I sang songs to myself. I loved how the moist clay responded immediately to every motion of my fingers.

Every day I'd come home from school, rush through my homework, then descend into the basement feeling unbelievably alive. After a mandatory dinner break, I was back down in the basement, incessantly refining my sculpture. Eventually, one of my parents would force me to go to bed, well past my usual bedtime. I was too young to understand the concept of an obsession, but in retrospect, it was the first time I recall my zeal to master something. I came in second place, finishing only behind a boy who was two grades ahead of me.

***

My stomach growls, so I pour myself a glass of flavored seltzer and wash and cut an apple. I plop down on the couch with my Kindle, exhausted. Too much stress takes a toll on the body, just as I witnessed with Jay. Outside, the trees sway from an early fall breeze. The colors of the birch trees are just starting to turn. The brilliant colors of the maples are still a few weeks away.

I'm starting to doze. This happens a lot these days, where I'll fall asleep on the couch and then I have to rush through my nighttime routine because I'm too tired. I think a part of me doesn't want to get ready for bed because I think Jay will be home, and then we can get ready together.

I get up, turn off all the lights, lock the doors, and head upstairs. Tonight, I slept straight through the night. I look around when I awake and do my best to orient myself. It's the landline that wakes me up at 6:45 a.m. Who would be calling me this early? The sound of the ring echoes loudly throughout the house. It's a West Virginia area code so I answer the phone, a number I don't recognize.

"Hello, Jay?" I say in a shaky voice.

"No, ma'am, my name is Chaplain Wilson. Am I'm speaking with Mrs. Jay Keller?"

"Yes. What is this in reference to?"

"I'm calling from FMC Franklin regarding your husband."

I feel dizzy and quickly rush to the chair. In the beginning of Jay's incarceration, I kept my phone by me at all times and would jump every time the phone rang, never wanting to miss his call. But I got used to his schedule, and now I know the times when he can and cannot call. He's never called this early or on the landline.

"Is he okay—is everything okay?" My voice rises in panic.

"I'm afraid not, ma'am. I regret to inform you that your husband passed away late last night. He was found in his cell, unresponsive. I assure you the medical team did everything possible to resuscitate him, but he didn't respond to their efforts. I'm very sorry to be the one to give you such news. The good Lord has taken your husband to his Kingdom where I pray he will have eternal peace. The Lord—"

The room spins and black dots fill my vision. I'm going to faint. I don't want to believe it—no, it's not true. Jay is sleeping right now, in his bunk. I feel it in my heart and bones and he is alive.

"What are you talking about? I spoke to Jay on Tuesday and he was fine. I visited him a month ago. Jay doesn't have a cell. He's in an eight-man room in the Antioch Unit. You've made a mistake. Nothing you tell me makes any sense. Can you please check to make sure you're calling the right person?" My hand is shaking.

"I know this is hard, ma'am, but I performed Last Rights on Mr. Keller a few hours ago, and I was the one who went through his file to get your number. As head of the Chaplain Service at FMC Franklin, I make these kind of phone calls quite often. I'm very sorry, ma'am."

I scream. "I'm sorry, Chaplain, but Jay is healthy, doing well, and he's ready to come home soon! Everything you've said just isn't possible."

"Ma'am, I have his photo ID in front of me. Five-ten, brown eyes, his date of birth is correct, gray-brown hair. He also smiled for his entrance ID photo. No one smiles when they come in here. It's him, Mrs. Keller."

There is nothing but silence because I can't speak. My mouth has stopped working and my stomach wants to eliminate its empty contents.

"What the *fuck* did you people do to him?" I say more bewildered than angry. "You're telling me that I'll never see him again, I'll never hear his voice, I'll never touch him? I don't believe any of this."

As much as I want to explode, I'm still not convinced that Jay's dead. I stand motionless, with the phone to my ear, and my mind races with questions, coming and going a million miles an hour. *What do I do now? Do I fly out there? Does anyone know what happened? Any details at all? And what cell is the chaplain talking about? No, this has to all be a mistake.*

The chaplain breaks the silence. "I'm so sorry, Mrs. Keller. What I do know is that he was moved to the SHU I believe on Thursday or Friday for medical reasons, and by this morning he expired. The good Lord needed your husband today."

"Oh, cut the 'good Lord' shit! If you knew a goddamn thing about Jay, you would know he was a non-believer. Believing in a benevolent god these days, that's just a bit too much to swallow." My voice is growing louder with each passing word.

"Ma'am, please, calm down and listen closely. I must explain to you the process when an inmate dies here—"

"No! You listen to me! I've had it with all of you. FMC Franklin is nothing but a morally bankrupt fucking cesspool! You didn't punish him enough, so you had to kill him? I need answers and I'll get to the bottom of this, believe me. Do you hear me, Mr. Chaplain?"

My body is shaking with pure rage. I'm seeing red.

"Mrs. Keller, I understand you're upset—I do. But please let me get a few words in. As you probably know, everything is done a little differently within the BOP, and I want this to be as simple as possible for you and your family."

"A little differently? I ask. "You mean, they do whatever the fuck they want? Wait, wait, wait. Stop right there. Is his body in the prison right now.?"

"Yes it is, ma'am."

"Good. I want an autopsy performed by someone other than the BOP, an autopsy done by real doctors. Do you understand me? Jay made that *very* clear to me. He told before he entered FMC Franklin, if he died in prison, he wanted an autopsy to find the cause of death. I want an autopsy."

"Okay, Mrs. Keller, here's what I'll do. I'll check with the assistant warden who handles these matters, and I will get back to you shortly. I'll call you as soon as I get an answer. Again, I'm sorry for your loss and will have you and your family in my thoughts and prayers."

I slam the phone down, drop to my knees, and let out the loudest scream until my throat burns and gives out. My breathing becomes shallow, and tears pour down my face as the snot runs from my nose. *This isn't happening, this isn't real.* Nausea like I've never experienced curls my stomach. I want to die, right here and now. Rage takes possession of my body. While kneeling, I pound the bed, faster and faster. Here I am, lonelier than I have ever been, mentally paralyzed to do anything. Finally, I fall to the floor where I remain powerless in a fetal position, writhing back and forth for what seems an eternity. Abruptly, the landline phone rings, which forces me to return to my nightmarish reality.

"Hello, Mrs. Keller, this is Chaplain Wilson again. I wish there was an easy way to tell you this in your period of mourning. I spoke to the assistant warden. You do have the right to have an autopsy. That's the good news. The bad news is that you will have to pay for the autopsy. It is BOP policy that autopsies are not routinely performed. Also, any transportation costs of the body from this facility are your responsibility."

"So what you're saying Chaplain is that although the BOP sent him to West Virginia for his sentence and ultimate execution, I have to pay to bring him back to me? No one has a shred of decency? No wonder Jay hated the people who ran the prison, from the slimy unctuous warden on down. Everything Jay said was true!"

"Well, ma'am, this is BOP policy. I'm a preacher. I don't make policy. It doesn't matter whether I think something is right or wrong. We can keep his body in the morgue until you arrange for the transportation. Just so you are aware, the BOP charges families $500 per day to store anyone in the morgue after an initial forty-eight-hour period."

I'm seething. "And you labeled my husband a criminal? You are all evil people, all part of a corrupt cult. You're the corrupt ones, not Jay. Every cent of every paycheck you get is nothing but blood money. This is not over, Chaplain."

While trying my hardest to take some deep breaths, I compose myself just enough to tell the chaplain that I will make arrangements as soon as possible. He gives me a number so I can forward it to the funeral home.

"My thoughts and prayers are with you and your loved ones. May Christ comfort you in this most difficult time," he says."

"You didn't listen to a word I just said. He didn't believe in your fairy tale! Fuck your 'thoughts and prayers.'"

I hang up again, this time with no intention of answering the phone when it rings again. I collapse onto the bed and cry until I can't cry anymore.

CHAPTER 37

Circling the Wagons

It's all a blur. I rise up with a pounding headache. The clock reads 7:17. My eyes are swollen with burning tears, but I refuse to let them fall. I'm in and out of a dream-like reality, trying to come to terms that I will never see my husband again. And yet, I still have a sliver of doubt. There's too much that doesn't make sense.

I peel myself off the bed and head into the master bath to splash cold water on my face. Maybe, just maybe, I can wash all the sadness away. I walk in circles in the bathroom. As painful as it is, I will have to tell my children that the father they loved, adored, and cherished, the father who went to prison to satisfy the agenda of overzealous prosecutors, is now dead. Where will I even start? I can barely stand up or make sense of my thoughts.

I quickly dress and head downstairs. The house feels emptier. Even the air feels different. How will I get through this? In a rare and brief moment of clarity, I start to plan out a sequence of events I know must be done ASAP. I'll need a ton of help organizing the monumental tasks that lay in front of me. Some moments my mind is clear, other moments I'm completely pixilated. I have to call the kids, I have to call the world, but I can't get myself to do any of it. I can't bring myself to say the words, "Jay's dead." Instead, I call my neighbor Jill.

"I need you to come right over," I say. "Please, right away." I'm crying.

"Are you okay, Lily, what's the matter?" she says in a concerned tone.

"It's Jay. I'll explain when—when you get here," I choke on a sob.

I hang up the phone and wait. It takes less than three minutes before Jill is knocking at the door. When she sees my face, she pulls me into a hug, not to embrace me, but to hold me up.

"Lily, talk to me. You're shaking. What happened?"

"I just got a phone call from the prison. Jay's dead."

Jill could no longer support me while I collapse to the tile floor of the foyer, sobbing uncontrollably.

"Oh my god, I'm so sorry, Lily. I don't know what to say. Tell me what you need me to do."

We remain on the tile floor. With her left arm around me, she rubs my back and my hair, comforting me as if I was a child. And I am a child right now. Jill reaches into her pocket and calls her husband, who's on a train bound for New York City.

"Bobby, where are you right now?"

I can only make out a few words of what Bobby is saying.

"Get off at Yonkers and come home. It's Jay. He's—I'm here with Lily. We need help."

Jill hangs up. Then she says, "Come on, let's get up. Have a seat, Lily." She manages to get me to a seated position. "Do you know what happened?"

"No. Nothing. I just got a call from this worthless prison chaplain who didn't know anything other than my phone number and that I'm Jay's wife."

"Did he say anything else?"

"All he told me is that Jay was moved to the SHU over the weekend and was dead by this morning. That's it. That's all I know." Those few words took about a minute to express as they're squeezed out between countless weeps. I collapse into Jill's arms, and she does her best to keep me from falling.

"It's okay, Lily, stay right here," she says as she hugs my limp body. "We'll get through this, we will. I promise. Just stay with me."

We cry together, our bodies rocking to a soothing rhythm.

Jill stops after a moment and says, "Lily, look at me for a second." I peel my head up from her lap and stare into her eyes. I feel so empty. "Do the kids know yet?"

"No. I can't do it. I can't. What am I going to tell them? What will I say? I can't do it to them."

Jill sighs. "I know this is hard, but we're going to do it together."

"I have to tell them, don't I?"

"I'll help you. Let me know when you're ready. Where's your cell phone?"

"Try the bedroom."

Jill slowly rests my limp body on my side before going upstairs in search of my cell phone. A few moments later, she comes back to where I'm seated on the tile floor and places the phone in front of me.

"I'll help you when you're ready. Only when *you're* ready."

This is what friends and family do in times like this. It has felt as if I have been living "in times like this" for years. Even the most frightening rollercoaster ride eventually ends. But I feel myself spiraling downward, faster and faster.

Jill sits on the floor next to me with a pen and a pad in hand. "Let's write down what we need to do in the next hour. Can we do that?"

"We have to call my children."

"Who else do you want me to call?"

"Call Jay's cousin Vanessa Miller. She'll let the rest of the world know."

"Anyone else?"

"Cynthia. Between Vanessa and Cynthia, everyone will know. We also have to call a funeral home. I can't call the kids yet. Shit, I also have to arrange for an autopsy and—"

Jill gently places her hand on my shoulder. "Let me make a suggestion: Let's call Sara and Richard first. I'll help you. I'm right here. We'll do the other calls after. Are you ready?" She hands me the phone.

It's a foreign object in my hand. All I have to do is press a few buttons, and then my small world will know, and that makes it real. I don't want it to be real.

With a shaky hand, I make my first call, putting it on speakerphone in case I can't find the words. "Hi, Sara," I say faintly and sniffling. "I have some bad news." My sobbing intensifies.

"Mom, what's the matter?"

"I'm sorry, Sara—I'm so sorry." I break down again.

Sara's voice sounds faint and far away, and she keeps saying, "Mom, Mom, Mom—"

"I got a call this morning from the chaplain at FMC Franklin. He told me your father—your father—died. That's all I—"

"Oh my god!" Sarah starts crying. "Mom, I'm on my way home. I'll be there as quickly as I can. Is anyone with you now?"

I hand the phone back to Jill before collapsing to the floor.

"Hi, Sara, it's Jill. I'm here with your mother. Just come home."

"What happened? How did he die? Does my brother know yet?" Her voice is frantic.

"They didn't tell your mother anything other than he was placed in the SHU all weekend for medical reasons. That's all she knows. Just come home, your mother needs you here. We are going to call Richard now. Love you, Sara."

Jill has her arms around me, my wet face on her shoulder. I remain on the floor and listen to Jill make calls to our mutual friends and my family members, all responding with shock and sadness. In my mind, I am still waiting for a phone call from the prison that this is all a mistake. Jill's husband Bobby finally arrives to lend his support. My dearest and oldest friend Cynthia is also on her way. The village is circling the wagons.

CHAPTER 38
Emotional Spectrum

Sara is the first to arrive, and Richard is not far behind. I hug them both, embracing them for what seems an eternity. How many tears can the human body produce in such a short period of time? I would have crumbled to the ground if it isn't for their embrace of me. Here's the Keller family, all but Jay, sitting on the floor of the foyer, trying our best to survive this moment of sadness, anger, pain, uncertainty, and grief. Somehow, we make our way to the living room, all cuddled near each other on the sofa and the floor.

Cynthia soon arrives, embraces us, and asks, "Does anyone know what happened to Jay?"

Sara sighs. "Nothing."

They all escort me into the kitchen and I'm grateful.

Everyone gathers around the kitchen table except for Cynthia, who's looking through the fridge and pantry. She plops a box of crackers onto the table, a pitcher of iced tea, and goes about cutting up some cheese.

It's all so overwhelming. The next tasks are more vague. Arrange for the transport of Jay's body back to New York. Arrange for an autopsy. I tell everyone what Jay said to me just before he entered prison. I didn't want to listen, but he insisted. He took my hands in his and told me that he if were to ever die in prison, I had to make sure an autopsy was done. Arrange for a funeral. Jay had lost his parents and I lost my mother all within the last five years, so I have the names of funeral directors to call.

Sara does her best to get me to focus. "Mom, which funeral home do you want to use?"

"Try Aden Funeral Home in Larchmont. The director's name is Barry Fine. I think he did your Grandma and Grandpa's."

Richard is scrolling through my contact list. I've been meaning to update it. "Found it," he says. He takes my hand and stares at me. "Are you okay, Mom?"

My son looks so innocent in this moment. I stare into his big brown eyes and see the little boy asking me to help him with his homework, but calling a funeral home is not what little boys do. There is no childlike innocence anymore.

"I'll manage," I say to him softly.

Richard leaves the room to call the funeral home, and a few moments later he returns.

"Barry sends his regards. He knew Dad from the Chamber of Commerce, and he genuinely was saddened at the news. I told him we wanted to get the body back for an autopsy. He said there are a lot of logistics, and in his limited experience with the prison system, there are always some strange rules. I gave him the number, and he's going to call the prison himself," Richard explains.

I grit my teeth. I know this isn't going to be an easy task.

Sara emphatically tells Richard, "I already made some calls to Columbia, and I also left a message for Zack."

Zack Edwards is my nephew and a fourth-year medical student at Boston University. He's a talented jazz musician who Jay loved to ski with. He will be an outstanding physician.

"Richard, do you think anyone at your law firm would know the best hospital to get an autopsy performed in New York?" Sara asks.

"I'll ask around," he responds.

And just like that, I crumble to tears.

***

Barry Fine, the funeral director, empathetic and helpful in contrast to the prison chaplain, calls the house later that afternoon to say that despite a lot of red-tape obstacles, Jay's body will be arriving tomorrow at LaGuardia Airport, assuring us it will be in a state that will not interfere with any of the autopsy results.

The serene kitchen of Richard and Sara's childhood is suddenly transformed into a Control Central. Jill, Cynthia, Bobby, Richard, and Sara are all on their phones. I make one phone call to my closest cousin but recognize immediately that I need other people to make the calls. Every call is like tearing open an unhealed wound.

"So far, everyone has said to contact NYU for the autopsy. Zack was able to contact the Chief of Pathology at BU who said unequivocally that we should have the autopsy done at NYU. I'm going upstairs to call them."

Despite the overwhelming heartache, I'm amazed how Sara and Richard have responded. They have just lost their father. Yet, in front of my eyes, on this most painful day, they are the adults. When I see them functioning in the midst of the chaos and sadness, it gives me a little added strength. Regardless of their personal accomplishments, I have never been prouder of my children.

One by one, the Keller Village makes the calls, makes the arrangements, and is there to comfort each other in what is undoubtedly our darkest moment. Within a few hours, the house is filling up with friends and family. Everyone is here to answer the barrage of phone calls, texts, and emails. It's so distressing for me to see my children's eyes filled with tears. Nonetheless, Sara and Richard smile when they see me attempting to prepare food for all the people at the house. Even I have to laugh when they point out my instinctive behavior of feeding everyone. I laugh for the first time since the chaplain's phone call earlier this morning. Laughter and tears, opposite poles of our emotional spectrum.

CHAPTER 39

Standing Room Only

It's only six days since I was notified of Jay's death. It feels more like a decade. It's only two days since Sara, Richard, and I went to La Guardia Airport to identify Jay's body. I don't think I'll ever forget that moment.

There was a black body bag lying on a long table with wheels. The airport official unzipped the bag halfway. Richard and Sara were holding on to me, maybe to support me, maybe to support themselves. Jay's body was cold and lifeless.

"That's my husband," I said as I swiftly turned around, pulling my two children with me. I wish the director of the BOP had been standing in front of me, or better yet, the U.S. Attorney who prosecuted Jay. My tirade would be endless.

I recall the moment years ago, when Jay was first diagnosed with MS. We talked about wills, dying, funerals—all the discussions you never want to have. I just never thought it would be this soon. Jay insisted on being cremated. He wanted his ashes spread on his favorite mountain top, rather than have his body take up room on an overpopulated planet.

Funerals are sad, some sadder than others. My mother's funeral was sad but buffered by the fact that she "lived" in a nursing home the last seven years of her life with minimal cognition of her existence after suffering a massive hemorrhagic stroke. Others are more a celebration of life accomplishments. Jay's funeral will be sadness on steroids.

I woke up this morning in a daze, perhaps from circumstances, perhaps from the sleeping pill. I shower, dress, put on makeup, and do what I need to do, all by rote muscle memory. I have no recollection of being driven to the funeral home.

The funeral director looks out into the crowd and turns to me. "I can't remember this funeral home ever being packed like this. I added a few rows of seats in the back and the sides. Let's hope the Fire Marshall isn't here for the funeral. I think they'll be many who will have to listen to the service outside. We're setting up a screen and speakers outside right now. Quite the tribute to your husband."

"Thanks. Jay touched many people in his lifetime," I say.

Richard leads me to the front row and I sit. I'm afraid to look up, but I must. There's no casket, only an urn placed on a small cloth-covered table.

We decided this morning that Richard and Sara would speak first. I still wasn't sure if I would speak or not, as much as I wanted to. After the funeral director signals to us that we can begin, Richard makes his way up to the podium. He speaks to the packed room, eloquently but with a few pauses to regain his composure.

"When I was still in college, I remember shooting hoops with my father, just the two of us. Out of the blue, he asked me which was more important: a great résumé or a great eulogy. It took me a minute to process the question before I realized what he meant. Today, that question has a great deal of relevance. Do you want to have the greatest résumé but go through life being a horse's ass? Or is it better to have people speak with lavish praise at your funeral? I am here today to speak about the effect my father had on people because that is what *he* valued. He had a great résumé, but he knew it wasn't worth a damn unless you've had a positive effect on people. If you want to honor my father, do it with your actions. Let those actions affect others for the better."

Richard continues for a few more minutes, but my mind isn't able to focus on his words. I picture Jay carrying three-year-old Richard around the house on his shoulders while singing "Zip-a-Dee-Doo-Dah."

Sara walks up to the podium, paper in one hand, a handkerchief in the other. She pauses for moment, and I think she's going to fall apart. Not Sara.

With her hands shaking and her breathing labored, she begins to speak. Her words are steady and heartfelt.

"My father was the wealthiest man I knew. It wasn't because he had the most zeros at the end of his bank account; it was because of the life he led, the relationships he built, and how he affected so many lives in such a positive way. That is wealth. I got to grow up in a house where my mother and father deeply and genuinely loved each other." She pauses to look at me, and I wipe tears from my eyes. "That is wealth. I was loved by a father, unconditional love, someone who was always there for us. He was there for the good times, and he was there for our roughest times. To my dad, being a father was never a chore—it was simply what he was programmed to do. That is wealth. He loved hosting friends and family at our home. That is wealth. I remember reading his letter not too long ago when he said something so simple, so obvious, so true, yet overlooked by so many. 'It is relationships with others that gives meaning to life.' That is wealth."

There isn't a dry eye in the house. I am filled with pride only a mother can receive from her children.

I debated about speaking but my children told me that if I have things I want to say I should get up and say them. There is more than a short pause before I stand up and walk to the podium, trying to be graceful, perhaps dented, but still walking. I stand at the podium but before speaking, I motion to my children to come up and stand at my side. I need them beside me in case I can't finish the words I have written down. I look out into a sea of faces and see a funeral home filled to capacity, and then some.

"We wish to thank all of you for coming today. Jay meant a lot to all of you, and you meant a lot to Jay. I believe a man is judged by how much he is loved by others, and this funeral is testament to how much Jay was loved. Our sincerest thanks."

I open the piece of paper containing my eulogy and lay it on the podium. I stare at the paper before finally looking back up and into the audience. I never look back down at my prepared words. Instead, after a long, deep breath, I speak from the deepest crevices of my heart. Yes, I pause every so often to compose myself. I cover a great deal of territory and even address the eight-hundred-pound gorilla in the room. "As someone who spent a lot of time in Jay's office, I am here to tell *everyone* that Jay was not a criminal as our government depicted with jubilation and triumph at his sentencing, as well as in the newspaper."

Other than that one reference, I spend all my time in praise of my husband, trying my best to be insightful, loving, and even a bit humorous. "Jay had obstacles in his life, but no one was more tenacious in defeating them. How sad that he didn't have the time nor the power to defeat the last of his obstacles. I see that resolve in my children. It will serve them well."

I maintain a constant theme about a life of good deeds snuffed out too prematurely for reasons beyond me and everyone else. "We shared so many wonderful moments. I will be forever grateful for the time we did have together, but it was too short a time."

I turn to look at Richard and Sara before finishing. "Our love grew exponentially with each passing year. No matter what obstacles were in front of us, and no matter how difficult things became, it only confirmed our belief that we would do it together. No matter what, we knew there would still be the two of us, together as a team." I take a deep breath.

"Jay, I hope you know how much happiness you brought into my life. When it was time to leave Jay after my last visit to Franklin, he told me how he looked forward to soon saying 'good night' instead of 'goodbye.' In the last letter I received from him, he ended the letter by quoting a line from a children's book he used to read to our children: 'I love you forever. I like you for always. As long as you're living, my *wife* you will be.' Yes, I will Jay." I pause for a moment to gather myself. "The heart that has truly loved never forgets. I will never forget you, Jay."

Upon the conclusion of the service, my son and daughter, each holding my arms, escort me to the exit at the back of the funeral home. I'm amazed at the number of people in attendance. Many could not find a seat inside. They listened to the service via loudspeakers and a screen while standing outside the funeral home. Beyond the masses of humanity are two news trucks from the local TV stations, their reporters begging for a story, trying to shove a microphone into my face.

"Mrs. Keller, any comments on your husband's prison sentence?"

"Mrs. Keller, can you tell us how the family is holding up?"

Richard immediately steps in front of me and addresses the few hungry reporters. "Are you guys crazy? This is a funeral, not reality TV. Get the hell out of here and show some respect. None of us have anything to say."

We enter the limousine for the ride back home. "I'm kind of surprised to see news trucks and reporters," says Sara. "We always used to tease Dad that he was a 'big deal' and how many people knew him, but to have reporters at the funeral home, what's that about?" Sara says.

The limo ride back home is mostly periods of solemn silence, broken occasionally by conversation.

I find the strength to speak. "I want both of you to know how proud I am today. It's not easy to give a eulogy, at any age. You both were sublime. Dad would have been very proud of you. Now we have a few days of Shiva to get through, and if it's anything like the funeral, there's going to be a lot of people to welcome and embrace. I remain silent another minute as if my brain cannot fabricate sentences.

"What do we tell people when they ask us how Dad died?" asks Richard.

Without hesitation, Sara responds, "Keep it simple and say 'we don't know.'"

Richard adds, "Personally, I think it was something the prison did. Dad was doing too well to die all of a sudden."

The limo turns off Route 24 and onto the more local roads filled with potholes. "I don't know what happened and that's why we are doing the autopsy," I say. "Things happen to people my age. I don't think it was his heart, but he could have had a brain aneurysm like his mother, or maybe a blood clot, an infection. Who knows? That's why we're doing the autopsy."

CHAPTER 40

Never Share Again

Jay and I have a big home, not over-the-top big, but big enough. One by one, people show up to offer their condolences. Friends. Immediate family. Extended family, the kind you only see at weddings and funerals. Patients, scores of them. Colleagues who worked with Jay over the years. They came from far and wide to pay homage to Jay. The mayor. The police chief. Neighbors who moved away years ago. Friends we hadn't seen since soccer games decades ago. I want to greet everyone and talk to everyone, reveling in what Jay meant to all these people. My emotions swing from sadness to anger, but never do I find peace. Peace remains an illusion that neither I nor Jay have known since the days of Jay's first MS attack.

I don't recognize him at first, but once he starts to speak, a lightbulb goes on. It's Dr. Dana Feinstein, the local neurologist who first diagnosed Jay with multiple sclerosis and the subsequent immunological problems. Dr. Feinstein had also written to the court on three separate occasions, warning of the inherent danger of putting Jay in prison. It was, of course, to no avail. I met him once or twice when I had to drive Jay to his office.

"So nice of you to stop by, Dr. Feinstein."

"Please, call me Dana," he says, "How are you, Lily?"

"I'm still standing, right? Come, let's go into the study."

Once secluded, I close the door, blocking the noise of the rest of the house. "Jay appreciated all you did for him prior to him going to prison. Unfortunately, the government disregarded everything. Did he ever write to you about how they ignored your letters?"

"Yeah. He was hurting."

I explain that when Jay first arrived in prison, he knew all the doctors' letters sent to the Court weren't worth a damn. His letters described blind inmates, limbless, demented inmates, psychotics, cancer patients, the mentally challenged, a dwarf in a wheelchair, you name it. He knew immediately that *no one* in America avoids prison time due to their medical condition.

Dana thought for sure his letters, worded as strongly as they were and combined with his credentials, would have been enough to keep Jay out of prison. He, like everyone else. had no idea why the government was so hell-bent on putting someone like Jay behind bars. Finally, he asks what he's been dying to ask.

He whispers, "Was an autopsy done?"

"Funny you should ask. Jay always lived with the fear of getting sick in prison. You know, bad doctors, uncaring bureaucracy. Even before he went away, he told us that if anything happened to him, he wanted an autopsy. We had an autopsy done at NYU. I'll let you know what they find."

"He should have never lost his life this way. I'm truly sorry. He was a fabulous physician, a great man, a gentleman." Dana pauses for a moment, then says, "Lily, on my drive over here, I was wondering, you know—just kind of—"

"Dana, just say it."

"I was giving some thought to all that's happened to Jay. You know, depending on the autopsy results, there could be a lawsuit to pursue."

"I've been told, but can't think about it now. Just know Jay was appreciative of all your support. He always said he was very comfortable with you as his neurologist. And please, try some sandwiches. We ordered way too much food."

Throughout the day and evening, I move from one group to the next, and the next, with barely time to digest the tributes. People keep coming. Doctors who trained with Jay. The owner of our favorite restaurant in town. My coworkers. Little League coaches. Jay's barber. Musician friends. The owners of the local hardware store and local market all stop by.

On the third evening of Shiva, I'm talking with Cynthia about putting out more sandwiches. What would I do without Cynthia? We met decades ago when she worked for my father at an ad agency. I was visiting my father after work one day when Cynthia saw me in the waiting room. Only a few years ago did Cynthia tell me when she saw me that day, how she had to know, "Who is that beautiful hippie chick?"

After Cynthia leaves the kitchen, I spot Stephen Conklin, one of the attorneys who represented Jay. Like most former US Attorneys, they leave the government for the more lucrative private sector.

Stephen is well dressed as usual, wearing an expensive well-tailored suit, suspenders that only lawyers seem to wear, oversized cufflinks, a light gray shirt with a white collar, slicked back gray hair, and shiny Italian shoes. If anyone has the stereotypical look of a defense attorney, it's him.

Stephen lives in New York City, so this is a big trip out to the suburbs of Westchester. Perhaps more significantly, Stephen and Jay never really bonded in any sense of the word. Jay always felt his case was too insignificant for a man of Stephen's stature. It became our contention Stephen was more interested in executing a plea deal expeditiously rather than defending Jay or negotiating the best possible plea deal.

"Hi, Lily. Nice to see you. I was devastated when Andrew called me and told me Jay had died. How are you holding up?"

He is making an effort to show his respect. My unenviable task is to appear gracious. I flash a smile. "Thanks for coming. I'm holding up because I have to."

"How are the kids doing? I'd love to meet them. I feel as if I know them from all the meetings we had. One went into law, right?"

"They're having the battle of their lives. Like everyone, they're in shock. Richard finished NYU Law School and is pretty angry the government decided to make his father a sacrificial lamb. He knew it was a senseless case more than anyone."

Stephen takes a sip of his drink and looks around. "You have a beautiful home. I'm glad you were able to preserve your assets. Do you remember all the discussions we had about choosing your 'best–worst option'?"

"Discussions I'd rather forget. I used to drive home nauseated after your meetings. And Jay, he was sick for months, the MS, the legal nonsense. Everyone who saw him during that period thought he was dying of cancer."

Stephen looks uncomfortable. "Listen, Lily, I don't mean to rehash the case but taking it to trial could have killed Jay as well."

I can't believe he just said that. It confirms my suspicions of him being an insensitive narcissist. Jay and I both felt he was too imbedded in the judicial system to really do what was needed for Jay. And how could he have not known that there are no medical exceptions to prison in America? How could he not have known that going to an FMC is like going to a real prison rather than a prison-camp for white-collar crimes? Suddenly, I see Richard who I hope can be my buffer in this already awkward conversation.

"Richard, come over here for a second. I'd like to introduce you to Stephen Conklin. Did you meet him at the sentencing?"

Richard walks over and appears irritated. He knows all about Stephen. "No, we haven't met," he says. "Nice to meet you Stephen." He extends his hand.

"The pleasure is mine. Jay was very proud of you, Richard, your sister too. A real tragedy what happened to your father."

The combination of stress, not eating, and my animus toward Conklin is making me feel faint as Richard and Stephen begin their legal-speak chat.

"My mother said you had been in favor of a plea from the very beginning. I want to ask you a few questions about that," Richard says.

Stephen looks a bit nervous. "Sure, ask away."

Richard looks at me, and says, "Mom, do you mind if I ask some questions?" I nod my head.

"Why were you in favor of a plea deal from the get go, even told my father to accept the feds' first offer? You also knew that my dad agreed to things in the plea that weren't true. You told him, 'in a few years, no one cares about the details of a plea deal.' In retrospect, do you think that was the right course?"

Stephen smirks. "You can't think like that, Richard. You're a lawyer. It was the *United States of America vs. Jay Keller*. Not exactly a fair fight, *and the* feds aren't in the business of losing," he says with conviction. "Federal judges, in my experience, go along with recommendations of prosecutors close to 100 percent of the time meaning the prosecutors are the judge, jury, and executioner."

"How come there never was a discovery phase?"

"We never got far enough to have a discovery period so I was never sure of what they had or didn't have. The government's position was that the signed contract between your father and the lab was enough to make a case against him. And with the number of federal laws that exist today, they can always find a law to support their case."

Confused, Richard asks, "A signed contract was enough evidence to enter a plea? What am I missing?"

"The purpose of the law is to prevent physician-decision making to be based on any financial arrangement. Your father had a financial arrangement, and that's all they needed."

I flash back to a meeting in our lawyer's office. Conklin told us the AUSA told him, "this wouldn't even be a case if Jay Keller was the only doctor, nor would it be a case if the laboratory billed responsibly, but come on Stephen, you know how the system works."

"That was it?" asks Richard.

"Look what happened when another doctor did take it to trial to argue the validity of the contract. His legal team got shot down. The judge decided any discussion about the legality of the contract was inadmissible at trial."

"Hard to believe there were no other options. You couldn't argue my father's actions were no different before, during, or after his relationship with Accurate Labs?"

I cut Richard off and stare at Conklin. "The whole reason for having those laws is to prevent doctors from ordering unnecessary tests. If the government had issues with Jay's actions, make it a civil case. He never had criminal intent. You knew it and the feds knew it."

"Listen, I could have made many arguments, but in the end, very few people win against the feds. My impetus for a plea was from first-hand experience of how the feds operate. If they didn't have an iron-clad case against your father early on, they would have by trial. Been around long enough to sense how cases will end and Jay's case was pre-ordained. US Attorney Bob Keenan is a smart, powerful, and brutal prosecutor."

"That means you just capitulate to his whims?" I ask.

"Not at all. What I mean is the feds can *always* get someone to flip to support their case. It's amazing how that happens, especially in low-profile or no-profile cases like we're talking about. I'm not saying it's right; I'm saying it's just how it is. Your father was collateral damage who didn't have the resources to go up against the government."

Richard stands there stunned. "You didn't know the feds lock up everyone regardless of their medical conditions? Really?"

I know my face is red because I can feel my veins pulsing. The nerve of this man! He claims he's so knowledgeable about the outcome of the case, that Jay had no hope, yet claims ignorance about where Jay ultimately ended up?

Stephen bites his lip. "I'm sorry, maybe I shouldn't have even brought up the details. Having been a US Attorney, it's likely they got someone to say stuff against your father, and the other doctors in exchange for a lesser sentence. It's not right, but it's just how it's done. Every day. Everywhere." He looks at me. "I hope this gives you answers."

It's too much for me to handle. I leave the conversation without a word.

***

I make it through my husband's funeral and a few days of Shiva. Exhaustion is all around me, similar to how Jay used to describe the fatigue of MS. It goes down to the bones. This evening, after all the guests depart, I crash onto the king-sized bed, fully dressed, fully spent. Lying on my side, my eyes dart around the bedroom to each article in the room. Every piece of furniture, painting, sculpture, photograph, and lamp reminds me of our life together. My mind remembers where we were and why we bought what we did. Every artifact carries a story and a mental picture.

There is only one photograph of me and Jay in the bedroom. It was Jay's favorite photo, taken in the Italian countryside. We were gently kissing, my left arm resting on Jay's shoulder, his right arm holding me around the waist. A small pond in the center of the piazza was behind us, and in the distance was an eighteenth-century building with a red-tiled roof. Under the roof, a chamber orchestra was playing on a Sunday morning. We were staring into each other's eyes as our lips touched ever so slightly. Despite the exhaustion, it's impossible to quiet my mind. Staring at the ceiling, I'm suddenly flooded with a wave of sadness, once again reminded that I will never share this bed with Jay. Never again will I touch his lips.

Dear Jay,

I don't know why, but I have to write to you. Tonight was the last day of Shiva. People came out of the woodwork to pay their respects to you, people from every era of our lives. You should have heard Richard trading father-son stories with your basketball buddies. Sara was so graceful. Our children have amazed me. We must have done a something right because they are special people, much stronger than I am. They both have your tenacity, which will serve them well.

Stephen Conklin, of all people, showed up. Richard asked a ton of questions. As I was listening to their exchange and reliving those moments, I realized how blindsided we were. We were total novices to the justice system going up against professional prosecutors who do this as a career. If that wasn't lopsided enough, it reminded me how pixilated your brain was during that crucial time period.

You meant so much to so many people. You touched so many lives in such a positive way. Everyone misses you, but no one more than me. We had a wonderful life together. Tonight, I feel so empty, as if I've been violated and robbed of my most valuable possession. You're right. You can never say "I love you" enough. You can never share too much. I keep thinking I'm going to get a call from the prison telling me there's been a huge mistake and you're really okay. Pretty silly, isn't it?

Anyway, I'm sad, angry, and miss you every day. I never could have imagined it would have ended this way.

I only wish you were next to me. I love you, Jay.

Your loving wife, forever.

Lily

CHAPTER 41

Now We Know

Six long weeks pass before I return to work, running the HR department of Herman, LLC, a large New York accounting firm. The days are getting shorter, the trees are almost bare, and the holidays are just around the corner. Working is therapeutic for me as my workdays fly by. The weekends move slower, but my children continue to visit, barring a major social event. I have either forgotten how much there was to do after someone dies or my brother did more than I remember. What's certain is I'm up to my eyeballs with paperwork regarding Jay's death.

Exactly ten weeks to the day Jay died, I come home from work and see a light flashing on my landline phone. Probably another robo-call.

"Hi, Mrs. Keller, this is Gavin Sandler from the NYU pathology department. We finished all our work, which means you can call us to make an appointment to go over the autopsy results. Some people prefer us to just have the results sent to them. We'll do whatever is your preference. Let us know how you would like to handle it. Please give us a call at your earliest convenience."

I feel my stomach churn, that same feeling of nausea I had after every attorney meeting, after every time I didn't hear from Jay on the day we were supposed to speak, that same feeling I had after the chaplain called from the prison. I'm not sure why this voice message upsets me now. After all, this is a good thing. We finally will know why Jay died.

***

On a grim December day, with a few snow flurries blowing in the strong breezes, we arrive at the pathology conference room of NYU, a long rectangular room with several smart boards and large cushy leather chairs. Gavin Sandler is the administrator of the department, and Dr. Anusha Patel is the pathologist. Dr. Patel first tells us her credentials and how many autopsies her department performs each year. We know most of what she is saying because that's why we chose NYU. Her lack of an accent suggests she is second-generation Indian-American in her early sixties. A streak of gray hair highlights an otherwise head of long black hair tied back in a braid. She exudes confidence and professionalism.

Before diving into details, she tells us everything is on a disc we'll take home. This is hardly Dr. Patel's first autopsy presentation. She now plunges headfirst into specific results.

"Don't worry about a few technical terms I'll be using. I'm sure you can Google everything or have it clarified by the doctors who cared for Dr. Keller here in New York. My team will also be available for questions. If you need us to meet with lawyers, there will be additional charges. We are often asked to provide expert witness testimony."

Dr. Patel pulls out a few pages from a manila envelope. "Your father, your husband, died from two infections. The first was a viral disease called progressive multifocal leukoencephalopathy, PML for short. Have you heard this term before?"

I let out a gasp. This was what Jay feared—I can't believe it.

Richard jumps in, "This is what his doctors feared. They all were worried about being in prison without a functioning immune system. Everyone knew our father was at risk for it."

"Well, the autopsy findings are pathognomonic of PML. There are nuclear inclusions, severe demyelination, swollen oligodendroglias, perivascular leukocyte infiltrates of CD8 cells, presence of JC virus DNA, virtually every sign of PML. Apparently, the virus overwhelmed him because it was all throughout his brain, probably as bad a case as we've seen." Dr. Patel takes a sip of water.

"He also had cryptococcal meningitis, a fungal infection that falls under the category of an opportunistic infection which is common in someone whose immune system is damaged. Lastly, his kidneys and liver shut down from the high fevers he was running combined with a lack of fluids. He was extremely dehydrated, which I have to say in this day and age, in a hospital setting, is very unusual. We understand he was in a prison hospital, a federal medical center?"

Spewing venom, Richard says, "In name only. Why didn't they transfer him to the hospital?"

"That's a good question which I don't have an answer for. I'm a pathologist. I answer why someone dies. What I can tell you is that dehydration should never happen in a hospital setting."

It's the first time we unequivocally know that negligence killed Jay. For weeks everyone reserved judgement. Now we know.

The pathologist goes on about a bunch of other findings. It all confirms Jay was immunodeficient, had MS, was neglected when he got sick, and that's why he died. Richard and Sara can't hold back their tears. My head drops as I labor to take a few deep breaths. Richard is mumbling and cursing, out of control. We nicknamed him Sonny Corleone because he's the hot head in the family. Sara is ostensibly more in control, but her face is filled with rage. She bows her head and cries some more. How much more can we take?

Sara whispers to me, "Now I know why you were so fearful when the pathology department left the voicemail. You were afraid of hearing this."

I could have accepted a heart attack, a stroke, cancer, a blood clot, a burst aneurysm, all things that happen to people as they get older. It would have still been painful. But now I know Jay got sick, thrown in the SHU, and left to die.

With Dr. Patel's presentation concluded, we all shake hands while thanking her for her efforts and honesty. Then she and her staff exit the room, leaving the three us of sitting there shell-shocked.

Sara reaches out for my hand. "He was never treated, not even with basic IV fluids. Zoo animals in the crappiest zoo in America would have gotten better care. How the hell does that happen in this day and age?"

I take a few long deep breaths, close my eyes, and gaze upward at the ceiling. I stay in this position for a long time while trying to control my sniffling. Finally, I gain my composure and stare at my children with my tear-filled eyes, and shake my head as my lips purse tighter.

"Dehydration in a 'medical center'? How is that even possible?" After a few moments of rubbing the skin of my temples, I stand up abruptly and announce, "I have to use the bathroom."

"You gonna be okay, Mom? Want me to come with you?" asks Sara.

"Thanks, sweetie, I'll be okay. When will this *ever* end?"

***

Later that night, I need to write another letter.

Dearest Jay,

There is so much I need to tell you. The autopsy proved you died from PML, cryptococcal meningitis, and get this, dehydration. Everyone was warned about the risk, but no one cared. All they cared about was putting another notch on their conviction belt.

When I got home tonight, I pulled up the letters Dana had written a few years ago. He wrote, "As for determination as to where to place him, there simply are no good options. Anything other than home confinement carries serious exposure risks. The potential for a life-threatening infection or irreversible progression of his MS far exceeds the intended punishment. As with the JC virus, constant monitoring and immediate specialized intervention are absolutely essential in treating patients like Dr. Keller." Why didn't our government give you the immediate specialized treatment you needed? They promised us you would be cared for.

Knowing what killed you, and how painful those last few days were for you, has been haunting me. I can't get the image out of my head of you begging for help and no one answering. You lived your life with such honor and dignity. Your death was so inhumane. I feel as if I let you down, not being there for you in those final hours. You must have been so thirsty, but no one was there to give you a glass of water. Jay, this is the pain that I fear will never leave me.

Whenever I drive my car or ride the train, I ruminate on a different thought. What evidence did the feds have and where did they get that evidence? I muse on what we could have done differently, yet I know it's pure folly because I can't change the past. Over and over I hear the false words of the slovenly prosecutor at sentencing. The prosecutor looked right into your eyes before telling the packed courtroom, "Jay Keller, a spoke in the wheel of a giant conspiracy, sold the blood of his patients for profit." Those words, Jay, spoken so sanctimoniously by a shamelessly mendacious prosecutor, still haunt me.

Several weeks ago, I didn't have the strength or will to get dressed or make my bed. I want you to be the first to know that after today's autopsy report, I must pursue a wrongful death suit. How much fight is left in me? Enough to sue the federal government? Today, my answer is an unequivocal yes. Just in case my reserves run low, I have the full backing of our children. We will start our search for firms who have the needed expertise. Sara said you left us a magnificent Michelin roadmap in your letters. Who knew a millennial like Sara knew what a Michelin roadmap was?

Like you, we will be strong, tenacious, and resolute in bringing a suit against your captors. We thank you for your masterful job of documenting what went on in FMC Franklin. Honey, learning the autopsy result has been hard to swallow, yet in an odd way, it has given me the conviction that used to be such a part of me. Less time wallowing in self-despair. More time pursing goals.

I yearn for peace. Oh, how I wish I could hold you in my arms!

I love you forever,

Lily
P.S. The deer are taking over the garden without your vigilant spraying.

CHAPTER 42

Quicksand

Three days later, I leave work an hour early. Sara has two surprises for me. The first is getting tickets to the Museum of Modern of Art. There is a special Matisse exhibit that is closing in a week and Sara knew I wanted to see it. An even bigger surprise is convincing Richard to join us. We all meet outside the subway station on Fifty-Third and Fifth. I marvel and envy the resiliency of youth.

"How exciting," I say as we huddle together, protecting ourselves from the northern winter winds. I toss my empty coffee cup into the trash can and turn toward the museum. "I've been wanting to go for a while. I can't believe you convinced Richard to join—a minor miracle," I say with a chuckle.

"I'm taking one for the team, Mom," quips Richard.

Henri Matisse is one of my favorite artists. His pictures are not complicated nor encumbered by the minutiae of subject matter or technique. He expresses freedom and movement in the simplicity of his lines and forms. I feel optimism and joy in his use of colors and shapes.

Sara hands out tickets and we enter the museum atrium. It's been so long since I've been here. Lots of renovations. Flashbacks of coming here with Jay swirl through my mind. I feel a bit overwhelmed which my children pick up on. Richard's also compelled to remind me what wonderful children I have as we wait in front of the large bank of elevators.

"Before we start the exhibit, I just want to say one thing. I want you both to know we are pursuing a wrongful death case."

"Of course we are," says Sara.

"Mom, I'm like one of those guys at the poker table," Richard says as I flash him a confused look. "You know, the guys in the poker tournaments, wearing sunglasses and backwards baseball hats, when they suddenly stand up from the table and move all their chips to the center of the table because they're *all in*. Well, that's us, Mom. We're *all in* for you. Whatever you need, we're here for you."

Sara rolls her eyes. "Do you really think Mom sits at home watching those morons on ESPN play poker?"

"I think I get the picture," I chime in with a smirk. "Let's have some fun this evening. For a few hours, let's not think about the justice system."

We spend the next two hours walking through the Matisse exhibit. During our time together, my children share their struggles at work, what's up with their friends, love interests, roommates, sports, upcoming ballets, you name it. Listening to their voices puts me at ease because *that*'s what moms do best. Just listen.

As we meander through the random permanent exhibits, Richard ducks into the bathroom. Sara and I sit on a bench in a room full of large bronze sculptures in the center and paintings on the walls. I remain seated while Sara inspects a few Heinrich Steiner paintings more closely.

When Richard returns, he and Sara notice my demeanor has suddenly changed. They sit down next to me. "How often did you and Dad visit museums?" asks Richard.

I'm staring at the distant wall, lost in my own thoughts. I'm thinking back to when I dropped Jay off to self-surrender. I can still see his labored gait as he made his way to the entrance. There was nothing I could do.

"Mom, are you okay?" Sara asks.

My breath becomes shallower and more rapid. "I never told either of you about the last attorney meeting I went to with your dad. I know our intent isn't to talk about legal stuff tonight, but I have to get this off my chest. I probably should have told you about this meeting a long time ago, the Saturday morning when our lawyers told us that your father was going to 'hang.'"

Richard clenches his jaw. "Mom, who used the word 'hang'?"

"Conklin." I pause a moment to gather my thoughts and composure about the day. I remember every detail of that day. "Your father and I parked the car and were walking to the office of Andrew Marconi, and I asked him if he knew why the attorneys insisted on a Saturday meeting."

Sara chimes in, "Was this the first time you met on a Saturday?"

"First and last time. Your father was relaxed. He knew Conklin spoke with the feds for an hour the day before and was hoping he convinced them that Dad didn't know anything. They'd finally be off his back. We were so naïve."

Looking off in the distance, and speaking to no one in particular, I start my catharsis.

"Conklin started by telling Dad he quit working for the US Attorney's office because they were a bunch of heartless pricks. Then, we learned we were screwed. Conklin told us the feds rescinded the signed 5K letter meaning your father was of no use to them. We—"

Sara interrupts me. "What's a 5K letter?"

"A 5K letter is a "get out of jail free" card," says Richard.

"It means you have information that will help the feds convict someone else and in exchange, lessen your sentence," I state. "When Dad sold his practice, the new owners installed a different lab. Turns out Dad discovered that the new lab was doing illegal stuff too, and on as big a scale. Our attorneys notified the feds that a federal crime was committed. They were all hot to trot until they had a change of heart, for who knows why. It just goes to show how the feds have the power to pick and choose who they'll prosecute and walks away. Anyway, the feds also said they had a sworn affidavit. Conklin didn't know if it was true or just a threat. The feds didn't say from whom, but they insinuated they had enough evidence to link Dad to the whole insurance scam. That he was a target and they were going to indict him on bank fraud, conspiracy, wire fraud, mail fraud, commercial bribery, etcetera."

I let out a long exhale while looking toward Sara and Richard.

"Conklin explained this was business as usual. The feds wouldn't have gone after your father and all the other doctors for receiving rental income if the lab didn't overbill. They had a dirty lab, and the feds could link a hundred doctors to this giant conspiracy, a new arrest every month, and now they were getting mileage out of the case. Dad got sucked into the quicksand. He started to lose it."

"What do mean he was losing it?" asked Sara.

"I remember him going off and asking Marconi and Conklin about the Pledge of Allegiance, 'What about those fucking words at the end of the Pledge of Allegiance, you know—with liberty and justice for all?' Marconi and Conklin offered no reply. They might as well have put a knife in his back."

To add insult to injury, Conklin told Jay, "You're a nobody. An internist in a quaint, little town, nice home, nice kids. Who gives a shit? He claimed he wasn't trying to demean Dad."

"Your father and I were speechless. I remember clenching my hands into fists. Dad excused himself and went to the bathroom. Later, in the car, he told me he'd thrown up. Conklin told us we had two options. The first option was for Dad to enter a guilty plea, take his lumps, and no charges would be filed against me."

Sara asks, "Mom, what did you have to do with any of this?"

"I was looking at jail time too. At that time, Dad's office manager left so I went in one or two days a week to do the HR stuff and deposit checks in the bank. Because I deposited the rental checks, they were going to charge me with the same bullshit as Dad: conspiracy, wire fraud, mail fraud, and I forget what else."

I hadn't thought about this meeting in years. It takes a few seconds for me to compose myself.

"Conklin told me I wouldn't be charged if Dad pleaded guilty, he would get his life back in a few years, and they go easier on people who accept a plea deal."

Sara puts her hand on my forearm.

"Our other option was to take it to trial and prove Jay's innocence. Those were the only choices we had. Everything else was off the table. Your father and I looked at each other in total disbelief. Conklin wanted to make sure we knew the price of going to trial. He told us he'd be happy to take our money if we chose the trial route and maybe we could win at trial, but there are a lot of statutes on the book that would have made it easy to win a conviction. There are too many laws that are simply unjust. There's one statute that says even if Dad had no knowledge or no intent to defraud, he was guilty if his actions led to someone else defrauding the government. We couldn't afford to take on the US government. Win or lose, we would be 100 percent broke by the end of the trial. We would have burned through all of our assets. If we won, and it could take years, his name would be cleared, but we would be flat broke, starting from zero. That was the best-case scenario. If we lost, we would still be broke, but Dad and I would both be in prison. That was never an option for him."

My eyes fill with tears.

"Dad's MS was the other factor. It was obvious to everyone that he wasn't healthy enough for a long and grueling trial. He was in terrible shape, couldn't tolerate the MS meds, lost about twenty-five pounds, one attack after another, and maybe more than anything, his brain was fried. He couldn't write a check correctly or drive a car. Conklin said they would portray Dad at trial as nothing but a rich, greedy doctor who cheated the system, that the feds could make Mother Teresa look like a crack whore. He told us it's nothing but culling herd to feed the system, a system's that's more self-serving, than serving its citizens. Thousands of people profit by making sure every jail cell in this country is full. So, Dad and I did what we thought was best."

As I finish my story, Richard and Sara are staring at me with their mouths wide open.

"Mom, I'm so sorry. I had no idea about so much of this," says a wounded Sara. In contrast, I feel relief. We sit silently for a minute until a guard comes by to tell us the museum is closing in ten minutes.

"Before we leave," I say, "there's still one more pebble in my shoe."

Sara and Richard look at me with confusion written all over their faces.

"Your father and I believed someone gave false testimony about him. I want to find out who."

"How would knowing that change anything?" Sara asks. "Don't start obsessing and making yourself crazy over this like you usually do."

"It's something that has always gnawed at me, and still does. I can't help it."

I can see the hesitation on Richard's face. "Mom, you sure you want to go down that rabbit hole? This isn't a pebble in your shoe, it's a frickin' boulder."

"That's why we have to talk about it."

"Okay, hire a private investigator," adds Richard. "Attorneys use PIs all the time. Give me a week and I'll have half a dozen names for you."

I ponder his idea before responding, "Not a bad idea, but I have enough bills to pay."

"How many times did you and Dad speculate about someone flipping?" Sara asks. "How many times did Dad write to us about how the whole criminal justice system is based on defendants telling the feds what they want to hear in order to lessen their own punishment?"

"Too many. The more we learned how many doctors were convicted, the more convinced we were of how overzealous the prosecutors were in order to make this into a much bigger case than it ever should have been."

As we continue in silence, maneuvering through the exiting patrons, my mind is still churning. I stop and turn to both my children.

"Oh, and one last thing, I promise. From now on, your father didn't die in prison, he was murdered. Are we clear?" I say.

"Very," says Sara.

"Crystal," quips Richard. Together, we enter the revolving glass doors and empty out into the crisp air and bustling noise of Fifty-Fourth street.

CHAPTER 43

Word Spreads

It's early Saturday morning with birds chirping, squirrels and chipmunks canvasing the backyard in search of endless treats, and the deer making their morning trek through the yard. Richard is in Philadelphia for a bachelor party. Sara is working in her lab all weekend. Just after nine, I slowly make my way down the staircase, still in my bathrobe, and sit at the kitchen table.

I take a few sips of coffee when my cell phone rings. Cynthia is calling to confirm that I am meeting her and Walter for dinner at her house tonight.

As I'm finishing my coffee, I see the mail truck and walk out to the mailbox. While walking back to the house thumbing through the mail, I notice a letter from the Department of Justice. My heart and stomach collide. Waiting until I'm at my kitchen table, I open the letter.

> Dear Mrs. Keller,
>
> In response to your appeal under the Compassionate Release Program, we are informing you that since Jay Keller is no longer in BOP custody, we consider his request for Compassionate Release closed.
>
> *In a million years, you couldn't make this shit up. Can they be any more callous?*

I spend the afternoon cleaning the garden from the winter storms, before devoting the late afternoon to paying bills. For the third month in a row, I have to transfer money from my dwindling savings account. I never share with

255

my children the precariousness of my financial situation. The last few years have taken their toll on us financially. Because of his MS, Jay wasn't working, but he did receive a little income from a disability policy. That ended when he died. I began to tap into our retirement funds, but that comes with penalties nor is it really enough to sustain me indefinitely. While I still have my own income, it's not enough to give me a positive cash flow. Financial strains only add to my stress and constant feeling of anxiety.

***

As word spreads within our village that we are going to pursue legal action, a barrage of suggestions starts gathering force like a summer thunderstorm. Everyone knows the best lawyer or best law firm to handle our case. I quickly understand we need a firm that specializes in medical negligence combined with the experience and gravitas to do battle with the federal government.

Early Saturday evening, I receive a call from Janice Kalter, a cousin of Jay's and a veteran Supreme Court Judge in New York City. Janice is older than me and Jay, and a bit closer to retirement. She and her husband always enjoy frequenting the New York City jazz clubs, so at least once a year they would join us for a night of music. She knows firsthand who are the best attorneys and the firms with the best results. She's heard through the family grapevine we're pursuing a case.

After an hour of phone chat, Janice's tone changes. "Do you have the stamina to initiate a lawsuit against the government?"

I tell her there's no way I'm going to let the BOP get away with another murder. Plus, Richard and Sara are full of piss and vinegar. If I wear down, I'm confident they'll pick up the slack. Janice offers to reach out to each of them which I know they would welcome.

"Do you realize you're ultimately going up against the federal government? I just want you to have realistic expectations," Janice says in a serious tone. "They have unlimited resources, and I don't just mean money. Your resources are limited regardless of the firm you choose."

"I know it's not a fair fight, but I don't care. His letter writing had a purpose—to tell the world what really goes on behind the barbed wire. I believe he left us a roadmap just in case of an eventual lawsuit and I'll do anything to make sure that what happened to Jay won't happen again."

Janice chuckles. "There's a saying: 'Justice is best served when both sides are equally well represented.' I've been on the bench for a long time and believe that to be true. But that's not what happens in the real world, and certainly not against the federal government. The team with the most resources usually wins. Just how it is."

I let out a sigh of disappointment while absorbing her words of wisdom and experience. Regardless of what she tells me, there's no way to let this go without a fight. That's not in my DNA. Janice continues.

"Lily, there are a few things you have to promise me you'll do. You must do the case on full contingency. Don't lay out your own money. No large retainer fee, okay? Legitimate law firms never take on cases they don't think they have a chance of winning. They have to be pretty sure of a handsome reward before investing their time and resources."

I'm taking down notes. I appreciate all of her advice, but it's overwhelming.

Janice continues, "During the interview process with the different firms, pay close attention to the level of enthusiasm. I want you to find an attorney who is as passionate about your case as you are. This is crucial. If you interview several firms and none of them want to take the case, what is your next step?"

"I'm not sure what you mean," I say.

"You call me immediately."

"Why?"

"Because I need to be there for you and Sara and Richard to help you walk away from the case, to let it go. Walking away is the hardest thing to do. You have to be able to walk away. Understood?"

I fight back tears. Doubt fills my brain.

CHAPTER 44
Translation Please

Maybe I was waiting for Jay to come home and he would read it to me. Perhaps an element of fear prevented me. The only thing that matters now is finally translating Jay's diary.

Joanne Scibetta is a local high school language teacher. She was born near Florence, Italy, and moved to America when she was five. Italian is her first language, but she also teaches French and Spanish. Her son played on soccer and Little League teams with Richard, and her daughter danced for years with Sara. Joanne and Jay would speak Italian as they watched the games. This was a treat for Jay since he rarely had the opportunity to speak Italian, a language he acquired as an adult.

The last time I had seen Joanne was when she was at our house for Shiva. I call to ask her if she'd be willing to translate Jay's diary, something my children asked me to do when Jay first started mailing page after page. I explain that in addition to his voluminous letters, he also kept a diary in Italian, in an effort to hide his words from the guards. Joanne is surprised, but delighted to hear from me. After I further explain why Jay's diary needs to be translated, she's only too happy to help. I scan all the papers and print them out before meeting Joanne at a Starbucks on a Saturday morning.

Three weeks later, Joanne calls and says she's finished translating Jay's diary. We decide to meet at a Starbucks for her to drop off the translation.

I arrive early and get a cappuccino. Ten minutes later, Joanne enters with a large bag slung over her shoulder. We embrace, she orders a coffee, and we find two seats near the window.

"Lily, what a story. I couldn't put it down once I started reading it. I must say, it was horrible what Jay had to endure. I had no idea, but then again, I never knew anyone who served time in prison."

"Neither did we. It was a shock for all of us."

Joanne reaches into her bag to take out the translation. "I took the liberty of making four spiral-bound copies: one for you and the kids, one for the attorneys, and a few thumb drives."

"Joanne, you shouldn't have. I have to pay you for all this. How much is it?"

"Don't even think of it. It's my gift to the Keller family. End of discussion," states a resolute Joanne. "Besides, you already paid me by letting me read Jay's personal writings."

I'm humbled. "Thank you so much. It means a lot to me and the kids. I'm assuming you got a firsthand view of life in prison, the doctors, the warden, guards, inmates, nurses, case workers, counselors, you name it. Systemic rot from the top to bottom. That's why we are going to file a wrongful death suit and not let the BOP get away with another murder."

"Oh, I just hope it helps your case. It was my privilege. Jay was such a good man. To think this was how he spent his final months—that this is how they treat sick prisoners in a federal medical center? I couldn't believe one doctor would actually inflict pain on another doctor just for the hell of it."

"Pain? What are you talking about?"

"You know, his prison doctor, Dr. Huff. Sounds like he should be the one in jail," replies Joanne.

I'm taken aback. Jay always complained about Huff, and it was clear they didn't like each other. "Jay never mentioned physical pain," I respond.

"It was during his first visit with Dr. Huff. Let me see if I can find that letter." Joanne thumbs through the pages until she finds the passage. What she reads next makes my body go numb:

> While pretending to examine me, Huff kept pressing his thumb into the top of my eye socket until the pain forced me to pull my head away by rolling off the exam table.

I'm stunned. I feel like I'm going to throw up.

Joanne senses my discomfort. "Are you okay, Lily?"

"I thought I was done with surprises, but it never ends," I say. I suspected Jay's diary would unearth terrible things, but I just pushed that aside. It's clear to me that this information will open wounds and create more. "Any other spoiler alerts I should know before I read your translation?"

"He was never beaten or anything like that. I will tell you one thing: Bruce dying really scared the hell out of him. His writings became more fearful after that debacle. It was the first time he realized getting out alive was not a foregone conclusion."

I pause a few seconds before blurting out a question I've kept inside for too long. "Did he ever mention suicide?"

"Sure, he thought about it. During the first few days, he realized the sprinkler pipes were strong enough to hang from, 'just in case.' He also kept a large plastic bag in his locker."

I let out the breath I was holding and remind myself to breathe.

"Lily, I loved Jay's descriptions of the inmates and the staff. I know he was fearful of many inmates, but seems like he was most fearful of the staff. Oh, I take that back. The murder in the Bus Stop freaked him out."

Joanne once again leaf's through the pages and finds the section. My eyes well up as I listen to Jay's words:

It's only three days since I moved out of the Bus Stop and transferred into Bruce Hellman's room. There was a murder there two nights after my departure. An old man named Gus, with six weeks left on his sentence, was constantly complaining to a group of inmates that they made too much noise all night long and they need to turn the lights out so he could sleep. He's referring to the young men who play cards and dominos at night on a table right by his bunk. They ignored him completely until the other night.

The old man had enough and turned the lights out. A few of the card players beat the shit out of him. The guards found Gus dead on the floor in a pool of blood when they did their three a.m. rounds. Within a few hours, the Bus Stop was swarming with COs. The FBI was called in the next day and they interviewed every inmate who lived in the Bus Stop. The Bus Stop was emptied by sending every Bus Stop inmate to the SHU. Now all you see is yellow police tape.

All thirty-one inmates were placed in the SHU. If this happened while I was still there, I'd be in the SHU and you'd be wondering why you haven't heard from me for weeks. The beating took place at a time when virtually every inmate was sleeping. No one witnessed it. After multiple interviews by the FBI and the prison lieutenants, each inmate had to sign a sworn statement that they witnessed a Black inmate as the one who beat up Gus. If they refused to sign the statement, they remained in the SHU indefinitely. The esteemed Department of Justice, the moral compass of American society, forced thirty-one men into signing false statements so they would have closure on a murder and proudly say they got their man. Around here, truth and justice are nothing but catchphrases. I have to get out of here.

I reach for a napkin to dry a few stray tears while suppressing a wave of nausea. "Jay never told me that story. Guess he knew it would have freaked me out." I stare aimlessly out the window before finally standing up to give Joanne a hug. "Thank you for all your hard work. I promise to let you know how it all turns out."

CHAPTER 45

Dad Unplugged

It's a chilly winter evening and I'm curled up on the couch with Jay's diary. I've gathered enough strength to read Joanne's translation. The wind courses through the room, blowing the curtains. Goosebumps dot my legs and arms, but I'm not sure if it's from the air or the diary.

I flip to his first encounter with Dr. Huff, and as much as I don't want to read it, my eyes can't pull away.

> Huff had no intention of doing a physical on me. The physical exam lasted only twenty seconds and consisted of a few breaths and listening to a few heart beats. He told me, "In here you're not a doctor, you're nothing, just another inmate that fucked up in life."
>
> What I never expected was when Huff placed his thumb under my right eyebrow and exerted more and more pressure until I had to quickly pull my head back and roll off the exam table to get away from the pressure and pain. Huff just looked at me with a big smile and said, "Oh, was that hurting you? I'm sorry, Mr. Keller." His evil smile immediately transformed into a scowl. "You think that was painful? That was just a sample of what you'll experience if you try to make any trouble for me, or anyone else up here in Medical. Having doctor inmates as patients is about as welcome as a turd in a punch bowl. Here's my prognosis. If you don't give us any shit then maybe, just maybe, you'll walk out of here when your sentence is over. Nod your head if you understand every word I just said, you goddamn New York piece of shit. Now get the fuck out of my office."

I clench my jaw tighter and tighter. *Breathe in, hold for five seconds, breathe out.*

I'm trying to calm down and focus on my breathing, just as my psychotherapist told me to do. I've been seeing Dr. Dannert once a week for the last six months, and it's been helpful. Being a widow is new territory for me, and I'm not sure how to navigate it. It helps having a neutral experienced professional guide me and tell me that my feelings, moods, and sadness are all normal. Friends and family all mean well, but they're not neutral. Plus, I can vent to her all I want.

Sleeping is still hard for me, but I have noticed I'm becoming less dependent on medications. I fall asleep easier. Staying asleep is more problematic. Residual PTSD I suppose.

I turn back to the diary. It isn't what I expected. I was expecting venom to be spewing on every page. Turns out, it's entertaining—most of the time. Joanne warned me about the one story with Huff, but I just love listening to Jay describe, editorialize, and pontificate on the entire prison-industrial complex, how it's all so wrong.

Jay's anger in those early days leaps off the page. He was shell-shocked by the prison experience. Murderers, or the guy who had a ninety-day sentence for fishing in a lake owned by the Federal government—they're all treated the same. I could hear his acceptance of what happened to him as time went on. His acquiescence seemed to coincide with his gradually improving mental clarity.

How many nights did I stay awake fearing he was beaten, stabbed, or raped, but there's nothing in the diary to indicate any of that happened to him, and for that I'm grateful. I have nightmares of Jay suffering, of being alone and cold and sick in a dark cell. I know why Jay initially wrote in Italian, so he could slip his inner thoughts past the mail guards. But as time went, I think the real reason was because he liked writing in Italian. It was another mental escape from that awful place, like his music and yoga. I instead escaped my reality by drowning myself in *Downton Abbey* and other British dramas, accepted every social invitation that came my way, or passed hours on end working in my studio.

I come upon one entry I had to read twice.

The doctor was treating a patient on the next stretcher when he was called out of the treatment room for something urgent. As the doctor ran out, his stethoscope fell to the floor. I picked it up, put it to my ears, and listened to my own heartbeat. It felt so good to use a stethoscope, as I have done so many times in my career. But here's the thing. The stethoscope was broken. I couldn't hear a thing with it. He was carrying around a stethoscope only for show. I flip to the next entry.

I'm sitting next to a man in a jam-packed waiting room who was ranting and raving to another inmate. Apparently, two years earlier he had a hip replacement. For two years he was complaining to the medical staff of worsening pain in his repaired hip. It was finally discovered after an open surgical exploration that a sponge was left in his hip until its removal one week ago. For two years, no one in Medical bothered to find out why he was in so much pain. Instead, he was reprimanded for constantly complaining. As tempting as it was to learn more details of the medical negligence, I decided not to engage this inmate. With the cornucopia of swastikas and other Nazi insignia tattoos, I returned to reading my book. If I don't write out these stories, there's no way I'm going to recall all the zaniness I'm witness to every day.

My children have named Jay's diary *Dad Unplugged* as he described details of inmates, from Dwight Gooden's cocaine dealer, to Vinny Gallardo, to the Native American inmates who tell Jay how they've been fighting terrorism since 1492. I read Jay's description of his first haircut.

After almost two months in prison, I need a haircut. The prison has a barbershop, which is run by inmates. I waited from 12:30 until the 3:30 recall. The barbers cut everyone's hair except mine. That gave me three hours to survey the barbershop. The chair I sat in was torn plastic held together with duct tape. The barbers use the same combs and trimming devices on all the inmates without an attempt at sterilizing anything. Combs fall on the floor but are picked up and reused without cleaning.

Maybe they think I'm a cho-mo, maybe it's a racial thing, but they won't cut my hair. I go back to my room, take my mustache scissors, and cut off my hair while looking in the dim mirror. I feel like Fantine from *Les Misérables* who cut her own hair to earn money to feed her child.

Come to think of it, there's another *Les Misérables* analogy. Jean Valjean served twenty years in prison for stealing a loaf of bread yet a prison guard, Javert, continued to punish Jean Valjean long after Jean Valjean was a free man. Twenty years wasn't enough punishment. I don't know what life will be like for me once I'm released, but I hear horror stories from other inmates how carrying the stigma of a criminal conviction in America follows you for the rest of your life. I hope it's hyperbole, but I hear the same theme from one inmate after another. They say I'll be released from prison but won't be able to find a job, get a credit card, or open a bank account. All for a crime I was unaware was a crime.

I leave the diary on the couch but the stories continue to swirl in my head. I pour a glass of Pelligrino, turn the lights out, and head up to bed. After an hour of my favorite British detective show, I open my iPad to read a novel but the monkeys in my brain would rather dance. Instead of wrestling with my agitation, I write.

Dear Jay,

A week ago, I met with Joanne Scibetta who was kind enough to translate your diary. What I now understand is how you sheltered me from much of the fear you lived with. At first, I was angry you didn't tell me everything, but I guess you figured I had enough to deal with. You were right.

You devoted many words to your survival tactics, reaching deep down to find the strength and conviction to survive *Dante's Inferno*. Writing helped you make sense of the insanity.

Let me tell you how your diary has helped me. From day one, everyone who is part of our village wanted revenge, no one more than me. I was fearful of going down that road, but little by little,

I'm convinced it's the right thing to do. Your diary has not only given me confirmation to pursue justice against the BOP at all costs, but it has made clear why I must hold Huff accountable.

Thank you, Jay. I love you.

Lily

CHAPTER 46

Sense of Fulfillment

Ten months after Jay's death, I appreciate how differently my children support my ever-changing state of mind. Sara's support is unconditional. Richard's sentiments are more testosterone driven. He is a champion of the "snap out of it" school of psychotherapy. But I have noticed it's becoming easier for me to remember moments of laughter from the past, the joy of watching our children grow up, family gatherings, dinners with friends, and the sharing of countless moments with my loving husband. I remain very conscientious about keeping my weekly appointments with Dr. Dannert and writing letters to Jay at her suggestion. Not every psychotherapy session is productive nor life-changing. In fact, most are not. Sometimes what Dr. Dannert suggests doesn't sink in until months later.

Recently, I've gotten involved in the Fortune Society, an organization based in Queens, New York. The wife of an inmate at FMC Franklin, Martina Havel, lives in Rochester, New York. She and I will occasionally be in contact through email. Via our husband's introductions, it's common for spouses to be in contact with each other. Martina is going to be coming to New York to visit an elderly, ailing aunt. While in New York, she plans to attend an event at the Fortune Society and wanted to know if I'd be interested in joining her. With a bit of curiosity about meeting another "prison wife," we set a time and place to meet and attend the event together. It's a beautiful July afternoon.

The mission of the Fortune Society is to promote successful reentry from incarceration and foster alternatives to prevent recidivism. I went online a few times to learn all I could about the organization, but it wasn't until I attended the seminar that it all made sense.

The lecture about post-incarceration obstacles reminded me of what Jay often wrote about, the obstacles inmates will have to face once they are released, including himself. It's an uphill battle to find a job or housing. It's even more daunting if you have no particular job skills, and only minimal command of basic math or English. As if those aren't enough obstacles, banks refuse to open accounts or give credit cards, and getting a loan for anything is impossible as long as you carry around the stigma of a convicted felon. It's as if the letter "F" is tattooed on one's forehead. *This* is the price of a conviction in America. It doesn't matter if one has paid his or her debt to society. The punishment is never-ending.

After the lecture, I register to volunteer for the Fortune Society. As the months roll along, I begin to conduct mock job interviews, work on résumés, and tutor ex-inmates in English and math. Many of the men and women, for one reason or another, have never learned basic life skills. Everyone is so excited and grateful of my support. Whenever an ex-inmate asks why I volunteer my time to the Fortune Society, I tell them what happened to my husband. That's all I need to be given instant "street cred."

Dear Jay,

It has come to me slowly but I'm finally emerging out of my cocoon. Honey, now I understand why you kept writing about the incalculable cost of convictions on all of American society. Fixing a tiny element of the criminal justice system gives me a sense of fulfilment that I have not felt since being a full-time mom. Helping those in society who need the most help gives me purpose. I volunteer a few hours a week at the Fortune Society and it literally has changed my life. On top of that, I'm good at it. At first, I was palpably uneasy around ex-inmates. That changed quickly. It has become easier and easier to connect with everyone I work with.

My favorite student is a woman in her thirties named Tanya who maintains a perpetual smile. She finished a seven-year sentence for drugs and offers incredible social insight. With minimal job opportunities despite completing high school, she turned to drugs, a decision she laments to this day. I knew how horrible the living conditions were for you, but a woman's prison seems just as bad. She described in graphic detail, in addition to the daily violence, how one woman took her used tampon and smeared the walls and bathroom mirrors with her blood, writing the words, "Death to the Warden." The commissary suddenly had all feminine hygiene products backordered for over two months. My tiniest act of kindness brought this woman to tears—I gave her a birthday card. She strives to be trained for a real job so she can afford her own apartment. She lives on her grandmother's couch because her felony conviction excludes her from any federally funded housing. She served her time, is making amends, but archaic laws set her up for failure.

I remember you talking about the bank robber who led a normal life until he started hearing voices, but once he received the proper medication, he was the nicest and most normal guy in Antioch Unit. I've now met some whose criminal acts were 100 percent a function of their mental illness. Now that they're treated and have the ability to be productive citizens, ex-inmates are still thwarted because they carry the indelible stigma of a criminal conviction during this era of mass incarceration and over-criminalization. There are so many obstacles for anyone with a conviction that a good part of my time is helping them deal with the enormous feeling of despair. The system should be helping these people succeed, not putting up more roadblocks and insuring they fail.

Jay, I never thought I would write this, but there are days when I truly shine.

All my love,

Lily

CHAPTER 47
Choosing the One

Our first meeting is with the firm of Gardner and Dunham on Madison Avenue and Sixtieth. Five weeks would pass before our meeting with the second firm, the earliest we could coordinate schedules. The second law firm of Cope, Clark, McKenzie is in Midtown, Forty-Third and Lexington. We meet in the lobby, show our ID, and head up to the fifty-first floor.

Nine days later, we were doing it all over again, a four o'clock meeting at Fifty-Seventh and Seventh, the Sotloff Turner firm.

We're feeling more relaxed having appreciated that both firms we have met with so far have preliminary interest in taking on our case. As we enter the offices of Sotloff Turner, I watch my son, who's dressed in a beautiful suit and tie, interact with the receptionist. This time he walks up to the receptionist and instead of saying he's Richard Keller for an appointment with so and so, he asks the receptionist for an espresso and two coffees, milk only, and heads for a seat.

"Of course," says the receptionist. "But who are you here to see?"

"Sara, Richard, and Lily Keller for Joe Linnard," Sara pipes in as she rolls her eyes at her brother. The receptionist returns a minute later with Richard's coffee order.

I track three attorneys leaving the office, all wearing the stereotypical lawyer wardrobe of suspenders, cufflinks, white collared shirts, and coiffed hair. I watch Sara scan the artwork on the walls. She looks back at me with a self-assured smirk. I know exactly what she's thinking.

"Be respectful," I say with an exaggerated smile. It feels good to be light in these types of moments. "Not everyone knows the difference between Picasso and Pissarro."

We sit in the oversized seats and wait. Sara says, "I've been reading many of Dad's letters—not all, but a lot. I never realized how dangerous that place was, how many guys died there—"

"You okay, Sara?" Richard asks.

Sara takes a deep breath. "Fine, but there are times—sometimes the most unpredictable of times—when I can't control myself and the tears just come out. I might be crossing a street in Midtown, thinking about who knows what, and boom, it hits me, and an outpouring of tears are streaming down my cheeks."

"You're not alone," confesses Richard. "It happens to me, too, at the strangest times and with no warning."

Ten minutes later, Joe Linnard comes to the reception area to introduce himself. He looks to be in his mid-sixties, wears a tie loosely around his neck, no jacket, and the sleeves of his solid light blue shirt are rolled up. His thick wavy white hair is swept back. "Joe Linnard. Nice to meet all of you. Follow me. We can meet in my office since we're a small group." After we all get settled, the meeting begins.

"My father being sentenced to prison was a travesty of justice," Richard says. "Let's leave it at that, because the only thing that matters now is what happened after he was sentenced. The case will focus on his time in prison, what care needed to be delivered, and what care we believe was not delivered."

We show Joe eleven letters from experts written before Jay was incarcerated, plus the one letter from the BOP hired expert, the immunologist from WVU. All twelve doctors stated their objective arguments against incarceration. We hand Joe the autopsy results along with a few other documents which he scans quickly.

"I see your husband filed a BP-9, 10 and 11," Joe says.

"He had the time for it," states Richard.

"What's a BP?" asks Sara.

"A BP is an administrative appeal," replies Joe. "Your father was asking for home confinement rather than prison because of his medical conditions. It's a good thing he filed even though they were all denied."

"Why?" asks Sara.

"Your father probably knew the BOP would have had immunity from future lawsuits if the BPs weren't properly filed on time. It's just one of the many shields they employ."

Joe thumbs through some papers and is quiet for a moment. I feel nervous for some reason, like this is a mistake, but then I remind myself of why I'm doing this. "Excuse me. I'll be right back," Joe says. "I'd like one of my associates to join us." He makes a quick exit.

"I'm impressed," Sara says. "And let the record show I love that Joe isn't wearing cufflinks and suspenders. You have to promise never to dress like that Richard."

"Me? Come on, I'm way too cool for that look."

Joe returns with his associate, makes the necessary introductions, and the meeting continues. By the end, Richard outlines, with me and Sara adding facts here and there, the problems with Jay's incarceration, what transpired, and our theory of how and why Jay died.

"Nice presentation, Richard. I predict a long and prosperous career for you," Joe says with a sincere smile.

"Thank you, sir."

"I don't think I could have presented such a concise argument when I was your age. You were schooled well." Joe turns to Sara and me. "My sympathy is with all of you and your entire family. You've withstood a lot."

Joe moves the papers in front of him to the side and leans forward. "I understand you're going to other firms, as you should. Your decision should be based on whom you feel comfortable with and whom you trust. Let me tell you why this case interests *me*."

Joe doesn't say anything for a moment as he gathers his thoughts, and I feel like my heart is going to beat out of my chest. He cracks open a small bottle of water in front of him and takes a swig.

"I was in high school at the time when my mother's brother, Uncle Bob, was sent to a federal prison on charges of conspiracy to commit bank fraud. Something happened while he was in prison and he died. No one ever really knew what happened but everyone had their suspicions. That was my introduction into the abuses inherent in our criminal justice system and specifically the BOP. I came by it honestly, and that is what I've spent much of my legal career doing."

"Can you help us?" I ask while catching my breath.

Joe reminds us the devil is in the details so he will have someone look through the thumb drives in more detail, conference on it, and get back to us.

The meeting ends. We say our goodbyes and head off to dinner. I'm quiet as we navigate the busy streets of New York, trying to process everything Joe said, Janice said, and what this will entail. I like Joe's persona, and I know Jay would have liked him. He's someone you want on your side.

We arrive at a cozy Manhattan restaurant and are seated at a cramped table near the window. A waitress brings over drinks and takes our order. We hash through the pros and cons of all three firms. Richard and Sara confess they've never hired anyone beyond just a simple moving company, but they both remember what Jay always preached— *No one cares how much you know, until they know how much you care.* It warms me to know they listened to their father's words. I can't remember how he came up with that saying, but he said it often.

"And Joe Linnard was one of the two firms Janice recommended," adds Sara. "This meeting had a whole different feel to it."

"So if Joe Linnard's firm does this on full contingency, is this who we go with?" asks Richard.

"I think, for our case, he's the one," says Sara. "What do you think, Mom?"

"I'd be very comfortable with him representing us. I loved his passion."

We enjoy our dinner, and for the first time in a while, it feels like old times. But there is that underlying sadness, especially with Sara. When she talks about her father, her eyes get a tinge of sadness to them. She's been far more interested than Richard in reading Jay's letters. Though she's never said a word to me, I think she's disappointed I didn't share more of the letters with her.

***

Within two months we learn all three law firms are willing to take the case on contingency.

We arrange another meeting to sign the retainer and contingency agreements with Joe Linnard of Sotloff Turner. An enthusiastic Joe Linnard outlines what the case will look like, how it would progress, how long it could last, what he'll need from us, how often we'd be meeting, etc. Although he knew I had been through the mill when it came to legal cases, he reminded all of us how litigation takes on a life of its own.

Joe goes out of his way to prepare us for a bumpy road. A settlement before a trial would be a best-case scenario, but that would only happen if there was compelling evidence for the government to do so. Joe tells us a lengthy trial is a more likely scenario.

Preliminaries out of the way, Joe introduces the other attorneys and administrative staff who will be working on our case, all under his lead. The attorneys ranged in age from late twenties to early seventies, all with varying expertise. We also meet Dr. Geraint James who works part-time for Sotloff Turner as a medical expert after he retired as the Chief of Medicine from Cornell. When all the introductions are out of the way, Joe, now alone again with us, summarizes it all.

"Listen, here's what I think happened. Your father never should have been incarcerated. He was a non-violent first-time offender where home detention would have served the same purpose as incarceration, especially in view of his rare combination of MS and a damaged immune system. That's just common sense, but the DOJ is always under pressure, internally and externally, to incarcerate. Put everyone in prison. That's just what they do."

I'm holding back tears, but I'm grateful that we have found our ally. I'm sitting here in this room, surrounded by my children, as we all seek justice for Jay. An overwhelming feeling of calm washes over me. "I want justice for my husband," I say. "I don't want anyone to have to go through what we've gone through."

Joe smiles. "Lily, me and my team will do everything in our power. Your husband had the misfortune of being sent to a shitty prison in West Virginia, where I suspect bad physicians providing poor medical care was the accepted norm. When he got sick, no one read his medical records to even know about the possibility of PML, so they threw him in the SHU instead of sending him to a hospital. Without the needed medical attention, he dies of dehydration, a raging viral infection, and an opportunistic fungal infection. That's what I think. That's probably close to what you think happened. My job is to convince a jury that is in fact what happened. The jury must be certain why a wife lost her husband, and two children lost their father. Plain and simple negligence."

And there is it, all laid out for me.

Within three weeks, we fire the first shot. The opening salvo in any legal action is the filing of a complaint by the plaintiff. Sotloff Turner emailed me, Richard, and Sara a copy of the complaint. It's the first time we see the words: "*The Estate of Jay Keller v. Federal Bureau of Prisons and John Doe 1-10.*" Just seeing the word "federal," I'm reminded of the tale of David and Goliath, with the Keller family attempting to take down Goliath. For the last few years since we first learned of the case against Jay, we lived witness to the unbridled power and wrath of the federal government. Now it's our turn to exert some pressure. In many ways, exerting pressure on the federal government is an oxymoron. How can you exert pressure on the world's most powerful government? I know *we* can't, but that's exactly why we hired Sotloff Turner, hoping their expertise can find a tiny crack in the government's armor. I know this whole suit is a long shot, but Richard and Sara keep reminding me that three of the largest and most powerful law firms in New York think otherwise.

CHAPTER 48

Tying the Knot

Weeks go by while Joe Linnard and his team continue their quest for information pertinent to our lawsuit. I had forgotten how slowly the wheels of justice turn. Meanwhile, I've decided to dive headfirst into my volunteer work, which is a big factor in keeping me balanced these days.

Without a bit of traffic, I pull into the parking lot of the Fortune Society twenty minutes early. In years past, I would have been in my sculpture studio or garden rather than spending my morning in an industrial part of Queens, in a non-descript building a few feet away from an elevated train. For months, I have spent my Saturday's coaching, tutoring, and mentoring those who society has given up on. I'm working with men and women Jay described in such detail, most of them who started life with two-and-a-half strikes against them. A good chunk of their education came from surviving on the streets.

After logging in and saying hello to a few friendly faces, I sit at a table in an open lounge as I prepare for my mock interview sessions. I'm approached by a man with a visible limp. He looks to be about sixty. He has kind eyes, but I can tell he's been through quite a bit.

"Hi there, may I have a seat?" he asks.

"Sure, make yourself comfortable."

He labors to sit down opposite me and smiles. He seems nervous. "I'm Dan," he says, extending his hand. We shake. "You're Mrs. Keller, right?"

"Why yes, have we met before?"

"No, but it's a small community. I've seen you around and asked someone your name. You're Jay Keller's wife?"

"Yes."

"I knew Jay from FMC Franklin."

I wasn't prepared for that answer but felt an immediate connection to this beat-up stranger in front of me.

Dan proceeds to tell me how he was transferred from a prison in Tennessee to FMC Franklin for a much-needed hip replacement. He was serving a seventeen-year sentence for falsifying the financial statements of his hedge fund; seven of those months were spent in Franklin. The first time he met Jay was when Jay played a Sunday night concert with The Convictions. Once Dan learned he could make an appointment to review his medical records with Jay, he and Jay became friends.

"He was the only bright spot in a pretty dilapidated prison. I used to meet him in indoor rec where he knew there were no cameras and wouldn't get busted by Dr. Huff."

"Don't talk about Huff—Jay's nemesis and his executioner. Guess you heard he got a bad infection and Huff left him in the SHU to die."

"Our co-workers here told me what happened to Jay. I can't tell you how sorry I am. Jay was a good man. I got lucky with my hip, no complications or anything, but believe me, that place was more fraudulent than my 'altered' financials."

We talk for fifteen minutes. It's hard to describe the bond I have with other people who have been touched by the criminal justice system. I never met Dan before this morning, but none of that matters. Perhaps "war buddies" have the same immediate bond as I have with people touched by the hands of justice. I could have listened to him speak about Jay all morning but I had to start my mock interviews. We stand up and give each other a heartfelt hug.

One of the first men I started tutoring was Tariq Johnson, a thirty-three-year-old Black man from New York City. At twenty, he was busted selling $5 vials of crack within one thousand feet of a school. The public defender worked out a plea deal for him. Instead of facing a mandatory minimum sentence of twenty-five to thirty years, Tariq spent twelve years in a state penitentiary. Tariq may be covered in mental and physical scars from years of institutional abuse, but deep down, he is a bright man who earned a GED in prison and is searching for an alternative to selling drugs on a street corner. He comes to the Fortune Society every day, yearning for a better life. I noticed right away how math came easier to him than to either of my two children. He struggles with English but is determined to study and practice all the communication tools I share with him.

When I first met Tariq, he was a janitor at a large department store in Manhattan. Six months after I started working with Tariq, he was promoted to a mailroom clerk.

As we sit in the classroom, I encourage him. "You're missing the point, Tariq. An entry level job means just that: a starting point. Now you're a mailroom clerk. When you perform your job well, you get promoted, get a pay raise, and eventually have better opportunities."

"Ain't never gotten past an entry-level job," replies Tariq.

"That's what we're working on. With your capacity for math, I think you can go way past entry-level jobs but you have to start somewhere. What are the three things we've talked about that will get you to the next level?" I ask.

Tariq speaks slowly and pensively. "One: I have to be reliable. Two: Do the work. Three: Take initiative."

"You do those three things and you'll be rewarded. That's a promise."

"I hope so, Mrs. K."

Two weeks later, he arrives with a bounce to his step. "Did I tell you the store just posted a data entry clerk job?"

"Excellent. Let me see the job description." Tariq retrieves the job description from his cell phone. "Then today, we're going to work on your résumé."

"I've been in prison for the last twelve years. Do I put that on my résumé?"

"We have to be honest, but we can still make you look good." I write a few things on a yellow notepad. Tariq tells me that the first three years in prison he worked in food service. Then he worked as a clerk in the library for about four years. In the last five years, he worked in accounting helping with accounts payable.

"My husband told me that most inmates switch jobs all the time, sometimes every few weeks. You only had three jobs, which tells me you're reliable. Let's see what we can do with all that."

After an hour, I transfer all my notes to the computer and finally show Tariq his freshly printed résumé. His face lights up. "Wow. I've never seen my résumé before."

Half an hour later, Tariq is reading the cover letter that just came out of the printer.

"Wow. Is this really me?"

"Sure is. The next step is to fill out the application and send it in with your cover letter and résumé. If all goes right, you should get an interview in a week or two. We'll work on interviews next week. Don't forget the proper handshake we talked about a few weeks ago."

"Thanks, Mrs. K., I appreciate it," he says.

My heart swells with gratitude that I've been able to help Tariq. "One more thing." I reach into my purse and hand him a bag. Tariq opens it and looks surprised. "Here are some of my husband's ties. Even in the mailroom, you can still wear a tie. People will notice."

Tariq looks down at the floor. "I don't know how to tie the knot."

A few online tutorials and twenty minutes later, Tariq proudly ties his first tie. He looks into my small makeup mirror. "Damn, that's one handsome guy. This has been a good day, Mrs. K. Never had a teacher like you my whole life."

"Tariq, you're a wonderful young man with a lot of potential. It's my pleasure to spend this time with you. I truly believe you're going to succeed," I say with sincerity. "One more thing, are you free this Wednesday evening?"

"Other than torturing myself watching a Knicks game on TV, yeah. Why?"

"Wednesday evenings is when I meet my son and daughter at a restaurant. I'd love for you to join us. Let's see if they recognize that you're wearing one of their Dad's ties."

My mind wanders to thinking about how much Jay would have loved meeting Tariq. I haven't felt this happy in a long time, as if I have a purpose in this world. Jay was right in what he always shared in his letters:

Focus on what you have, not what you don't have.

CHAPTER 49
Documenting the Negligence

As expected, the BOP responded to our complaint by filing a Motion to Dismiss. Joe was happy to share with us that Judge Jonathan Park of the Southern District in Bluefield, West Virginia, denied the BOP's motion. The BOP will now have to respond to the complaint within the next two weeks. It's a tiny victory in what we realize will be a very long, drawn-out war. If there is one thing history has taught my family, the US government is like the "house" in Las Vegas. It may lose every once in a while, but in the end, the system is set up such that the "house" always wins.

The wheels of justice continue turning at a snail's pace. We've waited months for the discovery documents to come in. Joe asks the BOP for all relevant and reasonable documents in a case like this, yet receives only a few grains of sand at a time. The FMC office notes of Dr. Huff contain nothing but contradictions to Jay's letters, his conversations with me, and his diary.

Some documents are helpful. We learned Beth Hurst was the nurse who saw Jay on Friday afternoon when the guard, who was concerned about Jay's toxic state during the four-p.m. count, transported him to the medical clinic. Hurst wrote that Dr. Huff said he wouldn't come to see a sick patient because he was buying a new truck. Joe surmised from her meticulous notes that she knew Jay was not being appropriately treated; therefore, she wanted to ensure her notes documented everything to minimize her complicity. She later penned Huff's exact words: "I'm supposed to drop everything for a fuckin' inmate. Don't call me unless he's dead or dying—and he better be dead."

Joe was surprised at not only how Beth Hurst documented her interaction

CONVICTIONS: A TALE OF PUNISHMENT, JUSTICE, AND LOVE

with Dr. Huff on the day that started Jay's demise, but the fact that the BOP sent notes with such damaging details. He speculates there was an honest whistleblower in the medical records department. He tells us how he can now fill in the John Does of the complaint with real names. The guard John Tackone. Beth Hurst. Dr. Harley Huff. The guards who transported him to the SHU. They will all be deposed. Joe filed a second request for all the medical records relating to when Jay was in the SHU. There is no doubt that the RFP (request for production) is being stalled by the BOP, or worse, documents are being deleted.

While waiting for the additional records, Joe is ready to depose the first round of BOP employees. Joe plans to do the depositions himself. It's one of the things we like about him. He wants to win the case, even if it means leaving his Manhattan corner office and traveling to Franklin, West Virginia.

A few days after the deposition, I go to Joe's office to watch the deposition video. Butterflies are dancing in my stomach. I'm mostly nervous to see these people, what they look like, what they sound like, knowing that they had a hand in harming my husband.

"I need to warn you," Joe says, "hearing your husband mentioned and talked about in this context may be difficult. Please, if at any time, you want me to stop the video, tell me."

"I'm ready," I say.

Joe dims the lights and the video plays.

In the conference room for the deposition is Joe Linnard, one of his younger associates, a stenographer, videographer, and an attorney representing the BOP, Ms. Louise Fleming. Officer John Tackone is the first to be deposed, followed by Beth Hurst, and then the guards who transported Jay to the SHU. The last person to be deposed would be the intake guard in the SHU. An ambitious lineup for one day by anyone's standards.

Officer Tackone is articulate, which makes the deposition move at a quick pace. He is diligent, shows no hesitation in his answers, and the BOP attorney representing him offers very little input or objections to any of Joe's initial questions.

"Officer Tackone, you stated earlier that you had worked at FMC

Franklin for about ten years. How would you describe Jay Keller's behavior as an inmate, especially compared to all those you have interacted with in your career?" Joe asks.

"He was easy. Kept to himself, didn't gamble, didn't fight. Seemed to read and write a lot or play his guitar in outdoor rec. Was always respectful, even when some of my colleagues would hassle him. He had a short sentence, which made most things easier to tolerate," Tackone says.

"Did you know him well?"

"Not really. Like I said, if an inmate gave you no trouble, your interaction with him was minimal. He was used a lot by the guards for random alcohol breath tests. We never want to find a guy who is positive because we'd have more work to do. We knew testing someone like Keller was safe. I did it. Lots of guards did."

Joe continues, "Can you tell me why you were concerned enough that Friday afternoon to insist on getting Mr. Keller to medical clinic?"

"Yeah. It was a no-brainer. He was delirious, sweating, could barely stand up. He was sick. I ain't trained in medicine, but anyone who saw him knew he was sick."

"What did you do next, Mr. Tackone?" "No big deal. I called medical, told them I had someone who needed immediate care. The nurse, Beth Hurst, came down and we brought him up to the medical clinic. Last time I saw him alive."

Next up is Beth Hurst, RN. After the boilerplate questions, Joe dives into the crux of the deposition.

"Ms. Hurst, did you know Mr. Keller well?"

"Yeah. He was up in my clinic at least three times a week for his MS injections, so I would say I knew him well."

"Describe him for us."

"Well-dressed, which around here means his shirt was tucked in and his pants were around his waist. Always had reading material. Respectful. You could tell he was educated, just had that air about him. Walked slowly, but otherwise you wouldn't know he had MS. Gave himself the injections, which made my job easier. Oh yeah, he always sat as far away from other inmates as possible. I think he was a little germophobic. Don't blame him in this place."

"Scratch 'don't blame him in this place' from the record," demands the BOP attorney Louise Fleming. "No opinions, Ms. Hurst, facts only. Continue."

"Thank you, Ms. Hurst. Now on the day in question, was his appearance any different?"

"Different? Different as night and day. He was sweating like a pig, talking nonsense, weak as could be, disheveled. He looked terrible. Never saw him like that!"

"What did you do next, Ms. Hurst?"

"I called Dr. Huff."

"What did you tell him?"

"I described the inmate in front of me and told him I was nervous about having such a sick inmate in the clinic. Temp of 104 is really high."

"What was Dr. Huff's response?"

"Well, like my notes say, it was after regular hours and he wanted no part of treating Mr. Keller. First, he said he was in the middle of purchasing a new truck. Second, Huff made it very clear to me that he just didn't like Mr. Keller."

"Objection," says Ms. Fleming. "Ms. Hurst, please refer accurately to titles. His name is Dr. Huff. Is that understood?"

"Yes. Sorry, ma'am," says Beth.

Joe continues his questioning. "Do the doctors frequently come back to evaluate patients after they've left for the day?"

"Not very often. They're supposed to, but they usually have some excuse why they can't come in, especially Dr. Huff. For a guy who is a prison doctor, he really is hard on the inmates."

Ms. Fleming abruptly stops her. "Objection to form. Ms. Hurst is rendering opinion and describing events in a prejudicial manner. That answer should be scratched from the record. No editorials, Ms. Hurst. Just answer the questions factually."

Joe was just about done with his questions. "Nurse Hurst, does Dr. Huff behave differently than the other doctors?"

"Let's just say he is the laziest—no, I'm sorry, I can't say that—but Dr. Huff is probably the least sympathetic of all the doctors. Can I say that?"

"No, you can't," yells Ms. Fleming. "This is your last warning, Ms. Hurst. Only the facts, otherwise I'll call the judge to explain that we have a witness who is not following deposition instructions."

"Understood, ma'am. Now that I think of it, I can't recall a time when Dr. Huff did come in after hours. In all fairness though, a lot of times things can be managed by phone, by all the doctors."

"Was Dr. Huff helpful to you in caring for Mr. Keller?"

"No. He just said, 'Put him in the SHU and I'll see him in the morning.'"

"Were you satisfied with that answer?"

"Hell no. I knew Mr. Keller was really sick. I told Dr. Huff he was really sick, but Dr. Huff didn't want to hear any of it, he just kept repeating, 'Put him in the SHU and I'll see him in the morning.'"

"Was there anyone else you could have called to get a second opinion?"

"Well, not really. Dr. Huff was the doctor on call. No one else would respond to my call."

"You mean another doctor?"

"Yeah."

"Could you have called the warden, or an assistant warden, or anyone else in administration?"

"That's not what protocol states. It's the doctor who has the final say on all medical matters."

"Are there any circumstances when calling an administrator is part of the protocol?"

"Not that I'm aware of. We are taught to follow a chain of command and that's what I did."

"If you appreciated how sick Inmate Keller was, why—" Joe pauses for a moment. "No, scratch that. I have no further questions."

Joe stops the video. I'm speechless. I cannot believe what I just saw and heard. I'm shaking.

"Lily, are you okay?" Joe asks.

"I'll be fine," I say without sincerity.

Joe tells me the reason he stopped asking questions to Nurse Hurst is because he didn't want to pursue any questions that might point to her negligence. He also didn't want to risk turning Beth Hurst into an adversary, that she'd be too valuable a witness at trial, so he let her off easy. He was considering asking, "Ms. Hurst, you're trained as a nurse to advocate for your patients. Why didn't you break protocol to advocate for Mr. Keller?" He explains that he didn't want to give the defense any reason to see her as negligent so he thanked her for her deposition and called it a day.

CHAPTER 50
Chasing Demons

After parking my car in a lot piled high with snow, I enter the three-story office building which houses mostly medical and dental professionals. The stairwell takes me to her second-story office suite, a small, modest, but cozy office. Dr. Dannert is a youthful looking woman, probably close to sixty-years-old with longer hair than most her age and usually tied back in a ponytail. She wears very little makeup because she's one of those women who needs very little, wears dresses all summer, and slacks in the colder weather. Her shoes are chosen for comfort. The only photos in her office are of her two young grandchildren.

There's a sense of serenity in Dr. Dannert's waiting room so I like to arrive a few minutes early to think about what I'd like discuss today. Fifteen minutes later, Dr. Dannert opens the door from her inner office and says goodbye to her patient, a young woman with multiple tattoos and piercings. A white-noise machine drowns out the rest of the world.

"Come on in, Lily. I love that scarf."

"Thank you. Sara picked it up when she was at a conference in India."

"The colors look great on you," she responds as I settle into my chair. Dr. Dannert asks if I'd like a cup of tea which I decline. She pours herself hot water and quickly returns to her seat with a cup of tea in hand, something she always has by her side during my visits.

"What would you like to discuss today, Lily?"

"Remember Jay's roommate who died, Bruce Hellman? Well, I finally met his widow this weekend."

"I remember you telling me about her. How is she doing?"

I tell Dr. Dannert how we met at a restaurant in Bucks County Pennsylvania near Iris's apartment, embraced as the oldest of friends, and yet, this was the first time we've met. Tears trickled down our faces as we squeezed each other for support.

There is an inimitable bond among people whose spouses are incarcerated. It's as if we are in on a secret that no one else knows except us. Both of our lives have been indelibly changed by the cruelty and malfeasance of the BOP.

Here I was, seated across the table from a woman who not only endured thirty months in prison herself, but lost her husband, all her assets, moved from a McMansion to renting a single room, and stripped of her full Social Security. Despite all that, she had the most sincere and beautiful smile. A sense of peace radiated from her. I was envious of her.

"How are you at peace with it all?" I ask, mystified to be envious of a woman who has lost everything.

"The peacefulness comes by accepting all that has happened to my family. The comfort comes from my children, religion, co-workers, my own good health, my new grandson, and so much we all take for granted."

Dr. Dannert laughed at my description of me and Iris laughing far more than we cried, while drinking a bottle of wine. We dined from six until the restaurant closed at ten. It was one of those evenings you didn't want to end.

I drove from the restaurant to a nearby Holiday Inn Express. During the two-minute drive, I realized how helpless I was from preventing the same fate for the next Bruce Hellman or Jay Keller. I felt a sense of clarity when I began to fantasize about a publicized trial with reporters putting their microphones in front of me as I descend majestic courtroom steps, a giant soapbox for me to pontificate.

"Lily, of course you're envious. She's not chasing demons like you are."

"What do you mean, demons?"

"She's accepted all that has happened, and is moving on. You want revenge, justice, punishment, which you may get. Then you'll be at peace?"

"I don't know. Guess I'm angry because I screwed up. Is that so wrong?"

"What do you mean you *screwed up*?"

"Jay was sick, and I wasn't there for him."

"I don't follow you. You were there. You visited him all the time in West Virginia. You held the house together. You earned a living. You helped your kids. What didn't you do?"

"I wasn't there, damn it! Jay's brain was scrambled from the moment we started dealing with the lawyers until I kissed him goodbye at the prison gates. He couldn't remember the house alarm code we had for over twenty years, or write a check correctly. Renee, it got so bad I wouldn't even let him drive."

"Lily, calm down. Breathe slowly."

I feel something inside of me, like a volcano about to spew its lava into the air. "Jay died because I should have fought the charges more. I should have sought more opinions, different expertise, instead of foolishly listening to the attorneys who only wanted to execute a plea deal and move to their next case. Jay was too sick to mount a fight. So no, I wasn't there for him."

"Lily, don't you think—"

"Let me finish. Every night Jay was in prison I would lie in bed beating myself up. Why couldn't I get him to a low security facility where he would have had more freedom? Why wasn't he with safer inmates where he didn't have to fear being jumped? Why wasn't he closer to home? Did someone sell him out? If you pay someone over $100,000 dollars, doesn't it make sense to take their advice?"

For the first time since seeing Dr. Dannert, I stand up, walk once around the room, and pause to glance out the window. "Why did we blindly follow the attorney's advice right into Dante's Inferno? So yes, I screwed up."

"Lily, you're being way too hard on yourself. Most people would have done the same thing."

"I don't care about everyone else."

"Lily, please, show *some* kindness towards yourself. You're—"

"I know what I am. I'm obsessed." Neither of us say a word for what seemed like forever.

"I don't know if that's the word I'd use, I—"

"Well that's what it is. I want to look into the eyes of the people who harmed Jay. I've always been able to read people by looking at their eyes. So yeah, I'd love to look into Huff's eyes, or the other guards, or all of them."

"Interesting. So, looking in their eyes will rid you of all your demons?"

"I don't know, but it's something I want to do."

CHAPTER 51

Pulling Teeth

At five p.m. on a beautiful spring evening, we enter the Fifty-Seventh Street office building, show our IDs to security in exchange for visitor passes, walk through the turnstiles, and head to the Sotloff Turner office on the twenty-third floor. Sara engages the receptionist in small talk while Richard finishes up his phone call. A few minutes later, Joe Linnard walks into the waiting room.

"Nice to see all of you. Come on in. How's everyone doing?"

Richard answers first. "Nothing's changed on our end."

"Then let's get right to it." We follow Joe to his office and sit around the small table across from his desk. "Okay, Richard, you do litigation work. We've asked the BOP three times for all discovery documents and we still haven't gotten most. What would you do next?"

"Hmm, I'd file a Motion to Compel. Have the judge force the BOP to hand over everything."

"Very good. That motion will be filed Monday. How much will he lean on the BOP to hand things over? He's been favorable to us in the past, but reality is that they work for the same team. *Many* federal judges, like Judge Park, were former prosecutors at some point in their career. Don't need to explain more."

"Are you telling us that we can't get the BOP to hand over public records?" Sara asks, enraged. "What kind of banana republic are we living in? This all seems so blatantly wrong. Am I missing something?"

"You're not missing anything," Joe responds. "There are some major imperfections in our judicial system as your family knows all too well. The

BOP may still not cooperate even after a Motion to Compel."

Sara leans back in her chair and throws her arms up in the air. "No wonder my father was so incensed. He wanted everyone to know the goddamn obstacles everyone faces when fighting a powerful and malfeasant bureaucracy."

"Sara, I hear what you're saying, but we have a Plan B," says Joe. "While we're waiting for the judge to order a Request for Production, an RFP, we're going to arrange to depose the nurse Beth Hurst a second time."

"Damn," says Richard after a few seconds. "Why didn't I think of that?"

Sara and I haven't put the dots together. "I'm still confused," I interject. "Why are we deposing her again?"

"I'm betting that after Jay died, on that Monday, Ms. Hurst learned who cared for him in the SHU."

Joe sees my expression change immediately.

"She's worked there for over a decade," Joe adds. "Knows all the players. Only natural for Ms. Hurst to have a conversation with some of her colleagues about who worked the SHU that weekend. We already know she's not going to save Huff's ass. It's worth another trip down to West Virginia to find out."

"I never learned shit like this in law school," Richard says to me and Sara.

"I'll take that as a compliment," replies Joe.

We say our goodbyes and leave Joe's office feeling somewhat frustrated. I'm trying my best to shake the sense of doom and gloom I have since Joe informed us how obstinate the BOP is being. The streets are filled with the pedestrian rush hour as we walk east on Fifty-Seventh Street. Standing at the corner and waiting for the traffic light to change before heading down Lexington Avenue, I stop them from crossing.

"You know, we never talked about this, but I don't want a settlement unless the BOP agrees to fire Huff. We could win all the money in the world, but if that son of a bitch is still able to practice his sadistic brand of medicine, that's a deal breaker for me."

"I'm with you," says Sara.

"Goes without saying," Richard adds. "It's a discussion we need to have with Joe."

***

Sotloff Turner files our Motion to Compel. Judge Park agrees with *The Estate of Jay Keller.* The BOP is given three weeks to produce all requested documents. Three weeks go by without the firm receiving anything. On the twenty-second day, Joe files the necessary paperwork to depose Beth Hurst, RN, as well as notifying Judge Park of the BOP's delinquency. The firm makes travel arrangements for another visit to Franklin.

One month later, I'm in Joe's office to view another deposition. And once again, I have that visceral feeling of melancholy, as with most times I walk into an attorney's office. I'm also lacking the comfort from my children who are both tied up at work.

"Remember, you can always tell me to turn it off," Joe says.

"Understood," I say.

"I just want you to know that the deposition was scheduled for ten a.m., but Ms. Hurst was running late. You'll see why this is significant," Joe says.

At two p.m., Ms. Beth Hurst arrives. Although she's grossly late, she offers no apologies for her tardiness. Joe is accompanied by a stenographer, videographer, and the same BOP attorney, Louise Fleming.

Joe begins, "Good afternoon, Ms. Hurst. We are still confused by the events that transpired the weekend Jay Keller died. We have a transcript from your previous deposition if you need to refer to it at any time. Any questions?"

"No, sir."

After twenty minutes of softball questions, Joe launches into his witness. "Do you know who in the medical staff cared for Inmate Keller after he was sent to the SHU?"

"Yes."

"And how do you know who cared for him? You stated previously that you had no contact with Mr. Keller once he was put in the SHU."

"When I came to work on Monday and found out Inmate Keller died, I made it a point to speak to the charge nurse in the SHU."

"And who was that?"

"Her name is Madeline Delacroix. She was in charge of the SHU's medical care."

"Did you know her well?"

"Sure, I met her the first week I started working here. Ten years ago."

"What did Ms. Delacroix tell you about how Inmate Keller died?"

"I'm sorry, I don't remember all the details. But she told me how frustrated she was with trying to get Dr. Huff to care for her patient."

Joe continues to squeeze every bit of information out of Beth. In addition to Ms. Delacroix, she names the two guards who worked the SHU that weekend, as well as another nurse who worked the nightshift in the SHU.

"Ms. Hurst, when were you made aware that you were to be deposed again?"

"This morning, when I showed up for work."

"I see. Did they tell you what time the deposition was to be held?"

"Yes sir. Two o'clock sharp."

"Thank you, Ms. Hurst. You've been very professional," as Joe glares at Louise Fleming.

CHAPTER 52

My Gut Feeling

As I ride the train back to Westchester, I hear my mother's words, "Be self-reliant. If your friends are busy, do something to entertain yourself. If you need to solve a problem, tackle it until its solved. If you want to be happy, first be happy with yourself before searching for a boyfriend or someone else to make you happy." It's almost a decade since Jay was diagnosed with MS, five years since his legal problems started, and about a year and a half since Jay died. I fear the BOP will figure out a way to avoid responsibility for killing my husband, and I still know someone is out there who lied about Jay's involvement with the lab. Is it any wonder I sleep so poorly? Sometimes I have to ignore well-meaning people and go with my gut feeling.

Monday morning, I call Betsy Simon, a medical assistant who still works Jay's old office. Sure enough, Betsy remembers the sales reps name, Stanley Blacker. That evening I ask Richard to research the name in the Southern District of New York archives. There's no record Blacker was part of the Accurate Lab case, nor has any legal action ever been taken against him. I knew it didn't mean much because virtually all the employees of Accurate Labs were honest, hard-working people who had nothing to do with the hundred-million-dollar insurance scam. Now almost five years later, the evidence to date points only to the owners of the lab who concocted the scheme. They were the first to be arrested but are *still* waiting for sentencing. Regardless, I relish the chance to speak to Stanley Blacker in person.

Via social media, I find out Stanley is forty-five and married with four children. He's now employed as the general manager of a successful steak house on Long Island. I drive out on Saturday and sit at the bar waiting until the lunch crowd thins out. I know from Facebook what he looks like. I see him speaking with customers who always walk away with a smile on their face. He's tall, thin, well dressed, well spoken, and friendly. A quintessential restauranteur. When I see him moving about the restaurant, I pounce.

"Mr. Blacker, my name is Lily Keller. I'm looking into the circumstances of Jay Keller's incarceration and murder."

"Jay Keller?" he asks very calmly. "The only Jay Keller I know is a doctor in Westchester. Sorry, can't help you."

"That's who I'm talking about. I'm his wife."

"Dr. Keller died? When? How?"

"He died while in prison. I'm trying to understand how he ended up in prison."

"Wow. I'm blown away. Dr. Keller. That's really sad. Good guy. I'm going to grab a drink. Want anything from the bar?"

"Sure. Whatever you're having is fine with me."

"I'll get the drinks. Let's talk in my office. Second door on the left. I'll be right in." He points to the hallway leading to his office. While I wait for Stanley to return, I study the photos in his office. Many pictures are of the Little League teams he has coached, others of family vacations.

He returns a minute later with two glasses of whiskey in his hand. "So, Lily, tell me what happened."

While looking directly into his eyes, I say, "My husband pleaded guilty to one count of commercial bribery. Because Jay was sick, they placed him in a Federal Medical Center prison. He was doing fine until he wasn't. Got a bad infection and died."

"Wait, the Dr. Keller I knew was healthy as a horse, played a lot of sports. You sure we're talking about the same guy?"

"We are. When was the last time you saw Jay?"

"Shit, had to be seven or eight years ago when I was still a lab rep."

"Why did you leave the lab?

"Because I found out that the owners were shady." Stanley lifts his glass for another sip. "Never would have thought Dr. Keller to be colluding with the owners. He always seemed like a pretty straight guy."

"Yeah. Hear that from everyone."

"Wait a minute, what kind of illness did he have? Cancer or something?"

"No. Multiple Sclerosis. Got a bad infection in prison and died."

Stanley stares at his drink while stirring the ice cubes. "It's not like we hung out together, but I saw him at his office once in a while. Occasionally brought lunch for his office staff. I feel really bad. Of all the docs I knew as a rep, he's the last I thought—"

I cut him off. "Did you know the owners of the lab were making millions?"

"We all knew they were doing pretty well, but never to that extent," replies Stanley.

"How did you hear that Accurate got closed down?"

"From a few people. Went online. Never imagined the owners were stealing that much money, and *never* imagined the government would throw a hundred doctors in jail."

"So you had no knowledge of their business model?"

"Not really. Come on, I was a lowly sales rep."

"Did you know whether doctors were offered bribes?"

"What I can tell you is when the owners wined and dined the sales team, they urged us to 'help our clients in any way we could.'"

"Really. Like what?" I ask.

"I just knew the tip of the iceberg, but I heard the owners talk about exotic vacations, apartments for mistresses, tons of theater and concert tickets, cars, cash, stocking entire wine cellars, even diamonds. I think the owner had a friend in the diamond business. Money was no object."

"Putting the contract aside, do you think my husband took bribes?"

"Not him. Wasn't a flashy guy. Kinda straight."

"Did you ever offer him a bribe?"

"No, but from what I heard, the feds considered the whole rental contract a bribe."

"Were you involved in the contracts?"

"Every rep was, that's why I know it was written by a top healthcare law firm in New York, Norton Cole I think."

"But as far as you know, no wining and dining while you were his lab rep?"

"Nope. Not Dr. Keller. I'm still digesting that your husband died while in prison. That's so sad."

"Stanley, it was really nice to meet you. I appreciate the kind words you said about Jay. It means a lot. Do you think I can have your cell number in case I have any other questions?"

He hands me his business card. "It has my cell number. Feel free to call. It was nice to meet you."

I take a few steps toward the exit before turning back. "One last question: When you left Accurate Labs, did anyone replace you?"

"Can't say for sure, they might have expanded another rep's territory. If they did, it probably would have gone to a guy named Bill Bauer."

I hand Stanley my business card after we shake hands. "If you think of anything else that may be useful, please give me a call."

We shake hands as I look directly at him. His eyes were telling me that what he said, was true, but I think he had more to say.

CHAPTER 53

A View to Kill

I tell my children all the details of my encounter with Blacker. Richard thinks it was "kind of cool" that I drove out to Long Island and met the guy. Sara is more reserved in her response. I know she wishes I would let sleeping dogs lie and focus on rebuilding a new life, not running around pretending to be a private investigator. Two children, raised in the same house, same parents, same schools, yet so different.

After being beaten up, battered, and bruised from the last several years when I was stuck in survival mode, I'm following my gut feeling. Only two weeks after meeting Stanley, on an impulse and against the strong advice of my children, I'm gazing out an airline window on my way to Franklin, West Virginia.

I open up my iPad and reread a flagged email I wrote to friends and family who were going to visit Jay. Hard to believe I wrote this letter three years ago:

Get there early so you don't get turned away because it's too crowded. You will look around at the rolls of barbed-wire fencing and guard towers and think, *WTF are we doing here?*

After you hear the clicking of the metal gates, you will walk through the first set, they close behind you, and the second set will click and unlock. You will walk through and up to the main entrance. On the left side is a table with a clipboard holding a form each of you must complete. Enter Jay's name and his ID number. You also need to remember your license plate number. All you can have on you is your photo ID and money for the vending machines. Leave all else in the car. You will go through security similar to an airport, removing shoes, keys, belts, or even under-wire bras. You will finally enter the large, open visiting room as the guard tells you where he wants you to sit. The inmates always sit facing the guards. The guards sit on an elevated barricade-like platform overlooking the room. Once you are seated, they will call for Jay. I think I can safely say it will be an experience like no other.

Definitely eat a good meal before you go. Please bring some single dollars and a few dollars in quarters in case the change machine has run out or is not working. These are for the vending machines. While meeting with Jay, please purchase some trail mix or nuts or granola bars and some water or juice because he cannot go to the vending machines himself. He may not ask you to get him food from the machines, but get something anyway as he will be missing lunch or dinner during the visit. He will want you stay for the whole time, and you will want to. The vending machines are horrid, stocked with expired food items and junk. There is very little for him to eat in prison, so you will understand why Jay looks so thin.

Last, be prepared to be treated like a criminal. Don't even think about challenging the guards on anything. You will lose. They rule with an iron fist and don't get paid to make your visit more enjoyable. Your visit will mean so much to Jay.

After landing, I summon up all the memories I've tried to suppress. All the bad karma is instantly stirred up as I make my way through the tiny airport. With my carry-on bag in tow, I rent a car, and I'm on my way.

On a drizzly Saturday morning, with nausea and dread, I pass through the barrage of security officers who exhibit nothing but disdain for the visitors. No "good mornings." No "welcome." I sit in the same uncomfortable plastic chairs in the visitation room as I wait for the first inmate to arrive. Here, amidst the filth and dreariness inside the institution that killed my husband, I look at the guards and wonder if any of them had abused Jay. I stare at them as they go about their jocular banter with each other, wondering if they sense my contempt. Off to my left are the infamous vending machines filled with nothing but empty calories from out-of-date food items. Half an hour later, I have a visit with my first inmate.

He's short and stocky, dark hair with specks of gray, and bright blue eyes. Jay's description was spot-on.

I stand up and approach Diaz who has just handed his ID to the guards. "Good morning, Mr. Diaz. I'm Lily Keller, Jay Keller's wife." I could see he was happy to see me. I wasn't sure if it was because my visit was a welcome change to his daily drudgery or it was because I was his friend's wife.

"Holy shit! Prettier than Jay described. Hey, call me Diaz. My father is Mr. Diaz. I'm just Diaz. Really nice to meet you. Shame that your husband died in this shithole. Man, he was a helluva guy. Nicest guy I met in prison. Most of the guys in here are scumbags. Not Jay. Hey, how your kids doing?" Jay was right. Diaz is a talker.

"No matter how strong someone is, a Category 5 hurricane will knock them over. They're gradually getting used to life without their father."

"Man, I miss Jay. His name still comes up once in a while. Tell you one thing, he was the best doctor in this fuckin' place. He helped me; he helped more people than that whole motherfuckin' medical department. Lotta fucked-up inmates here."

It doesn't take long for me to appreciate that left to his own devices, Diaz would talk away the entire weekend, just as Jay had written. After an hour or so of listening to Diaz go off discussing other inmates, his entire family, and the medical department of FMC Franklin, I know I have to be extremely specific in my questions.

"Diaz, did my husband ever discuss the legal side of his case with you? Actually, let me be more specific: did he ever talk about who he thought ratted him out?"

"Ya know, in prison, lotta guys wanna talk about 'their case.'" Diaz raises two fingers to make air quotation marks. "They love working on 'their case.' Jay wasn't a talker in that sense, he was a writer. Always had a pen and paper, hoping to write a book and tell the world what goes on in hellholes like this."

"Anything at all you can remember Jay saying in connection with the lab?"

"Not really." Diaz pauses for a few seconds, then says, "Ya know, Jay had a short sentence. Eighteen months ain't nothing around here. My old cellie, Ken Brady, now *he* was a library rat. Wouldn't surprise me if Ken had some legal conversations with your husband. Might wanna talk to Ken Brady, wherever the fuck he is these days."

"So as far as you know, Jay never mentioned who lied just to save their own ass?"

"Hold on, now that you mention it, I do remember Brady grilling Jay when I first introduced them. Jay was brand-new here and scared shitless because of his mac problem. Brady was a straight shooter. I remember him asking Jay, 'Who has something to gain by ratting you out'? Pretty common question when you're in prison. That's when Jay said something like it had to be someone from the lab."

"You sure?"

"Sure as anyone can be after being locked up for five years. Yeah, he said he had a tenant that fucked up. Poor guy was shell-shocked and Brady was grilling him hard. Prison ain't easy."

"Tell me about Dr. Huff."

Diaz grits his teeth. "That fat fuck Huff is still here abusing inmates. Amazing no inmate ever killed that fucker. You should go after Huff. He killed Jay's cellie Bruce, a whole bunch of others guys in here, and I know Huff hated Jay. That is one mean motherfucker."

I lean forward and cover my mouth so the guards can't see what I'm saying. "I learned it was Huff who killed Jay."

Diaz arches his brows. "What did that asshole do?"

"It's what he didn't do. Jay had a bad infection that should have been treated. Huff just ignored him. Left him to die in the SHU. Goddamn gross negligence."

"That lazy, sadistic fuck! I'd pay money to watch that motherfucker get filled with fifty thousand volts of electricity."

"Trust me. We're going after him."

"Let me know if you need my help." Diaz mimics a chokehold around his own neck.

"Diaz, I appreciate your time. You're even kinder than Jay described in his letters. He said if it weren't for you, he would have drowned in here that first week. He was never going to forget that. He also said that whenever he would play *The Godfather* theme on his guitar, you were the only one in West Virginia who recognized the music."

"Come on, man. I grew up in the Bronx. Arthur Avenue. The Spics and Waps got along good back then. Who else you visiting while you're down here?"

"Henderson and Robitelli. That's assuming they let me visit with that many people."

"Hey, please tell your children their dad was a great man."

"I'll certainly pass that along. Diaz, stay healthy in here. From what I understand, this is no place to get sick."

I hugged Diaz goodbye and understood why Jay liked the man. What he lacked in polish, he made up for in sincerity. I spend the remainder of the afternoon in the squalid visitation area, but none of the other inmates offer any useful information. As I exit the prison, the last guard asks me where I'm staying and if I want some company tonight.

Jay warned me about this behavior from the guards but this is a first. I pause, turn, and look first at his name tag and then into his eyes before responding. "You're a disgusting pig! I wouldn't choose you if you were the last man on earth, but I will write a letter to your superiors, Mr. Vaughn."

I hurry to my rental car, take more than a few deep breaths, and begin my drive through a rather scenic part of West Virginia. Beautiful mountains and trees take over the horizon. I'm feeling incredibly sad and helpless after leaving the prison. The last time I was in Franklin, I was with Jay, and he was alive. I remember holding him. I remember kissing him goodbye.

Once back at the hotel, I read though my emails including one from Joe. He finally spoke with the nurse Madeline Delacroix long enough to know that "angry ex-employees always have a lot to say."

After confirming my flight home early tomorrow, exasperation begins enveloping me. Not one of the inmates I met with talked about being trained for a job or any preparation for when they inevitably get released. None spoke of the obstacles they will face. Maybe it's better they don't know.

My thoughts turn to what Diaz said about Huff. The truth is I've been obsessed with Huff from Jay's first description of him in his letters. Now I learn from Sotloff Turner that the BOP won't touch him. This is the man whose eyes I need to see.

I open my laptop and Google Harley Huff, MD as I have done several times. I had been searching for this man's face, but after Jay died, I couldn't even bring myself to type the devil's name. Still, no photos of him online. I go to the same website as once before and learn his home address hasn't changed.

I get into my car to make the ten-minute drive to where he lives in Waitsville. I park my car diagonally across the street from Harley Huff's home for no other purpose than to look at the man who killed my husband. Along with snacks and satellite radio, for the next ninety minutes I sit there lost in thought, thinking of my conversation with Diaz, the last time I saw Jay, the prosecutor assuring the judge that Jay would get the medical care he needed, all the bureaucrats who did nothing about the inadequate medical care in prisons, if there is something more I can do to help Bruce Hellman's widow.

With maybe an hour of sunlight left, a large pickup truck pulls into the driveway. When the driver door opens, a man matching Jay's description of Dr. Huff slowly exits the cab. He's large framed with a shiny domed head. He flicks his cigarette onto the driveway before proceeding to the back of his truck to retrieve a cased rifle.

I see the face of Jay's assassin. My heart pounds and I'm frozen in place. He's everything I envisioned him to look like, but even more grotesque in person. Jay's letters captured this man perfectly. Rifle slung over his shoulder; Huff disappears into the garage. That's it? Ten seconds?

Before I have a chance to decide what to do next, the front door of the house opens slowly. Out comes Huff, his hands carrying a tray of snacks and a beer can. He makes his way to an Adirondack chair on the front porch. I try taking a picture but my cell phone camera is useless from such a distance and impending darkness. My memory will have to suffice.

Huff eventually puts down his empty food tray, which frees up his hands to remove a cigar from his shirt pocket. The beer rests on the arm of the chair while he lights his cigar. As the evening darkens, the porch light comes on giving me a better view of Huff, slowly puffing on his cigar, occasionally taking a swig of beer. I flash back to Richard at my house saying how he would relish the chance to put a rope around Huff's neck.

I'm engulfed by a massive wave of nausea. Should I confront Huff face to face? What would I say? I suddenly recall an anthropology course I had in college when I wrote a term paper claiming revenge is part of human nature. Humans have had revenge killings throughout history. Our specie is built for revenge, complete with a concomitant release of endorphins that the revenger feels. An eye for an eye. Today my thesis is validated. Here I am, sitting in my car staring at the man who took my husband's life. What if I had a gun with me today? Could I pull the trigger? Would I feel remorse? Could I hire a hitman? Could Richard really hang this man? I race from one virulent thought to another.

Then I remember what Diaz said earlier today. I wonder if I could pull the lever that would send fifty thousand volts of electricity through Huff's body. One thing I know for sure. If I couldn't, Diaz could.

I'm looking at a man content as could be, sipping a beer, puffing a cigar on a beautiful summer evening. Does he ever think about Jay Keller? My bet is he doesn't even know the pain he inflicted on my family. I remain staring at Huff pulsing with emotions until I see him laboring to lift himself out of the Adirondack chair. On his third try he gets up and walks into his house, closing the front door behind him.

As he enters his home, I realize there is nothing more for me so see in West Virginia. I put the car in drive. I feel angry, helpless, and a bit satisfied.

CHAPTER 54

Lady Justice

Families are complicated. They just are. You don't choose families; they're selected for you. Jay and I had always talked about how lucky we were to both have large extended families whom, for the most part, we enjoy being with.

Our cousin Janice is a perfect example of someone who is both family and friend. Janice called me a week ago to get together and we agreed on a simple lunch in her judge's chambers, a novel experience for me.

At 11:30 a.m., I leave my office and hop on the subway, which takes me to a stop downtown directly in front of her courthouse. Her text reads:

"When you exit the subway station, go left half a block and the eatery Morsel's is right there. The order is under Kalter."

After picking up the food, I walk toward the steps of the courthouse, an iconic-looking building with high Corinthian columns probably built in the early 1900s. My pace slows but my heart accelerates as I climb the granite stairs. At the top is a large bronze statue of Lady Justice with her eyes blindfolded, a sword in one hand and a scale in the other. I remember Jay and I passing a similar statue the day of his sentencing. He paused and said to me, "I don't think justice is blind." Hours later, after Jay was sentenced to prison, we walked past the same statue. This time he said, "Told you, the blindfold is just for show."

As I walk into the atrium, I realize this is my first time in a courthouse since Jay's sentencing. Courthouses, similar to places of worship, have disproportionately high ceilings and excessive grandeur. I believe architects design these buildings to make feel people feel intimidated and subservient to a higher power.

I weave my way through security feeling a bit nauseated, anxious, and angry. I proudly drop Janice's name as my destination.

"Elevator to the third floor. When you get off, you'll see another security officer. Tell him you have an appointment with Judge Kalter," states the humorless officer.

Once out of the elevator, a security guard leads me to Judge Kalter's chambers. He knocks on the door. A well-dressed man in his mid-thirties opens the door, introduces himself as Judge Kalter's administrative assistant, and escorts me to her private chambers.

"Lily, come in," states Janice with a big smile. "You look beautiful as always."

I thank her assistant and enter a room far larger than I envisioned. It's well appointed, slightly dark, and Janice is sitting behind a desk piled high with papers and manila folders.

"Thank you, Janice. Nice digs. This is my first time in a judge's chamber. Also, the first time I've been in a courthouse since Jay's sentencing."

"Today will be more enjoyable. I promise."

"It has to be. What a train wreck that day was with the judge fumbling through papers. I know in my heart he never bothered to read the valid arguments Jay's lawyers presented to him."

"Yeah, I'll never forget that day either," replies Janice.

"For the life of me, I still don't understand why the judge followed everything the slovenly prosecutor asked of him. Enough of the past."

"I think my cousin needs a hug." Janice gets up and gives me a warm embrace.

We finally sit down at a large table with high-backed chairs, lay out the food, and immediately catch up on kids, her husband Sam, and common relatives.

"Guess who Sam performed gall bladder surgery on yesterday?" Janice asks as she reaches into her mini-fridge for two bottles of sparkling water.

"Bill Clinton?" I ask. Janice smiles and shakes her head no. "Woody Allen? Spike Lee?"

"Good guesses, but no. Ronald McIntire, the warden at the infamous Manhattan Correctional Center."

"Oh my god. That's where Jay's friend Jeremy Gordon was for a week after he left FMC Franklin and before he was extradited back to the UK. They made him wear the same clothes all week, wouldn't give him a fork, spoon, or a plate. They delivered all his food on old newspapers. Poor guy had to eat his meals using his fingers. No soap, toothbrush, nothing. And we lecture other countries on human rights?"

"Then you won't be surprised to hear Sam said the warden was a pompous ass." Anyway, how's the case going?" asks Janice more cousin-like than judge-like.

I tell her Sotloff Turner has been great to work with but express my frustration with the sluggishness of the legal system and the intransigence of the BOP. Janice reminds me of our first conversation about taking on the federal government, and unfortunately, her words were all too prescient.

Once I tell her about watching the video of the first round of depositions, she looks relieved. I think in her eyes, there is far more progress than I appreciate, especially after I tell her the nurse called Huff negligent and incompetent, although not as precisely as my adjectives.

"Reliving events is hard," states Janice. "I see it every day when victims have to listen to testimony about their son or daughter being murdered."

"Tell me. I've spent two sessions blabbing to my therapist about the video."

"*Good guys* don't always win and justice isn't always served," says Janice slowly.

I feel the veins in my neck filling as my stress hormones suddenly surge as I flash back to Huff sitting on his porch. What if Huff is never punished for what he did? I debate telling Janice about my excursion to West Virginia but I dread having to explain my actions. Instead, I reply, "We can only hope the good guys win this time."

As soon as those words leave my lips, I make an *X* with my two index fingers signaling to Janice that I don't want any more legal-talk. At my insistence, we spend the next hour discussing everything else from the joys and sadness of being empty nesters, to current museum exhibits, my volunteer work, and catching up on our wacky but lovable relatives.

CHAPTER 55

Two Little Fish

The legal system can move painfully slow. Months go by. I know Joe and his team are working hard because I get frequent emails, but to me, nothing is happening. Work is work. Volunteering, yoga, and sculpting takes up most of my free time while my children are focused on their lives. I continue to wrestle with my demons.

It's a beautiful Saturday afternoon on Long Island, and a perfect day for watching an end of the season Little League game. I find a spot on the upper bleachers. Stanley is on the sidelines, coaching his son's team. He's an enthusiastic coach who supports all the kids. When the game is over and all the equipment is being packed away, Stanley chats with some of the parents. I watch as Stanley kisses his wife goodbye and gives his son a high-five. The second Stanley is alone, I approach him.

"Stanley, nice game today. Your boy plays quite a shortstop."

"Wh-what the hell are you doing here?" he stammers, looking at me with confusion.

"I remember your team's name, Huntington Fire Department, from a picture I saw when I was in your office. I went online and saw you had a game today."

"You drove all the way out here to watch my son's Little League game? I'm honored, but why do I have a hard time believing that's the reason for your visit?"

"Loved the way he turned the double play to end the game."

Stanley crosses his arms in a defensive stance. "Why are you here?" He glares at me. "I told you everything I know."

"I just want to put my cards on the table," I respond. "I'm here because I'm having a hard time believing you know nothing about why my husband went to prison."

"I already told you you're wasting your time," he says, staring directly at me.

"I was intending to come out here, maybe try to bluff you, make up some story how Bill Bauer, the rep who took your place, already confessed to signing false statements, but I'm not. Stanley, the reality is, I need your help."

"What the fuck are you talking about?"

"I'm talking about what you did to keep yourself out of prison."

Stanley takes a step back. His face pales. "This is bordering on harassment and I'm in no mood for it." He picks up the last two bats leaning against the backstop and places them in the equipment bag.

"There were two little fish," I say. "You and my husband. Insignificant lives to prosecutors with power."

"Lily, enough of this. What the fuck are you trying to say?"

"Listen, I understand what you went through with the feds because I watched my husband go through it. I went through it. The feds had you by the balls and you didn't want jail time. I get it Stanley, I do."

Stanley picks up the equipment bag and walks across the field heading to the parking lot. I follow a few steps behind him but can't help but think this is not the behavior of an innocent man.

"You did what you had to do. I don't think you could've imagined the consequences of your actions."

Stanley pivots suddenly. "Are you on drugs?"

"I can assure you, no drugs. Please, Stanley, I'm suffering. I just want to know how my husband landed in prison. That's it. I need your help. It's been eating at me from day one. At this point, you're the only one who can heal me. I just want some peace of mind. Can you help me?"

Stanley ignores me and continues walking.

"Why don't you just tell the truth?" I yell.

Stanley pauses and remains silent while smoothing out the dirt in front of him with his feet.

"I think you have something to say, but you're afraid of getting yourself in trouble. Am I right so far?"

Stanley turns to me and shouts, "How do I know you're not wearing a wire?"

"Check me." I open my arms and legs, keeping my arms fully extended upward. "I have a sports bra under this T-shirt if you really need to see." Stanley doesn't move, so I'm thankful I'm not forced to prove myself. I'm shaking in anticipation.

"I think you, Bill Bauer, and maybe others signed statements for the feds saying you gave all sorts of bribes to Jay and the other doctors. I ask myself two questions. Why would Stanley do that? Answer: So he doesn't go to jail himself. Why would the feds do it? Answer: As a guarantee that if the case ever went to trial and a jury found the rental contract legal, your signed statement was their backup evidence to guarantee a conviction. It was worth giving a few little fish full immunity."

Stanley's jaw drops. "Listen, even if everything you said was true, no one in their right mind, especially me, would admit to that."

My gut feeling was right. I'm speechless as I stand here under the beating sun, face to face with the man who turned on my husband.

"I get it. Four kids, wife, house, and looking at real jail time. The feds gave you an offer that was an easy, simple, clean way of making it all go away. All fun and games until someone gets their eye poked out—or dies in prison."

"Never thought they'd put all the doctors in prison, especially a guy like your husband," replies Stanley in a remorseful tone. His gaze is to the outfield. "Made no sense."

"Just tell me what happened," I whisper. "Please."

Stanley looks away to the outfield and sighs. "I was looking at about five years in prison, maybe more depending on what charges they ultimately brought against me. On my third meeting with the feds, I was in a conference room with my attorney and three Assistant US Attorneys. They said if I was willing to sign the statements they just gave my attorney to read, the whole ordeal would be over for me. The AUSA's left us alone for a few minutes. My lawyer recommended I sign the statements, that it was a good deal. So, I signed. Bet most people in my position would do the same."

"How many doctors did you sign against?" I ask, finding strength in my voice.

"I think a dozen, maybe more. My lawyer was handing me the papers and I kept signing."

"Was anyone else besides the three AUSA's in the room?" I ask.

"No, except when the big Kahuna, Bob Keenan, popped in for a few seconds."

"How'd you know it was him?"

"I've seen that asshole on TV a few times. Short, skinny, nerdy-looking guy with a vest and a bowtie. Looked like the kind of guy who was stuffed into lockers or garbage cans by the other kids when he was in junior high school."

"Did he say anything?"

"Not much. I remember him looking at me and saying, 'Smart of you to sign.' Then he whispered something to one of the AUSAs before leaving the room. Kind of smug, self-righteous. All those AUSAs are heartless bastards."

"Those same bastards sent the doctors to prison, Stanley, all of them," I add.

There's a moment of silence as we stand there staring at each other. I feel like the world is crashing down all around me.

"Stanley, of the papers you signed, how many doctors actually took bribes?" I ask.

"Only one."

"Was it Jay?" I already know the answer, but I have to hear this man say it to my face.

"No. He wasn't even offered—too straight."

"Fuckin' DOJ, or more accurately, *Department of Convictions*. They don't have a clue how they unnecessarily destroy lives every day. All convictions are life sentences."

"Listen, this meeting is over," Stanley says firmly. "I hope this helps you, but let's be clear about one thing. I'll deny this entire conversation. If anything about this case ever comes up again, my lawyer and I will do everything to make sure you are seen as nothing but an angry and crazed wife, still mourning the loss of your husband."

"Understood."

"One last thing. I don't ever want to see you again."

"You won't, Stanley," I say. "Thanks for helping me.

CHAPTER 56

The Ripple Effect

One week later, Janice opens her apartment door, we greet each other with a warm embrace, I follow her brisk pace back to the kitchen where she is pulling appetizers out of the oven and a bowl of fruit from the refrigerator. At her request, I lean over the island placing freshly rolled grape leaves onto a tray.

A few minutes later, the doorbells rings, and Janice asks, "Can you get that, Lily?"

When I open the door, Joe Linnard smiles at me before giving me a two-handed hand shake.

"Good to see you, Joe. Thanks for coming tonight."

"Same here, Lily. How are Sara and Richard?"

"Doing well, working hard."

Janice emerges from the kitchen and warmly embraces Joe.

"You look wonderful, Janice. How long has it been?"

They catch up while I uncork a bottle and pour everyone a glass of wine before joining them around the dining room table. I enjoy watching Janice and Joe as they reminisce about the last four decades of the New York legal scene, the good, the bad, and the ugly. I thank them for making time for me and inform them I found out who flipped on my husband.

Joe smiles and raises his brow. "Oh yeah, I remember talking about it a while back. Did you hire the Private Investigator I recommended?"

"Nope, I never hired him because I found out on my own," I say with confidence.

They both flash me confused looks, but I explain that like most things in

313

life, you figure it out. I tell them all about Stanley Blacker. When they wanted to know the details of how I got him to confess, I summarized, simply saying I narrowed things down, and with little luck, Blacker told me what really happened. He confessed.

"What am I missing here?" Joe asks as he refills his glass. "They had the doctors because of the signed contract with the lab. They didn't need more evidence. Hmmm, how does this affect our case going forward?"

Janice jumps in. "It doesn't. You're pursuing a wrongful death suit against the BOP. What we just heard, if true, is a whole other mess to clean up that I don't even want to think about. My guess is the feds had a sliver of doubt and were afraid a talented defense attorney would convince a jury the contract was in fact legal."

Joe turns to me. "Lily, didn't one doctor try to argue the validity of the contract in court?"

"Sure did," I say. "A doctor by the name of John Egan. Judge denied his legal team from bringing up any discussion about the contract at trial. Ended up screwing the poor guy. Five-year sentence. He died in prison at the age of eighty-three. Lymphoma I think."

"So, getting more evidence was just an insurance policy," proclaims Joe.

"Sounds like it," adds Janice. "I hear the US Attorney out of that office, Bob Keenan, is pretty tough on his AUSAs."

"Shit," says Joe. "I hear Keenan hasn't lost a single case in his tenure."

As I pour a little more wine, Janice says, "The AUSAs might have gotten a little cavalier in their tactics. It happens when you always win."

"I can't believe AUSAs are still doing stuff like that," adds Joe.

I pause for a few seconds. "Guys, this is why I asked you come here tonight. I need your advice. How do I go about bringing the prosecutors to justice?"

"Why don't you start by telling us exactly what Blacker said," Joe responds.

"Stanley was in a room with three AUSAs and his lawyer. If he signed the twelve or fifteen statements in front of him, he'd go scot free. His lawyer told him he'd be crazy not to sign, so he signed. Keenan popped in for a second and told Stanley he was making the right choice."

"Did Blacker say anything else?" asks Janice.

"Yeah, two things. He told me that he'll never admit to any of it, and if he ever sees me again, he's going to file harassment charges against me."

I pass around a tray filled with stuffed grape leaves. As I look at each of them, I focus on their uneasiness. Both of them speak hesitantly, expressing their concern that this would be a "he said— she said" situation and who would believe Blacker over the word of a US Attorney. My stomach is back in knots.

Joe sighs. "I just don't think there's enough for the Inspector General to launch an investigation."

"Bullshit," I yell. "Put Stanley in a room with the FBI. Then tell him if he lies about anything, he's in jail for at least five years and proceed from there!"

I get up from the table, walk to the window overlooking the Hudson River for a few moments, then slowly return to the table. I ask Janice her opinion. She used to work for the Office of the Inspector General when she first graduated from law school. She too was in agreement with Joe.

"This conversation is not making me happy," I lament. "You're both content with prosecutors being above the law? This is crazy."

Joe takes a sip of wine as he and Janice exchange glances, but no words.

"And Janice, I met Melvin Hartwick at your son's wedding."

"Come on," she replies. "You want me to call the US Attorney General on your behalf? Lily, think of what you're asking."

"I can't believe this. After what I just told you, you're not willing to make a call?" Nausea and anger fill my gut.

"Okay, let's play this out," suggests Janice. "Imagine they were found guilty of prosecutorial misconduct. Then in theory, every case out of that US Attorney's office for the last ten years could be considered tainted."

"They would have endless appeals, a real shit-show," adds Joe.

"I just don't think Hartwick, or any AG for that matter, would open a can of worms over a case like this," echoes Janice. "It's the ripple effect. Would be the biggest scandal to hit the Justice Department since the U.S. Attorney General John Mitchell served nineteen months in prison for his involvement in Watergate."

"Supreme Court, *Imler v. Patchman*. 1976," says Joe. "Made prosecutors immune from any civil suit no matter how egregious their actions. Sounds absurd, but it's law."

"Fuck the Supreme Court," I plead. "You can't give full impunity to people who have the power to destroy lives and reputations. This is what happens when you combine a twisted culture with extreme ambition and unbridled power."

Janice says she agrees with me but is just trying to be practical and realistic. I yell loud enough to be heard in the next apartment. "If US Attorneys conceal or fabricate evidence, make false statements, or cut sleazy deals with jailed informants, then they should be disbarred and learn first-hand what prison is really like. The days of prosecutors being immune from lawsuits must end."

Janice shakes her head. "Remember when we had lunch in my chambers awhile back. I told you then how the system is 'okay,' but has a long, long way to go. Even if I make the call you want, I just don't see anything happening."

I can't believe they're both content with a system that incentivizes prosecutors to seek 'wins over fairness' regardless of the wake of destruction it causes. Joe and Janice remain silent. After more than a few moments of awkward silence, Janice leans over and places her hand on my shoulder.

"I'll reach out to Mel, but please, don't get your hopes up."

"Thank you, Janice."

I turn and look at Joe. He flashes me a smile and runs both his hands through his thick white hair. "Lily, you're right. Changes in the system have to come from within the system."

"Thank you. Thank you." I exhale loudly as my eyes well up. "You're doing this for Jay." We share another two hours together, never once speaking of any legal matters.

CHAPTER 57
Nailing a Broken System

With a bluebird sky on a warm September day as I approach the two-year anniversary of Jay's death, my best friend, Cynthia, her husband Walter, and a few neighbors sit in my den on a Sunday morning awaiting my television debut. I've prepared fresh fruit, pastries, and Bellini's for everyone. I'm excited to see myself on TV for the first time in my life. The Fortune Society knew Channel 7 was coming but no one told the volunteers. My words were spontaneous and heartfelt, but how will I look on TV? This crowd will give me an honest review.

"This is Investigative Reporter Laverne Sanders coming to you from the Fortune Society in Queens, New York. Today we'll be speaking with Mrs. Lily Keller whose husband, Dr. Jay Keller, died suddenly while serving a two-year prison sentence. Lily now volunteers at the Fortune Society helping men and women who have recently been released from incarceration. We are with Lily in her tutoring classroom. Mrs. Keller, what do you see as the biggest obstacle facing ex-inmates?"

"It's hard adjusting to life on the outside after being locked in a cage for years or decades. Throughout his incarceration, my husband spoke about all the obstacles inmates face upon their release. It's not as if one day someone is released from prison and all is forgiven. He or she must find work, housing, reunite with family and friends, get a credit card and bank account, clothing, all while having the word 'felon' tattooed on their foreheads. In America, a conviction, a criminal record, follows you forever. I'm trying to make the transition a little easier for them. Some of the older inmates are seeing the letters *www.* for the first time."

"In the time you've been volunteering, have you seen an increase in the number of ex-inmates who come to the Fortune Society?"

"Yes. The number of ex-inmates is staggering. Let me share one statistic with you. Between 1990 and 2005, a fifteen-year period, a new prison opened in America every ten days. *Every ten days.*"

"We're talking about the prison-industrial complex, aren't we?" asks Laverne.

"Yes. Do you think politicians are going to pass funding to build prisons and not pass laws to make sure they're full? That's how we went from 200,000 prisoners in the US in 1970 to about 2.5 million today, and another 4.5 million on probation or parole. Welcome to the over-criminalization of America."

"Those are amazing statistics and certainly explains the uptick in volume here at the Fortune Society. For your husband, what was the most difficult part of being incarcerated?"

"My husband wrote countless letters about horrid medical care, overuse of solitary confinement, and rampant violence. He used to quote Nelson Mandela: 'If you want to know about a society, look inside its prisons.'"

"Do you think inmates' human rights are being abused?"

"No doubt. For example, my husband regularly witnessed wheelchair-bound inmates forced to go up and down flights of stairs on their hands and butts because the elevators were broken for weeks at a time. Can you imagine that scenario being acceptable in a public building in New York?"

"Let's change the subject for a moment," says Laverne. "Before we went on the air, you and I were discussing mandatory minimum sentences. It's a complicated concept. Can you tell our listeners what you shared with me?"

"I'll try to simplify things. Every federal crime carries a mandatory minimum sentence. When someone is convicted, a federal judge *must* apply that mandatory minimum. The cruelty is that the mandatory minimums are too severe, about four times longer than in all other developed countries."

"That sounds very Draconian," interjects Laverne.

"It is. Here's the problem—sentencing power has been transferred from judges to prosecutors. We must eliminate mandatory minimums and return sentencing to judges."

"Don't judges do that now?" replies Laverne.

"Absolutely not. When my husband was forced into accepting a plea deal, the judge had to sentence him to a mandatory minimum amount of time in prison. There is zero consideration given to the specific circumstances of a crime, the characteristics of a defendant, or the threat to society."

"Why didn't your husband's case go to trial?"

"If we didn't accept a plea, the prosecutor could have easily added wire fraud, mail fraud, and conspiracy, all statutes originally passed to get at organized crime, but now applied to any case they need. Each of those charges carry additional mandatory minimums. Now we're looking at a ten-year sentence in a system where federal prosecutors rarely lose a case. Do we take twenty months or risk ten years?"

"Seems like the prosecutors hold a lot of power."

"Too much power. We need to change the culture of the prosecutors by getting away from *conviction notches on a belt* as the benchmark for their performance. Convictions do not equate to justice. In two hundred and forty-plus years of our democracy, the only punishment for committing a crime is locking someone in a cage? Shame on us!"

"One last question. If you could wave a magic wand to fix the criminal justice system, what would you like to see?"

"America has only 4.4 percent of the world's population, but one out of every four people locked up in the world sits in an American prison. That has to change."

"You're saying of all people in prison in the entire world, America holds twenty-five percent of them?"

"Yes, sadly. Let me phrase it another way. Most of the developed world has about 100 people in prison per 100,000 citizens. Russia, China, Israel, and North Korea are outliers at about 175 per 100,000. America has 750 inmates per 100,000. Are we out of our minds? We need shorter sentences whenever possible, especially for non-violent crimes. Give judges discretion in sentencing and let them apply alternative forms of punishment. And by the time an inmate is ready to be discharged, we must do a better job of transitioning them back to society. We know that ninety-eight percent of the people we incarcerate will eventually be released. They need jobs. They need housing. They need hope. That is our mission here at the Fortune Society."

"Thank you, Mrs. Keller, for helping—"

"I need to add one more statistic. Unless someone has been touched by the judicial system, very few know, or care. However, America must reexamine the use of grand juries. It was created in England in 1164, originally to protect the public from abusive prosecutors. Today it's used to protect abusive prosecutors from public scrutiny. In 2010, over162,000 cases were brought before Federal Grand Juries. All were indicted except for eleven people. If prosecutors present evidence to a federal grand jury, there is a 99.999933% the grand jury sides with the prosecutors. Why wouldn't they since *only* prosecutors can present evidence? It's almost impossible for a citizen dragged before a Grand Jury not to be indicted. It's like the Salem Witch Trials. Back then, if someone was accused of being a witch, the townspeople would weight her down and throw her into a pond. If she rose to the top of the water and lived, that proved she was a witch, and they would burn her at the stake or hang her. If she drowned, she was judged innocent. No good options."

"Thank you again Ms. Keller for enlightening all of us. Please join us next week to watch Part Two of our interview with Volunteers of the Fortune Society. From Queens, New York, this is Laverne Sanders."

Oh my god, you were fabulous, Lily," says Cynthia as she and everyone else extends their arms to hug me. "You looked so calm and composed. You're the only person I know who can rattle off statistics so effortlessly. You're amazing. This calls for a fresh round of Bellinis."

Sara calls my cell phone. "Mom, you were so good. I loved it. You nailed the broken system perfectly!"

"Thanks, sweetie. It felt good to tell people the truth."

CHAPTER 58
Here's What We Have

A few weeks later, Joe tells us Madeline Delacroix is returning to America. Ms. Delacroix is the nurse who cared for Jay when he was in the SHU. A few months after that fateful weekend, Ms. Delacroix retired from the BOP and temporarily moved back to her native Haiti to help her mother who was recovering from a hip fracture. Now back in the U.S., Joe's plan is to depose two guards and Ms. Delacroix all in the same day. This time his team would arrive in the morning, travel to the prison, and hope that it will go as uneventfully as possible. Wrong again. The first deposition didn't start until one p.m.

This time, the three of us are in Joe's office to view the deposition. It's becoming easier for me to watch them, though I need to mentally and emotionally prepare a few days in advance.

With the same cast of characters as before, they begin the deposition. The first witness is a middle-aged Black man named Paul Jackson, a Correctional Officer whose job is overseeing inmates housed in the SHU. He towed the party line, offering nothing useful. The next guard to be deposed is John Starker, a thirty-something Caucasian man who sports a shaved head, not from baldness but rather in the typical ex-military style haircut. His tight shirt exposes his chiseled arms and neck muscles. Jack summarizes the deposition rather than make us sit through worthless testimony. I'm thankful for that.

Ms. Delacroix is sworn in, answered all the boilerplate questions, and is ready to give the substance of her deposition.

"You see many inmates in the SHU for all sorts of medical reasons. Why would you remember Mr. Keller?"

"He was sicker than most. A good chunk of the medical stuff in the SHU is nothing but getting ready for routine outgoing medical trips. Maybe they have a doctor's appointment or surgery the next day so they put them in the SHU the day before. Maybe it's a colonoscopy in a day or so, perhaps a cataract removal, joint replacements. Most aren't that sick. If they're really sick, they're usually sent over to University Hospital right away. The SHU is designed to separate inmates from other inmates, not to treat their medical problems."

"If he was sicker than most, why was he in the SHU?"

"I was told by the medical clinic they thought he had the flu. Many flu patients, patients with infectious diseases, bad rashes, scabies, are put in the SHU to separate them from the general population."

"September is an odd time of year to diagnose influenza. Was there a flu outbreak that September?"

"Not that I was aware of."

"Is the SHU a good place to put an inmate with the flu?"

"Objection," says Ms. Fleming. "The witness is here to only state facts, not opinion."

"Scratch that question. What is the average ambient temperature of the SHU?"

"It's pretty cold in the SHU, all year long. Usually fifty-five to sixty degrees."

"Can you objectively describe Mr. Keller's cell? What kind of bed did he have, how many blankets, pillows, towels, the lighting in the room?"

"Inmates sleep on metal beds. We never have enough pillows or blankets for everyone, but most inmates have a sheet or two to wrap around themselves. I can't remember if Mr. Keller had a pillow or not. The inmates are all alone in their cell, but it's pretty noisy from all the banter and trash-talk from other cells. Lights are on 24/7. I wouldn't want to be there if I had the flu."

"Objection to the last sentence. It's purely subjective," exclaims BOP attorney Louise Fleming. "Ms. Delacroix, you are only to state facts."

After the small interruption, Joe resumes his questioning. "Ms. Delacroix, you were in the SHU that Friday and Saturday. Are all medical patients in the SHU seen every day?"

"I would say most days. I usually do rounds with the physician on-call that day. A guard will unlock the door and stand outside unless it's a violent inmate."

"Did you check on Dr. Keller regularly that weekend?"

"Objection," says Ms. Fleming. "There is no reason to refer to Jay Keller as 'Dr. Keller.' He is 'Mr. Keller' or 'Inmate Keller,' the same title as every other inmate. To refer to him as 'doctor' is prejudicial."

"Disagree. Whether Jay Keller is an inmate or not, he earned his medical degree. He is still a doctor. I see no reason for your objection."

"Let's stop here and get the judge on the phone," says Ms. Fleming.

After a few moments, Joe says, "I will concede on this issue."

Ms. Delacroix continues. "No. I didn't check him regularly."

Joe fast forwards. "What about Saturday?"

"I showed up at seven a.m. as usual."

"Did you do rounds with the doctor that day?"

"No sir."

"Why not? I thought you stated rounds were done with a doctor every day."

"Dr. Huff was the doctor on call that day, and he didn't come in during my shift."

"He just never showed up for work that day?"

"No sir. Not on my shift."

"Did you look into Mr. Keller's cell often?"

"I remember that Saturday morning walking past Mr. Keller's cell and peering in. This time he was sleeping but facing me. I could see from where I was standing that he was really sweating and his breathing was labored. He just looked bad, sick, no other way to describe it. I then asked a guard to go into the room with me for a closer look."

"What did you notice?" asks Joe.

"He looked septic, you know, toxic, a bad infection," replies Ms. Delacroix." I checked his temperature which was around 102 as I remember."

"What did you do?"

"I called Dr. Huff and told him about the inmate."

"What was Dr. Huff's response?"

"I told him my clinical findings. He told me to give Mr. Keller two extra-strength Tylenols every four hours and force fluids on him."

"For the record, can you explain what 'force fluids means'?"

"Basically, make sure he drinks a lot of water. That's when Dr. Huff told me he may be in later but couldn't say what time. I ended up calling him an hour later because Mr. Keller looked so sick. Dr. Huff told me the same thing—two Tylenols and force fluids."

"Was Mr. Keller able to swallow the Tylenol pills, Ms. Delacroix?"

"I had to hold his head up and help him swallow."

"Did Dr. Huff ever come in on that Saturday?"

"He never came in during my shift. Heard through the grapevine that—"

"Objection," says Ms. Fleming. "Facts only, Ms. Delacroix. The 'grapevine' is hardly factual."

"I'm sorry. Dr. Huff never showed up that day or Sunday," says Ms. Delacroix.

Joe takes a sip of water, then says, "Ms. Delacroix, how do you know Dr. Huff never showed up the entire weekend?"

"My next shift was Tuesday. I had a conversation with Mary Osborne, the evening nurse in the SHU who took over when my shift ended. That's when I found out Mr. Keller died."

"Were you surprised to hear such news?"

"Shocked, but not really surprised," replies Ms. Delacroix. "She told me Dr. Huff never came in."

"Did you write any notes about your phone calls to Dr. Huff?"

"Sure, if you read the computer entries from that day, you would have seen I called him twice, then called the AW once."

"I'm sorry, Ms. Delacroix, but for the record, what is an 'AW' and can you tell me his name?"

"*Her* name. The 'AW' or 'assistant warden.' Her name is Meredith Kramer. She listened to what I had to say and said she would handle it. Never heard back from her."

"I see. Why did you feel the need to call the assistant warden?"

"I could tell Dr. Huff was pissed at me for calling him at all, so I called the assistant warden who oversees the medical unit hoping she could offer an administrative remedy. I told her I had a really sick inmate and needed input from anyone who could help me," replies Ms. Delacroix.

"What help did she offer?"

"She thanked me and told me she would handle it."

"Did any of your colleagues hear back from the AW?"

"Not that I'm aware of, sir."

"I'm sure it's all in the computer records, Ms. Delacroix, but I haven't had a chance to read those yet." Joe flashes a wrathful glance at Ms. Fleming. "Ms. Delacroix, were there any other inmates you would describe as 'sick' patients in the SHU that weekend other than Mr. Keller?"

"No. Mr. Keller was the only one who was really sick. Pretty quiet weekend. The SHU wasn't crazy-full like it is sometimes."

"Let me summarize for you, and I'm going to ask you to correct me if I misstate *anything*. Mr. Keller went to the SHU on late Friday afternoon for what was presumed to be the flu. On Friday, you saw Mr. Keller only briefly through a window in the hallway. He was sleeping with his back to you. On Saturday, after getting a close-up view of Mr. Keller, you called Dr. Huff twice, the AW once, documented those calls, gave them your clinical impression of Mr. Keller, and twice Dr. Huff's only response was to 'give the inmate Tylenol and force fluids.' The assistant warden Meredith Kramer's response was that she'd 'handle it.' No doctor or administrator saw Mr. Keller on your shift," states Joe.

"Yes sir. That's correct."

"No more questions. Thank you, Ms. Delacroix."

"I have one question on re-direct," says Ms. Fleming. "Ms. Delacroix, you stated none of your colleagues heard back from the AW. Is it possible that the AW did speak to one of your colleagues even though you didn't hear back?"

"Of course that's a possibility."

"No further questions for the witness," says Ms. Fleming.

Joe stops the video and gives us a moment to sort through what we've seen.

"This is bullshit," Richard exclaims. "The warden, Huff—they should all be held accountable!"

"I understand your frustration," Joe says. "We all knew this wasn't going to be easy. However, we now have an autopsy report performed at NYU stating Jay Keller died from exactly what his doctors warned the BOP about. We have depositions from two nurses saying the doctor in charge was grossly negligent. We have some medical records from the BOP to support their claim. We have documentation that an assistant warden, Meredith Kramer, participated in the negligence. We have twelve letters from top New York doctors stating why incarcerating Jay would be extremely dangerous to his health and have consequences far beyond the intended punishment. We have a thousand pages of letters written by Jay—letters to his wife and a diary he mailed to her separately—describing the gross deviations from the 'standard of care within the medical community.' And, we have a beautiful, humble family who lost their husband and father."

"This is all good, right? It will strengthen our case?" I ask.

"Yes and no," Joe says. "I talked with others on the best strategy to convince the BOP to settle rather than risk a public trail. Every attorney I asked in our firm, and a few outside the firm, had his or her own opinion and their own slant on how to proceed. With all this damming evidence, I hope you give me the green light to settle and hopefully avoid a long, drawn out, and costly trial."

"I just want the people who wronged my husband to pay for what they did. I can never get my Jay back—" My words trail off as Sara stands behind as she gently rubs my back.

Joe looks at me sympathetically. "Lily, trust me on this. I have your best interest at heart."

CHAPTER 59

We Want Huff

Ten weeks have passed since Sotloff Turner sent a settlement proposal to the lead in house counsel at the BOP, Harmon Allison. I'm losing my patience. We all are. Even Joe and his team are dumbfounded by the sluggishness of the BOP. It doesn't make sense to us, but Joe confirms this is typical in cases like ours.

Three more weeks go by before Sotloff Turner receives a call from BOP headquarters in Plano, Texas. Harmon Allison, calls Joe to arrange a face-to-face meeting. Joe tells Mr. Allison that without the prospect of a settlement, no one from Sotloff Turner is flying to Plano. Joe sends an email to me saying he assumes the case will go to trial. It's time to depose Dr. Huff, perhaps the most important witness of all. Meeting him in person will give Joe the needed insight into how Huff will come across on the witness stand.

Sotloff Turner makes all the arrangements for Joe's next trip to FMC Franklin. The key deposition is obviously going to be Harley Huff, MD. In preparing for the deposition, Joe's colleagues discover Huff has twelve grievances filed against him over the last decade with the State Board of Medical Examiners of West Virginia. Joe ponders how he could use this information at trial. If Joe told us once, he's told us a thousand times: he's salivating to know what makes Huff tick.

The day before he and his team are to go back down to Franklin, Joe receives a call from Harmon Allison, lead counsel for the BOP. He is calling to set up a videoconference. During their brief conversation, Mr. Allison utters the word "settlement" for the first time.

"Lily, good news," Joe says. "I got a call from the BOP and this time they used the word 'settlement.' I have scheduled a videoconference at my office for Monday at eleven. You're welcome to watch it live if you like."

"Can I ask why?"

"You'll be able to see what's going on and know who the different players are. Ultimately, any settlement is *your* decision, so having you right here to discuss and debate on the spot would be great, just in case they make a legitimate offer."

"I'll be there but can't speak for Richard and Sara. Joe, are they going to make us an offer?"

"I think so. They clearly know people at FMC Franklin screwed up. They've read the autopsy, depositions, computer records, and expert's letters, everything. The real question is how much you settle for versus what you could win if it goes to trial."

"But I thought they don't want a trial?" I ask.

"Exactly. If it goes to trial, the case could blow up for them or blow up for us. Does the BOP want that publicity? If not, that has a price tag."

"Joe, I've never asked you before but what do you think this case is worth?"

"Lily, you can never predict a jury. With the evidence we have so far, with the supposition your husband got his medical license back and practiced another twenty years, with the wanton cruelty of how he was treated, $25 million is a realistic number from a jury, maybe more."

"I'll see you Monday, Joe."

***

That evening I have a conference call with both Richard and Sara, reminding them, despite all the damming evidence, winning at trial is not a guarantee. I reiterate two critical pieces. Huff is one, confidentiality is the other.

Sara speaks up first, "What's your point? Dad wanted us to tell everyone what went on at FMC Franklin so we can't have a gag order with any settlement?"

"Exactly. I have to be able to speak my mind," I reply. "You agree Richard?"

"Yeah, on the confidentiality issue. Huff is more problematic."

"Why should that be problematic? Hang the son of a bitch," says Sara.

"If I had a rope and was alone with Huff, I would. The reality is we all want his medical license revoked, plus criminal charges," states Richard. "The problem is the BOP doesn't have jurisdiction over a state board of medical examiners or any board that grants licenses. We may be asking for the impossible. Don't risk a settlement over the Huff issue."

"Can we bring criminal charges against Huff?" I ask.

"I don't know, but I'd bet good money Joe would know," replies Richard.

"We agree about a no-confidentiality agreement," I say. "And we agree we want Huff however we can get him. But the more I think about it, the more a trial makes sense. Your father documented all the mistreatment and malpractice for a reason."

"Mom, even if we win at trial, how will that change the medical system?" asks Sara.

"I'd like all of that too, but let's be realistic," says Richard.

"After all I've endured—I don't want to be realistic."

"Mom," says Sara, "everything you say is true, but think this through. Suppose the jury sides with the BOP, which is a real possibility. Then we've lost all we've worked for. Who knows what they'll make up at trial? Didn't Stephen Conklin talk about the DOJ doing whatever it needed to get a conviction? Have to think defending a case is no different."

"I think I've stated my intent. One way or another, I'm telling the world what goes on in prisons."

"I'm still not clear what we tell Joe on Monday," quips Sara.

"We listen to the BOP offer, but you know where I stand. Get Huff. No confidentiality. Got it?"

CHAPTER 60

Time to Write

Cynthia and I have our yoga mats slung over our shoulders as we exit the yoga studio and dodge the rain until we're in my car.

"That was a fabulous class. Michelle is such an incredible teacher," exclaims Cynthia. "Before I forget, I want to invite you to an art history lecture at SUNY Purchase. It's on Matisse, next Monday evening. Think you can make it?"

I'm so fortunate to have her as my friend, how supportive she's been these last few years. "I would love that," I say. We hug each other within the restraints of our seatbelts.

Continuing to drive back to Cynthia's house, my thoughts bounce around like a pinball before turning to an idea I've been mulling over for a while, but I have yet to tell anyone.

"I've been thinking about writing a book using Jay's letters. I know how good it would feel good to put it out there. On the other hand, part of me is hesitant about allowing the world to view my husband's suffering. But, doesn't America need to know what happens to people like Jay every single day?"

"Don't think about it, do it," Cynthia quips back.

"Really?"

"It's a great idea. You have the perfect perspective to let people know how broken our criminal justice system is. When did you start thinking about doing this?"

"Jay would often joke about it when he was in Franklin, saying 'if anything happens to me, make sure people know what happens on this side of the barbed wire.' I never gave it much thought until one of the men I tutor, Tariq, suggested to make a book out of Jay's letters because I'm always quoting from them. He once asked me if I can bring in some of Jay's letters for him to read."

"I think it would be a great project for you. You know how therapeutic writing can be. It certainly was for Jay, and certainly is for you. You're still writing letters to Jay, right?"

"True. I've been thinking how I could write it but change my mind every few hours. Maybe I could write something based on Jay's letters, or maybe a book for all the spouses who have a loved one in prison, sort of a *How to Survive and Thrive While Your Husband Is in Prison*."

Cynthia fires back, "Or how about a novel about a woman whose husband was murdered by the negligence of the criminal justice system, but after a period of mourning she musters the conviction to pursue justice. I think you must tell your story to anyone who will listen about the human toll of mass incarceration, being convicted of a crime in America, the over-criminalization of society, the oxymoron of achieving a productive life after incarceration. You know, something you know nothing about, LOL."

As I continue to drive, my mind wanders away from writing a book. Thoughts, especially dark thoughts, creep into my mind like pernicious viruses. All of sudden, Huff is front and center. "Cynthia, what if Huff is never punished for what he did?"

"That's what you're worrying about now?"

"Well, I think we're close to settling with the BOP, but after speaking with Joe, and my kids, I just have a sinking feeling that nothing will ever happen to him. I don't know if I can live with that."

"Lily, get your mind off Huff. He's not worth it."

"Easy for you to say. It's as if your neighbor just robbed your house, took all your valuables, a lifetime of photographs, and kidnapped your children. You saw him do it, but he retreats back into his hermetically sealed home, and no one can punish him."

While paused at a red light, Cynthia barks, "Stop it Lily. You're eating yourself up over him. Think back just ten minutes ago to Michelle's dharma talk. She'd be the first to tell you to let it go. Let me see if I can pull you out of your black hole. She pauses before cracking a smile. "As your biggest fan, I have to ask. Have you given any thought to putting your toe in the dating arena?"

"Why do you ask?"

"Because I get asked that question all the time and I feel like being a *yenta* once in a while," answers Cynthia.

I chuckle, trying to keep a smile on my face. The truth is, I haven't thought about dating. "Not there yet—but you'll be the first to know."

CHAPTER 61

Justice

I arrive at Sotloff Turner by 10:45. It's easier for me to get away midday than my children so I will call them tonight with an update. A staff member sets me up in the conference room where I'll be watching the negotiation. Joe enters the room with two associates, his demeanor visibly energized.

"Let's get started," he says. "We'll be next door. Enjoy the show." He disappears from the room and reappears on the TV screen.

Joe's team listens as Mr. Allison explains why the BOP is willing to settle. No one is expecting an admission of guilt, but they did say, "Things could have been handled better, more professionally." Finally, a taciturn Mr. Allison proposes his offer. "I can offer $8 million that includes a confidentiality agreement binding the plaintiffs from ever discussing any details of the settlement or the case." My eyes grow wide. Eight million dollars is a lot of money.

Joe pauses for a moment, then says, "Thank you for your offer, but it's only a little more than Dr. Keller's future earnings. There's no compensation for what the family has endured. I will present this to the family, but I can tell you it falls way short of what we believe we will receive by going to trial. Way short. And, they want no part of confidentiality. I'll contact you tomorrow with their response. Have a good day, counselors."

Without batting an eyelash, Joe's ends the conference abruptly and walks back into the room. Looking directly at me, he smiles and says, "Well, we have an offer. It's a good sign."

"I must say, Joe, eight million dollars is a lot of money, meaning that part of the offer we could accept. But what we can't accept—and won't accept—is the confidentiality agreement he spoke of, and he never mentioned Huff's name," I say.

"I hear you. Remember, this is their first offer," replies Joe.

"What I'm saying is money's one thing, but more important to us is having people know about the negligent medical care in prisons and putting an end to it," I say. "No confidentiality agreement. That's non-negotiable. If we have to take it to trial, then that's what we do."

Joe nods. He doesn't even look surprised. "If those are my client's wishes, that's what I'll relay to the BOP tomorrow. A confidentiality agreement may mean more to them than money, who knows?"

My stomach remains in knots.

"Now that we're in one room, Lily, tell me what is and what isn't a deal breaker. After listening to you, it's my impression that a confidentiality agreement is a deal breaker and that's it. Anything else I need to know?" Joe asks.

I pipe up immediately. "What about Huff? Huff must be part of any settlement."

Joe crosses his arms and looks deep in thought. "Lily, you're willing to risk a settlement based on Huff's staying employed by the BOP?" he asks.

"That's exactly what I mean."

"Let's prioritize and remember—"

"Huff murdered my husband, so don't lecture *me* about priorities. Tell me how we can get to Huff," I snap.

"Lily, no one gets everything in a negotiation and only the State, not the BOP, can revoke his license. I'll have my firm research some options," replies Joe. "Anything else? Tell me now. Good. If we're clear so far, I will give them your answer tomorrow and let them know we will arrange to depose Huff."

A week goes by, and still nothing definitive. Joe checks in with me often to keep me abreast of what is going on—negotiation after negotiation. Finally, almost three weeks later, Joe calls me at home with some answers. I'm sitting at my desk looking out the window as a few snow flurries are beginning to fall.

"I've got some good news and bad news," he says.

"Good news first," I say before sitting down at my kitchen table.

Joe explains that it's been back and forth negotiating with the BOP, as often as twice a day. At one point, the BOP offers as much as $24.5 million but only with strict confidentiality.

Joe continues his synopsis. At their next negotiating session, Harmon Allison informed Joe that $24.5 million was the BOP's final offer. Joe wasn't pleased with this and said, "Mr. Allison, looks like we're going to trial. Please have the BOP give me dates so I can complete my deposition of Huff and the others. And one last thing, Mr. Allison. We've retained the Landow Group, the largest PR company in the US. I can assure you Fox and CNN will be reporting on this case. Every sordid detail of this trial will be public knowledge. Look forward to getting those dates."

My heart is pounding as Joe relays this information to me. To be honest, I don't know what to think. If anything, this raises my hopes that this will be a high-profile trial, perhaps with news coverage on major outlets.

A week later, Mr. Allison calls Joe with another offer. A watered-down confidentiality agreement, but with less money—$20 million. The amount of the settlement is prohibited from ever being disclosed. I'm free to speak about the case as long as I don't slander, libel, or defame the BOP.

"This is great news. It means we've beaten the BOP in the form of a financial settlement and in reality, the only part of the case I can't discuss is the amount of the settlement."

"There is some bad news," says Joe. "The BOP reviewed Huff's yearly evaluations for the last twelve years. They show nothing but *stellar* performance grades, not a single demerit." Joe explains they won't fire him or revoke his medical license. Licensing is a State issue and has nothing to do with the BOP.

Shit. My palms begin to collect moisture, my heart and respiratory rate accelerate. This is not what I envisioned. "After everything that has been said and written about Huff in the depositions, and the BOP has no problem with him continuing to mistreat inmates?"

"Lily, I know this is a huge blow, but I would like for you and your children to come to my office to discuss this."

Two days later we are at Sotloff Turner. The secretary greets us and ushers us into Joe's office, where we are offered water and coffee.

Joe offers his analysis of the latest settlement proposal. "I've read this three times. Lily, as long as your future statements are 100 percent accurate when you say anything in public and don't talk about the settlement amount, you should be fine. But let's not kid ourselves, the federal government can indict and convict a ham sandwich if it chooses. Don't be reckless."

"Didn't Justice Antonin Scalia say that?" asks Richard.

"He might have. It's a term used by many, but I think it was the Chief Justice of New York, Sol Wachtler who is credited with the saying," replies Joe as he turns his attention back to me. "I know your family is more concerned about letting the world know what goes on in US prisons. You can do that with this agreement."

"And Huff?" I ask.

"You and I both know we're negotiating with a morally bankrupt bureaucracy. They won't touch him. Getting at Huff will need to be separate from this settlement. Guys, let me give you time to talk."

Alone with my children, I look into their eyes hoping for answers. No one is saying a word until I ask, "Is Huff a deal breaker?"

"Mom, we have two-thirds of what we want. Let's trust Joe that there are other ways to get at Huff," says Sara.

"She's right," adds Richard. "It's a good settlement. Better than good. I say we take it and go after Huff later."

I know my children are right. It's me, and only me, who can't let go of injustice. I can't let my thinking be impaired by my hatred of Huff. Hatred only clouds one's thinking. And why am I expecting an entirely fair settlement when I know life isn't fair? *Breathe deeply and slowly, Lily.*

I want to take down Huff more than anything, but this settlement would afford me the luxury of speaking my mind. And I have so much I want to say. I fantasize about speaking at large public forums. I hear Jay's words, "A half of loaf of bread is better than no bread to a starving man." I drop my head to avoid their stares, trying to breathe slower. All the pros and cons swirl through my mind at dizzying speeds. I don't say anything for more than a minute before nodding my head affirmatively.

Sara tells the receptionist to let her know we're ready to meet with Joe.

Walking back into the conference room, Joe asks us, "What's your verdict?"

I extend my hand to shake Joe's hand. "We accept their offer."

"I'm happy for you Lily, and your family."

"Thank you, Joe," I say. "Never in my wildest dreams did I expect to beat the BOP."

"I know Huff is still out there. Call me if you want to pursue him."

Richard and Sara give Joe a hug and a big thank you. We all share the blissful feeling of an upset victory. "Guys, from my point of view, this is the most satisfying victory of my career. My Uncle Bob is smiling down on us."

***

After we leave Joe's office and are on Seventh Avenue, I hug and kiss both of them as I feel years of stress departing from my body. I let Richard and Sara pick the restaurant as I usually do when we dine together. They choose a local Italian restaurant around the corner from Joe's office. We are all anxious to dine in celebration.

While seated at the table, I think back to my dinner with Bruce's wife Iris and how content she was with what she had, never focusing on what she lost. I look at the faces of Richard and Sara and think how fortunate I am to be their mother, to have these two wonderful people in my life. And being their mother, I remind them, as I usually do, that if they take out their cell phones during dinner, they must pay for the dinner. It's amazing how they temporarily detach from their phones.

Tonight however, is different. I feel like I'm floating. Maybe it's shock, but it feels like an out-of-body experience. *We've defeated the BOP,* echoes in my head, and I don't quite believe it.

"You guys pick the wine," I say. "I'll drink anything tonight."

Richard turns to the waitress, "We'll have the 2010 Brunello di Montalcino, Tenuta di Lupinari." I look at my son with a wry smile. "What? Did I do something wrong?" he asks.

"Not at all. You sound just like your father when he ordered wine."

"I happen to know that was one of his favorites," says Richard as he leans over to hug me.

"I remember being in the town of Montalcino with your father years ago. Your father had feather-light gnocchi with truffles and a Brunello. Happiest I had ever seen him."

The waitress brings the wine, which Richard approves wholeheartedly. We raise our glasses for our usual toast of "To Dad." Sara adds, "And to justice."

Over the next two hours, we talk about nothing the least bit serious, and I'm grateful for it. The last two years of my life have been consumed by the aftermath of Jay's death. I'm hoping my children see the joy on my face. I actually feel—dare I say it—*happy*. I ask the waitress for the check since neither of my children took out their cell phones.

As I finish the last few sips of wine, I look at my children and reach for their hands. "I'd like to discuss with both of you what we should do with the settlement money, assuming the BOP eventually hands it over."

Richard chimes in, "You mean how you're going to invest it?"

"No, no. What we should do with the money," I reply.

"Have you given it any thought?" quips Sara. "Because I certainly haven't."

"The money went to the Estate of Jay Keller, and we're all a part of that. It's a lot of money, certainly more than I need and more than you need. I think we should give a chunk of it to people who need it more than us."

Richard changes his tone. "I have an idea, and I think Dad would have agreed with me. I was speaking to Zack the other day. Get this. When he graduated medical school, he had over $300,000 in loans on top of his undergraduate loans. The federal government is charging him 7.4% interest on his loans, money they borrowed for 0.5%."

"So what are you suggesting?" I ask.

"Mom, sure would be nice to wave a magic wand and make his debt go away," proposes Richard. "That guy worked his ass off."

"I'd love that!" says Sara.

"Then if we all agree, I'll call Zack and tell him the good news. Who knows when we'll actually get the money, but we can put his mind at ease."

"Anything else we need to discuss?" asks Sara.

"Yes. One other thing I'd like your input on. Dad's roommate, Bruce Hellman, also died at the hands of the BOP. His wife Iris was left with nothing. As if her family hasn't been punished enough, the government is taking part of her Social Security to pay for Bruce's restitution. I'd like to gift her $100,000 to help her get back on her feet. Any thoughts?"

"Mom, you're like Oprah Winfrey. We're all in," exclaims Richard.

CHAPTER 62
Happy Birthday

Dear Jay,

I've been waiting all week to write you, my love. Today is your birthday. I remember so clearly your first birthday we shared together. I made a dinner I knew you would love. But when you came home, you were so tired from your night on-call and needed to change out of your work clothes first. After a few minutes, I called to the bedroom to make sure everything was okay, but you didn't answer. When I went to the bedroom you were fast asleep, still in your scrubs. You crashed before I laid out the appetizers.

I remember celebrating your fortieth birthday in Italy. We were in southwestern Tuscany for over two weeks. Most people want to sightsee and dine in wonderful restaurants when they are overseas. You chose to celebrate your birthday covered in dirt with the goal of completely redoing the landscape of your friend's country home. I will never forget the look on your face when you placed the last jasmine tree in the front yard. You looked up at me not realizing your face was covered in sweat and dirt. At that moment, I thought how lucky I am to have you as my husband. We worked our asses off but, in the end, we had completely transformed Enrico's gardens. I hope to visit his home soon and bear witness to the fruits of your labor. What a glorious but exhausting vacation. If that didn't prove my love for you, nothing will.

Jay, you were right. It was Stanley Blacker who signed a bunch of false statements against you and at least a dozen other doctors. It was his only way to stay out of prison. With a little help from your friend Diaz, we now know the feds forced Stanley Blacker to fabricate evidence. I can finally put that pile of angst to rest.

Speaking of justice, I'm planning to use some of the settlement money to fund a research project at the John Jay College of Criminal Justice with the goal of determining the best punishment for various crimes. Imagine, evidence-based punishment just as you had written about in so many of your letters. My hope is the research will facilitate real changes and perhaps signal the end of mass incarceration.

My volunteer work continues to be enormously gratifying. I've been working with one woman who spent seven years in prison after being busted for stealing FedEx packages. Now Tanya is working for FedEx, just graduated from junior college, and supports herself and three children. She stopped by last week to give me a present, a picture of Tanya receiving her diploma. She inscribed, "To the woman who gave me encouragement and confidence."

Travis is a fifteen-year-old boy who was sentenced to juvenile detention on drug and burglary charges. The judge must have seen something in Travis and gave him a last chance. We discovered he's an innately gifted jazz drummer. He just got accepted to finish high school at the Fiorello LaGuardia High School of Music and Performing Arts. Every once in a while, I hit a home run.

Life has gotten better for me despite feeling your loss every single morning. I still want to touch the side of your unshaven face, watch you make cappuccino in the morning, and I so miss being on "nose hair patrol." What I've learned from Dr. Dannert has helped me appreciate that all the memories I have of you aren't just memories, they're treasures I get to keep forever.

I am eternally grateful for the love we shared.

You may have been stolen from me, but I will never stop loving you. I love you forever, Birthday Boy.

Lily

CHAPTER 63

Darwin's Dinner

Just getting started and wanting to do more, I've attended several lectures over the last year at the John Jay College of Criminal Justice, a fifteen-minute walk from my office. During my frequent visits to attend lectures, I've had the opportunity to meet the president of the college, Dr. Arthur Schwartzman. Today I'm attending an all-day conference at the college titled *Time to Reform*.

Dr. Schwartzman is a warm, distinguished-looking man in his early sixties, perhaps carrying a few extra middle-age pounds as well as a mane of thick white hair. He has a booming voice to project his erudite vocabulary, a voice that rarely needs a microphone. Like many college presidents, he knows how to work a room, welcoming everyone in a manner that makes them feel as if he's their best friend.

The conference begins with President Schwartzman introducing the keynote speaker, Senator Bryan Whitfield of New Jersey, a staunch and long-time advocate for criminal justice reform. I have admired Senator Whitfield for years, read his books, and follow him on Instagram. Senator Whitfield gives an impassioned speech illustrating the lunacy of the status quo.

Senator Whitfield talks about being a first-hand witness to the full consequences of mass incarceration and over-criminalization. He spent several years voluntarily living in the public housing projects of Newark, New Jersey. He openly talks about his time in the projects, visiting homes with one or both parents incarcerated, the violence, the struggle to survive all the collateral damage to the family unit, especially the children.

The senator slams his fist several times on the podium as he concludes his speech, calling mass incarceration a stain on the democratic principles our country was founded on. He challenges the audience to urge their legislators to embrace alternative punishments and sentencing guidelines that are in line with other developed nations.

Senator Whitfield concludes with this final thought. "Mass incarceration has been a colossal failure. It is our duty as citizens of this great nation to find another solution."

I jump to my feet with the rest of the audience to give the senator a rousing standing ovation. I love hearing him confirm so much of what Jay wrote about during his sixteen-month imprisonment.

There are several hundred attendees from all over the country and from all the various spokes comprising the criminal justice system. With about fifteen different break-out sessions to choose from, I select two for the morning and two in the afternoon.

The first session, *Family Values*, has several speakers, all touching on the subject of how families are destroyed when even a single member is incarcerated. One woman speaks of how she and her brother were raised by their ailing grandmother. She never met her biologic father, spent three years in prison herself, and regretfully is now watching the cycle repeat again as her daughter is currently serving six months in juvenile detention on drug charges. A man in his early thirties speaks of how hard his mother struggled to raise him while his father was serving a twenty-year sentence in Leavenworth, Kansas. I leave the session grappling with one statistic that I can't get out my mind: eighty-five percent of all incarcerated young people come from fatherless homes.

The next session, *The Need for Transparency*, corroborates what I experienced firsthand when Jay was in prison. There's money to be made by keeping prisons full. The speaker, Hal McMurphy, the executive VP from the Southern Poverty Law Center, wrote his doctoral thesis on profits in the prison industrial complex. He spends the first few minutes informing the audience about the prison phone industry, a market dominated by a few large, private companies earning $1.2 billion a year on the backs of those who can least afford it. Jay had it easy, in a relative sense, because I sent him money.

He was able to afford the obscene twenty-four-cents-per-minute phone calls, but most inmates don't have the means to connect with people on the outside. I'm incensed when I learn private phone companies transfer a percentage of their revenue to state and local authorities, a practice most people consider a blatant kickback.

Throughout Dr. McMurphy's presentation, he gives numerous examples of how companies profit handsomely from the prison-industrial complex, now an $85 billion-dollar-a-year industry. If you add in the costs of prosecution, indigent defense, bail fees, forfeitures, criminal policing and the costs to families, you are at $182 billion-a-year. He talks of how as a nation, the rate of spending on prisons is three times more than spending on K-12 education. His contention is many people benefit from this era of over-criminalization and mass incarceration. Prison commissary companies have earnings of $1.6 billion. Here's another statistic I can't get out of my head. Corizon Health is America's largest prison healthcare firm, earning $1.4 billion last year. In just the last five years, that same firm has been sued 660 times for causing death or permanent injury.

Between sessions, I hydrate with some water and coffee. I'm in awe of the number of people whose lives are devoted to the various elements of criminal justice. I glance at the titles on everyone's nametag, sometimes with reverence, sometimes with disdain. One nametag reads *Warden, Rikers Island Correctional Facility*. All I could think of was Jay's letters about the unctuous warden of FMC Franklin whose only concern was preventing a full-blown prison riot. Beyond that, he had no interest in anything the inmates had to say or how they were treated by his staff. I'm extremely forthright when explaining to people how my husband was murdered in prison. Everyone's first reaction is to think he was stabbed or killed by an act of violence. When I tell them he was murdered by the medical staff, I'm surprised by the number of similar stories people share with me.

Before I can exhale, it's lunchtime. I opt to eat at the school cafeteria. Before I take a spoonful of my soup, a middle-aged gentleman asks me, "Is this seat taken?" I glance up and see he's a conference attendee and warmly reply, "Have a seat. I'm Lily."

"Nice to meet you. Hank Loman. I'm a prosecutor from the Bronx DA's office. Where are you from?"

"Live in Westchester. Work in the city," I reply.

We exchange pleasantries for several minutes as I have my soup and salad while Hank consumes his bacon cheeseburger, fries, and a Coke. As we're finishing up our respective meals, I say to Hank, "Being a prosecutor, I would love to ask you a question."

"Sure. Fire away."

"My husband was a physician who broke a law he was unaware of, there were no victims, he was a first-time non-violent offender, and had medical problems that cost him his life while he was still in prison. Why would a prosecutor say things about him at sentencing that made him out to be Charles Manson?"

Suddenly disarmed by my sincerity, Hank replies, "Your husband died in prison?"

"FMC Franklin. Gross medical negligence."

"Sorry to hear that."

"Thank you," I say, "Jay could have been punished in so many other ways, aside from incarceration."

Hank sighs and rolls his eyes. "I still believe that if you break the law, you go to jail. We're a country governed by laws. But I will admit sometimes prosecutors can be overzealous."

"But why lock people in cages instead of exploring alternative forms of punishment and shorter, more appropriate sentences? Can we at least agree on that?"

"No. We need jails. That's where we put bad people."

"So, you believe the only punishment should be locking people in cages?"

"Yeah. That's my job. Trust me, the scumbags I deal with every day deserve to be in prison."

"Can we at least agree that prisoners should receive the same medical care as you or I would receive?"

"Interesting point." Hank pauses to finish his drink. "On this issue, I believe you're right. I've been privy to how much the state of New York pays out every year because of medical malpractice in prisons. It would be much cheaper to do things right the first time."

"See that, Hank, we can agree on something," I respond.

Hank excuses himself, as he has a panel to get to, and I watch him carry his tray away. All I can do is shake my head and smile, realizing I just had a friendly, civil conversation with a state prosecutor.

The first afternoon session, *The Education Train*, focuses on job training. This is by far the most well-attended session, because every expert knows education and training are essential to ending mass incarceration and reducing recidivism. Everyone has an entrance date and most have a release date. One ex-inmate speaks extremely eloquently about how his life changed after learning HVAC during his twelve-year sentence. He now has a marketable skill and found a job after his release. He's been with the same HVAC company for the last seven years.

The second session, *Changing the Rules,* is given by a law professor from the University of Chicago. He tackles the absurdity of the number of laws we have. In 1790, there were thirty federal crimes. By 1980 there were over 3,000. Today, he says, there are about 4,500-5,000 federal statutes and 300,000 regulations that carry federal criminal penalties. Trained as a lawyer, he explains that having so many criminal statutes makes it possible for prosecutors, not a judge or jury, to decide how undesirable conduct is punished, or not punished if they so choose. They can decide to imprison people who deserve fines or social censure. With so many laws, clever and determined prosecutors can threaten a defendant with decades in prison for their acts that were the result of merely bad judgment. But such a system allows prosecutors to coerce plea bargains, raises the stakes of a day in court, and undermines respect for the law itself. This is the opposite of the system of limited and clear laws that the framers of the constitution had intended. If ignorance of the law is no excuse, then every American is ignorant and in peril. Nobody can know all the laws that govern their behavior.

I'm emotionally exhausted after attending the four sessions. But my day is far from over. After a quick pick-me-up at a local coffee shop, I head back to the college. Dr. Schwartzman has invited me to participate in a working dinner to discuss a research project designed by the college. On one hand I'm excited to be part of this special session arranged by Dr. Schwartzman. At the same time, I'm nervous walking into a dinner with some of the largest philanthropic organizations in America.

Dr. Schwartzman invites everyone into a room where dinner is to be served around a large circular table. I'm seated between a woman from Google and a gentleman from the Ford Foundation. Dr. Schwartzman stands up for introductory remarks. Using his mellifluous voice, he begins by sharing with everyone that all the food servers and kitchen staff this evening are ex-inmates who have been trained for jobs in the hospitality industry. He asks the entire staff of fifteen workers to come out to receive a round of applause from the dinner guests. Dr. Schwartzman then asks everyone to stand up and introduce themselves, starting with the representative from the Ford Foundation.

Before I'm about to stand up, Dr. Schwartzman asks me if it would be all right if he introduces me. I agree, and remain seated while he speaks.

"We are very lucky to have Lily Keller with us today. Ms. Keller received her education in criminal justice in the most painful way imaginable. Her husband, a respected physician in Westchester, was sentenced to two years for a white-collar crime. Because of his medical problems, he was sent to a Federal Medical Center in West Virginia where he died from gross negligence on the part of the prison doctor and the entire institution. Since that time, she has volunteered at the Fortune Society. By chance, a few months ago I happened to see Lily on a local news segment about criminal justice reform. A week later, I introduced myself when I saw her attending a lecture here. Since then I have gotten to know Ms. Keller as a tenacious advocate for criminal justice reform and hopefully a donor for our research study."

The group applauds. I stand up as butterflies dance in my stomach. "Thank you so much, Dr. Schwartzman, for your kind words. I'm honored to be with all of you tonight. The truth is, I didn't know anything about criminal justice reform until the last few years. But, the study of outcomes is something my husband wrote about extensively from prison. Being in a Federal Medical Center, my husband saw a large cross-section of prison society from gang members, to drug dealers, sex offenders, and white-collar.

He came to one conclusion: Prison sentences are nothing but arbitrarily chosen numbers with no science behind them. I would love to see this project result in evidence-based sentencing as well as alternative solutions to punish offenders that does not include incarceration."

Dr. Schwartzman spends the next fifteen minutes detailing the College's research project. He uses a PowerPoint presentation to give everyone an overview and its potential to be a landmark study. At the crux of the research is the concept of evidence-based punishments. What punishment of a crime will yield the best outcome for society?

"To date," he explains, "there has been almost no research to objectively determine how we punish criminals. We can and we must do better to narrow the gap that exists between American sentencing guidelines and internationally accepted norms for punishment, between punishment for people of color, and all others. This is why my colleagues and I here at John Jay have designed a randomized, double-blind controlled study to finally answer the question: What is the best way to punish people who have broken the law?"

Dr. Schwartzman pauses and allows his words to sink it. "All of us in this room know there is no proof that locking away a drug dealer for twenty years gives a better result to society than giving him or her a two-year prison sentence with three years of mandatory job training. Make people leave prison with basic skills to be productive citizens in society. Where is the proof that locking white-collar criminals in a cage for ten years gives society a better result than having that person tutor or mentor others? I could go on with a million examples of sentences that have nothing to do with protecting society. I propose we study justice outcomes and finally prove, with evidence-based results, the best punishment for a particular crime and a particular defendant. Until then, all we are doing is nothing more than what 'feels right' to the prosecutors. That is not justice!"

The next hour and a half is spent exchanging ideas and dining on deliciously prepared appetizers and entrees. Often the conversation digresses from criminal justice, which the dinner guests welcome after spending all day hearing about alternative punishments, mental healthcare, and sentencing reform. I'm rather quiet during most of the dinner. Finally, after all the others at the table give their final thoughts on the proposal, Dr. Schwartzman says, "Lily, anything you'd like to add?"

"Being new to the world of philanthropy, I wasn't sure if contributing to this study was the best use of my resources. But after hearing all of you speak, and learning more about the research project, it's exactly what I want to do."

I have never had a fear of public speaking, but speaking in front of this group about something so personal brings on some nerves. I take a few sips of my water.

"My husband, Jay Keller, was a physician, a man guided by science who based his medical decisions on evidence. Please indulge me as I tell a quick story my husband often shared with our children, family, and friends:

Charles Darwin was thirty years old when he completed his theory of evolution. Why did he wait another thirty years before presenting his theories to the European scientific community? Because he was unable to provide the evidence to support his theory. Darwin was tormented for decades because he knew good science was about having proof. Genetics had not yet been discovered. In 1859, the elderly and ailing Darwin finally bit the bullet and presented *On the Origin of Species* to the world. His theory was not immediately embraced, especially because it was contrary to religious dogma. Here's the tragic part. Three weeks before Darwin died, he received an envelope from a Czech monk named Gregor Mendel. Sadly, Darwin was too sick to open his mail and died before reading the contents of the envelope. In that envelope were all of Mendel's findings from his genetic experiments that proved evolution's mechanism of action, the proof Darwin had sought for decades. America, too, needs objective data so we can put *justice* back in the term *criminal justice*."

The room erupts into applause. I quickly scan both the eyes and faces of each donor. Everyone is happy for me. The patrons hold up their glasses and I do the same. A feeling of warmth and light spread throughout my body. In that moment, I entered the world of philanthropy.

As President Schwartzman is saying his goodbyes, he promises to keep everyone apprised of the project's design and funding status. A few people thank me for sharing my story. We all head toward the exit when a gentleman from Bloomberg Philanthropies and a woman from the Pew Charitable Trust invite me to join them for a drink. I accept the invitation wholeheartedly.

CHAPTER 64

OMG

Time flies. Almost six months have passed since I beat the BOP. I am slowly accepting my new normal.

I dart to an empty seat as soon as the train door opens. Placing my briefcase on my lap, I pull out my cell phone and scan the NY Times headlines. My eyes are drawn to the third headline, a statement from US Attorney General Melvin Hartwick. The video of his press conference shows the Attorney General announcing the formation of a Commission on Prosecutorial Misconduct. The Commission will have the power to investigate any and all allegations and issue sanctions against prosecutors who have broken laws, superseding the Office of the Inspector General. Hartwick lamented that those trusted to enforce our laws are completely unaccountable when their own unethical actions are discovered. Hartwick made his announcement but did not respond to any questions regarding his impetus for establishing such a commission. I put my phone in my pocketbook and smile while looking about the packed train car. I can only think my discussion with Janice and Joe, in some way, contributed to the formation of this Commission.

A few weeks later, I'm at work in the middle of a meeting when my administrative assistant interrupts as I'm speaking, discreetly whispering in my ear.

"I'm sorry, but he said it's an emergency and has to speak to you immediately," he says. The color drains from my face, as the last few years have primed me to be ready for the worst. I leave the room with trepidation before slowly picking up the landline phone in the next room.

"Lily, it's Joe Linnard. You must get to a TV right away. Do you have TVs in your office?"

"We do, but what's going on Joe?"

"Just put on any of the local news channels. They're all covering the same story. It's *your* story, Lily."

I rush to the lounge area and put on Channel 2. Plastered across the bottom of the screen are photos of five US Attorneys. I recognize them all. Above the photos is a reporter outlining details of the raid.

"This is what we know so far. At 7:05 in the morning, twenty FBI agents conducted a coordinated raid at the Charles L. Brieant Jr. Federal Building and Courthouse in White Plains, New York, where US Attorney Robert Keenan and four of his AUSAs were assembled for a seven a.m. meeting."

"A stunned Robert Keenan, Ray Bradley, Victor Stallworth, Tyler Hoskins, and Griffin Jackson were all arrested and brought to different parts of the Federal Building for processing, all charged with five counts involving prosecutorial misconduct. This is the first time in modern history that US Attorneys have been arrested for their work-related misconduct, truly a stain on the Department of Justice. We will be following this story all day long, right up to Attorney General Melvin Hartwick's press conference. This is John Manfred, Channel 2 News, from the Federal Building in White Plains, New York. Back to you, Eileen."

"Oh—my—god!" I say, over and over, smiling ear to ear, feeling relief pass through every cell in my body. The federal prosecutors, who so zealously put my husband in prison on the pretext of curbing fraud and abuse, have become victims of their own hubris. For the first time in their careers, they will now experience the inhumanity of prison.

I take my time walking back to the conference room. Everyone in the office is going about their day as if nothing has happened. As much as I can't wait to talk to Sara and Richard and hear the joy in their voices, I wish Jay was standing next to me to witness this historic event. Jay was right—you can't predict life.

EPILOGUE

It's 3:40 on a sunny but cool afternoon in FMC Franklin. Diaz and two other seasoned veterans are sitting at a picnic table in the Antioch courtyard talking to Dante, a new inmate.

"What do you mean there's no medical care here?" Dante asks. "That's why they transferred me. Spent over a week on a fuckin' bus getting to this World War I museum."

"I've been here five years," says Diaz. "Ain't no one gives a shit about you up in Medical. Best doctor we had here was killed a few years ago."

"A doctor was killed here?" asks Dante as his eyes widen.

"Two doctors. First was an inmate, Dr. Jay Keller," answers Diaz. "Got sick and instead of treating him, the prison doctor threw him in the SHU. Died a few days later. Jay wasn't here that long, but a lotta inmates used to make appointments with him for all sorts of medical problems. He was great."

"Man, I forgot about Jay," Andy says, the quiet but forceful Canadian. "I remember the first time I met him. Profiled him as another cho-mo, but I was wrong. Man, I miss his yoga classes. No one was as driven and willing to put up with the lazy fucks that ran recreation."

"Jay was the man," Diaz declares. "Still can't believe those motherfuckers killed him. Anyway, he was the voice of reason to all the bullshit the medical staff used to feed us. Couldn't get away with their shit as easily when Jay was here."

"And the other doctor?" Dante asks.

Diaz is laughing before he can get his words out. "Huff was the prison doc here for years. Abused all of us. A real shithead. Even after he got a slap on the wrist for killing Jay and some other shit, he continued to work here. You know, innocent till proven guilty."

"How'd he die?"

"Died the way he deserved to. Got into it with an inmate up in medical clinic, a guy serving a life sentence. Wanna guess what happened?"

"The inmate killed him?" Dante asks incredulously.

"Oh yeah." Diaz chuckles. "I was in the clinic that morning. In front of a packed waiting room up in Medical, he decked Huff with one punch. Once Huff was on the floor, the inmate grabbed an empty chair and smashed it into Huff's head probably ten times or more before the guards could pull him off. Huff's brains were splattered *all* over the waiting room. Motherfucker got what he deserved. The nurses tried to save him, but his skull was flat as a pancake."

Dante looks scared and amazed.

"Don't expect no real medical care here," Diaz continues. "Fucked-up Medical Center is what FMC stands for. If you're lucky, they send you out to University Hospital. You'll learn soon enough. How much time you got left?"

"Seven years."

"Better off going down to the chapel and praying," adds Andy.

Diaz pats the new inmate on the back. "If you got any questions about this place, just ask me. I'll show you where we eat after count. Been locked up for a long time and I've learned a few things. One thing about prison is you get a good sense of who belongs in here and who got fucked by the system. No way Jay should have been in here."

"Let it go, Diaz," says Andy. "Enough of your bromance with Keller. We gotta get inside for count. Good luck, Dante. Learn to pray."

Diaz and Dante head inside for the four-p.m. count.

"Keller did something really stupid when he first got here so don't you go making the same mistake. Don't take anything from anyone. Nothing in here is for free. Got that?"

"Got it," says Dante.

"Ya know, Dante, I grew up in the Bronx, Arthur Avenue," Diaz babbles without pause as he walks alongside his new friend. "Where you from?"

The courtyard slowly empties as all the inmates make their way back to their rooms for the mandatory standing count.

Diaz makes his way over to his bunk and stands there while the two COs do their count. He clasps his hands in front of him and closes his eyes. He didn't sleep well last night and he's tired.

"Diaz!" the CO barks, and Diaz jolts his eyes open. "Come down to my office after count clears."

"For what?" asks Diaz, "I ain't done nothing wrong."

"For once, you're right. Someone sent you a book. Been sitting in my office for three fuckin' days." The guard spits his chewing tobacco juice into a jar.

After count clears, Diaz meanders down to the COs' office and knocks on the window before being waved in by the disinterested guard who continues talking on his cellphone. The CO points to the corner of his empty desk where a lone book is sitting. There's a piece of cardboard concealing most of the cover. Diaz grabs the book, walks out into the lounge area, peels away the cardboard, and reads the title:

CONVICTIONS
A Tale of Punishment, Justice, and Love
by
Lily Keller

Diaz's smile stretches from ear to ear. "Son of a bitch. She wrote Jay's book."

ABOUT THE AUTHOR

Dr. Leslie graduated magna cum laude from Fairleigh Dickinson University with a bachelor's degree in biology. He received his medical degree from Midwestern University's Chicago College of Osteopathic Medicine and completed his internal medicine residency at the University of Medicine and Dentistry of New Jersey in 1985. He is board certified by the American Board of Internal Medicine.

After a few years in private practice, Dr. Leslie founded Mahwah Medical in 1987. He served as the medical director for almost three decades, practicing both internal medicine and occupational medicine. Dr. Leslie also served as the Director of Occupational Medicine for Good Samaritan Hospital, Suffern, NY.

While in practice, Dr. Leslie was designated by the FAA to be an Aviation Medical Examiner in which he performed physicals on pilots. He was also certified as a medical review officer by the American Association of Medical Review Officers.

He was actively involved in community affairs for many years. He was a two-term president of the Mahwah Regional Chamber of Commerce, the police physician for the Township of Mahwah for over two decades, and advised many local corporations on medical issues.

Dedication

To Lynda, whose love nourishes me in good times and bad, in sickness and in health. A better partner you will not find.

To Alec, Ray, and Juliana, whose love, hard work, and character will make the world a better place.

Cover design by Juliana Leslie, **jsievleslie.com**

Made in the USA
Middletown, DE
09 March 2021